THERE
ALL ALONG

THERE ALL ALONG

LAUREN DANE
MEGAN HART

HEAT | NEW YORK

THE BERKLEY PUBLISHING GROUP
Published by the Penguin Group
Penguin Group (USA) LLC
375 Hudson Street, New York, New York 10014

USA • Canada • UK • Ireland • Australia • New Zealand • India • South Africa • China

penguin.com

A Penguin Random House Company

This book is an original publication of The Berkley Publishing Group.

Library of Congress Cataloging-in-Publication Data

Dane, Lauren.
There All Along / Lauren Dane, Megan Hart. — Heat trade paperback edition.
pages cm
ISBN 978-0-425-26376-1 (pbk.)
1. Erotic stories, American.   2. Love stories, American.   I. Hart, Megan.   II. Title.
PS3604.A5T48 2013
813'.6—dc23
2013032687

PUBLISHING HISTORY
Heat trade paperback edition / December 2013

PRINTED IN THE UNITED STATES OF AMERICA

10 9 8 7 6 5 4 3 2 1

Cover photograph by Claudio Marinesco.
Cover design by Rita Frangie.
Text design by Laura K. Corless.

CONTENTS

LAND'S END

LAUREN DANE

1

oyal led the escort up the wide expanse of Highway, up the ramp and the steep roadway. To Silver Cliffs.

To Verity Coleman.

He had a shell in his pocket. One he'd leave for her on the morning they pushed on to the next garrison. He knew the pink insides would delight her. Knew the swirling shape and smooth surface would bring a smile to her lips.

Escorting a transport to Silver Cliffs was his job. The same as he escorted to other garrisons up and down the Highway. But *she* drew him there. Like a magnet. He found himself rushing through his last day any time Silver Cliffs was next on the list.

He was a lawman. He didn't just take official traffic to the garrisons; he brought law and order. He brought the hammer down when necessary. He was the face of a government that could be beneficent, or brutal.

Every day he had to be hard. He *was* a hard man. Had seen a lot. Had done worse. He was a killer when he had to be. Solved disputes along the Highway when they pulled into town. Sometimes that included putting men down for crimes that put the rest of the garrison in danger.

He was good at his job. And for most of his life he'd been happy to do it with no real ties to anyone outside his crew. The men and women he traveled with were also lawmen. Also trained. Under his command they did whatever was necessary and he counted on that over and over. They were the only people he considered himself close to.

One of the escort vehicles at the rear hailed him. "Road is clear behind us. I, for one, am looking forward to some quiet downtime in a room with a bed and none of you anywhere near me and Marcus. A hot meal, a warm bath and a good night's sleep. Heaven."

Trinity, one of his men, and her partner, Marcus, traveled together in their crew. The two of them had a deep and abiding connection. Intense and physical as well. It softened a hard-edged job to have that. Trinity had her own demons to deal with, and since she and Marcus had ended up together, she'd been stronger, steadier.

Being constantly on edge was hard on a body. Their world was hard enough, even for those living in the garrisons. But out there on the road they saw things daily that chipped away at their humanity. Made them jaded and cynical about humanity. Sex was a way to blow off steam. To work out the kinks in your heart as well as your muscles. But he sure as hell didn't need love to get sex.

Sure he liked fucking. A whole hell of a lot. It chased away the brutality from his skin and the taste from his mouth for the time he'd buried himself in a woman. When he felt the physical need to be with a woman, he filled it. There were plenty of women all along the Highway who had no problem laying with a lawman. He'd never needed to pay or barter for it.

He'd been fine with that for years. Until Verity.

After a time on the Southern Highway, he'd been assigned to the northern sector. The first time he laid eyes on her, she'd been standing out at the loading dock where the official transport would unload goods into the back of her mercantile.

Red hair rode in a long, braided rope down her back. She'd been young then. She was young now. Back then she'd been capable, as most were out there on the edge. But she had a hesitance about her too. Her eyes had flicked up, gaze locking with his, a sweet smile on her face, and that had been the moment she'd begun to capture his attention.

He knew he should have kept away from her. She wasn't a woman he'd come to bury his cock and his sins in. She was a woman you couldn't walk away from. The kind of woman a man gave himself to body and soul because she was worth that constancy.

But he found himself asking her if she had a room to let, or if she knew where he and his people could stay while they were in Silver Cliffs.

And that's how he found himself in her guest room. Biting his lip as he fucked his fist every night he was there, wishing it was her.

They'd leave and he'd think of her daily. And when it came time to go to Silver Cliffs again, it was as if he came home. Not to the garrison, but to her.

The horns heralding visitors coming over the bridge and approaching the gate brought Verity's attention from her perch on the ladder. Certainly whoever might be arriving was far more interesting than dusting off jars and canisters of dry goods on high shelves.

There'd been a blip about a shipment of goods and mail

coming. That had been three days ago so it was still a little early. The herald could be traders from one of the other garrisons. But just in case it was official traffic, it wouldn't do to have messy hair and be covered in dust.

She nipped around the back to brush and rebraid her hair after washing her hands and face. On her way out, she unlocked the large doors at the loading bay behind the store. If it was an official transport, she'd be taking deliveries through there. Best to be prepared as the folks from town would be lining up to see what she was getting.

Being past midday, the sun was high, and though it still wasn't quite past the threat of the last snowfall, the day was clear and warm, a hint at the long, warm season to come.

Verity hoped the seeds she'd ordered would be in the shipment if it was indeed a big delivery. Many of the farmers within the high walls of Silver Cliffs had their own seed stores, but since a lot of folks in town kept kitchen gardens, she put in large orders for seeds at the end of every harvest season, knowing they'd show up after the last of the regular snowstorms as the ground readied for planting.

As she walked down the hill toward the garrison gates, she passed the power station. The river was full of melting snowpack so the generators hummed, recharging the banks of batteries that would keep the lights on even in the coldest part of the annum.

She had some solar collection banks James had bought but never did anything with. Last harvest season she'd paid Byson Carter, one of the local boys, to install them on her roof. Her share of payments to the garrison board had gone down by half. She liked that very much. Keeping her freedom was important. Especially in a town where a woman her age remaining unmarried, even after she'd been widowed, was frowned upon.

She paid that no nevermind. She'd done her time under the

thumb of a man who used fists and drink as easily as he took a breath. She had no great desire to hitch herself to another anytime soon.

Though that didn't mean she wouldn't enjoy the company of a certain lawman the few times each annum he rolled into Silver Cliffs with official transports.

They'd allowed a crowd to gather along the walkways to either side of the gate so she figured it had to be friendlies of one sort or another. Otherwise they'd have sounded an alert and men would be running down the street with rifles, heading to their stations.

They all stood, going up on tiptoe to try to get a better glimpse of the outside world, hungry for news of what was going on down the valley, up and down the Land's End Highway.

The guards stood on the walkway above the gate, calling out to whoever was beyond. Verity cursed her impatience. If she'd gone to the front bedroom upstairs she'd have been able to see more.

Bits and pieces of chatter reached her ears. People hoping for mail, some awaiting parts for needed machinery. Verity had a list of goods that'd been on backorder for some time. If it was official transport, she'd have some pretty-smelling soaps she'd traded for some of her preserves with a friend down in Banyon Pass.

And there'd be some time with Loyal. She smiled just thinking about him. Her tall, taciturn lawman.

The large wheels that worked to open the gate began to move and a burst of pleasure shot through her as she caught sight of the lead vehicle, a lawman escort. Another just behind it and then the large official transport followed by another two escort vehicles.

Happiness coursed through her. She waved, being unable to see through the heavily fortified front windows, knowing though that he always drove the lead. Hoping he'd feel at least a whisper of the happiness she did.

The excited tone of the gathered crowd pulled her out of her thoughts about Loyal. She needed to get back to the mercantile to take the delivery. The transport always offloaded its goods and deliveries to her. She handled the dissemination to the garrison's citizens. Well, of everything but munitions, and that was something the lawmen did in private, behind the big steel doors of garrison headquarters.

They'd give her no more than half an hour before townspeople began to mill around. She hustled back up the hill, her mind already on work, as the various vehicles went one way or another.

Tobin, her nephew and her assistant at the mercantile, tipped his cap at her from where he stood on the raised loading porch.

She grabbed a pair of gloves and slid an apron on. "Ready?"

"Indeed I am. I'm under orders from my mother to dibs anything she might like." He rolled his eyes affectionately as he spoke.

"By that she means anything sweet or perhaps shiny." Constance was her big sister. She'd been fortunate to marry a man who adored her, who was a true partner. She was satisfied with her life in Silver Cliffs and sometimes had difficulty understanding Verity's wanderlust.

The transport's back doors slid open and the driver tossed up two large burlap bags. Mail then, which would make everyone happy. She took those to the little locked room she delivered the local and outside mail from. As soon as they got everything off, loaded and inventoried, she'd begin the process of sorting the packages and letters.

They passed crates up. Bolts of fabric. Brown paper sacks holding nails and other household needs. Colorful ribbons tied the opaque bags of the sweets her sister loved so much. Jars and cans of all different types. Tobin took delivery of the grain and seeds. The doctor came through the crowd and signed for a shipment of much-needed basic medication for folks in town.

There'd been thin times. Enough that the knot of fear that always began to tighten when she could begin to see the bottom of the drawers of basic foodstuffs in the mercantile loosened. Yes, they could weather lean times. Mostly. But having enough and a little to spare was a good thing. It kept the town easy and satisfied.

And with the days beginning to lengthen and planting season and the hours upon hours of labor that came with it, satisfied was a far better mood for people than the drawn face of worry.

Once she'd signed for everything, the transport would head over to the lot they used while in town. It was at the outer edge of the business center and the residents of Silver Cliffs would be able to drop off things to have them be delivered all up and down the Highway. Verity handled official mail, but there was a steady barter business between all the garrison towns.

"Tobin, get the news and other periodicals out first. I'm going to start on all the mail. Don't unlock the doors until I say so." She headed up to her apartments above the store to check on the stew she'd started that morning. Extra glad now that she knew she'd have a guest.

The place smelled good, the savory herbs and baby onions she'd found on her walk the day before near the river beginning to rise, accompanying the meat from a plump Muscat she'd been paid with. Muscats were nice and fat this time of the annum as they fed on the snow mice that bred in abundance. Her customer had even plucked and dressed it, saving Verity the less than pleasant job.

Another quick look in the mirror in the room Loyal always rented out when he came to town. When she'd received the blip that a transport would be arriving she'd aired it out, giving all the bedding a wash and leaving them in the sun to dry. Mountain lilies sat in a vase on the dresser, lending a deep red splash of color. Readying it for him.

———————

n his sector there were twenty garrison towns. A few were little more than bends in the road of less than a hundred people. All had their own charms in one way or another. But Silver Cliffs was not only beautiful, sitting up on the cliffs above the Highway, it had several farms, a river full of fish, woods full of game and two waterfalls that powered a mill.

There was a sense of plenty in Silver Cliffs that some other garrisons lacked. They took care of themselves and each other.

He took a leisurely walk up the hill from the garrison offices, his pack slung over his shoulder. The air was so clean up there.

Where Shelter City had thirty thousand residents—far more than Silver Cliffs' five thousand—it had more industry, more traffic. More noise to the peaceful quiet in Silver Cliffs.

He'd grown up in the back streets, running games for his father to put food on the table.

He shoved that memory away. It'd be good to stay a night or two in Silver Cliffs before they headed for the last two stops, the northernmost garrisons on the Highway.

It seemed as if half the town was lined up at the mail window and the other half milled around inside the mercantile. He knew there'd be extra staff on to help Verity with the crush. Knew she'd be busy.

But he stood in line to see her at the mail office anyway.

He watched her, smiling here and there, scolding anyone who got impatient or rude, laughing and joking as she worked quickly and efficiently.

Nothing about her was wasted. He liked that. Though she did have an abundance of beauty, he noted she always made an effort to tame it when she was in public. Yearned, he could admit in his secret heart, to see all that flame-colored hair down, wild about her face. Desired to rest his hands at the curves hinting at the waist of her wide-legged trousers or the long skirts she wore on days like this one.

He thought of her often when he was out on the road. Miles of emptiness only broken by the memories of her scent, or the way she sounded when she laughed. Even times when he'd had to face the violence of the brigands she came to his mind. The personification of why he did what he did. To make it possible for Verity to continue on in their world.

She looked up and caught his gaze, her smile brightening. "Lawman, well met!"

He tipped his chin. "Good day, Ms. Coleman. I came to see if you had any lodging available."

"Aye. Your room is ready. If you see any of the others, please inform them the bed and breakfast has three rooms available and the Sorens have beds available out at their farmstead as well. You can go on up when you're ready."

He tipped his head again. "Thank you." He moved out of line and headed around back to the stairs leading to her living quarters. He liked that she trusted him enough to give him free rein in her personal space. Most did, of course. Lawmen occupied a revered part of the culture. The lawmen had served on the front lines against the brigands for generations. The populace understood that, respected that. Having one stay in your home was an honor and why he, a single man, would be allowed to stay here in a widow's home without any raised brows.

Or, if there were any rumblings, they'd be kept quiet. The garrisons needed the lawmen to get delivery of goods from all up and down the Highway. Naturally, they'd all need to be put up when they came to town.

Some garrisons had hotels and other traveler lodging. Usually those closer to the capital city. Most had what Silver Cliffs had, rooms to let in various homes, sometimes beds at the garrison headquarters or police stations.

The others would know, of course, each having their favorite places to lodge. Trinity and Marcus would take one of the rooms at the bed and breakfast as they always stayed together. There was a bar down the other end of town, along with two cafes.

He wouldn't need either, of course. He didn't drink in public when he was on a ride. And Verity's cooking would keep him well satisfied while he was in Silver Cliffs. He'd dine with her. Though she tried, always, to refuse his payment, saying without him, she'd lose business. He knew her store made months' worth of revenue on the days an official transport came in. Knew too, she received a salary from the central governance to distribute the mail and be responsible for dissemination of official communication from them via the blip system she maintained in the office downstairs.

But he paid. As he always did elsewhere, though here it made a difference knowing it helped her.

At the top of the stairs his mouth watered as the scent of her kitchen hit. Herbs, some foul. Freshly baked bread. There was a basket on the nightstand in his room with a note that he should eat and bathe until she finished up downstairs.

Bathing sounded mighty fine, as it happened. They'd been on the road two days, having only briefly stopped just down the Highway in Table Mount to deliver fuel. They'd slept in their vehicles and tents as Table Mount was little more than a way station. They could have all slept in barracks, but Loyal preferred to be outside or in his vehicle instead of the confines of a barracks, weather permitting.

She had running water and a decent-sized tub. He ate a few of the corn patties and drank several glasses of water before he headed into her bathroom to wash the road from his skin.

When she'd finally finished with the mail, and knew there'd be another line up in the morning when she opened again, she headed into the store to help there. The first people allowed in were those who'd preordered goods. It kept the traffic manageable that first day of the deliveries.

And, she couldn't lie, it also encouraged people to preorder and put down payments on goods, which kept her credit account healthy. She liked the numbers, liked knowing that should she ever need to up and leave Silver Cliffs, she had the means to do it. Liked knowing she'd be able to get herself on a travel list at some point too.

That didn't mean she had the opportunity, not all the time anyway. But she liked having some options in any case.

The store bustled with business, customers wearing smiles as they took their paper-wrapped bundles from the counter. Her storeroom in the back was still full so she'd spend some time stocking after she closed up as well. But for now, she had plenty to do.

Constance worked alongside Tobin, going through the order cards and settling up accounts. Verity pulled out orders as she caught sight of people coming in. Constance's husband, Emeril, also came in a few minutes later, after he'd left his job down at the credit office for the day. He worked there during the snow season but everyone cut hours back during planting and harvest time. They had a sizable plot of land and grew grain they ground at the mill and sold in town.

The mercantile had belonged to James, but it was *hers* since he'd gone and gotten himself killed three years before. Good riddance to him. And in that time, it not only became hers, but her nephew had come on as her assistant and her sister and brother-in-law helped on delivery days in exchange for goods.

Emeril was wary of her. She knew he didn't like her curiosity. Had made multiple comments to Constance about how she needed to settle down and get married at last instead of flitting around town. But he was there to help and that's what mattered.

She also liked knowing that right above them Loyal stretched out those long legs on the bed in her spare room. Or lounged naked in her tub. As she measured out fabric and cut it, wrapping it up for her customers, she went back to an old favorite fantasy.

One where she'd come upstairs and stand in the doorway to the bathroom. He'd look up, surprised, probably smoking one of his fancy cigars. But she'd put her finger to her lips to hush him up.

Each button at the neck of her blouse would come loose as he watched. Down, more and more of her skin would show and he would not move. He would only continue to watch her with those big pale blue eyes that were nearly the color of a snow sky.

She'd slide the blouse from her arms, letting it fall near the clothes he'd removed earlier.

The steam from the water would allow her to pretend they were somewhere far away. The hot springs in the hills above Silver Cliffs maybe. It didn't matter, only that she'd pull her undergarments up and over her head.

Still smoking, he'd look at her, one corner of his mouth quirking up just a tiny bit.

A few buttons and her skirts would slide to her feet in a pool of fabric, leaving her in naught but her drawers, which she'd shed, standing utterly naked before him.

But she wouldn't be a shy widow. No, she'd unbind her hair, shake it out and his pupils would swallow the color in his eyes. His lips would part and he'd hold a hand out. Urging her to step into the big tub and join him.

She'd take the cigar, maybe even take a long drag, letting the smoke inhabit her body. All while his lips cruised over her body, his hands caressing her.

"My goodness, Verity Coleman, whatever are you daydreaming about?"

Faith Ander patted Verity's hand, tearing her from that fantasy and back into her life at the counter.

She blushed furiously.

"I must admit, Faith, I'm starving. I was thinking about the stew on my stove cooking nice and slow all day."

She laughed and Faith joined her. "I imagine on delivery days you don't get much time to have two thoughts in a row much less luncheon."

Verity wrapped the cheerful yellow fabric up and grabbed the blue after she looked at the sheet Faith had brought along. Faith was a seamstress. In fact her clothes were sold in the mercantile all through the year.

"I am fair excited to see what you'll be making with this blue. So pretty."

"Have some skirts and dresses on order for the yellow. Thought the blue would compliment. I haven't forgotten you either, Verity." She patted the green already wrapped and ready to go. "This is for a skirt for you. I think the blue would make a pretty harvest season dress too."

"Yes. Please."

She chitchatted with more people, measured out dry goods and such until at last, long after the sun had begun to fall below the mountains beyond, they finally flipped the sign to *Closed* and she sent everyone home.

2

He sat in her living room, reading a book. Deep concentration on his face, yet his body was relaxed. It pleased her that he felt safe to do so in her home. Pleased her to have him there.

"Evening, Loyal. I'll be with you shortly and we'll have dinner. Unless you've already eaten?"

He stood and nodded, tipping his chin with respect in a very old-school way. "Evening, Verity. I will admit I ate the entire basket of baked goods you left for me. But I'm more than ready to enjoy that stew. Tempting me all afternoon with that scent."

She smiled. "Thank you. I've spent some time during the last hour or two just thinking about it. I need to wash the day off and I'll return. If you peek in my pantry, you'll find some ale and a bottle of wine. A trader from Charity Bay, he was. Always pays that way."

"I'll get us a glass while you clean up." He nodded at her as she left the room.

She chose a deep blue dress. Casual of course, the type worn in the evenings at home by many women. But the color complimented her skin and hair and she liked looking pretty for him.

In the bathroom she noted he'd left her a gift. He often did that when he stayed with her. Several small soaps shaped like shells. She picked one up and brought it to her nose. The scent was fine, as delicate as the shape. And more, these oval-shaped cakes of every day soap. Though these too had a lovely scent. River lilies, mountain violets and the lush, nearly velvet scent of orchidium, found far south of Silver Cliffs. Past the capital city.

She picked that one and soaped up a washcloth, choosing a quick lather-up instead of a long, leisurely bath. She wanted to be with him, to soak up as much time with him as she could before he left. Once he did, she'd have plenty of time for long baths. Alone.

Brushing out her hair, she spritzed it to keep the curls behaving and chose to bind it loosely so it hung on one shoulder.

Which had been the right choice as he paused, his lips parting slightly when she came back out.

"How's the wine?"

"I saved the first sip until we'd toasted." He handed her a glass and clicked his with it.

"Go dte tu slan." In the old tongue for *safe travels*.

She smiled and repeated it back before taking a sip.

"Sit down and I'll get some bowls filled. There's fresh-churned butter in the cooler."

"Some days, usually while I'm in Silver Cliffs, I wonder if being paid in credits doesn't rob a man of the finer things like cream, honey, fresh butter and the like." He lifted his glass. "Fine wines on a cool evening as well."

"Ah well, I'm sure in the capital you can buy all those things and more with credits."

She ladled up the stew in two large bowls and placed them on the table, returning to her cooler to grab a jar of pickled vegetables.

"Nothing in the capital tastes anything near this good and fresh. Though I'm of a mind to bring some butter I favor the next time I come. It's caked with salt from the Great Sea. I think you'd like it."

Once she'd settled, he sat, placing the linen napkin across his lap.

"And how do you do, Loyal?"

The stew filled him, warm and delicious. She would have made a good wife. Though from the bits and pieces he knew, the man she'd had before didn't deserve her. Not so very uncommon.

"I do just fine, Verity. And you?"

"The same. My sister is with child again. The rumors, and I know how much you love those"—he snorted at the tease—"are that the garrison chief is sneaking through Madeline Johnston's back door most nights. Course, they're both of age, neither is married to anyone else. He's fine looking, which I suppose is part of it. The jealousy, I mean. The river is full of sweet, fat silver fish. There will be plenty drying all around town this week. You'll be of a knowing when the wind shifts. Planting will begin soon. The ground is softening up. You only just missed the mud." She sighed. "Takes too much time to deal with the floors downstairs when we get a few days of mud. Like all of my life is about sweeping and mopping and sweeping some more. Telling people to kick their shoes a bit afore they come in."

He knew she was hungry for details of the world outside the walls. So when she finished, he'd give them to her. Part of his pleasure in visiting her was sharing those details, watching the delight on her face, hearing the rushed pleasure in the way she asked for more.

"This is a delicious stew. The pickle as well. Did you make it?"

"Yes, thank you. My garden was heavy last season. Had so much extra it seemed a shame to not pickle and put some by. Sold quite a bit downstairs to folks my mother would have termed the grasshoppers, aye?"

He smiled at the memory of the story of the ant and the grasshopper. The ants worked hard to prepare for lean times but the grasshopper lazed about and was caught unawares when the snow fell.

"If she were still alive she'd laugh to know those grasshoppers keep food on my table all snow long."

"Indeed." He shifted in his chair, settling in to speak. "The grass is very tall now down in Solace. They had their thaw two moons back."

"More temperate to the south, yes?" She leaned in, eyes alight as he started to give her those details he knew she wanted.

"Yes, doesn't snow much south of Shelter City. Only round the annum end. Powerful hot in the mid year down there though. No icy cold river to dip your toes in. Though in Solace there's a mighty large lake. In the mid year the town guards it often so folks can go on down after the workday is over, or on off days to cool off."

"Solace has those little cookies?"

"Yes, they're green because the flour they're made with is cut with the sweet grain that grows with the grasses. Seem to recall you have a powerful like for them."

She blushed. "You brought me some last annum. They were delightful with tea."

He'd remembered of course and would leave her a small bundle of them to find once he'd gone.

"And how is the Highway? Jackson down the garrison heard tell the brigands were active again on the southern passes?"

"Unfortunately, yes. Whole town was attacked, Brilliance. One of the furthest south, where the Highway begins."

Her hand went to her chest. "How did the people fare?"

"Many didn't." Including several lawmen who'd been nearby and had raced to help.

She shook her head. "A tragedy to be sure. I'm sure you heard when you checked in that we had some news of scouts."

He had and it had filled him with rage. And worry for her.

"You know if they come you're to head to your storeroom and lock yourself in."

She waved it away. "I know that's what everyone tells me to do. As if I would hide away when I could help. I'm a good shot with a rifle. I have extra ammunition here. If they come to our gates I will not hide while they burn us to the ground. I will protect my home. But the sentry towers are on alert. We're fine. I have a tunnel, from the cellar out to a plot of land a bit away. I've got food and water, supplies and the like, stored back there too. But I'm staying as long as I can."

He frowned. "Finer if you'd keep yourself safe instead of trying to do battle with scum like the brigands. They won't just burn things, if you take my meaning. Beautiful woman like you has far more to worry over."

"If you think women are unaware of such dangers, you have no idea what it's like to live in this world as a woman." She pursed her lips and sniffed as she delivered her set to and he had to grip his spoon to keep from touching her as the heat of want washed over him.

Prim and proper Verity was delightful enough, but when she got fire in her eyes? His cock grew hard and heavy and his mouth watered to take a taste of her lips. And other parts.

"I appreciate the way women are viewed." He nodded. "But I

know these brigands. They would rip everything you hold dear to shreds."

He spent the rest of the meal entertaining her with stories about all the garrisons he'd been in over the last moons. About what people wore, what they ate, how they celebrated this or that holiday. He colored in her world, adding details she craved about the world outside the walls.

"One day I want to travel down to Shelter City. Stay for a while. Stand on the shores of the Great Sea."

"It smells so clean. Like nothing else. The sand, so soft, like a cloud, aye? And the water chases away and rushes back. Over and over. Nipping at your toes. Cool and fresh. You'd like it."

People did travel for holiday. They could book space on official transport, but the price was dear and there was a wait list. A very long one. Extremely difficult too, for unaccompanied women unless they were visiting to be courted. She frowned at the idea.

She dried the last of the dishes and hung the towel on the peg.

"Would you like some music then?"

"I would. I brought you some books as well."

She smiled. When he visited he not only brought her little indulgences, but important things like books and periodicals. She loved to read and he did as well. He brought her all manner of things, from light and breezy stories of fancy and love to heavier, darker tales. Reference manuals she kept in her kitchen shelves. She traded the books around the garrison and they ended up in the library when she was done. She wasn't the only one who loved to read.

"Thank you."

Her music player was charged and soft music played through the room after she hit the switch. He'd built a fire earlier so the living room was cozy and warm. He handed her a large bundle and she settled on her settee to look through the titles as he settled in the large chair and pulled the newspaper out.

It was so lovely. Normal and yet a rare treat, as he'd be gone in just days and she'd be alone here once more. His smell filled the space and she breathed it deep, wanting to be bold enough to tell him how much she wanted him to touch her. Damning the world she'd been raised in, the world that had kept her from knowledge, had raised her to always use soft words, to keep her gaze averted and to wait for the man to do the talking and action taking.

It was a silly world and it had raised silly women all chafing at the rules that were supposed to protect them. From what no one ever seemed to want to tell her.

She only knew she was fortunate not to be under a man's thumb any longer. Her independence came at a cost. A price she'd pay a thousand times over to be in her own place, on her own terms. One she also realized wouldn't last forever, but she planned to enjoy it as long as she could.

"Loyal?"

He looked up, awaiting her question. He wasn't one of the silly men who'd fluttered around with flattery and charming smiles to talk her into sneaking a kiss, or far more. No, he didn't waste words except when he told her the stories about the outside world.

"Are women like this all through the Highway?"

He folded the paper once and then another time, sitting it in his lap. "How do you mean?"

"Overprotected, aye? Taught to only speak the sweetest of words?"

He struggled with a smile and she narrowed her eyes his way.

"There are garrisons where the women are not allowed to come out when we arrive. Where women cannot be unescorted by a male. Others where the women are equals, who have the same rights as the men. Silver Cliffs is a garrison on that side of the continuum, though not as open-minded as Shelter City."

"Hm." She nodded. "I wish to visit those places."

"Have some hard words you need to use, then?"

"Are you making fun?"

He laughed, the sound rusty, but lovely and welcome. "I would never dream of such a thing."

He picked his paper back up. "Should you like to use the bad words or get up to things men do, feel free. I can even offer you assistance should you need it."

Boldness burst through her. "Yes? Say if I wanted you to put your lips on mine then? Would you do that?"

His gaze snagged on hers. "I don't think that's a good idea."

"Is that so? And why is that?"

"Because you are fine and beautiful. You are feminine and graceful and I am not."

"If I had want of another woman I could find one and ask her for a kiss, Lawman."

He blushed for a moment, swallowing hard. "You know what I mean."

"No, I really don't. Do you not have a wanting of me? A woman back home?"

He licked his lips. "My wanting of you is not the issue. I'm not for you."

He went back to his paper and left her frowning.

Confused and frustrated.

But also, the fire in her belly lit. She saw it in his gaze. He wanted her and now curiosity and stubbornness worked together.

She wanted Loyal Alsbaugh.

3

She decided to go ahead and take a bath once he'd retired to his room. It would be an early start for her come morning. She'd get up, wash her face, braid her hair and, after a quick breakfast, would spend the rest of her day rushed off her feet in the mercantile.

The water was nice and hot as she disrobed before pinning her hair up. A few drops of oil in the water filled the room with scented steam, relaxing her.

Well. Most of her.

Just being around him sent butterflies into her belly and a bone-deep knowledge that if she should ever be so lucky to have him in her bed she'd never be the same. Loyal was the kind of man who would know what to do.

She sighed as she stepped in, groaning a little at how good the water had felt. The wine and company had loosened her muscles and the water did the rest.

Starting at her toes, she slid her hands and the cloth over her skin until she had to catch her breath at her mid thigh.

Her legs parted as she thought of his hands. The way he'd felt when he'd helped her up on the platform out back once before. Strong. And yet he touched her like she was precious. Not fragile, despite his earlier tease; he seemed to respect that she was capable and intelligent. But special.

Once, when she'd first been married to James, he'd rutted and passed out and she'd escaped the house, heading out for a long walk. And she'd seen Bethany Schaffer with Abel Temple. He'd pressed her up against the side of his house. Into a shadowed corner. If she hadn't been where she was, coming down the street quietly, she doubted anyone else could have seen.

But *she* had. She'd ducked behind a tree and watched with envy, knowing she'd never have that, not with James and his sour whiskey breath and his mean, careless fingers.

But the fingers she brushed against her pussy weren't his. Not anymore. Her fingers knew what she liked, what she wanted as they slid her labia apart, remembering how Bethany and Abel had looked together that night.

And the memory changed, shifted into fantasy as Bethany's eyes became Verity's, those hands sweeping up and over Bethany's breasts became Loyal's.

She soaped over her belly, one hand remaining at her pussy. She brushed the pad of her middle finger over her clit, breathing in deep as the wave of pleasure rippled outward.

The other hand tested the weight of her breast, a slippery thumb flicked back and forth over her nipple. Her eyes drifted closed.

His mouth would find her nipple, suck and draw until she rolled her hips, seeking more. He'd slide his hand down into her drawers, petting and then finding her hot and wet.

A teasing touch of his fingertip against her clit, all while his mouth was still on her nipple.

She'd whimper softly, urging him for more. Because she'd need more. And he'd give it to her with a snarl as he spread her legs apart with a knee. The teasing touch on her clit would turn into a gentle pinch of thumb and forefinger.

His cock would brush against her, pressing in just right until she arched her back on a gasp as he thrust all the way, all while he concentrated on her clit.

He'd whisper how much he wanted her, how sexy she was, how good she felt. His words a hot brush of breath against her nipple as he bit gently.

He'd fuck her like she'd dreamed all these years. She'd be the woman whose man took her as she threw her legs around his waist, her head falling back as she bit her lip, coming hard as he continued to thrust until he found his own end moments later.

Loyal had been standing at the window, staring out over the town, smoking and trying very hard not to think about Verity's suggestion that he kiss her.

He'd wanted to. Had even thought of ways to do it to teach her a lesson. But that would have been dishonest. And unfair to use that when she'd been chafing at the ways she'd felt restricted as a woman.

Especially when he wanted to kiss her so badly the hand holding the cigar shook a little.

She rustled in the bathroom next door and he tried not to imagine her in there, disrobing. All that pale, pretty skin exposed.

The scent of her soap, or whatever it was she was using, seeped under the door along with the steam.

He undressed, usually sleeping naked if he were home or in a hotel. But because he was there in her guest room, he kept his drawers on, along with his undershirt.

He was tired. Been on the road long enough that his muscles had ached for hours once he'd arrived. That had passed, but the exhaustion remained, blunted by the excellent dinner and company. He carefully stubbed the end of his cigar, saving the rest for the next day. He needed to sleep.

And that's when he heard the groan.

He scrubbed a hand over his face at the sound.

There was a splash here and there, enough he knew she was settling in the tub. The night was quiet enough that once he'd slid into bed, he could hear the sound of the water as she soaped herself up.

He lay there. Imagining her, slick and wet.

No. Fuck. No.

He tried to think on other things and then he heard it, another moan, only this was not a feel good sitting in the bath groan. No, he'd heard the sound come from a woman's lips as she'd been underneath him often enough to know. It was a moan of pleasure.

Which meant she was . . . The breath shot from his lungs. She had her hands on her pussy, on nipples he'd imagined way more than once or twice. She was just on the other side of the wall, making herself climax.

He should have put a pillow over his head and gone to sleep.

Instead, his hand found its way down to his cock, freeing it. Still hard from earlier, revived by the sound of her naked and touching herself just on the other side of a door.

She'd be a pale beauty, her breasts buoyed in the water, her nipples—they'd be cinnamon pink, he wagered—would peek just above the water line.

Knees up, perhaps?

He fisted himself, imagining slamming the door open.

"Seems to me, Verity, you need a cock deep inside you. No hand is going to make you feel the way I can."

She'd blush, caught with one hand delving between her thighs, the other frozen on her nipple.

He squeezed his cock harder, finding a rhythm.

He'd stalk over and pull her to stand as he sat on the side of her tub. He'd pull her down into his lap, right onto his cock. It'd be tight, that sweet cunt of hers. Most likely ripple around him as he seated himself fully.

Oh the sound she'd make. He cupped his balls with his free hand, speeding the grip on his cock as he imagined pumping into her body. The way her lips would part so he could kiss her, the taste of her as his tongue lapped at her.

"Later I'm going to lick your pussy just like this."

He had to bite his lip to keep back a groan at the thought of his face between her legs. He'd lay odds that old bastard she'd been tied to never ate her out. Never tasted her sweetness that way.

He heard her gasp next door. Heard a soft moan as the water splashed. Knew she was coming. Wondering if she thought of him as she did. Knowing, even as he told himself it was bad, that she did.

He arched, the hot, wet evidence of his climax hitting his hand as he worked to stay quiet, as he listened to her, thought about the way it would feel to come as he thrust so deep inside her body.

How old were you when you were married?" He asked her this as they walked side by side up the hill back from the picnic the garrison had just held for the lawmen and transit drivers.

She looked at him askance, briefly. "I was fourteen."

He frowned.

"My parents felt I was willful. Said I'd settle once I got married and had children. Thank the heavens James wasn't able to put a baby in my belly," she mumbled.

He raised a brow at her impertinence, liking it.

"Oh I know I'm supposed to want all that. And maybe I would have with another man. All getting married at fourteen did was make me hate my parents and end up dodging fists and tripping over sick and empty bottles for the next eight annum until he ended up dead at the end of a knife, bleeding out in an alley. No one missed him for three days."

"There were no good times then?" He shook his head. "Forgive my intrusiveness."

She waved it away. "Despite what I was raised to think and feel, I am not ashamed of what he was, or what he did to me. It was his sin, not mine. The blessing is that I have a way to remain independent now. My parents are dead. I did my duty and married. No one can force me into it again. No one can take my property. I'm a widow so that means they have to leave me alone for the time being. So I suppose that would qualify as a good time."

He'd never met anyone like her. Fiery and yet soft and sweet all at once. All that contradiction only made him yearn for her all the harder.

"So you're off tomorrow morning then?"

"Yes. Two more stops to make and then we start over at Shelter City."

"When will you be back?"

"Transports will be more frequent now that the weather is better. A moon or two most likely unless we pick up anything for Silver Cliffs in Charity Bay or Northern Tip."

"I wish I could come along."

He briefly let himself imagine her next to him as he drove. She'd most likely be a good companion on the long stretches of roadway. And then he remembered the fear, the heart-pounding danger the brigands posed him and his team several times every annum. The reason they all had to live behind walls.

"It's dangerous out there. I'd never want that life for you. Here you're safe. You can walk out in the sunshine. Have citrus punch and eat cakes. No one is trying to harm you."

"It's the same. Year after year. There's a whole world out there and I'm not living in it. You're out there and I'm not. I like having you around."

She blushed and he may have done so as well. As much as a man like him could.

"We'll be back before you know it. I'll be smoking in your spare room and eating all your eggs."

She shrugged. "Sure."

"It's your last night here. I won't be offended if you wish to join your friends down at the bar."

He snorted. "If I wished to have a drink with them, I could most days." He was of the opinion that it was best not to get drunk with the townsfolk of the garrisons they were responsible for protecting. They were supposed to be seen a certain way. Part of that was to hold themselves apart. It was hard to do that if you sat ass to ass on bar stools. Townies didn't need to see a lawman drink to excess. Though to be fair to his team, he doubted that would happen. They knew their jobs.

Moreover, he'd far rather have Verity all to himself his last evening in Silver Cliffs. He'd had to watch all day long as she helped with the preparation for the large cookout they'd had. Watched as men took her in with greedy eyes. And why not? There was something so very vibrant about her that others couldn't begin to match.

One of these days he'd come back through those big garrison gates and she'd be courted, or maybe even married to someone. And while it was an honor to lodge a lawman, he wasn't sure how he'd feel about sitting at her dinner table with another man at the head. A man who touched her in all the places Loyal dreamed of.

"All right then. You did promise to teach me a new card game. The last time you were here, remember? I have ale and some of the sweets left over from the luncheon today."

"Aye, that sounds like a very fine evening. I'm sure the men in town would thank me for teaching you how to be a card sharp."

She laughed, delighted. "That would be lovely indeed. I could build up a savings on the side to travel if I could do that."

"Travel?"

"I'm saving to visit Shelter City. I'm a ways off from a buy in for the waitlist. But I figure if I have another two good annum I can do it." She pulled a deck of cards from a drawer in her buffet cabinet and held them aloft.

"I'll get the ale." He headed into her kitchen. A woman like her in the capital would attract a lot of attention. A man would have to be blind to miss her.

"I'll be back in a moment. I'm going to change."

She stood in front of her closet, peering inside, frustrated. She *knew* he was interested in her in a romantic way. He watched her at times, the way men did women they fancied. He paused when she talked about travel or when she'd related the story about John William trying to argue her into letting him court her the season before.

But he kept his distance no matter.

It made her want to stomp her foot and toss a fit, is what it did. Though she was far too old for such silliness. And too smart. She knew that too.

Verity had to figure out how to shake him up, how to get him to abandon his silly insistence on not kissing her. Or bedding her. Or anything fun like that.

She pulled on a soft, long-sleeved blouse and some trousers. She unpinned and unplaited her hair, deciding to leave it loose around her shoulders before heading back out to her living room where he'd poured them both a goblet of ale and built a fire.

"Thank you for taking care of the fire. Clear skies mean cold nights this time of the season. A fair exchange I suppose, especially when the woodstove heats the house so nicely."

He stared at her long and hard without speaking and self-consciousness swept through her. "Is all well?"

He cleared his throat. "Yes, yes, I apologize for staring. Your hair . . . you . . . I don't know that I've seen it loose like that before."

She blushed, reaching up to touch it. "Does it look funny?"

He shook his head. "No. It's beautiful. Like sunset. Not a color you see often up and down the highway."

Warmth spread through her at the compliment. "Thank you. I have so much of it and it's so curly I keep it up or pinned back usually. My mother's hair was this color. My sister's is dark like my father's was. I guess . . . I guess you knew that as you've seen her around."

He pulled her chair out and she sat.

"I quite prefer yours." He studiously avoided her gaze as he spoke, pulling the cards from the leather case.

She sipped her ale, trying not to be nervous. Not nervous, actually, sort of . . . giddy. Yes, giddy. He'd taken notice of her in that way of his. But it was hard for him to shake off this time. She smiled at him when he looked up.

"That smile should make me nervous."

"Ah, but does it, mighty lawman? Do I make you nervous?"

He laughed then, hearty, a sound she rarely heard from him. "Any smart man would be advised to remain nervous around a beautiful woman who smiles like she's got a secret. It's what they call evolutionary learning, aye? Now, on to cards. We can't neglect your card sharp training."

They played cards for several hours as she coaxed stories from him about his travels. He rarely liked to speak about himself but she did something to him. Loosened him up before he even realized it. It was . . . nice to let his guard down around her. To feel safe within the walls of her cozy home and simply be Loyal.

She cleaned up, preparing everything for the next morning as she usually did, and for a moment he allowed himself to imagine this with her. This with her as his woman. Frivolous, and a waste of time, he tried to argue with himself, but he did it anyway.

She turned back to him once she'd finished. "I'm to bed. Since you're all leaving tomorrow there'll be a flurry of things to take care of. You know how people are. Always waiting too long to do the necessaries."

He nodded. It was the same in every garrison. The morning they left the townspeople would line up to get those last-minute letters and packages on the transport. The bits and bobs they wanted to barter with others up and down the highway.

"Human nature."

She stepped closer but he'd been leaning against the doorway to his room so he had no place to step away. Her scent wrapped around him, a fist of the glory of her womanhood, and he could do nothing but let it.

"I'll miss you."

He had to clear his throat to get the words out as she stood close enough that her hair brushed the back of his hand where his arms were crossed over his chest. Flowers and sunshine and a tiny bit of wood smoke. The spice of his cigar was what got him the most. His scent had marked her in a sense and though he didn't want to, he found himself moved by it. His cock hardened.

"I'll be back afore you know it. You stay safe. Brigand reports not too far down the Highway. Stay behind the walls."

"I can't always do that."

"You need to."

She went to her tiptoes. "And what'll you give me if I do?"

Her breasts brushed against his forearms and he groaned, grabbing her upper arms before he knew it, hauling her that tiny bit closer and his mouth came down on hers.

She moaned, opening up to his tongue as it swept into her mouth. She was sweet and hot, eager as he took and took. There was no artifice about her. She wasn't an expert at kissing, but what she lacked in experience she more than made up for in enthusiasm.

Even as his brain screamed at him to stop, his heart, his bones, his cock, everything he felt with urged him to take. To seduce and tease.

Her taste slid through his veins, gripping, digging in and rooting itself deep.

She made a startled sound—not distress—excitement, desire, when he nipped her bottom lip. He'd been trying to pull away, but the sound brought him back for more. Gods, more and more.

He kissed his way over her jaw, feasted on the spot just below her ear until she made another sound, a gasp of his name.

With every last bit of strength he possessed, he set her back from him, licking his lips as she looked up at him, dazed, her mouth kiss-swollen, skin flushed. So beautiful and carnal.

"I'm sorry." His chest seemed to burn as he fought his instinct to take her to the bed, to strip her of all her clothes and feast on her skin.

"Why?"

"This can't happen."

She frowned. "Ridiculous. It just *did* happen. I liked it. You liked it. Why shouldn't it happen more?"

"I already told you, I am not for you. Go to bed, Verity. Go to bed and thank your heavens above that I have the strength to make the right decision here." He pushed her back slightly to get around her and inside his room where he could close the door before he made any more mistakes.

4

When she'd woken up, he'd already packed his things and gone. A look out the windows showed the transport and escort vehicles lined up.

She didn't speed her pace. It was early still. She made herself breakfast and drank some tea before heading down to the mercantile and opening up. She handled all the last-minute packages and other mail and with Tobin, organized people into orderly lines to hand over their things to the transport drivers.

She caught sight of Loyal down the way at the garrison offices with the other members of his team. He looked up the hill and saw her, nodding his head. She waved, but kept at her work. The night before had simply been step one. He'd awakened something in her she hadn't even really known she possessed.

A sort of carnal awakening, a sense of her own power as a woman. She'd made him short of breath. She'd brought him so much need his fingers had dug into her upper arms hard enough to leave two fingerprint bruises. Not that she'd mention it. She got the feeling he would feel guilty and she didn't want that.

It had filled her with . . . a sort of satisfaction to see them. To see the effect of the loss of his control. His need had washed over her skin like a narcotic of sorts.

Loyal Alsbaugh wanted her. With so much ferocity it had set her aflame just being in contact with his body. She wanted more. Knew when it happened—and it would—it would change her. And hopefully him as well.

She could wait. For the time being in any case.

The townspeople used to the process of the leaving of the transport had been orderly and ready as their turn had come. Verity handed over the mail sacks and signed them in for delivery.

They'd all congregate shortly down at the bottom of the hill at the gates. But she moved to the lead vehicle where Loyal had just locked his rifle into the slot on the dash.

"You stay safe. And return soon. You didn't finish your card lessons."

He shook his head, a half smile on his mouth. A mouth that had been on her own, on her neck. A shiver went though her at the memory.

"Stay in the garrison like I said, aye? Please?"

She knew what that please must have cost him, so she nodded. "As much as I can, I will. Come back soon."

"Safe travels." He got in the vehicle.

"And to you." She stepped back to the walk and watched him close the door and click the side shield into place over the window.

"I don't know how they do it. How they face the dangers of that Highway each and every time the way they do." Tobin said it with some greed as he watched the procession head down the hill.

Perhaps she wasn't the only one in the family with a curiosity about the world outside.

"They do it because it needs doing." She waved at the transport and then the vehicles at the rear of the procession.

There were shouts and horns sounding at the gate as the sentries called out the all clear and the wheels began to turn as the gate slid to the side. Each vehicle drove through until they were all out. She knew they'd cross the bridge singly and then head down the fortified road to the Highway and drive north.

Her old life clicked back into place as the gate did.

"Come along then, Tobin. We've got some inventory to do."

She'd spent her time immersed in all the daily work she needed to do to get ready for the coming seasons. Out behind the mercantile she spent her late afternoons after she'd closed down tilling the soil and getting her planting rows in order.

She planted her seeds for the melons and root-based vegetables. Those she kept in the cellar below the store. The cool earth would keep them through the snow times. She'd be able to use them in soups and stews, baked in casseroles all through the coldest months. She trimmed back all her berry bushes near the low walls that separated her land from her neighbor's. Those would burst into life in a few moons and keep her in pies and preserves for the rest of the annum and also give her plenty to trade.

She opened all the parcels that had come with the delivery. Read the letters from her far-flung friends at garrisons up and down the Highway. She always saved them until he'd gone. For those first, hardest weeks when she felt his absence the deepest. There were little bottles of perfumed water, pots of healing salves for burns and rashes, muslin bags of dried herbs. Jars of preserves, of sauces, of flavored spreads to put on game and fish. Most she'd keep for herself, as they were little trades in return for her jars and bags of things she'd created. Others she'd use as payment for goods and services in the garrison throughout the annum. When her machinery needed fixing, or when she needed extra labor in the mercantile.

Over the weeks she'd received several blips from the central governance. Reports of increased brigand attacks on Highway traffic. And two incursions on garrisons.

Jackson Haldeman, the head of the garrison defense, showed up at the mercantile just as she was closing up. "Good day, Verity." He tipped his head and she smiled.

"Hello, Jackson. Do you have need of something from inside? I know the proprietor so I can open up for you."

He laughed, his smile spreading over his features, making him very handsome indeed.

"Appreciate that. But no. Not today. I came to let you know that, if you'd like, we're going to be doing some instruction. With the rifles. I know you have some first aid education and if you'd be of a mind to teach others, I'd see it as a kindness. With the increase in brigand attacks, I want to stay at the ready."

"Of course. To both. I know how to shoot. But I could use more instruction. I just put by some healing herbs and salves. I can make extras for the garrison barracks as well. They keep if you leave them in a cool, dry place. A root cellar or the like."

He nodded. "Thank you. On the morrow then, an hour before the sun sets we'll be starting with target practice."

"I'll be there. I can do some lessons on dressing wounds and the like on the off days. With harvest season ahead, it's a good knowledge. Always end up with injuries that time of year in any case."

He nodded. Pausing. His gaze sliding over her face with pleasure.

If it weren't for Loyal, would she wish he'd invite her for a walk? Should she go if he invited her? He would be a good catch, as her sister would say. Jackson with his broad shoulders and his easy smile. A provider. She'd never heard tales of him hitting the bottle or anyone else.

"I'll see you tomorrow then." He stepped down. "And perhaps . . . perhaps I will be seeing you at the fest this coming week's end?"

The fish were running. Every year the big, fat silver fish would come in high numbers to the river to lay their eggs and have lots of tiny baby silver fish. The town would net them and set them to smoke, to dry them, to jar them in oils and herbs and preserve them for the annum ahead. It was a unified effort. There was music in the evenings and a big dance out under the stars.

"Aye." She smiled, not really knowing exactly what she was agreeing to other than the target practice.

5

She'd been toting her rifle over to the field behind the garrison offices when she heard the horn sounding at the main gates.

She noted that the field was empty, so they must have all gone down already. Wisely, she kept the rifle. The horn wasn't the friendly note of non-hostile traffic, though not the alarm either.

She caught sight of Tobin. "Go back home."

"Why? I want to see who it is."

"Because there've been blip bulletins about the brigands attacking up and down the Highway lately. Because I said so and I'm your aunt, that's why."

He frowned.

"If it's bad, you'll need to be in a place you can hunker down and protect your family. Now get on home."

He nodded, grumbling, but he turned and headed back toward home. That was one less worry.

Men weren't running down the hill with rifles so that was a plus, but she headed up to her parlor to look out and saw the tail end of the procession. Lawmen.

Her heart skipped a beat and she put her rifle back in the closet and headed to her porch.

It had only been a moon since they were in Silver Cliffs last. Happiness replaced her worry at the rare treat to be able to see him again so soon.

The gates rumbled open as she watched.

Not the usual large official transport though. A smaller one. They used to be that size back when she was younger and the deliveries came about once a moon. The time between deliveries had lengthened as she'd gotten older.

Clearly something had changed. She wondered if it was a good thing or not.

Tobin came running up just a few moments later. "Guess I better get the mercantile open."

"Doesn't look like we'll be taking in a large order. But yes, let's get the back doors open and see what we're dealing with."

Loyal pulled up to the garrison offices and got out. One of the vehicles remained at the gates until they'd closed and would be along in a bit.

Haldeman came out with a wave. "Weren't expecting you back so soon. Everything all right?"

"Brigand attacks increasing. I suppose you been hearing?"

Haldeman nodded. "We've been doing target practice frequently to keep everyone sharp. Extra patrols. Verity has been doing triage and first aid for those wanting the lessons. Course, a pretty woman teaching you how to sew up a wound makes for some full classes."

Loyal wanted to snarl at the idea, but held it back. Nodding. Because he understood it. The world was dark sometimes. Hard living in these garrisons. Lots of work. You took your pleasures when you could get them. And most certainly looking at Verity Coleman would count as a pleasure.

"More lawmen out. They've cut our territory down, added two more escorts to each sector of the Highway. Figure it's better to let them see our increased presence and to keep folks happy with more mail and the like." And shorter trips for the escort edged the danger back a smidge, even as it filled the Highway with more guns and men and women who'd use them to protect those they were charged to protect.

"About a dozen annum back, aye? We had a lot of attacks then too. That's when we added the fortifications to the road leading up from the Highway. Is it that bad now?"

"Don't rightly know just yet. But if you can afford to add to your patrols, you should. Keep people up in those towers full time. They're leaving the Highway to come to the garrisons more and more often. Maybe they have a baby boom." He shrugged. They didn't know a whole lot about the brigands. They were nomads in nature, moving in large encampments.

He'd been a tracker first, before he'd hit the Highway with his escort team. Throughout history, especially after the big tech war, the central governance had tried to reach out to the brigands, to offer them land to set up, help with crops and the like. Urging them to leave peaceably. But what the governance had been confronted with was that the brigands weren't the same. They didn't want to settle. They *liked* their raids. Seemed to embrace the bloodlust of preying on the weak, of the raping and killing.

They were human still, yes, but not fully. There was something different. Less . . . civilized he supposed. And they had no hesitation in the burning and the pillaging of anything they could.

"I'm on it then. I'll be able to find you at the mercantile later?"

Loyal knew he should stay there at the barracks. After that kiss—and gods knew he'd thought about it constantly since he'd left—he should keep his distance. But he wouldn't. Couldn't.

He turned, catching sight of that sunset red as she took delivery of the mail. "Yes. I'm available to help with your patrols as well. We'll be here three days."

"I'll be up later then." Haldeman smiled as he looked up the hill. "Think I'll be getting the mail for my mother. Always nice to have an excuse to chat a spell with the widow Coleman."

Loyal wanted to punch the other man for even thinking about her. Instead, he nodded again and tried to keep his expression neutral. "All right."

He left his vehicle near the garrison and met up with the rest of his people.

"I've offered our services to Haldeman with the patrols. Trinity, I want you to be sure they're at least taking the opportunity to track on occasion. Bren, you work with them on their hand to hand. Marcus, take a look at their sentry points outside the walls. Haldeman says he's working on target practice so I imagine Indigo can help with that. Not tonight. Everyone get some rest tonight. Let's be sure we leave Silver Cliffs safer than we found it."

He headed up the hill, knowing she'd be there, needing it more than he should have.

The line for mail was the usual and he waited his turn. She caught sight of him and smiled. A smile just for him. "Head on up. I didn't know you'd be arriving, so there's no basket of baked goods. There's fresh bread on cooling racks in the pantry, though. I'll be up later."

He nodded and headed around back.

She managed to get finished and to close up within the hour. Since the delivery had come so late, most folks would wait until the following day to pick up their orders, which worked for her as she was hungry and tired.

And she wanted to see him.

The scent of his cigar hit her as she climbed to her front door. He sat at her kitchen table with a mug of tea at his left hand, a sheaf of papers before him on the table. She noted the red stamp at the top. Sealed blips, she noted. She delivered those—unread—to the garrison when they came. And there'd been a lot of them as of late.

"Good evening, lawman."

"Good evening, Ms. Coleman."

She squeezed his shoulder as she moved past. "Are you hungry then?"

"I am."

"I'll make us some supper and you can tell me what's happening with this new schedule."

She pushed her sleeves up and washed her hands before she began to pull together a meal.

"You're too bright for your own good."

She laughed. "If only you were the first person to tell me such nonsense. How is one too smart for their own good? In any case, I can read the blips. I know there are more attacks. Your change in schedule is most likely due to that. It's not mysterious."

"Aye. They've put more lawmen out on the Highway. It's good for citizens to see us, to know they're protected. But the shift only just happened a week ago so there's been some scrambling. We made a big jump and drove straight through without stopping. Stayed in Salt Flats two nights though, so it's better than we were before that."

"And how long are you here this time?"

"We're staying in all mid-sized garrisons three days now. Small ones we'll do overnights. The largest we stay for two days. My team will accompany patrols, do sentry duty."

"Good training for the garrison soldiers here. To see how you all do your job in that setting. Most of them are farmers. Aside from the full-time garrison sentries." She paused as she deposited a bowl of sliced fruit on the table. "It's bad then? Risky?"

"There's been a great deal of activity along this sector. We don't think you're at risk for an assault, but it won't hurt for their scouts to see us on the ramparts of the garrison walls."

"All right then."

"Been busy since I last left?"

"Gearing up for—" There was a knock on the back door. "Can you get that then? I need to turn the fish when it's ready."

He stood, moving carefully to the door.

Jackson Haldeman stood there with a smile. "Well met, Loyal."

Loyal stood aside to let Jackson in, hiding a frown as he headed straight to the kitchen.

Verity smiled when she saw who it was. "Good evening, Jackson. I was just making some supper. Would you like to stay?"

Jackson's expression lit in an entirely different way when gave his attentions to Verity. His smile softened as he took her in from head to toe. "I would very much, thank you."

That's when Loyal realized Jackson Haldeman had his eye on Verity as more than a passing fancy.

"I'll get another place set." Loyal moved past Haldeman to grab another plate and some utensils. He put them on the side away from Verity.

Jackson held up a sack. "I brought some sweets. My mother wanted to thank you for the poultice you made for her leg."

Verity took the bag and peeked inside. "Spiced fried dough? Your mother knows my weakness. We'll have them after dinner. Sit. Both of you."

She filled their plates with food and sat, chattering about her day and whatever else was going on for some time until she finally sat back. "All right then. I'm sure you're here for an official reason, Jackson. Go on."

"You might as well speak plainly in front of her or she'll pester you until you do."

Verity's surprised laughter came right as Loyal realized he'd spoken his thoughts aloud. He gave her a stern look but she waved it away and kept eating.

He and Jackson spoke then about their plans. About the news that the brigands had attacked Banyon Pass two days prior. The garrison had managed to repel the attack, but not without losing a third of its livestock and nearly twenty citizens.

Banyon Pass was roughly the same size as Silver Cliffs, though it wasn't quite as protected by the surrounding landscape as Silver Cliffs was.

"Why are they suddenly so much more active?" she asked.

"We don't know. It's always like this. It ebbs and flows, aye? We can go an annum or three with minimal activity and then suddenly they're everywhere, attacking. We don't know much about the other side of the mountains." Just that it was fairly inhospitable and crawling with brigands.

"I've got a meeting set for just after breakfast. Come down to the garrison offices and you can address my people. We'll double our patrols. I've already doubled the sentries on the walls."

"Smart."

Jackson stood. "I need to get back home. Thank you for dinner, Verity."

She smiled at him. "Thank you for the sweets. And your mother. If she needs more of the poultice let me know. I'm teaching a few in town how to make them and it's good practice."

He disappeared with one last nod at Loyal and a promise to see him the following morning.

"Looks like Haldeman has an eye on you."

She looked Loyal's way, one of her brows hiking. "Yes, I believe he does. Question is, Loyal, what are you going to do about that?"

"What do you mean?"

"I mean, you look like you just sucked on a lemon. Clearly you don't like it that Jackson is sweet on me. And I'm asking what you plan to do about it."

She moved out of the kitchen, pulling her curtains closed here and there as she moved through the house. He wandered behind her, breathing her in.

"I . . . Nothing, I suppose."

She spun, stomped over and poked him in the chest. "Nothing?"

"Are you sweet on him?"

"I'm on fire for you." Her voice was low. Urgent. Full of emotion and it set his world on its end. "There's no sweet on him, no room for that. Not when every time I think of you I can remember what it felt like to have your mouth on mine."

He licked his lips. Knowing he should step back. *Knowing it.* But he didn't.

"You shouldn't be. He's a better choice. Safer. He's here. I'm not."

She made a sound, frustrated. "Since when does that sort of thing ever play into it? I'm not my sister. I can't place my affections, my desire, based on a set of calculations about which man would come with more cows and pigs, who could chop more wood to keep my home warm through the snow. My desire doesn't care about that. It cares about the way your voice changes, deepens when I stand this close. How your scent rises to my nose as your skin heats. Spicy like your cigars. How when I see your vehicle my entire system seems to come alive and I realize all the time when you are not here is gray. You make me feel alive, Loyal. So stand there, why don't you, and tell me what you plan to do about Jackson Haldeman wanting to court me. Hm?"

He should have told her to back off. Hells, he should have backed off himself, retreated to his room and closed the door.

Instead, he slid his hands around her neck and yanked her close, his mouth falling on hers like he needed it more than his very breath. Which he was fairly certain was true.

She sighed, her body molding to his, her posture softening, submitting to his control and that only made his need worse. The roar of it harder to overcome and so he ignored all the voices telling him to stop and continued to plunder the sweetness of her mouth.

He sucked her tongue and she gasped and then moaned, arching. Irresistible. The need to show her what a real man could do in bed, how he could love her until she was boneless, raced through him. He wanted to show her that. He wanted to make her come so hard she sobbed, and the idea that anyone else wanted to do that, wanted to lay with her at night drove him on, drove him to burn into her memory just how much he desired her.

Wanted her to never forget him.

And it didn't matter that he shouldn't. It didn't matter that he'd told himself for years not to let himself get carried away with what he felt for Verity Coleman.

All that mattered was the need that beat at him, the way her breath hitched, the way her fingers had tangled in his hair, holding him close as he continued to kiss her.

Knowing a kiss, even hours' worth of kisses would not be enough.

Her grip tightened in his hair, bringing a grunt to his lips as he pulled her snug to his body, rolling his hips to let her know what was happening. Maybe on some level trying to scare her into breaking away. If she pushed him back or broke this off he could find the strength to end it.

He sure didn't have it on his own.

Instead she made a soft sound and pressed closer still, brushing her body against his cock, setting off licks of flame through his belly, low, hot, electric.

She let go of his hair and pulled back a tiny bit, but only to get her hands at the buttons on his uniform shirt. Unfastening quickly until she slid it open all the way, her palms caressing all the skin she'd bared.

It was his turn to groan, to hitch a breath as she pressed the heels of her hands against his nipples. She paused, breaking the kiss. "Yes? You like that?"

Surprising him, she pushed him back against the doorjamb and leaned, licking over his nipple. Gently at first.

"Harder."

Her eyes cut to him and she pressed her tongue, flicking it against his right nipple. Scoring her teeth over it until he gasped.

She kissed over his chest to his left nipple, kissing, licking that one until he hauled her back up, taking her mouth once more.

Then he pulled her blouse from the waist of her trousers and parted it, untying the ribbons holding it closed until she was left only in a chemise, the shadow of her nipples visible through the translucent material.

"So beautiful."

She swallowed hard, looking up at him as he looked down at her breasts. He cupped them briefly before he pulled the tiny, pearly buttons from the holes, one after the next until he stared at her, at the luscious swell of breasts he'd dreamed of since the first time he laid eyes on the widow Coleman.

"Better than dreams."

The hesitance washed from her face, replaced by a boldness that made him even harder.

"Touch me, Loyal."

He did. Brushing his thumbs over the hardened nipples until she arched. He kissed down her neck as he shifted, backing her into his room. To the bed he laid in when he was there, fantasizing this exact thing. Only now it was real.

She reached out as she hit the mattress, pulling him down with her.

"Don't go anywhere."

He pulled his shirt off, toeing his shoes away as he did. "I'm not. I have far too many things to do."

She unbuttoned the side of her trousers and shimmied out of them as he did the same with his pants.

The moon was high overhead, casting silvery light over her skin, now totally bare.

"You're so pretty, Verity." He swallowed hard, sliding his hands over the curve at her hips.

She grabbed his cock, squeezing gently. "You too."

"I'm . . . pretty?" He'd meant it to be a joke, but she'd slid her thumb through the slick at the crown and it sent a shock of pleasure through him, sending his words scattering from his head like birds going into flight.

"In your way, yes. Manly. Hard and strong."

He moved back to the bed, laying next to her. "I shouldn't be doing this."

"You plan to stop?"

He shook his head. "Not unless you want me to."

"I want your hands on me. Show me, Loyal. Teach me how to make you feel good. I'm not . . . not like the ladies you likely bed when you land in their garrisons."

"You aren't. Which is why you're impossible to resist."

She smiled and he pulled her hair loose so it fell against her pale skin like rivers of flame.

"And you're doing just fine at making me feel good."

She laughed.

"Now I want to make *you* feel good."

He bent to her again, kissing her mouth, nipping and licking until she was breathless. He left her lips and kissed over her face and down to her chin. Delicate and yet, as he'd realized after knowing her as long as he had, strong.

He licked over the hollow behind her jaw and she shuddered a sigh.

"Like that?" he murmured against that sweet, sensitive space.

"Y-Yes."

He continued, kissing down her neck, his hands sliding over

her chest, over her collarbone, down to her breasts—those glorious breasts. He tugged and rolled her nipples until she made a sound unlike any he'd ever heard her make. A sound he knew without a doubt he'd never forget. Full of need and pleasure.

He licked over one nipple as he tugged on the other. He sucked. Gently and then harder. When he bit she gasped and then her entire body seemed to heat.

She liked it hard.

He was in trouble.

Because he liked it hard too.

He tried again, a little rougher, pulling her nipple with his teeth as he moved back and she moaned, her hips jutting forward as she did.

He did this to the other nipple as she held on at his shoulder, her short nails digging in until he groaned.

He kissed over her ribs, across her belly and breathed over her mound.

She froze, the weight of the moment on them both.

He slid her thighs wide as he moved to the floor, settling on his knees between them, pulling her butt to the edge of the bed.

She gasped. "Oh. I . . ."

He kissed the back of her knee. Her skin smelled like nothing else he'd ever experienced. Hot and spicy and sweet. Up her thigh until he blew against her cunt.

He heard her swallow there in the dark.

"I take it no one has ever put his mouth here?"

He leaned in and slid the tip of his tongue over her clit for a moment.

"N-No."

"Shameful."

"Is it?"

He smiled as he spread her open and took a long lick, moaning at the taste of her.

"Not this part." He licked her again and again. "The part where no man has tasted how salty-sweet you are. I'm going to make you fly apart, Verity."

He sucked her clit gently, over and over until she breathed in soft little sobs.

And then he stopped. She reached out faster than he'd have thought of her and grabbed his hair, tugging.

"Shh. I'm not done."

Her breathing calmed a little as he watched her again, sliding his middle finger around and around her gate, pushing inside to stretch her. So tight his cock throbbed with want.

"How long?"

"What?"

"How long has it been since you've been fucked?"

"Two years."

He looked up her body as he took another lick. "He died three years ago?"

"Nearly four now. It was . . . doesn't matter. I was lonely. It was forgettable."

He licked again and again, stretching her as he added another finger.

Her muscles froze, tensing as she sucked in a breath.

"Let go. Breathe. Don't tense up." He spoke against her slick flesh as she came, as the taste of her, the sweetness he'd been lapping up, exploded into something else. Spice. Pepper. Heated as her pleasure bloomed on his tongue, against his lips.

He kissed his way up her belly, pausing when he caught sight of the tears on her cheeks and worried he'd pushed her too hard.

"Are you all right?"

"Yes." She opened her eyes. "Yes, yes. It was wonderful. I've just never . . . not that. Not with anyone."

He kissed her cheeks, tasting her tears. She wound her arms around his neck, holding him tight for a moment. And then she pushed him back, kissing his neck, down to the hollow of his throat. The cool silk of her hair slid against his skin like a caress, the scent of it, flowers and sunlight, seemed to dig into his memory with claws. He knew no matter what else happened, he'd never lose this memory.

She kissed across his chest, licking over his nipples and looking up at him. "I never realized men liked this."

He arched when she sucked his nipple and let her teeth slide against it as she let go.

"Can't say for anyone else. But when you do that I surely do like it, yes."

She smiled and went back to it, kissing him, sliding her hands all over his upper body. She licked a line down his belly until she got to his cock, grabbing it and looking at it closely.

"Kiss it."

She did.

Then she licked over it and licked again.

James had forced it on her many times. But this was different. *Loyal* was different. He tasted right. His skin taut and hot to the touch. She held him at the root, licking all the way from the head to her hand. Learning what made him jump, what brought that moan to his lips. What made him hiss with pleasure.

It was delicious to do this with him. It wasn't a requirement. Something she dreaded as a responsibility. She *liked* it. Her sister never said much about her intimate life with her husband, but she had said something once about how she looked forward to their time alone, when she could make him feel better and ease the day from his shoulders.

She hadn't understood it then, having wished daily that James would drink himself unconscious so she could avoid any intimate contact with him.

But she understood it now. Hoped that her sister had this with Emeril.

She licked around the crown of him, delighting in the sounds he made in response. She palmed his sac, pressing the pads of her fingers over the pucker of his ass. His answering groan told her he liked that very much.

She kept him nice and wet, up and down, around the head.

He was rather . . . large. Thick. A tingle of curiosity slid through her belly. Excited at the idea of having him in her, wondering how it would feel. Wanting it very badly.

His fingers had been tangled in her hair, holding loosely, but he shifted, wrapping it around his fist and holding her steady as he thrust into her mouth.

Her skin beaded into gooseflesh. She was wet again, aching to be filled.

And then he stopped with a snarl.

She was about to tell him if he stopped now he'd best sleep with one eye open. But he shifted, sitting up.

"On my lap."

"On top of you?"

He smiled and it sent a slither of want over her skin. "Oh yes. Never had it that way?"

She shook her head.

"Get over here. Straddle my waist. Knees on either side of my body."

She did as he said and realized it would be fine. She'd know what to do.

He grabbed his cock to angle it, sliding that fat head through her pussy. Teasing, she realized.

"Sit when you're ready. If I was on top I'd slam into your cunt hard and fast. But it's been a while and you need to go slow so I don't hurt you. You need to take control because when it comes to you, my control is weak."

What could she say to that? The things he said filled her with emotions she couldn't fully name.

She took him at the root where his hand had been. He moved his grip, one hand at her hip; the other found her nipple and began that tug, tug and roll.

"Mmm, you're so wet."

She would have been embarrassed perhaps if it was another man saying so. But his words weren't meant to shame. They were meant to incite. As he was incited by her.

The power of that built in her belly and she let herself be eased by it.

She began to move down on him. The head of him was thick and fat and she breathed, letting it feel good, letting the worry fall away because he wanted her. She didn't know what would happen in three days when he left, but she knew without a doubt that he wanted what was happening between them right then, and it was enough.

He stretched her slowly as she kept taking him inside. The burn at first would dissolve away into pleasure. James had never allowed for that. Had never let any of the pain dissolve and all it was was a burn.

This was what she'd dreamed of with her hand in her drawers late at night in the dark as she lay alone in bed. *This* is what it could be and she would enjoy it without shame.

He clenched his jaw, sweat on his brow, ordering himself to let her set the pace. Trying to ignore the screaming in his head that told him to take her. To slam his cock balls deep into her cunt and then let her adjust.

Instead, he looked at her features as she slid down. Watched the tension slide away as the pleasure took over. Never in all his days had he seen anything even approaching this sort of beauty.

The pleasure he felt was edged with near pain. She was so tight. The hot, wet embrace of her inner walls tortured him as she fluttered all around.

"Okay?"

Her eyelids came up and her gaze cleared. "Yes," she exhaled on a gasp.

And then she began to move. Slow, up and down. And he forced himself to let her do it. To find her pace, to see what she liked.

"There are other ways you can move as well," he said, his lips against the skin of her shoulder.

"How?"

He took her hips and helped her circle, wide and then tight. He showed her a back and forth slide that she seemed to really like given the warm rush of her as she moved.

"Like that."

Her head fell back as she slid herself back and forth, back and forth on him. She ground her clit against him, a ghost of a smile on her lips.

"Yes, like that indeed."

He moved one hand between them, letting his fingers brush

against her clit with each movement she made. She gasped, her eyes opening again.

"Embrace it. Let it come and let it feel good."

She nodded, catching her lip between her teeth as she did.

He let it go as long as he could before he began to move as well, pushing up as she moved back and forth. Her lips opened and he swallowed the exhalation as he kissed her hard.

"Yes. Do whatever, take it from me. Just . . ."

He did. Took over the pace, using his hand at her hip to continue to help her slide back and forth and he fucked up into her body over and over and over. She ground herself against his fingers, her cunt tightening around him as she turned superheated, as the hot rush of her sweet juices flowed and she exploded, sending him right over in her wake.

She sighed, sated, as he shifted to lay her at his side.

"I can't believe you made me wait years for that, lawman," she mumbled as he pulled her close.

He snorted a laugh.

"Me either, widow."

6

She was pulled from sleep by the repeated beep of the blip receiver.

She sat up, pushing her hair from her face. She smelled like him. On her hands, on her skin, between her thighs. She smiled as she got from bed as easily as she could, not wanting to wake him.

His eyes snapped open though, as her feet hit the floor.

"What is it?" Totally alert.

"How do you do that?" She pulled her clothes on quickly.

He shrugged, his gaze on her as she moved.

"Something important is coming over the blip. I'll be back. I need to go attend to it."

"I'll come with you. You don't need to be out so late, not all alone."

"How do you think I do it when you're not here?" She headed from the room, slipping her feet into her house shoes and grabbing a robe for the warmth.

"Ah, but I *am* here."

She didn't fail to notice the way he grabbed his weapon, sliding it into the belt he strapped on after he got his pants up. Dangerous.

She hustled down the stairs and out into the cool stillness of the pre-dawn hours outside. She unlocked the door to the mail office quickly, heading back, knowing the way, even through the darkness.

Three blips? She picked up the two that had fallen from the collection arm to the floor, handing them to him. Anything being sent at this time using the emergency channel would be something he'd need to see.

He turned on the light and read them quickly, his mouth drawing into a tight, disapproving line. "I need to go to the garrison office with these." He took the one that had just come in when she handed it over. "This one too. You go right back upstairs. If you hear the alarm I want you to go into lockdown, do you understand me?"

"What's happening?"

"Brigands hit Northern Tip. They've been seen just a bit up the road. They attacked an official transport as well."

She shivered. That was all so very close to Silver Cliffs. "All right." She handed him her keys. "You know which one unlocks everything. I'll be waiting for you."

He watched her carefully for long moments, before his gaze went back to the blip receiver.

"I'll run over to the garrison if any more come. Go."

He moved to the door with her but just before she opened up, he pulled her close, his mouth coming down on hers hard and fast. She pushed herself to his body, already getting used to it. Knowing she shouldn't and choosing to ignore that voice.

"I'll be back when I can."

She headed back upstairs, straight for her gun closet. Best to be prepared if things went the direction she feared they might.

H e pounded on the door of the garrison and it opened up rather quickly, the gun pointed at his face lowered once he was recognized.

"Blips." He stalked through the door. "Jackson here?"

"He's a'home."

Loyal gave the man a look. "Well go on then and get him. I'm going to rouse my people and we'll all meet back here as soon as possible."

The guard scampered off as Loyal headed down the hill to get the rest of his crew together.

Haldeman took the blips from Loyal's hand, reading them quickly. Loyal gave him credit for the way he simply took it in and formatted a plan.

"We need scouts down by the Highway."

Loyal looked to Trinity where she stood at the ready, near the door. "You go with one of Haldeman's people. Get down there and let me know what you see." He turned back to Jackson. "None better than Trinity."

Jackson nodded. "Good to know. Harmon, you go with Trinity. Take the trails. Stay off the road."

Trinity and Harmon disappeared out the door after Marcus squeezed her hand quickly. The two had been a couple since before they came onto Loyal's team. Some commanders didn't approve of partners on the same road crew. Loyal didn't care one way or the other as long as no personal shit spilled into official business.

And it hadn't, so he had no call going and having feelings one way or the other about it.

"At this stage, we don't know enough to get everyone worked up." Loyal eased back, leaning against the corner of a desk.

"Verity knows about this?" Jackson held up the papers.

"Aye."

But he didn't need to defend her, Jackson merely nodded. "She'll keep it to herself. She takes that seriously. I'm going to raise the watch level in town. We don't need to call a full alert, but people need to be sure they've got plenty of ammunition and some stores set by in case we get ourselves under siege."

Loyal nodded. "We'll postpone the leaving until we know for sure you're safe."

"Glad to have you in town should this happen."

He thought of Verity. He was too.

They stayed, going over the garrison's basic emergency plan, Loyal approving most of it, making suggestions where he saw they might be needed. Jackson Haldeman was a smart man. He'd have made a good lawman if he'd wanted to be.

"You know where I am when you hear back from the scouts. I'm going to send a few blips back to Shelter City."

"I'll be up in a bit."

He headed back up to Verity's place. Noting the lights burned in her windows. He went around back and into the blip office, sending back his official response, filling them in with what he knew for sure. Which at that point wasn't a whole lot.

When he'd gotten back upstairs, she'd made a big breakfast.

"I figured you might be hungry. I'm baking too. May as well lay in some supplies just in case."

He noted she'd lined rifles up at the various windows.

"The shutters are in good shape." Verity waved a hand toward the windows, meaning the siege shutters they'd draw should the garrison be overrun. They had slots for a rifle cut into them. "I just had them checked last harvest. Jackson had the whole garrison do a drill."

"Haldeman is setting the garrison on alert." He poured himself some black tea and she shooed him to the table, filling a plate for him and setting it in front of him.

"He'll be up soon I wager. To check the blips and give me the broadsheets to post."

Her store would be the nerve center for the town's citizens. The garrison was the law enforcement hub, but he knew the townsfolk would come to the mercantile for the news before they'd gather at the garrison offices. She'd post the broadsheets with the instructions for everyone to follow on the boards out front.

"You ever gone through this before?"

"An attack?"

He nodded.

"Once when I was eight or nine we were overrun. It was back before they built the wall to reach the mountains behind us. My parents hid us in the root cellar. They got pretty far into Silver Cliffs. Set fire to buildings near the gates. We've had alerts here and there since."

He stood and went to her, brushing the backs of his fingers against her cheek. "I'm going to protect you."

She nodded. "I know." Utter faith in him shone through her gaze.

"Come sit and eat with me. I'm sure it's going to be a busy day for everyone. You'll need to eat too."

She did, but before he could talk with her about what had

happened between them the night before, Jackson came in and sat with them, eating as he and Loyal went over next steps.

By the time they'd finished, she'd gone down to post the broad-sheets and open the mercantile for business.

And then Trinity had come back with news that sent everyone scrambling.

Brigands had been seen gathering on the Highway near the turnoff for Silver Cliffs.

Verity continued to work, trying to think on this as just another drill. Trying not to be afraid or to panic. There was no reason to jump into being afraid just yet. They were fairly well prepared. And they had something a lot of garrisons didn't when they were attacked, five lawmen working with the garrison defense.

Her sister came into the mercantile. "We want you to come stay with us until this is over."

Verity shook her head. "I need to be here to monitor the blips and to keep people informed. Do you have enough food and ammunition? Enough fuel?"

They were all advised to keep at least a moon's worth of sup-plies in case of a prolonged siege but people oftentimes put such things off.

"Jackson can put someone here to monitor the blips after you close. This is silliness. You're not a man. You're not a soldier. You should be protected."

"I'm also not helpless. I'm a better shot than many men in Silver Cliffs. My home is well fortified. I've got a lawman staying in my spare room. I'll be fine. I appreciate the concern, but I'm all right."

"He's not moving to the garrison barracks?" One of Constance's brows slid up and Verity braced herself for the lecture she feared would come.

"They've all decided to keep the lawmen scattered through town as they are now. They have personal communicators so they know if there's a problem. He can run and be down at the barracks in a flash. They all can. No use sleeping on a cot when he can stay here." She shrugged.

"You have anything you want to tell me?"

It wasn't a crime, or even a sin for her to take solace in Loyal's arms if she wanted to. As a widow, she had more freedom than she would have if she'd never married. But some people, maybe even her sister, might look askance.

She had no intention of confessing to her sister as if it was something to be ashamed of.

"Jackson is sweet on you. Is he all right with the lawman staying at your house?"

"I've been owned by a man. Owing him news and explanations of every moment of my day, aye? I will not, ever, owe that to another human being again. Jackson can feel however he wants about where Loyal is staying and it means no nevermind to me, understand?"

Constance sighed, nodding. "They're not all like James. Jackson would be good for you. I'm just saying maybe take how he feels into account."

"I know what you're saying." Verity closed the discussion firmly.

"All right then. Please come to our house if things get scary. I'll feel much better if you do."

"Thank you. I will."

"And Tobin says you've given him the week off until this blows over?"

"Yes. He should be home where he can protect you and the house."

Her sister rolled her eyes. "I want him here in the daytime. He gets under my feet at home. He's disagreeable because he'd rather be here where he can see everything. I know you'll send him home if things change."

"You sure?"

Her sister nodded.

"All right then. The windows need a good cleaning. I'll put him on that so at least he'll be too tired to argue with his daddy when he gets home at night."

Constance laughed. "Thank you." She hugged Verity, kissing her cheek. "You think on what I said." And left before Verity could argue.

7

People had taken to congregating there on her large porch, watching the street leading down the hill. Watching the gates and whatever they could beyond them.

She'd done a brisk business over the last two days. A few enterprising souls showed up several times a day with baskets of sandwiches and wrapped bundles of meat and rice or grains, selling them for snacks and luncheon. People found a way, she thought with a smile. Even in the darkest of times, people found a way.

There was a curfew in effect at sunset. She sent people home as she and Tobin pulled the shutters over the windows on the first floor, locking them into place.

"I'll see you tomorrow. Go on home and take that bundle to your mother. I made her some of the tea she likes. It'll settle her system."

Her sister tended to be violently ill in the early months of her pregnancies. Luckily, the combination of herbs and flowers Verity dried for her tea seemed to aid and ease her sister's discomfort. It was nice to be needed. Nice to be able to help.

Tobin nodded, kissing her cheek and running off home, the bundle under his arm.

Loyal hadn't been around the night before as he'd done whatever they did down the garrison offices. But he came in as she stood in her kitchen wondering if she should take some dinner down to them all.

He held up a basket. "Went fishing today since we were out scouting anyway. I even cleaned them for you."

"This is a division of labor I'm quite happy with." She smiled with a wink, taking the basket.

"Have I actually found something you aren't good at?"

"Gutting fish and scraping off the skin and scales?" She wrinkled her nose. "One does what one must. But if I can avoid such tasks, I'm pleased to do so."

He shrugged, a smile on his lips. "What'll you give me then if I do all the fish gutting and scaling?"

She put the basket on the counter and moved to him. "Whatever you want."

He licked his lips and she let the power roll through her. The ability to turn his head and keep his attention. The ability to make his cock swell and his mouth turn up into a rather wicked grin.

"Why don't you get on your knees. To get started."

She did, obeying immediately, looking up his body into his face.

"Let me check the door."

She grabbed the waist of his trousers, opening them quickly, pulling his cock out, hot and hard in her grip. She licked over the head, tasting the spice of his seed.

"You worried someone might come up and see me here, on my knees, your cock in my mouth?"

She had no idea where the words had come from. She'd thought such filthy things before, but never had she said them aloud.

He shivered, rooted to the spot. "Go on then." He rolled his hips as she put her mouth around the head, pressing in deeper and pulling back.

He undid her hair, his fingers sifting through it over and over as she fell under that rhythmic touch. Until he wrapped it around his fist and held her exactly where he wanted her.

At first he'd tried to tell himself he wouldn't do this again. But he'd been a liar because he'd been dreaming of this since he'd pulled out of her cunt the night before last.

The reality of this woman on her knees before him, that sweet mouth wrapped around his cock, her hair around his fist as he fucked her face was better than anything he'd ever dreamed.

"Breathe through your nose. Slow and steady." He nearly crooned the words, sliding his free hand over her head, down to caress her cheek even as he kept thrusting into that mouth.

"Can you take more? Hm?"

She whimpered, but not in fear. He had to close his eyes a moment at the way the sound affected him.

"I think you can. For me." He thrust harder, she hummed her pleasure and the sound vibrated up his cock, into his gut.

"I'm going to come in your mouth. And every time I look at you I'm going to know that. And you will too."

She dragged her nails lightly over his balls and he groaned, unable to tear his gaze from her, from the sight of his cock sliding into her mouth and coming back out, wet and dark.

He heard her breathe through her nose, deeply like he'd told her. Orgasm began to dig its nails into him as he watched her swallow his cock again and again.

He fought the urge to close his eyes when it hit, instead he watched as her lids closed, as she flushed a pretty pink when he came. She didn't let go either. Not until *she* was ready to be done.

And then when she let him pull back, she looked up and licked her lips.

He'd given life to this more carnal Verity. He saw glimpses of it here and there since that first night. Knowing no one else had noticed. No one but him. She seemed to ooze sensuality now.

And he let himself be fascinated by it. Later he'd have to deal with it, but for the time he was there, he'd soak it in.

He helped her up, kissing her hard.

"After dinner I'm going to feast on your cunt until you have to scream into the pillow. And then I'm going to fuck you so hard your breasts bounce."

She licked her lips again and swallowed, nodding.

"Yes. Please."

She moved around the kitchen on shaky legs as she put a meal together. He sat at the table, reading, making notes and watching her with covetous eyes. He made her knees wobble.

"So any new sightings?"

He looked up. "Nothing new. They're good at blending in. Not always so dependent on vehicles, which means they don't need the roads."

"Are you still leaving tomorrow?"

She hoped not.

"Most likely no. One of the blips today advised us to stay in place."

"You should take me then. When you leave I mean." Now that she'd blurted it out she felt better. Lighter.

She turned the fish in the pan, tipping it to get the oils so she could spoon them over the sweet flesh a few times.

"We've talked about this."

"No we haven't. You'd said I was better off here than traveling out there. I want to see the world. I want to know what it's like outside these walls. I've lived here my entire life. I've never been further than half a day's walk from Silver Cliffs. You've been up and down the Highway. You've seen how people live, you've eaten what they eat. You've seen how they dress. I know enough to know it's not all how we are here. I know people do things differently in other places. I want that. I want to see it."

"You want to leave here where the walls keep you safe from the brigands?" His gaze seemed to burn through her as she stirred the rice, fluffing it and putting it into a bowl she placed on the table.

"You're alive. The people you travel with are alive. The people who drive the transports are alive. Don't patronize me."

"I'm not patronizing you. I'm telling you it's safe here. You're better off here. The world outside will change you. I don't want that. Can't you see?"

"Why is it about what you want anyway? What about what I want?"

"And then what? Hm? You leave here to do what? Go where? With who?"

She rolled her eyes and put the bread, still warm from the oven, on the table. "Please pour us some juice."

He sighed, getting up to do so.

"With you, of course. Trinity and Marcus drive together."

"They're lawmen. You're a shopkeeper."

That hurt. He was right, of course, which didn't really negate the hurt.

"If you don't want me along, just say so."

He started to speak but a knock on the door interrupted them both. "Don't think I can't see the relief on your face. This isn't over."

He walked past her, pausing to give her a hard, quick kiss before he moved to the door, letting Jackson in.

"Trackers just came back. Brigands are about two miles down. They're sticking close to the river. But they're headed this way."

"I'll make this portable." She moved to sandwich the fish in the center of the crusty roll along with some of the pickle. "Jackson, would you like one?" She held up the bread after she'd wrapped it and placed it on Loyal's empty plate.

"Aye, that would be mighty fine, Verity. Much appreciated."

His eyes took her in, pausing at her mouth and then shifting over to Loyal briefly.

Loyal disappeared into his room and came back out with a leather roll, which he unfurled on the tabletop. He slid into an overvest, one she knew would repel bullets and blades. His gaze had gone flat and hard, his mouth set in a line.

She handed a sandwich to Jackson and he ate it as he watched Loyal take the weapons in the roll and strap them on.

Blades, guns, he tucked a few magazines for his weapons in a pocket of his trousers.

"I need to get to my people. Take the town up from general alert to full alert. I want everything locked down."

Jackson nodded as he ate. "Done. I'll send runners out." He turned to Verity. "Thank you for the dinner. I hadn't realized how hungry I was." He smiled, reaching out to brush some crumbs from her skirt. "You lock down too. Are you going to head to your sister's?"

She shook her head. "No. James let you all use the house the last time we had an incursion. He sure told the story often enough. You can see plenty from the attic and the roof." She took a key from a nearby drawer. "This unlocks the store and the stairs. Consider this my permission to use the roof and attic for your men as well."

"Don't go doing anything stupid, you hear me, Verity?" He took her hands. "You see them coming and you get yourself locked in your cellar. I know you have an exit from there to the pasture out back. You get gone if you need to."

She nodded. "I have supplies hidden out there. I'll be fine." He paused as if he were going to speak, but Loyal cleared his throat as he kept arming himself, though he kept his gaze down on what he was doing.

"I'll check in on you later." Jackson headed to the door and looked to Loyal before leaving. "I'll see you at the garrison shortly."

And was gone.

She moved to Loyal, bending to tie the laces on his boots. He hauled her to her feet when she'd finished. His gaze severe, hard. "You *will* remain here in this house, do you understand me? Green flare if you need to evacuate. You see two greens and you get that pretty little ass downstairs and into that cellar. Use the full locks and the big heavy door. You get yourself gone. I'll find you when it's safe."

"I'm not stupid. I won't stay if we get overrun."

"Nay, not stupid. But passionate." He sighed. "They will . . . they will savage every female in this garrison if they catch them. I don't want that to happen to you. Or to anyone here." He amended, but it was late enough that she knew he cared about her in a way he wasn't sure how to process. Which was good as she felt quite the same.

"I have no desire to be savaged. Though, should a certain lawman want to pillage?" She raised her brow and smiled. He shook his head.

"You're a handful, Verity Coleman."

"I am. Don't forget it."

He hauled her against him, the blades, though sheathed, pressing into her flesh through her clothes. A reminder of what else he was. It thrilled her though she knew it was dangerous.

His kiss wasn't safe. It was hard and fast, a gnash of teeth, the nip of her bottom lip. He branded her with that kiss. "Your lips are still swollen from my cock," he spoke against her mouth at last. "Haldeman noticed that."

"Yes." She tried not to pant, but it was difficult.

"Mine." He kissed her hard one last time and stepped back. "Watch out the window. Keep the lights off. Lock this place down and do not come out unless you get the signal or are escorted by one of us or Haldeman's men. Promise."

She nodded.

He grabbed two rifles and headed out. She went down, checked the locks on the windows and pulled the heavy plates down, covering the doors and windows. She slid the bolts and locks into place and headed back upstairs, doing the same on the main door from the back stairs. She'd keep the exit down the back stairs, up to the attic, down to the cellar and her tunnel to escape locked, but accessible. The lights went off all over town as the runners spread out. Shutters clanked shut, locks clicked out through the night.

She only hoped they were ready to repel the assault she knew in her bones was coming.

He gathered his team, who'd already been on alert and were all ready.

"They had a group of about twenty that I could see." Indigo indicated a map on the table nearby and they moved over.

Haldeman and several of his men were there as well, watching, ready for orders. In a situation like this one, Loyal would be the commanding officer.

"They were here." Indigo pointed.

"There's a trail just ahead." Haldeman drew a line from the river toward the garrison. "It would take them around the bridge, but they'd still have to cross the river. Right now it's swollen with melting snowpack. Several feet above the normal levels. And brutally cold. Too cold to swim across and live."

"Other than the main bridge, where else can they cross safely?"

"Nearer the pass." Haldeman pointed miles east of the garrison, higher up in the mountains. "There's a bridge up that way. They can cross there. Even if they ran it would take them an extra day, day and a half. The climb is brutal. Maybe it'll discourage them."

"Depends on the why of this attack." Stace looked over the map. "I can get to the bridge up on the pass. Blow it so they can't cross."

"What do you mean depends on the why?" One of Haldeman's men stood forward.

Trinity shrugged. "You can't count on the brigands to do things how you might. They don't think like we do. If they're hungry or angry at having to walk extra they may not give up like you or I might. Go pick an easier target. No, they might figure the extra work is worth whatever you got in these walls. Or they may be so mad that they see this as revenge for making them work so hard. Or maybe they're starving and they'll come no matter what. They don't think like regular folk is what I'm saying. They're brigands. Closer to animal than people at times, 'specially times like these when they're on a hunt."

Trinity knew them well. Her family had been taken by them. She'd been raised as a camp slave for several years until she'd escaped. Just ten years old, she'd leapt off a moving brigand vehicle and into the road in the path of a lawman's escort. It was lucky they hadn't shot her but stopped to help. Against regulations to do such things, but it had saved her life and she'd been with the lawmen ever since.

"I'm going to advise you let Stace blow that bridge."

"It's a way for us to hunt without having to go all the way around."

"I understand that. But if you can slow down a gang of brigands that's going to be better than having to deal with rebuilding it when it's warmer. You see my meaning? We may not be here the next time. You blow that bridge and they have no other choice but to come over the main bridge. It cuts down their avenue of attack. Makes it manageable."

Haldeman sent a hand through his hair and then nodded. "Go on. Tell me what you need and how many you want to come with you."

8

He shuffled back up the hill some hours later. He'd been up for far longer than he should have been and Indigo, his second, had shoved him out the door with orders to get some kip and a meal before he came back.

It was the calm before the storm. They'd prepared all they could for the time being. The team had left to destroy the bridge at the upper river with several of the garrison's best trackers so he had every reason to believe they'd finish the job and likely be back at the garrison before the brigands had even reached that far.

His people would also do a survey of the river to be sure there were no weak spots to get across. They could use boats to get across, but the current was fast as well as cold. And the brigands were many things, but sophisticated they weren't.

There was nothing to do at that point but rest while they could so he'd nodded and left.

The shutters were locked all over town, though some were out and about doing necessary business. But the mercantile was closed, he was pleased to see.

He went around back, unlocking the large blast doors covering the entrance and sliding them back into place when he'd finished.

She was curled in a chair near a shuttered window. He smiled at the juxtaposition of her there, small, the tumble of hair making her seem even smaller, and the rifles at each window.

He'd only gotten three steps into the room before she awoke.

"News?" She stood, stretching, and before he could think to say anything he was on her, his mouth on hers, his hands pulling her close. He *needed* that contact in a way that should have scared him. Most likely would later.

After.

He shoved her hair back over her shoulder one handed and slid the robe she'd been wearing off her shoulders, leaving her in a long nightdress that buttoned all the way up the front. He couldn't wait. Didn't want to wait. He grabbed either side and tugged hard, the material parting on the sound of buttons flying.

She gasped and he paused, waiting for rebuke, but got none. Instead she moaned, arching into his touch as he slid covetous hands over her bare skin. He'd had this well of need for her that appeared bottomless. And since the first kiss, he'd been unable to resist her.

She offered herself to him and he had no ability to turn away.

Pale and beautiful in the dim light that made its way through the shutters, he took her in as she stood, bare, the remains of her clothing pooled at her feet.

He fell to his knees. "I believe, before we were so unfortunately interrupted by brigand talk, I had plans for you." He leaned in to kiss her belly, below her navel. "For your pussy."

She shivered, sliding her fingers through his hair.

It was cool in the house and he noted the gooseflesh. "Wait for me there." He pointed at the settee, before he moved to the wood-stove and built up the fire within. The air began to warm a little and he moved back to where she sat, watching him without a word.

He took her mouth, still on his knees. She wrapped her legs around his body, holding him close.

"So beautiful," he murmured, kissing down her neck to her breasts, licking and biting her nipples until she made a whimper deep in her throat. "I've been thinking about the way you taste all night."

He'd come in looking haunted.

Long and lean, his hair close cropped so she could see the lines of his face. The lips, currently cruising down her ribcage, the blades of his cheekbones, the blue-gray eyes that failed to miss anything. He'd come in, loaded down, she knew, with the worries and fears of everyone in Silver Cliffs.

He'd stood looking at her as she'd shaken off her fitful sleep and managed to stand, moving to him as if he drew her by some magic.

But it wasn't magic, it was him. Her heart beat for him. Had for years now, she realized.

Big, strong hands slid down her torso and to her hips. He continued to kiss down her body until he got to her pussy and she shivered. Not from cold. From the sheer delight she knew she was about to enjoy.

"Sit back."

She did, obeying, watching down her body as he pushed her thighs open and spread her with his thumbs.

The room had warmed since he'd built the fire up, but his hands on her built the fire in her belly. His gaze found hers, locked as he kissed her knee and then up her thigh. He kissed her there, the heart of her, like it was her mouth. Fascinated, she kept watch, seeing his tongue lap, flick, taste her in such an intimate way it nearly sliced through her. No one had been this close to her and he reveled in it. She reveled in the way he touched her. Like he couldn't get enough.

This man of few words but for the occasional whispered dirty ones between them in the dim. He was thrilling. Exciting. Fearsome and not just because he was a walking weapon. But because he made her want things she knew she shouldn't. And did anyway.

Climax curled her toes, swept up her calves and thighs and burst over her until she indeed had to scream out, her face in a pillow from the settee should anyone be out on the street.

He stood. "Face the back of the settee. On your knees. Brace yourself with your hands."

Still shaking from orgasm, she rose up and did as he'd said, the thrill of whatever he'd planned washing through her. He moved behind her, the heat of his body against hers after he'd gotten rid of his trousers.

The head of his cock brushed against her and slid in easily as he grunted. "So wet."

She pushed back against him, her face burning with a blush. But not of shame. He never made her feel that for what they did together.

He set a pace, fast, deep. She held on as the settee moved just a little bit as he thrust.

"Want of you has set me on fire," he murmured against the skin of her shoulder. "This is what I think about. Your sweet, hot, wet cunt wrapped around my cock like a fist."

She stuttered a breath, curving her back to take him deeper.

Normally a chatterer, she found herself stunned silent by the things he said when it was just them, when it was this. Skin to skin, his body in hers. His hands caressing every part of her he could reach.

"Yes," she whispered.

"Mine," he whispered back, and she wanted to laugh. Yes, yes she was.

Instead she nodded quickly. "Yours."

That seemed to satisfy him for a time as he continued to thrust. His teeth dug into the flesh of her shoulder as he groaned. The pain silvered into something else, something pleasurable as she felt the jerk of his cock deep within her, as she knew she made him feel this way. *Her.*

She smiled against the fabric of the settee, the nub of it against her inflamed skin.

"Let us nap for a time." He stood back and picked her up, walking her not into his room, but hers. He pulled the blankets back and she moved over, giving him room to follow. Which he did.

She moved into the hollow where his arm met his body, resting her head there. His arms surrounded her and she closed her eyes. Satisfied and unafraid.

He awoke to the scent of coffee and fried meat.

She spoke in low tones to someone, which is what brought him to his feet and into his pants. He had nowhere to come out but through her bedroom door and realized he wanted to be seen. Wanted whoever it was to know she was his.

He froze, his hand on the knob. *Stupid.* Stupid to think in those terms. But there it was. He still tasted her, smelled her on his skin and he wasn't ready to give that up. Wasn't ready to give *her* up.

He'd lived through a lot. Survived the loss of his family, years on the Highway. Battles. He brushed a hand over his belly, against the ridges of the scars he bore from a nasty ambush that nearly ended with his death.

He'd driven up the Highway, seen the silvery gray cliffs rising up to the east and his heart had eased. Had eased because he knew he'd be seeing her soon. Knew he'd be in her parlor, listening to her voice as she told him about all the silly goings on in Silver Cliffs. Eating the meals she'd created. Sleeping with such beauty and perfection only on the other side of the wall and it had been enough.

Barely enough, but enough.

But it wasn't anymore. Now that he'd loosed the tide of desire that had lay within him for so long there was no going back. He couldn't drive back through those gates and not come to her. Not seek the solace of her lips, the sweetness of her touch.

He was sure his shirt was tucked in before he opened the door to find Indigo leaning against a counter in the kitchen, watching her as she cooked.

Verity looked up from where she worked, a smile on her face when she saw him. "I hope you're hungry. Indigo just arrived to fill you in on what's going on."

"My timing, as usual, is impeccable as I was also invited to stay and share the meal." Indigo flashed very white teeth as he smiled at Verity.

She blushed, patting his arm as she passed.

"You can wash up. I'm just about to get everything on the table."

Indigo tipped his chin. "Yes, ma'am. Thank you." He moved

past her toward the bathroom where he shot Loyal a smug look. Loyal barely resisted rolling his eyes.

He moved to her, kissing her quickly. "Smells good."

"Comes in handy when folks in town pay me with food and I've got a hungry lawman under my roof."

Hungry, yes. And not just for food.

"I'm sorry we've been invaded." He spoke quietly, standing close enough to smell her skin.

She shrugged with a small, satisfied smile as she began to put platters on the table. He moved around her, adding plates and utensils.

"It's all right. I like him and I like that because he's here, you have the opportunity to take some downtime to eat and get a meal into your belly."

Indigo came back out and they sat, digging in, the silence only broken by the sounds of utensils on plates. Finally, once they'd had a chance to fill up a little, Indigo sipped a mug of tea and looked over to Loyal, his gaze quickly cutting to Verity and back.

"Go ahead. You can speak freely."

"Bridge is destroyed. We left someone in place up at the pass to report back when the brigands arrived. Not back yet though."

"It's a goodly hike up that far. Should take a fair bit of time." She said this as she refilled everyone's glass.

"I'm not alarmed. Yet. Haldeman would have said if he was worried."

"So you mean to put them on the only possible path? Across the main bridge. Easier to defend that way I suppose. I read about it once in an ancient military manual. Killbox?"

Indigo sent Loyal a raised brow for a moment. "That's it, indeed. Smart as well as pretty and a mighty fine cook too. No wonder Loyal is always fussy when we have to leave."

She smiled, but said nothing else.

"We've got scouts out, keeping an eye on the road and the established trails."

"Is there a chance that they'll get up to the bridge and when they see they can't cross they'll move on?"

"They're . . . unpredictable. It could happen that way. But I don't think it will. I think they'll come because they'll be angry they were thwarted. Because they want this town and whatever is inside it. Because that's who they are."

"Like an animal who tastes human flesh."

Indigo looked back her way. "How's that?"

"We get big cats round here from time to time. Mainly they try to steal livestock. But every once in a while, someone is attacked and it changes the cat. Makes them . . . unpredictable I guess is a good word. As if taking that step somehow changes them and they can't go back. They have to be killed or they'll always be a threat."

He supposed that was a mighty fine metaphor.

"It's like their purpose is to raid. We can't even take them prisoner. They mutilate themselves while in custody. Try to kill everyone in sight. They'll kill themselves if they can." Indigo's gaze went distant, as if he was remembering. They all had memories.

She looked away, giving him that space, busying herself. "I think I'll make some sandwiches for you to take back to the garrison. I imagine people might be in need of some food."

Indigo got to his feet. "I'll take it over if you like. We don't need you yet," he spoke over his shoulder to Loyal.

Who stood. No matter how much he wanted to crawl back into bed with her, he had a job to do. Keeping Silver Cliffs safe meant keeping her safe. And that's what mattered.

"Go ahead on. I'll be over in a bit. I want to check on the blips and then I'll bring the food over."

Indigo stood, nodded and turned to Verity. "Thank you for the meal."

She took his hands. "It must be hard sometimes. All the traveling you do. Sometimes nothing is better than to enjoy a home cooked meal. You're welcome at my table any time."

Indigo ducked his head, charmed, it was plain to see. "Much appreciated, ma'am."

She smiled, so pretty. "I'm younger than you are I'd wager. So how about you call me Verity instead of ma'am?"

"All right then. Lock up and stay safe. I expect you know how to use those?" He tipped his chin toward the rifles.

"I do. I've even been doing a lot of target practice lately. Making myself better."

"Good."

A few more instructions from Loyal and he'd gone quickly, leaving quiet in his wake.

Loyal moved to her, pulling her close. "I'm sorry to eat and run off."

She shook her head. "You have a job to do. I understand that. People need you and your leadership."

He blew out a breath, nervous to be held up as an example like that. Knowing the whys of course—it was his job—and lawmen were important in their culture. Looked to for leadership. He would do it because that was what he was bred to do. And he'd hope he didn't let anyone down in the process.

"Go and wash up. I'll come down to the garrison with you with the food."

"I need this first." He dipped down to kiss her long and slow. All his angst and worry smoothed out as her taste took over. She sighed into his mouth and he took it, greedy for all of her he could have.

He should have broken the kiss several times, but he kept on, her lips curving up into a smile against his when he finally stepped back. "I really don't want to leave."

She laughed. "Yes you do. I can see you already starting to think on the garrison defenses again. I'm not going anywhere. I'll be here when your day is done and they send you back here to rest."

He thought about her words as they walked down the hill to the garrison barracks. He'd never had that before. A woman waiting when his day was done. *Anyone* waiting when his day was done.

Roots.

He'd grown up poor, without too many and then his family had been taken from him in a violent act. At fifteen he was thrust into the military and had gravitated to the lawmen because it had been solitary. He drove in his vehicle in a team, yes, but alone too.

It had suited him for a long time. The life without roots. But mainly it was that he did something worth doing that kept him getting back into his seat each time. He was needed. Necessary. He kept people safe, kept commerce moving. He'd been told plenty of times in his life that he was worthless. But each time they drove through the gates of a garrison town he proved his father wrong.

Jackson's eyes lit when he caught sight of her as they came through the doors some time later. She smiled back, holding up her basket. "I brought some food. Figured you all might need something to get you through the day."

They all set on her, though, Loyal noted, they were orderly. No one pushed and every single person said thank you. She seemed to evoke that.

Stace came in with some others just as she was packing up to leave. "They've turned back and are headed to the main bridge. They tried to burn the brush and tree cover on their side of the river but it's too wet to catch."

She turned and nodded. "I'll be getting back home. Jackson, I'll be up on my roof keeping an eye. I'll let you know if I see anything."

"No you won't. You need to stay inside."

She gave Haldeman a raised brow. "It's my house and my roof and heaven knows I'm safe there. No one can get to me. Especially from the other side of the bridge. They won't even be able to see me. But I have field glasses and I'll see them." She gave Haldeman her back, which was good because Loyal caught the annoyance on the other man's face.

Verity Coleman wasn't a female to be managed. Strong. With a mind of her own and if she wanted up on her roof she'd go there. Best to urge her to keep back and report anything she saw than to go forbidding her from something she was going to do no matter what.

"Stay back. They can't reach you from the other side of the bridge, but we don't want them getting any ideas as to strategic points to take either." Loyal escorted her to the door.

She smiled. "Of course. I'll send Tobin with any news."

And she was gone with a swish of skirts.

9

"You want to tell me what is going on with the lawman?" Tobin settled in next to her on her roof. She scanned the area with her field glasses.

"What do you mean?"

"You're more a friend than an aunt, really, Verity. I can see the way you look at him. Have looked at him for years. And the way he looks at you. The energy between you two has changed. Even my mother has noticed. He's . . . what do you think is next?"

She thought about it. Thought about telling him to mind his own business. She couldn't really talk to her sister. She loved Constance, but Constance would only tell her Jackson was a better match and the lawman's lifestyle was unsuitable for her.

And her sister would be right in a lot of ways.

"I'm in love with Loyal. I have been for at least a year. We've gotten closer lately." She sipped some water and kept her scan up.

"I don't know how he feels for me. Not precisely. I know he cares about me."

"You want to leave Silver Cliffs, don't you?"

She swallowed back her automatic rejection of the idea.

"I want to see the world outside the gates. I want to hear other accents, see how people live elsewhere. There's so much outside and I haven't seen most of it."

"Do you want him because he's your ticket out? Or because you want him?"

"I've been saving up for several annum now to get on the list to travel to Shelter City. Since before James was killed. I'm going whether I do it with Loyal or not. I don't know that I'd go forever. But . . . I am dying here. Slowly dying." She put the glasses down and turned to Tobin. "My heart aches to know. To learn. To see. And I can't. Not here. Do you see?"

He took her hand, squeezing it for a moment. "I do."

"I want him to take me with him. I know lawmen have lives. Families even. I wouldn't have babies out on the road. I don't think that would be fair, or easy. But Marcus and Trinity travel together."

"She's a lawman too."

"Yes, I know. I know all of this. I want to be with him. Before, when he left I was sad. But now? Now that things are different between us? It tears part of me away when he talks of leaving. I never had this before. If James had left for moons at a time I'd have rejoiced. I like being with Loyal. He makes me happy."

"Probably because you do all the talking." Tobin winked with a grin. She laughed.

"A plus of a taciturn man, Tobin, for a chatty woman. He says what he needs to say, but he doesn't waste anything. Not words, not movement. He's economical, but in the best sort of way."

"Dangerous world out there."

"Yes. But it's not always so. Most of the time they escort the official transport without incident."

"My mother is going to fight you on leaving."

She nodded, picking up the glasses again to scan the path on the other side of the river. "Aye. She will."

"She's not curious."

"She thinks curiosity is dangerous. It's how we were raised."

"I'm on your side."

Tobin settled back, picking up his own field glasses.

"Thank you."

"Will you support me then? When I tell them I want to be a lawman?"

She turned to him, not entirely surprised. "Is that what you really want?"

"I sent in papers, two visits ago, to apply to the training school."

And he'd said nothing. She nodded, reaching out to squeeze his hand. "Then yes, I'll support you. I can talk to Loyal if you like, see if he'll share what it's like."

"He has. I mean, mainly I've spoken to Trinity because she's a tracker and that's what I want to do. I'd have to go to their academy. It's a bit of money to get there. I'm saving for it."

He was one surprise after another.

"I can help you. I have credits set by."

"You do. But for your trip to Shelter City."

"I can do that too. So I have to wait longer." She shrugged. "This is more important. We'll make it happen for you one way or another."

"They won't like it. My parents."

"Probably not. It's not a safe or easy life. They'll want that for you."

"As if it's an easy life here? Behind a plow or whatever I'd find a place doing?"

"You could enter service at the garrison. They've always a need of strong soldiers here."

She wanted to be careful. She loved Tobin and wanted him to be happy, but at the same time, she wanted him to be safe too. Wanted him to make choices that would keep him that way. And without a doubt her sister would blame her for this turn of events.

"I could. I may still. It's an option after academy. I just don't want to be trapped here. I want options. Is it so wrong to want that?"

She shook her head. "No it isn't. You have every right to want that. Every right to pursue a life of your own choosing."

"Sometimes it feels like wanting that is selfish."

She shrugged. "Maybe it is. But if you can't be selfish about creating your own future, what can you be selfish about?"

He was silent for a while as he thought. "Is that what you're doing?"

"My parents traded me like livestock to a man more than twice my age when I was fourteen. I never had a life of my own choosing. Ever. The only freedom I did have was in my imagination. On the page of a book. After he was killed I had a sort of freedom I'd never had before. If it makes me selfish now to want to leave this and see what's out there? If I choose to come back here for good, so be it. I'm capable of more than having babies and wiping down counters in a general store. I may *choose* that in the future. It's not a bad life. I'm not saying that. I'm saying I want to know. I want my choice to be made with more information."

She'd been scanning the trail and saw movement. Verity leaned forward, peering carefully, noting the shiver of some bushes. Moments later the brigands emerged and marched in the open.

"Tobin, go. Run down to the garrison and tell them I've sighted the brigands near the big tree."

He got up and scampered away without argument and she kept watch.

Moments later it wasn't Tobin who returned, but Loyal. "Where?"

She handed the field glasses over and guided him to the spot, which wasn't hard as a whole band of them had emerged from the treeline.

They were fearsome. A shiver worked through her at the sight. The night was chilly, but they wore little more than some animal skins about their waists. The light of the waning moon, giving way to early morning lit them with purple-blue light. Their faces had been painted, or maybe marked with inks and tattoos.

"Their teeth are filed so they can tear into people when they attack."

She'd heard but had hoped it was rumor.

He turned to her and saw Tobin standing behind. "Go back to the garrison barracks. Tell them two score and five. They've got the usual weapons. I want full lights on that bridge and the sentry fires set immediately."

Tobin raced off.

"What next?"

"The sentry fires will be set along the walls. That'll let them know you see them."

"Obviously we can because they're standing out in the open!"

He turned, taking her hands. "I'm not going to let anything harm you."

She swallowed her fear back. There were twenty-five of them and at least five hundred fighters, more if everyone took up arms who had them and could use them. She could use a weapon. She was all right. They'd be all right.

He caressed her face. "I'd never let anything happen to you. I swear it."

Loyal Alsbaugh wasn't the kind of man she expected sweet words from, though certainly he said lovely things to her from time to time. But he made her feel safe. In a world like theirs, it meant everything to feel that way.

"You're not helpless. Even if I wasn't here, you'd be safe." He paused for several long beats. "But I'm grateful I am. If I'd been elsewhere and got the news, if I hadn't been here knowing you were under siege?" He swallowed and she stood, held by his words, the breeze sending her skirts swaying around her legs, catching a stray curl and bouncing it from her cheek. She could smell his skin. Woodsmoke and gun oil.

The sun was up somewhere, not quite there yet. But the promise of it lightened the sky and she looked up, caught by the masculine lines of his features.

"I'm grateful you are too."

He brushed his lips against hers. "I'm going to send someone up here to keep watch. I want you back inside. Please," he added after she'd given him a look.

"Can I be of help anywhere else?"

He chewed his lip for a time and sighed, deciding to just be blunt. "If you're safe in your house I'll be able to work better. I'll worry if you're out anywhere. I need to focus and gods help me, you're on my mind so much as it is."

The fierce look she'd been wearing softened. The fear and anxiety were gone, replaced by a smile that shot straight to his gut.

But she didn't push it. She nodded.

He escorted her back and resisted re-checking her weapons. He'd already done so when she hadn't been watching.

"You know all the warnings. If there's any emergency communication, use the whistle and we'll send a runner. I don't think they're going to get over the bridge. But it's best to be smart and prepared."

She nodded again. He pulled her close, kissing her until she lost all the stiffness in her spine. Until he throbbed with each heartbeat with the need to take her to the floor and fuck her senseless.

No time for it though.

He tore his mouth away. "I have to go."

She followed him to the door. "Don't get hurt or I'll be vexed."

He grinned and jogged away.

He was pleased to see his orders being carried out; the sentry torches lined the entire wall surrounding the garrison and could be seen from the highway.

"You think that's it?" Haldeman tipped his head toward the bridge where the brigands had begun to gather.

"I wouldn't count on it. They can travel in bands of several hundred. They often send out smaller raiding parties to reconnoiter the prey." He'd sent out three scouts to see if there were others hidden elsewhere on the way up to the garrison and expected them to report back soon. If they had indications there was a large gathering of brigands he'd put in a blip and send for soldiers from Table Mount.

Otherwise, they'd be expected to repel the offensive force themselves. It wasn't expedient or even possible to have the central government in Shelter City ride out to protect the garrisons outside the main security zone surrounding it. It was simply an accepted fact that the cost of independence for those who lived outside that safest zone was the necessity to protect themselves when they were threatened by outside forces.

"So do we tell them to back off or what?"

"They won't make an immediate attack. They're going to make a camp right out there on the other side of the bridge. So you can see them. It's part of what they do. Build up your dread and terror."

"We have sharp shooters. Let's kill them all and be done. Why are we so afraid of a bunch of animals?" One of the garrison soldiers shrugged a shoulder.

"You'll find that they're close enough for you to see, but just out of range for that. They're feral, yes, but they understand strategy. Don't underestimate them. They live this way. For generations this is how they have survived. Understand that."

"So what do we do then?"

"You need a show of force. Put men up on the sentry points in full view. With weapons. They'll respond to that. You make yourselves a poor target. Show them you can fight back. That you have excellent defenses and will repel an attack. They'll watch you, see how you react. Hold steady and if you're lucky, they'll leave. If they make a move we will react fiercely and immediately. You have to kill them. All of them. Your reaction is what will gauge whether or not they come back. And how soon."

10

He took reports from his scouts. It appeared a smaller party of brigands were down on the highway. Which meant they were waiting to see what happened up at Silver Cliffs before they moved.

It was his hope that they could get out of this without a breach of the bridge. Underlining just how strong Silver Cliffs was. Then the brigands would find another, weaker target.

He convinced Jackson to have some of the businesses open during the day for the residents of Silver Cliffs. He wanted to keep a sense of normalcy, though also on heightened alert. Keeping the residents emotionally well adjusted was key. A long siege could make people more prone to rash decisions, which put everyone at risk. So he wanted them out in their fields and doing their daily tasks to stave that off.

He put everyone on three shifts so that the wall would constantly have soldiers on it and after a long day, he walked back up the hill to Verity's place. He'd eat and rest a while before heading back. Brigands tended to move at night. He didn't think it would be that day, but likely the following if they moved at all. But there was no harm in being prepared.

Earlier that day he'd gone through Silver Cliffs to patrol. He'd wanted to be seen by people, to reassure them they were safe.

Verity had her mercantile open, Tobin at her side as she filled orders and chatted with her customers.

He wanted her.

Wanted to stride up to her, pull her in for a kiss so everyone in the place knew she was his. She'd looked up and smiled, waving. He'd tipped his hat and kept walking.

He'd realized at that moment that it wasn't so much that he planned to hide his involvement with her. Many people in Silver Cliffs had already figured it out. But he had a job and she had hers. He respected her, and considering the bits and pieces he knew about her husband, he realized that sort of possessiveness might not be welcome.

But now the streets were quiet. A sense of expectation hung in the air, but not as fervently fearful as it had been even the day before. He'd often found that once people knew what to expect they were less prone to panic. The show of force and the confident way the garrison defenses had been conducting themselves had given people a sense of direction and safety.

He headed up her back stairs, locking up again in his wake. He smelled something savory, but didn't hear her. Had she taken a nap? He smiled, imagining how he'd wake her up.

Then he heard the water and her voice as she sang. Not as pretty as the rest of her. Verity Coleman was incredibly talented at a lot of things, but those things didn't include singing.

Once he was sure they were alone and he'd locked up and taken a look out toward the gate to be sure things were still quiet, he headed to her, discarding his clothing as he did.

He knocked, not wanting to startle her as he opened up. She smiled when she saw him.

"Why good evening to you, lawman."

"Howdy, ma'am. May I be of some service?"

She took a leisurely look from his toes up to his face, a smile on her lips. "I can think of a great many services I'd be eager for you to provide."

Something about her always eased the knots in his belly. He let himself be happy as she got to her knees and he moved closer.

"Do you need a back scrub?" she asked as he got into the tub, settling between her legs that she wrapped around his waist. She pressed a kiss to his neck, hugging him to her, back to front. "Let me take care of you for a change, hm?"

She soaped the cloth up, sliding it against taut, muscled shoulders. Circle after circle as he sighed, relaxing as she ministered to him.

She wanted to take care of him. Wanted to ease things a bit in a life she knew was hectic and filled with a great deal of responsibility.

"Long as you don't sing to me."

She snorted a laugh. "Are you insulting my lovely singing voice, lawman?"

"Verity Coleman, you are beautiful. You're intelligent. Strong willed. You are eminently capable, you're sexy as sin. You taste like heaven. But you are not a singer."

She giggled, unable to deny his claim. "I had no idea you were out there listening to my rust voiced warbling. It's a flaw, but I keep it within the confines of my bathing tub, after all."

She massaged his muscles as he leaned back into her touch. The outside world was insane. Dangerous. Chaotic even. But right there things were wonderful. Her heart was lighter than it had been in ages.

"Close your eyes." She took up a nearby pitcher and got his hair wet, pouring some of the liquid soap she'd recently come by into her palm and then massaging it into his scalp.

He groaned. "You're mighty good at that."

"I have ulterior motives."

"Thank the heavens for that."

She rinsed his hair and got out to rinse the rest of him appropriately. He stood and she helped him out, grabbing a towel, drying him. Rubbing over his hair, across his chest and shoulders, down his arms.

He watched her. Quiet. Emotion in his eyes. She got to her knees and finished drying his legs and feet and he pulled her back to hers, returning the favor, buffing her gently with the towel.

"You're the most beautiful thing I've ever seen." He said it so softly it was almost a dream.

She blushed up from her toes. Empty flattery she could take. Dealt with it all the time. But this was something else. He didn't waste words. And it was him. Her lawman. Telling her she was beautiful and that made all the difference in the world.

"Thank you."

He folded the towel and placed it on the side of the tub as it drained. He held a hand out and she took it, allowing him to draw her into her bedroom.

"On the bed. On your belly."

She swallowed hard, but obeyed, her skin hyper aware of his gaze, and then of the cool, slight texture of her bedspread as she lay against it. Her nipples throbbed in time with her thundering heart.

The bed dipped on one side as he got on.

"Close your eyes." He kissed her shoulder. "Let yourself feel."

She did, with a shuddering breath.

"Trust me?"

"Yes." Her answer was immediate. She did. With her life. With her body. With everything she was.

"Good." He licked down her spine, pausing to give a quick nip of her left butt cheek. She giggled at the surprise and then moaned as he nipped again just beneath where her ass met her thigh. And then he licked.

Shivers flew over the surface of her skin. It was delicious and exciting and darkly taboo. His mouth so close to all sorts of places she should be embarrassed about.

He continued down her leg, licking at the back of her knee until she writhed against the mattress. He picked up her foot, kneading against her instep, over her ankle, kissing, nibbling and licking until she was nearly begging him.

But she wanted to know what else he had planned so she bit her bottom lip to keep the words inside.

He dug his thumbs into her heels, up her ankles and calves until she grunted. His touch was deeply sensual, but also reverent. She was glad her eyes were closed against the swell of tears.

So few people touched her in an intimate sense. Not necessarily sexual, but only her sister and Tobin touched her affectionately.

Like she mattered. Like there was nothing else they wanted to do than to touch her, feel her against them.

Loyal had unlocked something she'd buried deep, pretending it didn't matter because she didn't have it and to obsess on it would have killed her.

With him, like this, she was something more than the woman in town who gave you your mail. More than the pretty face at the mercantile or the little lady whose drunken lout of a husband had been murdered.

In Loyal's arms, in this bed, she was worthy of reverence. Worth the time and effort it took to touch her this way.

No one had ever made her feel this way.

Cherished.

He took her seriously. He listened when she spoke. When she talked about wanting to see the rest of the world he didn't chuckle, smug and self-satisfied as he patted her head and told her the big bad world was too much for her pretty little head. He *understood* her curiosity.

The allure of that. Of being understood and valued like that . . . she didn't have words for it. She only knew it filled her up until she was satisfied. Warm and happy and tingly.

His cock pressed against her leg as he leaned over her to knead her arms, as he brushed his fingertips against the sides of her breasts. His beard rasped against her ribs as he kissed her there.

He swept her hair from her back and kissed down her spine again. This time though, he said, "Head down, ass up."

Swallowing hard, her eyes still shut, she obeyed to his hum of pleasure.

His breath against her ass brought hers to a stutter. His fingertips slid against the seam of her pussy.

"When I'm on the road, far away from here, away from your scent and the feel of your skin against mine, I think about you. About how juicy your cunt is, about your taste. I think about the way you're so buttoned up and lovely outside your door, but in here, with me? You're open and eager. You want pleasure, you give it. There's no shame between us."

He spread her, dancing a fingertip round and round her pussy, up against her clit, down around her gate, just inside, and then back against her asshole.

The breath shot from her lips when he did that. Only once before in her life had anyone been back there. It had been done to humiliate her. To break her and bring her pain and domination in all the worst ways.

He paused for a moment, waiting for her to tell him to stop, but he'd asked her to trust him and she would. He wasn't James. Everything they'd done had been totally different.

A brush again, against her asshole and she made herself relax. Again the hum of satisfaction. She smiled though he couldn't see her do it.

Then he knelt, bending and licking her from behind, right up to her asshole, and she squealed. He cracked a hand against her cheek.

"Shh. Keep still."

He went back to it. Licking at her pussy, lapping, fucking into her with his tongue before he pulled back to flick the tip of his tongue against her clit. And then he moved back up again, licking against the rosette of her ass until her spine loosened and she let herself truly feel it.

He bit her cheek again, gently. "Sometimes it's the things we're not supposed to like that feel so good. Hm?"

Starting again, licking, stroking with his tongue until she was on fire for him. Because it didn't matter what he was doing, it felt good, and because it was him, it was all right.

Her slide into climax was slow and delicious and when it hit she breathed through and let it come. She was warm and really wet and ready for whatever he had in mind next.

"I'll be right back." The bed moved and she listened to his footfalls retreat and then return as quickly as he promised.

He got to his knees, looking at the creamy skin of her shoulders, still a little pinked from the flush of her orgasm. Grabbing his cock at the root, he teased her pussy. Sliding in for several quick, deep thrusts and pulling back, brushing the head against her clit until she began to tremble a little.

He wanted all of her.

With a depth of greed that surprised him. Even scared him a little. But he wanted her nonetheless. She gave herself over with ease. Trusted him. It humbled him even as it excited and thrilled him.

He opened the little pot of the cream he used on his skin when the weather was so very dry and he spent long hours in his vehicle. Nothing in it that would harm her or sting. But it slicked things up nicely and it was perfect for what he planned next.

He dug a bit out and, using two fingers, he slicked it over her asshole, and then quested inside, stretching her. She stiffened at the first intrusion, much like she had with his tongue. He'd gathered from the way she froze in certain situations, that her former husband had mistreated her. So he took it slow, giving her plenty of time to see he was different and for her to call a halt to anything she didn't want.

Smooth and very, very tight.

He stroked slow and sure into her pussy, one hand curled around her body to circle her clit gently, enough to keep her feeling good, relaxing as his other hand stretched.

Finally, he pulled out, still wet from her, and began a slow press into that tight rear passage.

She grunted and he petted over her hips. "Push out when I push in. Blow out your breath and if it's too much, say so."

He knew her. Knew how stubborn she was. She'd never say no unless she truly couldn't take it.

He wanted it to be good though. Wanted to show her that everything he did would make her feel pleasure.

"Reach back and play with your clit," he murmured, sweat forming on his brow at how good it felt to be in her. At the pleasure of her submission to what he wanted.

She angled herself, doing as he said. She squeezed around him even tighter once she'd reached her clit, but the tension in her muscles eased a little as she began to stroke.

Another time he'd sit in that far chair and watch as she made herself come. For him and him only.

For the moment though, he was a knife's edge from coming. He wanted her to go first, held on, jaw clenched. "Make yourself come," he gritted out.

She gasped but within moments she thrust back at him as she came, the scent of her body rising, holding him tight and yanking him into climax along with her.

So hard and total he saw nothing but white light as he closed his eyes and let it happen.

Then he pulled out, picked her up and headed back to the bathroom where he washed them both off, caressing her as she looked up at him, a small smile on her lips.

"I think we need to sleep a while." He murmured this as she slid a sleeping gown over her head and then braided the long coil of her hair.

She nodded. "I'll fix you a meal when you have to go back."

He took her hand and they climbed into bed. He was tired. Bone deep exhaustion. But there was something else there. Satisfaction. Happiness. A sense of rightness as he pulled her close, into his embrace, burying his nose in the softness of her skin. And let himself sleep.

By the time he arrived down at the garrison the sun was rising. His muscles were warm and he carried a sense that things would actually be all right.

"They're still out there. The ones down on the Highway are still there."

"I think we need to make a move at some point today. We can't just leave them out there indefinitely. They know by this point that you're resourceful. That the walls will protect you. That they can't get over except by that bridge. But that won't last forever. They'll be able to cross when the water goes down."

He and Indigo studied a map for a time.

"Is there a way we can get out where they can't see? Other than the back route the scouts have taken?"

"What do you need?"

He turned to see Verity standing there wearing trousers, her hair in a tidy braid back from her face. But there was no softness in her features. He'd left that Verity when he'd come down here. The woman who spoke now was strong and canny.

"A military trained scout." He shot back her way.

She smiled and he knew he was in trouble.

"I know more about the exits and entrances outside the walls than most everyone here. My grandfather designed the walls." She stepped up to their map.

Indigo snorted a laugh. "Show me, Red."

She grinned. "There's a culvert of sorts here." She pointed. "Tight fit, but you can all get through. There's a stand of trees here that should give you cover."

"And a perch for a sniper?"

She thought for a bit and nodded. "Yes. Many of the trees there are older. High branches are thick. Though you'd have to see how high that goes. At the top they're thinner. Probably could support you, but not if you needed to lay down or stretch out."

"Fine. Show me."

He was an expert sniper. Had specialized training and, in fact, several times each annum he led a training back in Shelter City where he taught a class for the military and lawmen corps.

He hated the idea of taking her out of the walls, but he also realized she lived out there on the Highway and hadn't survived as long as she had by being stupid or taking risks.

"When? Now?"

"Give me a bit. I need to get things dealt with here first. I'll come up to the mercantile to get you when I'm ready."

She nodded, holding up a basket. "I brought some food down. Nothing fancy, but it should get you through the next hours."

Jackson took it with a smile. But his gaze skittered to Loyal for a moment and Loyal knew the other man realized they'd formed a real relationship.

That didn't stop the appreciation in Jackson's gaze, of course. But the man had a sense of honor, Loyal knew. He wouldn't make a move now. Which didn't mean he wouldn't jump at a chance later, if Loyal cocked it up.

She waved and went back out.

"She's one of the best scouts in Silver Cliffs," Jackson said quietly as he ate. "If you're looking to get a sniper's position she's familiar with the geography around, especially given the time of the annum."

"I won't have a lot of time. Once I take out a few they'll take cover so I want to have people at the ready on the sentry posts on the wall in case they try a frontal assault. Indigo, I want you and Marcus in position as well." They'd take sniper positions in more than one spot and take as many down while they had the jump as they could.

And hopefully at the end, the brigands would take whoever was left and get the hell out of there.

11

She looked up when Loyal came into the mercantile with Indigo and Marcus before turning to Tobin. "I'll be back later. Close up at midday. Go home and check on your mother and brothers."

She grabbed her rifle and strapped it on after tucking the tail of her hair into the back of her dark coat. "Ready?"

Loyal nodded and they all headed outside. "Excuse us a moment," he said to Marcus and Indigo as he guided her away. "I'm agreeing to this on one condition."

She sent him a raised brow. "Is that so, lawman?"

"Yes, that's so. You will listen to me and do exactly what I say when I say it, no questions. You accept my expertise and I'll accept yours. If you can't agree, I'll have someone else show us out."

She snorted. "I'm not slow-witted, Loyal. I am perfectly willing to admit you know things about this that I don't."

"I'm not . . . I don't think you're slow-witted. I think you're headstrong and you want to help and you might make a mistake in that eagerness to protect your friends and family. I can't . . . if something happened to you I don't know how I'd survive. So do we have an agreement?"

What could she say to that? To that last admission she knew had been difficult for him to have made? Though to have heard it sent a thrill through her.

She nodded. "Yes, we do."

She led them around the garrison and behind the buildings on the main street in town. They skirted the wall, climbing up a sharp outcropping.

"The spot is just ahead. We need to go out single file. There's a copse of trees just outside, and then if you two are looking for other spots, there's another just up the ridge and you can most likely find cover in some of the rocks just south of where we'll come out. Keep low and you should remain out of sight."

"You will come right back through and stay on this side of the wall."

"I'll need to remain here to let you back in. There's a combination on the inner wall that will unlock the mechanism to slide it open."

He sighed, but nodded. He knocked in a certain rhythm. "That's the code. Aye?"

"Aye."

And then she led them outside, sending out a fervent prayer that they all returned safely.

She held the door until they'd all come out and turned. He squeezed her arm but his features were remote, his mind on the task at hand. She did as she promised, heading back to the safety behind the walls.

———————

He put her out of his head. He had to. A series of hand signals to Indigo and Marcus and he made his way up a tree, one that was close enough to the edge of the nearby cliff. He had a perfect view of the brigands' impromptu camp just on the other bank of the river.

They were in closer range than they'd have been at the gates on the wall. Close enough that if he and the others used their shots wisely they could cut that group in half before they had the time to respond. Jackson's men were already in position on the walls at the bridge along with Trinity and Bren. If the remaining brigands made a move to cross that bridge, they'd be cut down.

One way or the other, it would be over.

He heard Marcus' bird song and then Indigo's, signaling they were in position and ready to go.

It all fell away. No fear. No anxiety. Just the job. Each moment fed into the next, over and over.

He breathed out, looking through the scope of his rifle. He centered himself, took aim and squeezed the trigger. Again. Sliding the bolt into place again and taking another shot.

The brigands below fell. Six of them. Loyal took another shot, managing to hit one more as he attempted to take cover. Marcus got another from his position.

Eight down.

Indigo missed a shot and then took out two more.

By the time the brigands had managed to get under cover, the three lawmen had taken out twelve of the brigands and another two or three were wounded.

The remaining brigands shouted, pointing up in their direction. So the lawmen remained still until the brigands shifted their attention to another spot.

When he squeezed back through that narrow slit in the rock wall, Verity was there to open up, her rifle pointed at him until she was sure it wasn't a trick. Smart woman.

"Head back to the mercantile," he told her as she slid the door back into place, bolting it. "We're off to the gates."

She didn't question him, though he could see on her face that she wanted to know. But he didn't have time to explain and they'd be needed so he and the others ran full out to the gates as she turned and headed back to her mercantile.

Once she'd reached the front porch and heard the roar, knew the remaining brigands were charging across the bridge. The horns sounded, announcing a full alert in Silver Cliffs. She ran around back and headed up to her roof, pulling two other rifles along with her as she did.

Tobin was already up there with one of Jackson's men.

She took the field glasses and scanned the gates and the action on the top.

"I think they took out half of the brigands. Maybe more. I counted the shots. I won't assume they made every single one, but given the looks on their faces when they got back inside, they were overwhelmingly successful."

She checked her rifle again and sat, waiting. If they broke through, the rest of Silver Cliffs would rise to the town's defense. She was nervous, but at the same time certain things would be all right.

"Glad the lawmen are here," the garrison soldier said quietly.

She was too.

The chaos didn't last a long time and it wasn't more than an hour or so before the horns sounded again. Lockdown. But they weren't under siege anymore.

The soldier on the roof with them nodded. "I'm off to get news."

She waved, though she remained seated. Once he had gone she looked over to Tobin. "I didn't expect to see you here. I believe I told you to stay at home."

"Father is angry at me. I told him I'd been speaking with the lawmen about their training and would be seeking a position at the academy. He kicked me out as long as I'm *insisting on this foolhardy path*."

She blew out a breath. Tobin wasn't her son. It would be easier for her to let go than his parents. That was only normal. But he wanted more. And what he wanted to do was good. Honorable. They had three other sons who already worked their farm. Two daughters who would marry and create connections to other families in Silver Cliffs. Her sister would have to let go or lose Tobin entirely. She didn't envy that choice.

"To be fair, I told them you supported my choice."

She winced.

"I'll be hearing about that by nightfall I wager." Her sister would be angry at her for interfering in their family issues. Even if all she'd done was listen and support Tobin's desires. She was the younger sister, the widow. It was Verity who should be seeking their advice and support, not the other way around. That's how Constance would see it.

"I'm sorry."

She patted his shoulder. "Don't be. I *do* support your choice. I hope I can persuade them to do the same. They love you. Worry about you." She understood his position better than he probably knew. She'd had no one when she was younger, she'd be damned if she let a bunch of nonsense keep Tobin from his dreams.

She'd deal with her sister and brother-in-law and hopefully they'd listen to her.

"I know they love me. But I can't just give up what I want. I'm young, it's the time for me to try things. It's not like Silver Cliffs is going anywhere if I change my mind. Can I stay with you? Until things are smoothed over?"

"Of course."

"I'll kip in the blip office. There's a cot in there."

"I have a spare room. Loyal is . . . he's in with me."

Tobin nodded. "I know. I'll stay downstairs anyway. He'll be leaving soon, I'm sure you'd like the time. And my parents won't be as upset if I'm appearing to suffer on a cot instead of in your house where it's more comfortable."

She snorted a laugh. That was likely true.

"What are you going to do? When it's time for them to leave I mean? I guess they have families. Indigo told me some of the lawmen had wives or husbands, children and the like in the garrisons along the Highway as well as in Shelter City."

"I don't know, to be honest with you. I don't know how I'd feel about being with someone I only saw a few times each annum for just days at a time." And her life was sad, sad, sad that a nineteen-year-old boy was her confidante. "And this isn't just about me wanting him. Though I do. I want to see the world. Be out there. It's not enough to have him show up from time to time. I don't think I'd be satisfied with that."

He nodded. "Have you told Loyal that?"

"Sort of. We haven't even really discussed being together after he leaves this time. It's my assumption we are. There's a connection I know he feels too. He's not stupid. We clearly need a conversation. You know, after we're not under siege."

He laughed, patting her arm.

They watched down the hill. Eyes on the gates and the men and women who walked their tops, lit the sentry fires.

And hoped it was over.

12

The horns sounded again after darkness had fallen. They were still to remain on alert, still on a modified lockdown at night with a curfew. But it appeared that the immediate threat had passed.

She went downstairs, leaving Tobin up on the roof to keep watch. Jackson had someone come up and send a blip back to Shelter City. He told Verity they'd killed every last one of the brigands who'd attacked their gates. A scouting party had been sent to the Highway to see if the others had left or were on their way up.

She managed to deal with stragglers to the mercantile. She'd need more supplies soon as there'd been some major hoarding during the lockdown. Though people's pantries would be full, they'd still shop and want fresh goods.

She made some notes for reorders, and when the traders came to town—and they would after word of the siege got out—she'd be sure to restock from them as well.

The expected visit from Constance came not too long after that. Verity had looked up to see her sister come in wearing a frown.

The place was empty, but she didn't want to have that conversation where anyone could walk in. "Come on upstairs. We'll have some tea and cake while we talk."

She pulled the shutters closed over the windows and doors, her sister helping.

She went upstairs, Constance in her wake.

"I'll put on the kettle. Have a seat." She bustled around, pausing to look out the space in her shutters at the lane leading down to the gates. Still plenty of activity, but not frenzied. Which was hopeful.

"I think the threat has passed. For the time being at the least." She moved to the stove and measured out some tea, spooning it into the pot. "There's some cake there under the cloth if you'd like."

But Constance wasn't in the mood for cake. "I didn't come here for tea and cake."

"Maybe not, but cake is always welcome, isn't it?" She poured the water over the leaves and replaced the lid.

"You're turning my son against his family."

Verity sighed, turning back to her sister who'd moved to sit at the table. Her mouth a flat, angry slash on her normally pretty face. Verity told herself that her sister was upset and to try not to let the digs she knew would come get to her.

"How so?"

"He wants to leave Silver Cliffs. To be one of *them*. I know he got the idea from you. He told us you supported him in this ridiculous scheme. Just because you don't have any of your own children doesn't mean you can take one of mine."

"That's beneath you, Constance. I didn't give him any ideas about being a lawman. He came to me after he had applied to talk about it, to say it was what he wanted. I support that, yes. Not because I'm trying to take him from you. But because I love him. And you."

"You wander around this town like you're a visitor. Always looking for a way out. *Of course* he got the idea from you. If you can't leave, you'll push him away, live through him. I won't let you tear my family apart because you don't have one. Jackson Haldeman would be happy to court you and settle down. If you'd stop opening your legs to the lawman every time he came around."

As a slap, it was a good one. The kind only someone who knows you very well can deliver. "I'm sorry, am I interrupting your plan to keep him here, where he doesn't want to be so you can snuff out any dreams he might have that are beyond your ken?"

"Now who's acting beneath herself?"

"Maybe the sister who just called the other a whore? As for this situation with Tobin? It needs to be said, Constance. He's your boy. I respect that. I'm not putting ideas in his head. Because he's a smart young man. Because he has his own ideas. His own vision of his future. And because you can't punish him for wanting to know what's out there. Do you think you can just tell him no, put him behind a plow and he'll forget?"

"That plow puts food on your table."

"Sure it does. Just like this mercantile puts food on yours. Don't play the martyr game with me. He came to me to share his dreams. Not because he expected me to supply him with more, but because he knew I'd listen and not judge. I'm not his mother. I've never tried to be. I'm his aunt and his friend and I'm glad he has dreams. No matter what they might be. If he wanted to stay here to follow in his father's footsteps I'd be glad of those dreams too. It's not the what of the dreams, it's the fact that he has them. It's beautiful that even out here on the edge he has them. He's perfectly capable of his finding own wants and desires. He doesn't need me to give them to him."

"You're giving him a place to stay so he can avoid his parents."

"No. I'm letting him stay here until his father cools down and realizes kicking Tobin out of his home because he is afraid for his son's future is an overreaction and a mistake."

"That's not for you to decide."

"You don't get to tell me how to feel or react to anything. I love you and I respect your family. But Tobin is an adult now. He came to me and asked for my help and I'm giving it to him. I urged him to try to patch things up with you. But I won't urge him to stifle his wants for other people."

"Why not? It's dangerous out there!" Constance burst from her seat and began to pace, wringing her hands. "Can't you just tell him that? To wait a few years?"

"The world is dangerous. Shelter City is safer than Silver Cliffs. He'd learn to protect himself even better there. He could very well come back here, you know. He could be a garrison officer if he doesn't want to be a lawman. But if you push him away, what are his reasons to come back?"

"My husband doesn't want me to speak to you any more. He feels you're a bad influence."

That hurt deeply. She licked her lips.

"And what do you think?"

"I think your being unmarried at your age and status is dangerous. It leads the men in town to think things about you that aren't true. But that you won't do your duty for the good of everyone around you makes you, as he says, dangerous. Look at what you've done to my son."

"I already got married for the good of everyone around me. It got me years of beatings. Of rapes and abuse. It got me a drunk more than twice my age. That was for *your* good? Because if that's true, I don't want you in my life either. If you'd wish me back into that hell so your husband or the other men in Silver Cliffs won't want to fuck the widow, you don't deserve me."

Constance, probably for the first time in her whole life, seemed speechless. She stood, her mouth wide until she closed it with a snap.

"My husband doesn't want that. He's a good man. And I didn't know about the beatings. Or any of it."

"Lying is a sin, Constance. Everyone in this town knew. Just like everyone knows Loyal Alsbaugh is in my bed. Like everyone knows Shawna Parsons is sweet on Susan Anderson but will marry Susan's brother, Matian, instead. She'll bear his children and never act out on her feelings because everyone knows she's wrong for having wants. Right? Everyone in this town knows Floyd Rodders sneaks in Cesna's back door and has at her every time her husband goes off on a hunting trip. Everyone in town knows all sorts of things. I'm done living my life for the comfort of everyone else. Now you need to leave. You've said your piece. I've said mine. Don't push your son away. Let him have his dreams. Let him fail if that's what he needs to do. Have joy at the idea that he may find he loves being a lawman. But let the boy have his own heart. Don't stifle him until that flame he carries inside burns out and he's nothing but a piece of meat with legs shuffling around this town because *everyone* wants him to."

She went to her door and opened it.

Constance licked her lips, but said nothing else before leaving. Verity closed the door in her sister's wake and hoped it wouldn't be the last thing they ever said to one another.

But it didn't matter more than not being silent. She was done living her life for what everyone else thought was best for *them*. She'd suffered through a marriage far more like a prison sentence. She did her time and now she had moved past it. Oh yes, she knew some of the people in town felt that an unmarried woman in her circumstances was too big a temptation for the married men. As if it was a woman's fault a man couldn't honor his promises to his family.

She did have freedom. More than most. Certainly more than any other unmarried woman in Silver Cliffs. Since her father was dead and she was widowed, she didn't need a male to tell her what to do. Constance's husband had tried. He was a good man, she knew. Only trying to do his best in the world he knew.

But that didn't mean she would show her belly.

Not to anyone.

Never again.

Loyal came back to her place exhausted, but glad things seemed to have calmed down at last. He noted the light on in the mercantile and went to check, wondering if an emergency blip had come in.

Instead he found Tobin sitting on a cot in the corner, reading.

"I apologize, I thought Verity was down here. Is everything all right?"

Tobin sighed. "Not really. Can I talk to you?"

Loyal moved into the room fully, sliding into a chair near the blip equipment. "Sure."

"You know I want to attend lawman training. I sent my application in a while back."

Indigo had told him about that. Loyal had approved. They needed young people with the kind of honor and courage Tobin had shown.

Loyal nodded. "He and I talked about that. I may be able to get the fee waived. Each of us, the commanders, can recommend one student per class to attend on scholarship. You'd have to come to Shelter City, pass rigorous physical and mental tests. But if you do, I'm happy to recommend you for that slot."

Tobin's face lit. "You'd do that? Is it because of Verity?"

Loyal snorted. "Boy, you'll find, one of these days, that women can influence your behavior in many ways. But I've watched you grow up over the years I've come here. You're resourceful. Over this time with the brigands outside the gates you've been brave and clever. And you're from out here, from the garrisons. There are plenty of boys and girls from the inner core who attend training. But I think it's important all of the Highway is represented in the lawmen corps."

"My mother said some hateful things to my aunt earlier."

"About?"

"About my plans. Saying Verity put the idea into my head. She didn't. She just listens. She's a good listener. And she said she'd give me the credits. To attend the training I mean. She's letting me stay here. What are your intentions with her?"

"I think that's between me and your aunt. Did your mother bring that into the argument?"

Tobin nodded. "She's headstrong. They say that about her like it's a bad thing. But she's got backbone, my aunt."

Loyal pushed himself to stand. "That she does. I'll speak to her."

Tobin swallowed. "Thank you. For the recommendation I mean. And the advice. She cares about you. A lot. Don't . . . don't ruin it."

He headed around the back of the building and up the stairs to her place. To Verity's small home. She was in her front room, looking out the windows. Smoking a cigarette.

He'd never seen her smoke before.

"How are things?" She asked without turning around.

"Better out there than in here I wager." He moved to her, his front to her back. He took the cigarette from her fingers, drew the smoke into his lungs and gave it back. "Didn't know you smoked."

"I don't. Mostly."

"I hear you had a set to with your sister. That why you're smoking?"

"I want to come with you when you leave."

He paused. "That's what you and your sister argued about?"

"No. Not in so many words."

"Why did you argue then?"

She turned, leaning against the wall, looking him over slowly. Heat banked in his belly at this Verity. Bolder than usual.

"We argued because Tobin wants to be a lawman. She accused me of trying to steal him from her. Accused me of not getting married and popping out babies for Jackson because I was too busy whoring it up and being a general bad influence on all the good men of Silver Cliffs. I want to come with you when you leave."

"Because your sister is a fluffy-headed idiot?"

"Because I'm in love with you. Because I want to be with you. Because I want to see the world outside Silver Cliffs and I want to do so with you."

"You can't just toss out that you love me because you had a fight with your sister."

She rolled her eyes, her movements dangerous as she stalked past him and into her kitchen. "I'm quite exhausted with people pretending they can tell me what I think or what my motivations are."

"That what you think I'm doing?"

Perceptive eyes looked him over again, dangerously narrowed. His foolish, foolish cock liked it. Liked the air of danger flowing from her, tautening their interaction. He wanted to fuck her so badly his hands shook a little as he fisted them to keep from reaching for her.

"I think I told you several things. First that I wanted to go with you when you left. I've been quite clear since you first came to Silver Cliffs that I have wanted to see the Highway and everything beyond the walls. We talked about it before, though you avoided it at the time. I also told you I loved you. And if you didn't know that, you're a fool."

"Why are you telling me now?"

"You'll be leaving soon. Right? The brigands are gone or you wouldn't be back here. The threat level would still be on lockdown and it's not. Your job is out there. You've been here a week already."

He leaned close, taking her cigarette again and handing it back. One of her eyebrows rose slowly.

"I can't just take someone with me in my escort vehicle. That's not how it works."

"*That's* what you choose to say right now? Do you think I'll wait around for you to flit around from garrison to garrison? Being satisfied with the small bit of you I get?"

"If I said the first thing that came to my mind you'd kick me in the cock."

"And what's that then? I'll give you amnesty. For now."

"That you're dangerous and sexy and you make me want to bend you over this chair, flip your skirt up and shove my cock deep inside your cunt."

"Hm."

He satisfied himself with imagining what she'd feel like when he did get her drawers down and his cock into her. "As for the rest." He scratched his beard. "I may be leaving Silver Cliffs to run my transports, but I'm not leaving you. There are no others I'm flitting to. It's you. I'll be back. For you. Always."

"Which means what?"

He couldn't help his grin and he took a step closer. She gave him a raised brow but didn't move back.

"It means I love you too. Scary woman." He closed the last bit of distance, sliding an arm around her waist. "I'm sorry you had a fight with your sister. I'm sorry she was hurtful. I spoke with Tobin. I said I'd recommend him to the program for a scholarship spot. I can do one student per annum. He deserves the chance."

Her anger lifted and she stubbed out the cigarette, throwing her arms around him. "You did? You will?"

"Yes and yes. It'll be up to him to pass or fail once he gets in, but otherwise, I'm happy to help."

He flicked open the bodice of her dress, drawing a fingertip back and forth over the nipple he exposed.

"You still thinking about kicking me in the cock? Because I'm going to need it in a breath or two."

Her annoyance melted . . . a bit . . . replaced by a smirk. "That so?"

He leaned in, licking up the line of her throat, biting down when he got to a part he liked best.

Her spine relaxed as she gave over to him. Satisfaction roared through his system. *His.* Verity Coleman was his woman and he meant to have her. Again and again.

"You make me want to rut. No one before you has done that to my control."

Her fingers dug into his muscles as she held on. Held on as he licked over her collarbone. She made a sound, a near whimper as he pinched her nipples. Not too hard, but nearly. She arched into him and he let go long enough to back up, spin her.

"Ass out. You'd best hold on to the table. Good thing there's nothing on it."

He bent to pull her skirts up, flipping them to expose her legs. He pulled the drawers down quickly, one handed, as he unbelted his weapons holster and then unbuttoned his trousers, freeing his cock.

"You make me so hard, Verity." He teased her for a moment, his weight against her to keep her in place as he did. Gripping his cock at the root, he teased over her, through slick folds.

So wet and hot. No matter if she'd been angry at him moments before or not. She wanted him as much as he wanted her. A tussle was all right now and again. Especially because his woman was sexy when she was fired up. But he didn't like that she was upset. Didn't like that her sister had said those hurtful things. Didn't like that she'd doubted him for even a moment.

Or that he may have given her a reason to doubt.

"In," she whispered, pressing herself back against him as he teased the fat, blunt head of his cock against that sweet-hot entrance to her pussy.

"Like this?" He pressed in an inch or so, but pulled back.

She groaned and then snarled when he moved away.

He grinned, glad she couldn't see it and get back on her kick Loyal in the cock line of thought.

He wrapped the rope of her braid around his fist, guiding her head to the side, kissing her hard and fast as he thrust into her in one hard movement.

Her gasp of delight was so sweet as he sucked it down, licking over her lips, biting and kissing.

He fucked her as he'd wanted to all day. Deep and hard. Each sound she made, a soft squeal, a guttural moan, he made her feel. He brought from her.

Standing straight, he looked down and watched himself disappear into her body over and over. Loving the carnal way she left him slick and dark. Loving that he was the only man who had this view. That she was his and he hers.

He wasn't ready to come yet though so he changed her angle with his free hand. Grabbing her hip and moving her, canting her hips, staying deep.

She swayed a little though, circling him deep inside. It was his turn to gasp. His turn to nearly lose his mind and groan at how good it was.

That space between him and climax shrank to a razor's edge.

Not ready yet. Not ready to be done.

He pulled out, swallowing her sob of disappointment. He grabbed her, pulling her to the floor with him, laying over her body, kissing her hard, kissing her soft, trailing his lips down her throat.

He loved the way she sighed, utterly satisfied, when he took a long lick of her pussy. Loved the way she slid her fingers through his hair and tugged him closer.

"Get what you want, darlin'," he murmured against her clit.

"Give it to me."

Smiling, he did.

He nibbled, sucked and licked until she writhed beneath him. Until she sucked in a breath and blew out his name on a moan, coming on his lips in a hot rush.

While she was still gasping for breath he got to his knees and pulled her up, turning her body away from his as he lifted her to balance over his lap, arms braced on the floor.

So slick and hot, he slipped back in on a sigh before he bounced her a few times, finding a rhythm he wanted. One she responded to, tightening around him.

Instead of moving himself, he moved her. Bouncing her back against him over and over, drawing close to orgasm slowly but surely. Committing every sensation of her body around his, the way she sounded, her scent, to his memory. He'd be back, as he said. Eagerly. But while he was gone he wanted to call this moment up, remember what waited for him in Silver Cliffs.

When he let himself fall into her, again, that act of homecoming was poignant. Life altering. Beautiful. It grabbed him with sharp claws and didn't let go. Nor did he struggle to be free.

He helped her to stand and noted her smile before he bent to kiss her again.

"I'm hungry. And a little dirty now. What say you let me scrub your back and then I'll make a meal for a change?"

One of her brows slid up. "If you think I'm giving up on the idea of leaving with you because you pleasure me so well, you're a fool," she called on her way to the bathroom. "You can still scrub my back and make supper though."

He sighed, but followed her anyway.

13

She'd reached her limit.

Interesting.

After Constance had left, she'd paced the length of her living room until she'd hunted down the cigarettes she'd kept in her kitchen for the rare occasions she wanted to smoke one. She considered a quick belt of some liquor, but she needed to think.

Needed to decide just exactly what she wanted. What she needed and what she could live with.

She wanted Loyal.

She needed him too.

She didn't want to live without him.

So that was the first important thing.

She would continue to support Tobin. He needed that and she wanted it. So her sister would have to live with it.

She wanted out of Silver Cliffs with its too tight expectations on her behavior.

If she stayed, what then? Eventually she'd give in to those expectations. She knew that. It would be harder as each annum passed. As each planting season began, as the snow melted, as harvest came and went, she'd be pressured. And loneliness would be part of that choice. A man like Jackson Haldeman would be a fine husband. More than likely he'd let her have her way in most things. He was nice to look at. Seemed interested in her, but there were other women in Silver Cliffs and she'd eventually have to choose a probable future with a good man over whatever she could have the times Loyal rolled into the garrison for a few stolen days here and there.

Right now it was one thing to live for those times each annum when Loyal and his crew came to Silver Cliffs. But it wasn't enough.

She couldn't live with not enough. Not anymore. If she was selfish for wanting it, so be it. But she'd spent several years trying not to fall in love with Loyal and had failed. The last times he'd been in Silver Cliffs, ever since that first kiss, she'd been tumbling head over heels.

It was far too late to regret it. Though she didn't. He was a man worthy of her love. He was exciting and interesting and protective. He was also incredible in bed and seemed to enjoy her company.

He made her feel confident. Like she could tackle any problem. Sexy and smart too. Seeing herself through his eyes had made her everyday life harder in many ways. Made it more difficult to ignore the itch to be gone. The desire to see what was outside.

Tobin had been right that it was time to bring the issue up with Loyal.

But when she had . . . well. He'd gotten all hot and bothered by her attitude. She smiled to herself as she brushed her wet hair out and then twisted it all into a long braid.

He'd gone out to the kitchen to begin their meal after they both cleaned up. He hadn't said much but the way he'd touched her underlined his words of love.

But more needed to be said. She squared her shoulders and headed out.

"Take a seat at the table. I poured you some wine." He worked, chopping herbs as a pan heated on the grill top.

"So they're gone then? The brigands?"

"We sent scouts out to check the ones down on the Highway. Looks like a few escaped from up here and they left. They'll lick their wounds. But you held them off. Not only that, but you're well fortified and you had the guts to blow your own bridges and preemptively attack them. They'll move on to easier targets."

"So you're leaving for sure in the morning then?"

He eased the meat into the skillet, smiling at the sizzle, tossing in some spices before he turned to her.

"Not immediately, but yes tomorrow." He handed her a sliver of fruit. "I *will* be back. The trips will be more frequent for the next season or two."

"It's not enough. I want to be with you all the time."

He opened his mouth but they were interrupted by a knock on the door. He opened it, admitting Indigo and Marcus.

"I'm sorry to interrupt. But you wanted to talk when we got back." Marcus looked to Verity. "Evening, Verity."

She nodded to both men, smiling. Relieved they were all okay. That they'd been in Silver Cliffs when the brigands had chosen to attempt an attack.

"Evening. Come in."

"Thank you." Both men had wonderful manners. Courtly. Indigo had a hat on that he removed immediately upon seeing her.

They opened doors and pulled out chairs and, in general, were a delight to be around. Even if they all hadn't been extraordinary specimens of strapping masculine beauty.

They started to fill Loyal in on what they'd seen out on their scouting mission. On the plans they'd gone over with Haldeman for how to deal with the aftermath of the attack.

It went on as Loyal stirred and then his attention wandered. It was clear this was going to take a long time.

She moved into the kitchen and put the food off the grill before it burned.

"There's some fresh bread in the pantry there and some cold, sliced meat and cheese for you all to eat. Milk too, in the cold case. I need to go check on some things downstairs."

Loyal followed her out onto the stairs. "Wait."

"For what? You have a job to do. Just do it."

She knew it was petulant. He *did* have a job to do. But she'd been interrupted so many times it was wearing her temper and she didn't feel like being angry. "It's fine. I meant it. You have a job to do. Come get me when they're gone."

"We'll talk. I promise."

She waved over her shoulder but kept on downstairs.

Tobin came out to help her do a quick inventory so she could finish her orders to send back with the transport. It wasn't as bad as she'd feared. They had plenty of staples left. Flour, sweetener, spices, rice and the like. Building supplies were running low though. Nails and tools needed replacing.

She was hungry so she and Tobin had a meal of bread, cheese and fruit as they chatted about the lawman training he was so excited to start. She tried to avoid the topic of the fight she'd had with Constance, but he knew his mother had come.

"It was unpleasant. But I urged her to speak to you. Urged her to intervene with your father. I repeated my support of your dreams. That's not going to change. I'm sad she's unhappy. I understand, she's worried about your safety. But you want to fly and I'll cheer you on. She and your father will get over it. Maybe not before you leave, you should be ready for that."

"Indigo said a new class starts in a moon."

"Loyal told me he'd recommend you for a scholarship spot. Which will take care of a roof over your head and your meals. I'll send you some credits on a regular basis. You'll have time to see vids and maybe take a girl out to a meal."

"I can't thank you enough. I . . . it means everything."

"You're nineteen once in your life. That's the time to squire pretty girls to dinner. Or to have a few down the bar with your friends."

His lopsided grin cheered her up.

Loyal came down a while later, just about when she'd started to think seriously on going up and getting in her bed.

"I apologize but I need to go down to the garrison barracks to debrief with Haldeman. It may be a while longer. You should probably go to sleep."

She held back the annoyed sigh, but he saw it in her eyes. He lowered his voice as they moved away from Tobin, Indigo and Marcus.

"I really am sorry. I wanted to have this time with you. But—"

"It's your job. I understand. I do. But this isn't over. You need to know that. We have things to discuss."

He kissed her forehead. "I know. And we will."

She kept his gaze, underlining that. It was time to make a stand for herself. And now that she'd done it, she understood enough to know it had to be backed up.

She'd been asleep when he'd returned to her place many hours later. He could tell, given the folded blanket on the settee, that she'd waited for him.

Guilt stabbed his belly.

That was what her life would be if he took up with her. And he was too greedy for her, too selfish to walk away. He wanted her in a way he hadn't wanted since he'd been very young. She smoothed him out, soothed the rough edges, and he needed her. Needed her like he needed to breathe.

But the idea of her riding along? He'd need to get clearance for such a thing. If he wanted it and he wasn't sure he did. The road was dangerous.

He disrobed in the dark outside her room, moving to join her in bed. They'd need to be up and moving in a few short hours. Back to Shelter City this time to make a report. To get more ammunition and to pack up for more deliveries. He'd teach a class or two, as he usually did when they went back home.

And then he'd start over. Begin a new run on the Highway.

And he'd come back to her. Because he had meant it when he told her earlier. There was no one else for him.

She roused slightly, moving to him as if by instinct. And he guessed it was.

He let her settle, lay her head on his biceps as he tucked her head beneath his chin and breathed her in.

This was something dangerous. The way he felt with her body against his. Not that he planned to do anything else but enjoy it. He liked dangerous things. Lived on that edge all the time. Pretty face, luscious lips, smart eyes that didn't miss a thing, his woman was canny and dangerous, no doubt.

He smiled as he started to drift into sleep. He'd gotten used to this sort of contentment. Oh sure he fell into his job. He loved that too. It was who he was.

But something else was there now, deep inside. Verity had awakened something. A need to belong, a need to cleave himself to something more than his revolver and his vehicle. The badge that marked him as someone worthy.

He saw the same look on Marcus' face when he looked at Trinity. He had liked it because he cared about both deeply. But now he *understood* it.

This was love. Not the thing you said to someone you liked a lot. The kind of thing that was bone deep and inescapable.

14

She smiled when she woke with his arms around her. He'd come back very late. Or very early. Whichever. He'd stripped naked and slid into her bed, making room for her as she'd snuggled back into his body.

His cock pressed at her ass, which was another reason to smile. She could get very, very used to this life. Waking up with a man she loved every day. Waking up with his arms around her, his scent on her skin like a brand.

She managed to turn in his arms. He was awake, she could tell by his breathing. And the smile on his lips.

"Morning." She kissed his chin as his grip tightened.

"Morning, milady."

He filled her with butterflies and joy that floated through her veins like bubbly wine or the need to laugh really hard. And at the same time, he rolled his hips, brushing his cock against her and filling her with other things. Darker things that made her muscles tighten and a moan burst from her lips.

She'd never had this before him. And she didn't want to let it go.

She reached down, grabbing his cock, and squeezed the way she knew he liked. He'd awakened something in her. Well, many somethings. But a sensual thing. She'd wanted before. But the way he desired her had bloomed into something in her belly. An awareness of her sexuality, of the way she affected him. Of how good, how intimate and dark and dirty what she wanted from him was.

And that it was all right because she was his. It wasn't wrong to want him to put his hands all over her in any way he wanted. Because he was her man.

She liked the way that felt when she thought about it.

He rolled her to her back as his eyes opened slowly, focusing on her utterly.

"I want you so much I can't quite think straight. I just had you last night and I want you again. And again."

"Take me." She arched up to nip his bottom lip like he often did to her.

He groaned and followed her back to the pillow, his kiss starting off soft and sweet and deepening as his tongue swept over her lips and into her mouth.

He rolled on top of her, insinuating himself between her thighs so that the notch of her pussy was against the line of his cock. Every small movement sent a shiver through her, another wave of sensation that turned her to liquid inside.

"You're so hot. Wet already. Nipples hard. You want it."

She nodded as he spoke against her mouth. "Yes."

She tried to change her angle by pulling her knees up, bringing him flush to her, slick skin to cock. "In, in, in."

He obliged in one stroke that sent her eyes to the back of her head and her back to an arch.

He grabbed her calves, still kissing her slow and easy, and pushed her knees up, spreading her open impossibly wide. His weight on her kept her in place. Controlled exactly how she moved and when.

She liked it so much it nearly frightened her. But with his hands on her, his weight restraining her, she knew he could be trusted. Trusted to give her what she wanted. To take what he wanted and make it so good she'd ache afterward just thinking about it.

Gasping for breath as he got particularly deep, he nipped her lip, her chin. She cocked her head back to give him access to her neck, knowing he wanted it. Wanting to give it to him if for no other reason.

His beard scratched the sensitive skin of her neck but she didn't care. The burn was good. It sent shivers through her knowing she'd be red from it later.

Knowing others would understand just what made her that way. Maybe she'd wear a scarf. Maybe not.

She smiled at that.

He released her legs and his hands skimmed up her ribs to her breasts, fingers pinching and tugging her nipples until she saw bright flashes of color each time he let go.

"Your cunt tightens around my cock every time I do that."

His voice was rough. Burrs of desire woven through it as he whispered against her skin.

She rocked back and forth against him, pressing her clit to his body, getting just enough friction to drive her slowly, achingly up toward orgasm.

Each breath she dragged into her lungs, each nearly painful bloom of pleasure from the pinch and tug of her nipples, each thrust and drag of her clit against him was like a dance. Just the two of them, body to body, saying what words maybe never could.

She knew what he wanted and gave it to him. She gave herself to him freely, understanding he'd demand it, take what he desired and fill her with the sorts of things she'd never dreamed of wanting but now that he'd been in her in nearly every way imaginable, she craved.

"You want to come? Hm?"

She ground herself into him with a little more pressure as she tried to answer but only ended up whimpering a little.

He pushed her legs up even higher, nearly folding her in half. He got to his knees and continued to fuck her. "Give it to yourself. I want to watch you."

Her gaze locked on his face as he watched her hand slide down her belly. The greed in his eyes shocked her as she slid her labia apart and stroked a middle finger over her clit. Lightly at first. But it wouldn't last long. She didn't like it light. She liked it hard.

"Tap it."

He remained there, thrusting as he watched her finger herself.

She lightly tapped her clit, gasping.

"Harder. We both know you want it harder."

Her middle finger came down on her clit harder. Hard enough to make her groan. Hard enough to grab into her with talons and take her a whole lot closer to coming.

"Yes. Like that. Your pussy likes that."

She nodded, stroking with more and more pressure and tapping here and there.

"Wet your fingers. Don't want them to get dry and hurt."

She began to put them in her mouth but changed her mind, sliding them in between his lips. He groaned, sucking on them, the sound seeming to echo down her arm straight to her nipples.

When she moved back to her clit she knew within a few breaths she was going to come and come hard.

"Yes, exactly. Give me one."

Watching him as he watched her was too much and not enough. Stimulating to the point that she wanted to pull it down around her and wrap herself up tight with it.

And she came then, on the third stroke with her slippery fingers. He snarled a curse and then her name. Over and over again as he fucked harder and harder on each stroke until his gaze snapped up to hers and latched on.

He'd never come that hard, or that good. And looking into her eyes as he had tied them together in ways he didn't know how to process much less give words to.

So he didn't. Instead he rolled to the side and she moved close, burying her face in his neck, her arms around his shoulders as he caressed the curves at her hips and down over her ass.

She made breakfast and they sat in companionable quiet as they sipped tea and ate. He watched the sunrise on her skin.

"Nice to be able to have the shutters up."

He agreed. More because it meant everyone was safe. But the way the light lent her a pretty glow was good too.

"So."

He took a bracing breath.

"I'm sorry about last night. Sorry we got interrupted and that I was back so late."

She nodded. "I expect there was a lot to talk about."

"We wanted to keep an eye on the Highway here and the trails coming up to Silver Cliffs. We didn't want to drive away and leave you open to attack."

"Or get ambushed."

"That either. But it happens. We've been ambushed twice in the last few years. Other crews have as well. I lost one of my men. You're safe here. You won't be out there."

"I understand you're worried. But I don't want to wait around here for those few times each annum you come to town for a few days and leave. I want to be with you. I want a relationship, not a visit."

He groaned inwardly. She was . . . intractable on certain things. He'd seen the steel in her spine more than once, but this was the first time he was sorry for it. He wanted her to obey his wishes. So she'd be safe.

"I can come more often. I told you about the higher frequency of deliveries now. My job isn't only to run transport escorts. I teach at the academy too. We come off the road and have mandated off time every moon. I have a house in Shelter City. You can come stay there with me or I can come here. It'll be more than it is now. But I can't just toss you in my escort vehicle today. That's not how it works. There are regulations about it and even if there weren't I'm not sure it's a good choice for either of us."

"I'm not helpless! I can shoot. I can read maps. Do you imagine I'll sit next to you and ask if we're nearly there every few minutes?"

He wisely stifled a laugh at that. "No. That has not even crossed my mind. But I have to be utterly focused on the road when I am on an escort. Not on the beautiful woman next to me and her sweet pussy I'd rather be buried in."

"Are you serious? I can't come with you because you can't think with your head? You trust Marcus and Trinity and I know they have sex!"

"They're trained for the job, Verity. Trinity has been a lawman since she was sixteen. And they're not the leader of the crew.

Neither of them. They all look to me to keep them safe. It's my job. I can't just bring my woman on the road with me because she's lonely."

She narrowed her eyes and he held his hands up quickly, recognizing the danger he faced. "I didn't mean it the way it came out."

"How *did* you mean it then? You seem to think I'm asking you to come along, giving up everything here because I'm a sad spinster who wants to be entertained every moment."

"You're not a spinster. That's the first thing. And I don't think, nor did I say you were bored and wanted to be entertained. People try to kill lawmen on the Highway. In the garrisons I have to mete out justice. How will you feel when you watch me shoot someone in the head in the public square?"

"I'd feel bad for you because I know you'd hate it. But it would be necessary and I know that. Probably better than you do. I live out here. I understand the pressures of abiding by the law. I understand lawmen are the line between civilization and brigands."

He scratched his beard, wishing she wasn't so fucking perceptive and undoing all his arguments one by one.

"Damn it. Don't *you* understand what *I'm* saying? I can't bear the thought of anything happening to you. That I'd be the reason for it when you could be here, or in Shelter City, *safe*. I can't risk you out there with me. I can't and I won't. Not because of what I think you'd do, but of what could happen to you."

"I can't stay here. I realized it yesterday when Constance and I were arguing. I will always be . . . beholden here. Stuck in the ways I'm supposed to act. Every day I wake up and I'm alone. And I know it will only be allowed so long and I'll have to make a choice. A choice to marry a man like Jackson or to accept that I'll be unwed and asexual. Right now I'm given some freedom, yes. But my sister voiced something that is totally true. My remaining here without being married will turn people away. So I'd have to turn off my sexuality. No dating. No fucking. Nothing. I'd have to let that part of me dry up so I can remain unwed.

"Or I could just give in and marry a man like Jackson. If I'm lucky. If I don't move on that within an annum or two I'd have less choices. Worse choices. I can't wait for you to come to town the way I have been. Those times are ending. My freedom is drying up. I don't want to dry up and blow away like dust."

He started and stopped a few times trying to find the words. Finally she shook her head.

"You can't know what it's like. You're a man from the center. You don't have to make choices in the same way just to exist. I'm telling you I can't make that choice. I can't. I'm telling you I love you and I want to be with you. I want the world out there, violence and all. Better that than slowly dying."

The horn sounded outside, signaling the start of the day. And the time for him to be readying to leave.

"I *will* be back for you. There's no need to let Jackson in your bed just because you're mad you can't get your way." He said the last angrily and she wanted to throw her teacup at him because he still didn't seem to grasp what she had said totally.

"That's what you think? You think all this is a temper tantrum?"

She noted the wariness in his gaze as he realized the danger in her tone.

"No. I understand your frustration, but I don't like all this talk of other men. Especially when I've told you I loved you and we'd be together. I can't take you in my escort. I already told you. Stay here. Be safe. I'll be back. I swear to you."

She stood up, loving him so much it cut into her belly like knives. "Will you be back to take me permanently or will we have this discussion again?"

"What brought all this on? You haven't done this when I left in the past."

"I'm so tired. I'm done, Loyal. I'm done trying to make due. Being in love with you . . . having you in my bed it's . . . I can't pretend not to see it anymore. I can't be happy living half of a life. Not when I've had glimpses of what I could have otherwise. You woke something up. In my belly. My heart. It's torture to imagine having to go back to my old life when you drive away today. Last night after my sister left I realized I'd been living like a shadow. I had no idea I was capable of loving someone the way I do you. But even for you I can't do it. I'm giving Tobin half my savings so he has credits to live on while he's in training. I'll be stuck here now for several more annum. And I can't be a stop on your Highway map, truly alive for a few days here and there."

"I have to go now. I have to lead the team to get ready to leave." He stood, moving to her, taking her hands. "I love you, Verity Coleman. We can make this work. Please believe that. Believe in me."

She took a deep, shaky breath and pushed past her exhaustion and impatience to remember the feel of his mouth on hers, of the way he touched her. She'd find the patience to wait. For now. "Don't make me wait too long. I love you too."

He pulled her into his arms, hugging her. She tipped her face up and he rained kisses all over it. The tenderness mixing with ferocity and relief.

"I packed already. Will you walk me out?" He took her hand, wanting it to be known that she was his. All the talk about her lack of choices and it possibly driving her to another man had stirred something up inside and he needed to soothe it before he got in that vehicle and was trapped for the next four hours until they got back to Shelter City.

And he wanted to reassure her as well. He knew she remained

unsettled. Knew she'd wanted more than he could give just then. But he wanted to give her as much as he possibly could, hating to leave with anything unsettled between them.

He'd never really had concern for much more than his badge and his crew. Something deep had unleashed and flowed into the rest of his consciousness with the sort of completeness that felt like it had been part of him forever. Belonging. He belonged to her. He hated the idea of her unhappiness in a way he couldn't have imagined even just half an annum prior.

Whatever it was, he was old enough to accept it for what it was. It'd be stupid to fight it. He wanted her so he'd take the good and the bad along with it.

"I have to get down to the mercantile anyway. Constance won't be there to help. I've spoke with a few others who work for me off and on through the annum when we get real busy. But there'll be a crush now that the horns have sounded and folks know you're all leaving."

He kissed her again, taking his time.

"I'll be at the escort before you all leave though. I promise."

He kissed her before he grabbed his satchel and they headed out.

Silver Cliffs was buzzing with activity. After the restrictions of the last days and the fear of the brigands, people had places to go and things to do. There was a line up already at the mail window.

And on the porch in front of the mercantile Loyal pulled her close and laid another kiss on her right out in front of god and everyone. It left her breathless and a little weak in the knees.

"I'll see you in a bit then."

She watched him amble away, unable to hide her smile of appreciation.

"He does cut a fine figure going as well as coming," one of the elderly women said as she made her way up the steps heading into the mercantile.

Verity laughed. "Yes, ma'am, he surely does."

She worked a steady shift, taking and bundling mail and packages until she closed up and headed into the store. The crowd had thinned. Tobin nodded toward the door to the loading bay. All the mail was on a rolling cart she needed to get out back. But she wanted to check in with everyone first.

"Been stacking up orders, barter goods and the like near the bay doors."

"Thank you. I'll go be sure it gets on the transport."

She headed through the back and took a moment, standing in the dim behind a tall shelf to find her breath and gather herself.

She hated the fact that he'd be gone again in just a while. Hated that her life would slide back into that place it was before he'd arrived. Worse, she supposed since things had gotten so serious between them. Since she'd delivered an ultimatum and he'd taken it seriously.

If he decided to say no, or came back and tried to push for things to remain as they were, what would she do? She'd use the next break before he came back to really think on her options.

But for right then she'd do her job and also see him off. Store up all the last moments she could before he disappeared like smoke.

When she walked out into the brighter space, she pushed the loading bay doors all the way open and waved at the transport driver. "Ready to load up."

It was quick work from then on. Part of their routine in each garrison. She handed things off and smiled sideways at Loyal when he hopped up beside her and pitched in.

"We're off then. Heading back to Shelter City. Going to do

some quick check-ins at the garrisons on the way, make sure every-one is safe."

She nodded, hoping her fear for him didn't show too much.

He pulled her into a hug and she went, squeezing him tight, breathing him in. "Come back to me," she whispered.

"I promise. You stay safe. Keep up the target practice. Stay ready, and if they come and you can't hold them off, you get your pretty butt to that exit in the wall you showed me. In fact, I want you to take some supplies out there. Just store them in the space and if you have to run, you can. Or use the bolt-hole. Either way, be prepared to get out if and when you have to."

That was a very good idea actually. She nodded. "I know the back country well. I can head up into the mountains."

"Good girl." He broke the hug but kept her hand until he jumped down and then grabbed her waist and swung her down next to him, taking her hand again as they walked to his vehicle.

"Safe travels, lawman."

"Safe travels, milady." He slid into the seat and strapped himself in after he'd locked his weapon into the slot on the dash where he could reach it easily in an emergency. His face had lost the softness he'd worn for her and took on the wariness he'd need for the road.

She trailed to the gate as they drove away before she headed back up the hill to the mercantile to work her days through until he returned.

15

As they hit the Highway back to Shelter City they had a fairly quiet first hour or two. Loyal pushed thoughts of her from his head as he did the job. After a bit it became clear they were riding in the wake of a band of brigands. Whether it was the leftovers from the group that had attempted the siege on Silver Cliffs or not, he didn't know.

"You see this?" he spoke into the headset that connected him to the other vehicles in the escort.

They'd been ambushed before. Caution was a necessary thing out there on the Highway. But they couldn't just drive past without checking for survivors.

Indigo answered. "Yeah. I don't know how far behind them we are."

"The engine on that truck ahead is still smoking. It can't be that far at all," Stace added.

A snarl of vehicles littered the roadside. The tires had been blown, the windows broken. Loyal knew there'd be parts missing from the engines and whatever else could be stripped that the brigands might have needed.

There was no sign that people remained and most likely there wouldn't be. Brigands took slaves or killed everyone. They didn't leave much behind.

"Trinity, Marcus, you two ease up. I'm going to pull over. I want to be sure we don't have survivors."

He got out his field glasses and checked out the treeline. They had heat tech so he could see body signatures, even if they were invisible to the naked eye. Nothing but some small game, which was a good sign there weren't any brigands around.

He flashed his lights and let the rest know what he was going to do, popping the catch on his shotgun and easing from his vehicle.

The men in the transport truck had a mounted gun and once they stopped, everyone was on full alert. Indigo pulled up and got out, giving Loyal coverage.

Burning rubber and metal, blood, the stench of it never failed to clench in his belly. He'd gotten past the wanting to vomit part, but the juxtaposition of blood against the glitter of shattered glass glittering in the sun made a sort of aching, violent beauty.

Blood led him to the bodies. Three adult males with offensive and defensive wounds. So they'd gone down fighting at least.

The central government didn't approve of private traffic on the Highway, but it wasn't prohibited. There would always be people who wanted to do their own thing. He understood that sense of freedom and independence. Sometimes people wanted to holiday down in Shelter City. Or they moved from one garrison to another.

This group though—he looked around—were traders most likely, from the looks of the shells of the vehicles left on the road. Commerce made the world go round.

"Anything?" Indigo approached, his gaze shifting as he remained on watch.

"No. Let's take care of these bodies."

They had powder that would disintegrate the bodies. All lawmen transports carried it. Leaving dead bodies around encouraged disease. The powder got rid of the attractive and yet deadly target for predators and illness.

It took ten minutes to clean up. Ten minutes to erase the existence of these men, whoever they were. Fathers, husbands, brothers, sons.

A fucking waste.

"Let's go. We got some roadway to make up. Be on the alert, we may roll up on them as they're in action." He turned the engine over and the ferocious rumble slid up his spine. He didn't need to tell them to shoot to kill or anything of the like. They knew what to do. It was always the same.

You couldn't bargain with brigands. Couldn't take them in as prisoners. It was a waste of time and money, of space in the jails. There was one way to deal with brigands and that was to kill them. Period.

They tore up the Highway toward Shelter City. It loomed ahead, shimmering like a dream. If they didn't encounter any trouble, they'd be rolling up to the outer gates in less than an hour.

But of course, ifs were what they were and as they rounded a hairpin curve heading up a steep incline, Bren's voice barked over the comm system.

"Company about a click back."

Shit. They could probably run for it. The brigands would most likely peel away from a chase once they got a little closer to Shelter City where there'd be a higher chance of a patrol and they'd be vastly outnumbered and outgunned.

But they'd have to haul ass with a transport vehicle full of goods.

"Lead them around this corner. If we're clear, get the transport to the rear as we turn to head them off. Vests on. I've just sent a signal to Shelter City operations to let them know we're about to engage the enemy."

Once they'd cleared the turn and there was no sign of an ambush, the transport vehicle, with Indigo and Marcus on either side, pushed past Loyal, who spun his vehicle and got out.

Time seemed to slow down then.

All the training in the world can't prepare a man for this moment. When everything feels slowed down and sped up all at once. When all he'd really have was instinct and hope that his will to survive was greater than his opponent's.

He flipped the holster on his thigh open and chambered a round for the shotgun as he moved to the center of the Highway.

The surface of the roadway beneath his feet vibrated as he took a deep breath to center himself. Indigo and Stace fanned right and left. He knew the transport had pulled all the extra shielding into place and the gunner would have his weapon aimed.

Trinity's footsteps, along with Marcus as they all got into place.

There were no pithy sayings. No hoots or calls to arms.

They all stood and waited until the brigands came around that corner. His muscles burned from the way he held himself until he forced them to relax. This was what he was born to do and he would do it.

Going to one knee, Loyal allowed himself a smile as he aimed and shot out the front right tire and then the left.

The tanklike vehicle lost control and sailed off the Highway into the ravine that ran to the west of the Highway.

"Two more to go."

They came again, around the corner, no slower than the first vehicle.

Bullets peppered the roadway at Loyal's feet as he jerked his attention away from the blacktop to the van barreling toward them.

Still standing, Marcus took aim and shot out the windshield as Trinity took out the driver with a head shot. The last vehicle slammed into the back, sending them both skidding sideways.

Loyal hardened his heart as he pulled a pin and tossed a grenade into the gaping hole the windshield used to occupy.

They turned and went to one knee as the explosion sounded behind them and heat crawled over his back.

He turned again, standing, giving Trinity cover as she and Marcus headed to the next vehicle to finish everyone off.

"No civilians," Trinity said as she came back. "Everyone else neutralized."

But that was too good to be true as shots rained down from above.

"Sniper." They all headed for cover as the gunman on the transport aimed and gave them some time to get safe by shooting into the heavily forested ridge where the shots had come from.

"On it," Stace called out, shouldering his weapon and jogging into the treeline. Marcus followed, his rifle in his hands.

There'd be no more random shooting into the ridge above. They couldn't risk hitting their people. So for many breathless minutes they waited until the sound of a firefight drifted down.

As they cruised back through the first ring of gates around Shelter City, Loyal realized it was going to be a longer day than he'd thought.

"Head straight to defense HQ," the guard told Loyal.

The transport went in a different direction but now that they were in the city, they'd be fine. Loyal and his crew headed south, to the sprawling and heavily armed grounds of the defense headquarters.

The days slid into a week and then two. Life slipped back into routine. She normally had time with Constance, but her sister had frozen her out. An official blip came for Tobin, saying he'd been selected for the next training sequence and an official transport would collect him. It announced he'd qualified for a scholarship that would cover his room, board and tuition.

It also announced that the next sequence had been delayed by at least two moons because of rising tensions on some parts of the Highway with the brigands. While she was thrilled for Tobin, Verity also knew it would delay the opportunity to see Loyal again. Which had only underlined her position and the need to make a move one way or another when he made his way back to Silver Cliffs once more.

A positive was that despite the blip and his decision to go to Shelter City, Tobin had made peace with his parents and was back living at home instead of sleeping on a cot in her blip office.

But that blip, while not shoving Tobin further from his parents, had been a huge issue between them and Verity.

Despite the differences in their lifestyle and beliefs, Verity and her sister had always made an effort to be part of each other's life. She had dinner with her family at least once a week, babysat the younger boys, took them on hikes and the like.

But her sister's husband seemed to feel Tobin's wanting to go to academy was something Verity had done to them on purpose. A way to harm them and wrest their son from the house.

She'd tried—once—to speak with him about it. He'd been hard faced and angry and had told her she was no longer welcome in his home and to leave his family alone.

To have pushed Constance would have put her sister in a bad

place. She didn't want to make her sister's family life harder, even if she was angry. The last thing she wanted was to prove them right and actually work to bring disharmony to their family.

Still, Verity had expected her sister to at the very least try to speak with her about it, but Constance had patently avoided the mercantile and any contact and she felt that absence acutely.

Loyal was gone and things were clearly heating up outside the walls. Instead of the more regular deliveries he'd said to expect, they gotten less official transport with mail and goods and more military patrols passed through.

There wasn't much else to do but work to keep saving credits and to give herself something to do so when she fell into her bed every night she was too exhausted to think about anything.

It hadn't been all bad. She'd hired on extra help at the mercantile. She couldn't count on her sister anymore and Tobin would be leaving. She hoped to be as well, so it was a necessary thing.

Ruth Hannigan was a little older than Verity was. Married, but no children. Her husband had a herd of sheep and often traded the wool. She loomed beautiful textiles and had helped out on occasion during busy times.

Ruth took to full-time work easily. Learning quickly, working efficiently. They had the beginning of a good friendship already, but the concentrated time together deepened that. Giving Verity a place to go when she'd been rejected by Constance.

Verity found herself at the Hannigan's table several times a week. Sometimes for tea and a chat with Ruth, other times for meals. Jackson Haldeman was their neighbor and he also ended up at the table.

He walked her home from time to time and she liked his company. But he wasn't Loyal. Could she settle with him though?

Could she let Jackson court her and be his wife if Loyal didn't bring her an answer she could live with?

Only, she realized, if she could truly make a commitment to him or it wouldn't be fair. She didn't like living half a life, she most surely couldn't ask anyone else to do the same because she pined for a man she couldn't have.

It felt disloyal to even think on that. Disloyal to the man she was in love with. But as Ruth had pointed out reality was reality. She couldn't *not* think about her future in Silver Cliffs if things didn't work out either.

But she kept a firm space between herself and Jackson. A *friends only* space. She didn't want to lead him on or give him false hope. She wanted Loyal. Wanted a chance at a life with him.

They talked about all manner of things, but any time he moved too close to that moat, the place only belonging to Loyal, she gently, but firmly, pushed him back.

She stood on her porch with him after he'd walked her back. They'd had a rousing card game with Ruth and Garner and several other neighbors of different genders and ages.

"Been a while since the lawman came around."

She arched a brow at him. "You've seen the blips too. You know they're busy in the south with the brigands."

"What if he doesn't come back, Verity? Have you given any thought to that?"

She sighed as she moved to sit in one of the chairs. "He promised he'd be back. So he will."

"I know you're in love with him. And I saw how he looked at you. So I believe he'll be back if he can."

The last three words echoed in the near silent evening. The reality of what he did was something she lived with daily.

"If things don't work out with you and him, would you let me come around? Court you?"

She sighed. "I don't want to give you false hope. It's not fair. I love Loyal. I want to be with him."

"I respect that. You're a beautiful woman. Smart and independent. Man'd be lucky to have you at his side, is all I'm saying. I'd like it to be me if things don't work out. I waited, you see. I saw what James did to you. How you suffered. But he never broke you. When he ended up dead and you were free I told myself you weren't ready and I didn't want to push. But then Loyal came around and turned your head at the same time. I waited too long."

"You're a good man. Handsome. Charming. You're not a brute. You have a job, a nice piece of land. There are plenty of feminine glances your way when you walk up and down the hill. There's a woman for you here in Silver Cliffs."

He snorted. "Just so happens she's in love with someone else." His smile was rueful and tenderness flooded her at that admission.

"She is. But that doesn't mean she can't recognize what a catch you are for the right woman. This one? I can only offer you friendship. I like having you in my life. But I can't offer more than that."

He nodded. But she knew how he thought now. Had seen him play cards. Jackson Haldeman was a fan of the long game. He'd made a mistake in waiting, he thought—though he'd been right, she wouldn't have been ready for the first year or two after James' murder—but it wasn't a mistake he'd make again if he got the chance.

"I'll say goodnight then. And we're definitely friends, Verity. You're too good at cards to let that go." He winked, took a step back and faded into the dark.

16

Nearly a moon passed with no word from Loyal. Planting season had begun in earnest and everyone was busy in Silver Cliffs. They'd had some traders come through so her shelves were stocked, which was always nice.

But that didn't mean she wasn't thinking about Loyal all the time. Wondering how he was. Hoping he and his crew were safe.

Finally, two moons after she'd seen him last, a blip arrived saying an official transport would be arriving within the next moon to collect Tobin to take him to Shelter City to start the next training cycle.

Smiling, she headed out into the store where he stood with Ruth, helping her restock.

"Just got a blip."

He turned, expectant. Grinning, she handed the paper to him. He scanned it quickly and with a whoop he hugged her, dancing around the mercantile.

"I take it we got good news?" Ruth laughed at Tobin's antics.

"I'm going to be heading to training soon." He shook the paper. "Official notice."

Verity laughed. "It's really happening." And she'd be seeing Loyal at long last.

"I need to tell my parents." He sobered a little and her heart ached. She hoped they'd at least feign excitement for him.

"Go on then." She kissed his cheek before pushing him toward the door. "You can have the rest of the day off."

But of course Constance came barreling over shortly after Tobin had left to tell them.

"I can't believe you are still pushing this whole thing after all the trouble you've caused."

Verity looked up from where she'd been counting sacks of grain and then back to Ruth. "I need to step away for a little while. Can you finish this up, please?"

Ruth's gaze cut to Constance and then back to Verity. She nodded and then rolled her eyes. "Yes, of course." Verity nearly laughed but got herself back under control before she faced her sister.

"Let's go upstairs."

She led the way, not looking back over her shoulder to see if Constance was following.

"Now that we don't have an audience would you care to tell me what this is all about?" Verity asked once Constance closed the door.

"You know good and well what this is about. Tobin came running over with the blip about training. This is your doing."

"The last time you were here, I held back because I respected your fear for him. But this is my home and I'm done holding back for anyone. Just so you understand before we continue down this road."

"We just got him back home and now you're filling his head with this again."

"Is that really what you think or are you letting your husband get you all whipped up over something you know Tobin is in charge of?" Anger roiled through her system.

"You're pushing him."

"I'm *supporting* him, not pushing him." She threw her hands up. "Get over it, Constance. Or stop rushing over here to vomit your anxiety on me. You can't have it both ways. If you freeze me out and stop inviting me to family events you can't count on me to let you wring your hands in my parlor and take your abuse. Tobin is a man. He has an opportunity to go and do something he wants to do. You can support him or not, but you know as well as I do that he's going and it has nothing to do with me."

"It surely does. He told us you're helping him with an allowance."

"They're my credits. Mine to spend or save as I see fit. He'll need it."

"And what about you? He *left*. Without you. And you're giving your credits to Tobin so what do you plan on doing?"

Her sister's words, poisonous and full of anger, hit at her like fists, tearing at the walls she'd tried to build around her heart.

"Why are you here? You've already called me names and insulted me. What else is left but to underline it? This is beneath you. You're in my home, you're my sister . . . I'd never try to hurt you this way." She heard the unshed tears in her voice and wished she hadn't.

Constance drew back as if she'd been slapped and then she fell into a chair with a sigh. "I apologize. This tension between us is silly and I'm being a harridan about it. I feel out of control. Scared out of my wits at the idea of losing Tobin. It's been easy to pour all that into my upset over you. I'm afraid for you too. So afraid it's made me angry. I've missed you. I mean that."

"You shut me out. Like I didn't even exist. I've had all this stuff and I haven't had you to talk to about it."

"Please, sit. I'm sorry."

Verity sat next to her sister and Constance took her hands, squeezing them. "I didn't know how to deal with all my fear. And Emeril . . . he's been so angry. I stayed away to placate him. But you're my sister and I was wrong."

Tears shone in Constance's eyes and Verity let it go a little bit.

"Will you tell me? About the lawman. Distract me from the fact that my son will be going off to Shelter City to learn how to be one of them."

"He'll be safe in Shelter City. Safer than he would be here. And they'll teach him to be stronger. You need to keep hold of that when you're scared."

"He's my boy. I know he wants this. I know he'll be good at it. But I'm so frightened for him." Constance swallowed hard. "Enough of that for now. Tell me about Loyal. Please."

"I told him I wanted to come with him. On the road."

Constance gasped, her hand over her mouth. "You did not!"

"I need to be free, Constance. I want to go with him. I can't just wait around for him here. Content to only see him a few times each annum? No. I'd be half a person. I don't want that."

"It's so dangerous out there. How can you want that? For a man you barely know? Explain it to me so I can understand it."

"I don't know if I can. You and I are different." Verity shrugged, searching for the right words. "I can see how it might seem sudden, or that Loyal and I don't know each other very well. But I can tell you that I was married to James for eight years and he didn't know my favorite color much less my birthday. Loyal knows my hopes and dreams. He knows what I like, what my favorite flower is. He brings me books. I know him better than I've known anyone."

How could she explain something that felt so natural? So instinctive it went beyond words?

"I want to be with him. I know others have their wives or husbands with them. Even when they're not lawmen. I did research. It's not dangerous every time. Not more dangerous than being here, only feeling alive when he comes around."

Constance ran a hand over her belly as she thought. "I can't pretend to understand it. How you'd give up the safety of life behind these walls to ride up and down a Highway plagued with brigands."

"If it doesn't work out my heart gets broken. But I can come back here. Or to another garrison. It's not like my life is over. I'll just start another chapter. But if I don't at least try? Now while I can? I'll wonder what if for the rest of my days. I love him. He loves me. It's enough right now."

Constance took a deep breath and Verity knew her sister would never truly understand it. She loved her life in Silver Cliffs. Had never yearned to know things she wasn't told. It didn't make her bad or wrong, it just made them different. But the point would be how her sister reacted right then. Would she revert to anger and fear or would she accept that even if she didn't understand, it was what Verity wanted?

"I can't say that this is a choice I'd make. Or even one I like you making. I worry for you. I can't help it. But I do want you to be happy and I'm sorry, again, that I haven't been very nice about it. It is nice of him to help Tobin. At least he has that on his side."

"Tobin will be with other men and women his age. All wanting to make a difference. From all up and down the Highway. This will be good for him." Pride filled her. She had a very good idea that Loyal was the kind of man that if he had your back others would respect you just for that if nothing else.

"What if Tobin never comes back?"

Verity shook her head. "He will. They get time off. They can choose to staff the garrisons instead of work the Highway too. When that blip came he rushed to you. To share it with you. He loves you so much. He won't be living in your house anymore, but that would have happened anyway. But he'll always be back."

Constance stayed at her table, sharing tea and some cookies. It was the nicest time she'd had with her sister in a very long while and it gave her hope.

know better than to ask if we're staying the night here." Indigo spoke from where he checked under the hood of his vehicle.

They should. The last nearly three moons he'd been up and down that damnable Highway. Fighting. He'd been shot. Twice. Marcus had taken an arrow to the meat of his thigh and though he'd spent some time in a med facility and the muscles had been repaired, he had a slight limp.

They'd been ambushed. Been bloodied and battered. Had done their fair share of ambushing as well. And bit by bit had retaken the southern leg of the Land's End Highway that had been fairly overrun with brigands who'd managed to take over two garrisons.

Two garrisons where buildings had been destroyed. Where they'd liberated those who'd been tortured. Raped. Some of them anyway. Those who were left alive. The others? There'd been pits where the bodies had been thrown. The central government had to send in the health workers to stop an illness borne from eating human flesh.

The brigands had shifted into something far worse than they'd been before. A new type of band had emerged and there appeared to be some sort of internal battle being waged between this new breed, the flesh eaters, and the brigands they'd dealt with before and were fearsome enough as it was.

They were back to running official transports in the north once more. Exhaustion burned his eyes. But he needed to touch her. Needed to see her. Needed to hear her voice and feel her skin against his.

So yes, they should stay the night in the garrison. But Silver Cliffs was just up the Highway. They'd already stayed two days and it was time to go. He'd done his job and he wanted her so much his skin itched for her.

"The widow Coleman is good for you." Trinity cleaned her weapon at a nearby picnic table. "Being with someone makes you strong when they're worthy." Her gaze cut to Marcus, the corner of her mouth lifting as he turned and caught her looking.

"She wants to be out here with me. And after seeing what we did in the South, I can't. When we left last time it was my plan to make it possible, to get the clearance to have her with me. But now?" He scratched his bearded chin. "I can't bring myself to expose her to that. No matter what she thinks she wants."

He had an alternate suggestion. One he hoped she'd listen to and accept. But there was simply no way he could have her out on the Highway when they could be under attack by fucking cannibals.

He'd walk away before he'd do it. At least if he walked away, she'd be safe in Silver Cliffs behind those impenetrable walls. At least she'd be alive somewhere in the world. He had the stick as well as the carrot. For the time being the military had issued a ban on nonmilitary personnel traveling with lawmen. Even those lawmen who rode along with their husbands and wives had to leave them in a garrison. He'd lead with that before he made his proposition.

"What's the alternative, Loyal? You've seen life out here in the garrisons. Verity wants more. She wants to live outside those walls and she wants to do it with you." Indigo shrugged.

"You know as well as I do about the new restrictions. I have a proposal to make to her about how we can take the next half an annum or so. I guess I'll have to see what she thinks."

"Don't blow it. I've been riding with you for over ten years. I've never seen you do so much as look back over your shoulder when we left a garrison. This woman is the first. The only one you've been drawn back to and that means something." Indigo was far more perceptive than most people imagined.

"It does mean something."

"Let's roll then, shall we? Get to Silver Cliffs. Pick up our passenger for lawman academy. Have an ale at the bar. See Loyal go all cow-eyed at the widow Coleman." Trinity slapped his shoulder and laughed, heading for Marcus, who bent to kiss her before they headed to their vehicles.

They rumbled through the gates and headed back for the Highway. Their pace was harder than normal. He wanted to be there as soon as possible. The Highway was clear. Partially because of the increased military patrols. Partially because they'd beaten the brigands back.

No matter though, because it meant they could get to Silver Cliffs.

The time he'd been away had been torture because he'd missed her, yes. But it had also helped him get to the heart of how he felt about Verity.

Indigo had been right. In all the years of his life, there'd never been anyone who drew him to a place the way she did. Never been a woman who was so impossible to get off his mind.

He was a solitary man. He liked not being owned or having

responsibilities to anyone outside the job. His family was his crew, but otherwise no one else held much personal importance to him.

He hadn't been obsessed with fucking before Verity. He got it when he needed to, when he wanted it. When it was offered by a person he knew wouldn't expect anything more than a good time.

But Verity wasn't a woman he could tumble and walk away from. He'd known that when he'd crawled between her thighs the first time. It's one of the reasons he'd tried so hard not to give in to that burning need to touch her. For two annum he'd kept his desire leashed. But each time they'd driven through those gates it had been harder to resist.

Not just the sex, though that part made the blood heat in his veins. So smooth and sweet on the outside but behind closed doors, once they were alone she demanded her pleasure. He'd never really imagined that being as hot as it was. But there was something so deeply alluring in the knowledge that she was dirty but only he saw just how dirty.

She was someone who listened more than she talked. Curious. Vibrant. Full of decency and honor and caring. Verity was a person he could share his future with and it was long past the point where it scared him the way it did the first time he'd kissed her and left Silver Cliffs.

It was what it was. She meant something in his life. The totality of Verity wasn't just her. It was the Verity-and-Loyal of it all. The way she fit in his life, the way he fit in hers. The way the two of them made something else entirely.

He'd held on to that when they'd been out dealing with the death and destruction of the last three moons. He was part of something bigger than his job for the first time in his entire adult life.

And it was . . . good.

17

The horns sounded and she looked across the store to Ruth.

"Go on and see if it's him. Tobin and I will handle the loading dock doors."

Grinning, Verity patted at her hair. "They have to come up here anyway. And I can see from my parlor better than down at the gates."

Ruth laughed as Verity ran from the store, out the back. The view from her parlor was enough to show her the tail end of an escort heading over the bridge.

Her heart pounded, leaving her slightly breathless, and it wasn't until that very moment that she let herself confront the worry that he'd be hurt out there during this brigand uprising.

She sat in a nearby chair and let herself shake, letting it go so she could gather herself up again, put herself together so she could go back down and greet him.

The procession came up the hill, with the escort vehicles peeling off at the garrison offices.

He'd come when he could.

She smoothed her hands down her trousers and took a deep breath, heading to unlock the mail office. Three moons with no deliveries meant there'd be a lot of work to do.

Ruth's husband, Garner, had shown up to help with the store, closing up so they could get ready for the rush of preorders.

With Tobin going she was glad she'd hired on one more person to help, one of Ruth's cousins who ably dealt with the busy times and kept herself working when things slowed down.

She dealt with the sacks of mail showing Ruth just how it worked. It was bittersweet. Tobin had been so great, knew what to do and how to do it. He'd be gone and Ruth would take over. As much as she loved Ruth, as thrilled as Verity was for Tobin, she'd miss the boy a great deal.

New experiences for them all, she supposed as she handed out letters and parcels, checked names off the list and kept the line moving until she looked up to see Loyal standing there, looking tired and thinner than he had the last time she'd see him.

But he was hers and so much joy burst through her it was all she could do to stand there and smile at him. "Well met, lawman."

"I think you need to meet me out back. I have a message for you." He nodded his head solemnly, but the hint of a smile at one corner of her mouth belied the truth of what he was up to.

"I'll be just a moment," she assured Ruth, who waved a hand at her to go.

She forced herself to move at a normal pace until she'd closed the door and then she ran down the hall to the back door and barreled into his arms as he picked her up, twirling her, his mouth taking hers as he set her feet back on the ground.

His taste filled her to near bursting, his arms wrapped tight around her, his smell all around her.

"I missed you so fucking much," he muttered against her mouth. "You taste so good and I'm starving."

She smiled. "You're here."

"I told you I'd come back. I keep my promises."

"There's a mob in the store."

"I know. I have to go back to the garrison offices. I needed to come to you."

She hugged him again. "I needed you to."

"I'll drop my things upstairs."

"I'll see you when we close up."

He kissed her again, his tongue sliding over her lips and into her mouth. She sucked on it and he grunted, his hips jutting forward, holding her so tight she had the mad wish that he'd simply lay her on the grass and fuck her senseless.

"Playing with fire. I'll collect on that promise when I get you alone later." He kissed her one last time, setting her back.

She licked her lips and his pupils swallowed the iris.

"Looking forward to that, lawman."

The rest of her afternoon went by quickly enough. She was rushed off her feet between the mail and the folks coming in to collect their orders. They closed up and spent several hours more restocking the shelves to ready themselves for the next morning when the whole garrison would show up to see what new items had been brought from all up and down the Highway.

Tobin buzzed with excitement. Constance even stopped in with a smile, but didn't work a shift. And that had to be all right. Constance had to make her own choices just as Verity would make hers.

Hers sat in her parlor smoking a cigar, reading a newspaper and looking finer than anyone had a right to. This was often how she found him when he came to Silver Cliffs. But it was different now because he belonged to her.

He looked up at her entrance, stubbing the cigar out and moving to her.

"It was a miracle that I was able to get up here without Tobin in tow. I sent him off to talk to Indigo. Which was rather mercenary, I know. But I can't find it in me to feel bad."

He pulled her hair from the braid, running his fingers through it, bending to bury his face in it. "Three moons without the scent of you. Sometimes I'd wake up in the middle of the night and smell you, the phantom of your skin. It burned through me."

"You missed me then?" She ran her hands up his arms, loving the warm strength of his muscles. Over his shoulders and down to his chest where she began to unbutton his shirt.

"I did." He put his hands over hers, stilling them. "Not so fast. Aren't you hungry? I'm not going anywhere right now. Don't starve yourself to get something you can have—in abundance—after you've satisfied other hungers first."

"I'm starving for you." And it was true. It had been all day since she'd eaten, but three moons since he'd touched her. Since she'd had her hands on him, heard his voice.

"I made dinner." He put her in a chair. "Sit and let me take care of you. Then I'll take care of you some more."

He sauntered into her kitchen, pulling something from the oven that smelled very good, before dishing some onto two plates that he brought to the table. "I saw the bread, it's there under the cloth. I brought some butter as well. It's got salt from the Great Sea. I think you'll like it."

He bent to kiss her temple. "Don't pout or I'll give you something to do with that mouth besides eating."

Her gaze locked with his and she breathed in deep, letting what he did to her settle into her bones. So good. He woke up every bit of her senses. All her wants. Just looking at him made her ache.

It was a delicious sort of ache though. She licked her lips, loving the way his breath hitched.

"Promise?"

She watched, her nipples hardening, as he reached for his belt buckle and undid it, sliding his trousers open and pulling out his cock. Everything inside her stood up and cheered at the sight.

"Go on then." He tapped the head of his cock, wet with pre-come, against her lips. But she opened, licking across, tasting salt and skin and Loyal. She hummed her satisfaction at that.

He hissed and she took the head to the crown into her mouth with a swirl of her tongue.

"Yes."

She fought against the lure of closing her eyes and sinking into the sensation that way. She didn't want to miss the sight of him. Of the way he gazed down his body at her. Hungry.

Little by little she swallowed more of him. Taking him deeper and then deeper again. Finding her pace, getting her breath just right. His taste didn't flood through her, instead she absorbed it in increments until, before she fully realized it, he owned her.

He smoothed a hand down her hair, brushing her jawline, her cheek, the side of her mouth.

"So beautiful. There's so much ugliness out there and then there's you. You who washes it all away every time you touch me."

She moaned around the cock in her mouth. She tried to tell herself she'd be tough when she gave him her ultimatum, but how could she resist him? In the flesh as he said things like that with the truth of it written all over his face? She wanted him and she wanted things to work.

But for that exact moment she wanted to bring him pleasure. So she focused, licking up the line of him, delighting in his rough moan, of the way his hand had moved back to her hair to gather it, to move her at whatever pace he wanted.

"You want it in your mouth? Hm?"

She nodded.

His curse delighted her. Just a small slip, a tiny chink in his control. And she did it.

His hand tightened, her scalp tingled as the pain slid into something else, as the taste of him filled her, as his tortured groan was homecoming.

He had a plan, damn it. He'd make her a meal, strip her naked, bathe her, eat her pussy a few times, fuck her boneless and then they'd talk. But she was temptation personified. So lovely. Beautiful and sweet and soft but just beneath that softness there was an edge that drove him to possess her, to cosset and protect and take. Take and take.

He bent to kiss her, shaking his head at her satisfied smile.

"Welcome back, lawman. Now where's my dinner?"

"Can you wait then? For me to sate other appetites?"

She laughed, sipping the ale he'd poured. "I can wait. I know you'll make it worth it."

She buttered some bread and dug into the casserole he'd made, sighing happily. "In addition to everything else you're good at, you can cook. I'm not quite sure how you haven't been snapped up before now."

"Never wanted to be. Until now."

He took her hand after he sat. Squeezing it before digging in. "So fill me in on what's happened over the last three moons."

She waved it away. "You have a much better story, I'd wager."

"Not while we're eating. It's not a story that goes well with food. I see you have new staff in the mercantile."

"That's Ruth. She's going to take over when Tobin leaves. She's wonderful and a fast learner. I think she's better at running things than I am. Endlessly patient. A good friend too. Tobin is"—she shook her head, amused—"so excited. He fair bounces around town all day long. Any time the horns go off he runs to see if it's an official transport to pick him up. Jackson has been helping him with target practice and tracking. Most folks are proud to see him go and represent us down in Shelter City."

Most. "So you're still having trouble with your sister then?"

She told him about how they'd stopped inviting her over, about the things her sister had said. And about their recent attempt to patch things up in some way.

"I'm sorry I've brought you heartache."

"It's not that. It's . . . I think it's that I'm different now. I want different things and while most folks in Silver Cliffs are all right with that, some, like Constance and her husband, they're not. They're so frightened by whatever is outside the walls that my wanting to see it is threatening somehow. I don't know. But what can I do? Give up on what I want to make them comfortable? Why should I do that?"

They skirted around it, the gauntlet she'd tossed down when he'd left the last time. It was cowardly to avoid it, but he'd wanted a bubble. Just the two of them, no stress. Even for a brief time.

She smirked. "Just because we're not talking about it doesn't mean we're not thinking about it."

"How do you do that? Know what I'm thinking?"

She laughed, putting her head on his shoulder a moment. "It'll be our secret that you're really not so mysterious."

"Let's eat first. Then can we get naked and in your lovely tub? We'll talk. I promise. But let me have you, soak you up for a bit." He needed that more than he'd realized until right then.

"All right. The doors are locked so as long as we aren't beset by brigands or Tobin, we have time."

They talked of nothing too serious. She told him what she'd been up to. Training Ruth, making a new friendship. She skirted around her interactions with Haldeman, which amused him more than angered him. He had no worries about her constancy. The man *was* a threat, but not an immediate one.

"I'll clear the dishes if you'll run the bath?" He took her hand, turning it and kissing the heart of her palm. She shivered and he smiled.

"You're a rogue. I rather like it."

What he liked was the breathless way she spoke.

"Only for you. All for you." He pulled her close, swaying. She made him feel things he'd never understood. Had seen, knew existed between others, but had never begun to feel.

"You make me want things, Verity." He brushed a kiss against her forehead, pushing her hair back to expose more skin. More to touch.

"I'm glad I'm not alone."

He breathed her in deep. Needing that. She chased away the stench of death. Of misery and pain. Filtered it all out and left him better.

"I'll go run the bath."

"I brought you some candles and a few other baubles you might like."

She tipped her head back with a smile. "You did?"

He nodded. "I'll be in momentarily."

She tried not to rush as she lit the candles he'd brought. The scent of them filled her bathroom, casting a golden glow on the walls. The same walls she'd seen every day for so long. They'd been a different color when she lived here with James. But after he'd died she repainted. Changed things to suit herself and chase his energy away.

She disrobed, letting her hair stay free, knowing he liked it best that way. Several bundles sat on the bed. She unwrapped the red one first, finding earrings of deep blue glass. She smiled. No one gave her presents, not the way he did. Not always practical, but fun and pretty.

She replaced her other earrings with the blue ones and then opened the next. A scarf. She drew it over her skin. So soft.

"I thought it would look beautiful against your skin and I was right."

She turned to find him standing there, naked. She sighed happily. "You're the best present of all."

"I turned the water off."

She brushed her hair back to show him the earrings. "They're lovely, thank you."

"I have a confession to make."

"And what's that then?"

"My home in Shelter City is full of presents I've picked up for you over the years. I didn't want to scare you with how often you came into my thoughts. So I have them tucked in drawers and on shelves. I tell myself I'll give them to you bit by bit, but I keep finding new things that call to me. The scarf I picked up at a bazaar after the first time I came here."

She swallowed past a lump of emotion. "I don't know what to say that could do justice to how much that touches me."

"You were so lovely the first time I saw you." He took her hand and drew her into the bathroom. "We drove up that hill and I liked Silver Cliffs immediately. Well defended. Which makes my job easier of course."

She got in the tub and he settled in behind her, pulling her against him. Where she belonged. "It was the middle of the warm season. You came here and people were chattering because our old escort had retired. You got out of the lead vehicle and I just watched you."

"Yes. It was warm. You came out of the loading bay, your legs showing in a flowy dress. Pale blue. You had shadows in your eyes, but you smiled at me. I wanted you then. But you weren't ready."

She really was fortunate in the men who fancied her. Both Loyal and Jackson had said the same thing. Had given her time and space to find her feet in the time after James was killed.

"You weren't ready and neither was I. I suppose the more I got to know you, the more I understood that too." Their fingers tangled as they held hands. "I knew, deep down, that you were not the kind of woman I'd be able to walk away from. And once I took a taste." He paused to laugh. "Once you demanded I did and I finally let myself, there was no turning back. It's not just that I'm in love with you. It's that I cannot imagine a life without you. I need you."

Tears pricked against her lashes. The man barely said ten words in a row and there he was, making this most moving declaration of love.

"I don't know how I ended up with you. You're a miracle. My miracle and I cannot let you drive with me. Not right now."

Her heart got stuck in her throat and she forced herself to be calm, to listen to all he had to say and she hoped it would be enough.

"There's a schism in the brigand leadership. The ones we faced over the last three moons . . . " He held her tighter and she shivered at whatever could make a man like him speak with that tone of fear and horror. "They're cannibals. Not just the sharpened teeth to tear into foes when they attack. That's part theater, part weapon. But these new ones." He swallowed. "There's a new illness in some of the garrisons they overran. A virus that comes from eating human flesh. They are . . . I can't risk you. It's one thing to risk you when you can handle a weapon and would be riding along with my crew, who are all highly skilled. But they had mass graves. The women and children had been defiled in unspeakable ways. I've seen a lot, but this was . . . I've never seen anything like it. I tell you this level of detail because I want you to understand that when I came to the last few miles until the first gates of Shelter City when I left you last it was my plan to seek permission to have you ride with me."

Chills ran across her arms and he held her closer. "I can't protect you from that level of depravity. And the central government has issued a temporary ban on nonmilitary personnel riding along so it's not just me."

"So what do we do then?"

"It's a good sign you're not slapping me, I guess."

She snorted. "I want to be with you. But I'm not thick. I know this is bad. I know you have your reasons and they're good. I don't want to get tortured, raped and eaten for dinner by brigands any more than you want to."

"We get time off. I've arranged for some. I have this run to make but we'll be back to get Tobin and head to Shelter City. Would you like to come with me? Stay with me a while? I can show you around. We can have every day with each other. And, if you like Shelter City and my home, well, you could be my wife and live there. Or here. Once things get better you can ride along. But in Shelter City you can take classes, see vids, stand in the big sea. Be in my bed. I'm in Shelter City more than I can be here. But we can make it work. Whatever you want, if I can give it to you, I will."

She got to her knees and turned to face him. "Did you just ask me to marry you?"

He nodded, not speaking.

18

Driven to see her, he got out of the vehicle and nodded at Indigo. "Short of bleeding or something being on fire, if anyone disturbs me and my wife in the next two days or so, I will cut someone."

Indigo laughed. "Understood. Tell Verity I said hello and will see her when you're ready to unchain her from your bed."

Hm, that sounded like something he should try.

He waved and turned back to the house. A place that had been just somewhere he slept in between runs. For years. But now it was a home.

Dawn crept over the horizon as he let himself inside, heading to her. Always on his way to her.

She slept in their bed, a tousle of hair around her face, the blankets wrapped around her. A book lay open on the bedside table. One of the books from a class she was taking at the university.

She'd thrown herself into life in Shelter City with wild abandon. While he was away, she took day trips to some of the temples on the outskirts of Shelter City. She learned to swim in the ocean. Spent time with Tobin, who was thriving in his training. She'd made friends there as well. Neighbors, mostly, but people from her classes, some of the spouses and partners of the lawmen they knew as well.

They'd gotten married, just the two of them along with the officiant, on the sand with the roar of the big sea as their music. She was the heart of him. Vibrant and beautiful. Filling his life with music and love and so much desire his skin was tight with it.

She opened her eyes as she shifted to her back. "I heard you come in. What are you standing all the way over there for? It's been some time since I've been pleasured by anyone but myself."

He forgot everything else but her as he yanked his clothes off, sending things flying as he moved to her. Always to her.

Her skin was warm, fragrant with the soap she used, her hair soft, thick and cool against his arms as he got in bed, pulling her to him, kissing her hard and long. Taking all she offered so freely.

Two quick movements and he'd tossed away the nightgown she wore and her drawers, leaving her bare and eager.

"Your own hands though? Busy?"

"It helps me sleep." She arched as he kissed her neck. "Not nearly as well when it's your mouth or hands instead of my fingers, of course. I'm sure you're forced to make do with your hand while you're gone too. Especially as your wife"—she paused to growl when he found her nipple and licked over it—"mmm, would shoot your cock off if you put it anywhere near another woman."

"It's a sign of just how messed up I am, my love, that it gets me hot when you speak like that."

She laughed, squirming as he dragged his teeth over her nipple and sighed as he kissed down her ribs, dropping to her belly button and down, pushing her thighs open wide and breathing her in.

Hunger for her dug in deep as he slid her labia apart with his thumbs. He licked her over and over, taking her taste into himself until his restlessness, the restlessness that came from being away from her, eased.

She slid her fingers through his hair, tugging him closer, her hips moving back and forth against his mouth. Taking her pleasure.

It lit him up. Made him so hard he ached as his cock pressed into the blankets beneath where he lay. His face buried in her cunt so that he was surrounded by her. His tongue dug up into her, mimicking what he'd be doing with his prick shortly.

She made one of her sounds, a pleading sort of moan. He knew she was close. So wet against his lips, her thigh muscles trembling where he held her apart with his shoulders.

When she let go, she grabbed her pleasure up and wallowed in it. Trusting that there'd always be more when he was involved.

He'd been gone two weeks, which was better than three moons, to be sure. And when he stayed it was in their home. She woke up with him every day. He took her to breakfast or out to the ocean.

Her ring glinted on her hand as he surged up to kiss her. She wrapped her arms around him and her thighs, just as he slid into her body and she arched to get him deeper.

He didn't hurry. Just the slow advance and retreat. Filling her body over and over until she warmed up and accepted that he was home. She dug her nails into his ass, urging him on. "More. Deeper, harder. More."

"Greedy." He kissed her again, the scruff of his beard tickling her lips.

"Always. For you, always."

"I'm a lucky husband that way." He kissed down her neck,

changing his angle, hitching her hips up and giving her what she'd asked for. Harder. So hard her tits bounced as waves of pleasure shot through her with each thrust.

"Mine," he whispered.

"Yes."

"I surely do love you, Verity Alsbaugh."

"Thank you, lawman. I love you too."

She laughed as he came. Filling her up with joy and the wonder of connection that seemed to grow stronger each day.

He snuggled back down to the bed, remaining half inside her. "I'm home."

"Mmmm. Welcome back."

BY THE SEA
OF SAND

MEGAN HART

To my kids,
because you're the best thing I've ever done

1

ife was not easy by the Sea of Sand.

Perhaps it was not meant to be, Teila thought as she shielded her eyes against the searing glare of the triple suns overhead. If life were easier here, more would've come to homestead Sheir, stripping the planet's difficult-to-find resources faster than they could be replenished. It had happened in other places. It had made war.

Then again, she thought, there would always be reasons for war.

"Mao?" Beside her, Stephin tugged the sleeve of her robe. "Mao, I'm hungry."

Teila stroked her fingers through the length of her son's tangled blond curls, whipped by the heated wind and useless to comb. "What do you want, sweetheart?"

The little boy jumped and clapped. "Milka! Milka!"

Laughing, Teila scooped him up. She pressed her face into the warmth of his skin, relishing the boy's unique scent—milka, soap from his recent bath, a hint of her own perfume and, of course, the ever-present sand.

"Let's see what we can find for you in the kitchen. Come."

But before she turned from the railing of the balcony overlooking the sea, Stephin cried out, pointing. A whale calf had breached the sands, its burnished red and orange segments glistening with the oils that protected its skin from the constant grinding of sand against it, and also what made it so valuable to whalers. The calf rolled its immense tubular body over and over, exposing first its belly, then its back, to the suns' heat and light that fed it.

If there was a calf, there was a mother nearby. Sure enough, in a moment the female also breached the surface. She was twice the size of her baby, her segments a deeper, duller red. Feelers topped with sensory organs vibrated, sensing the air for disturbances that would indicate a whaler or other dangers, but the sea was clear as far as Teila could see.

She and Stephin watched the whales for a minute or so as the giant creatures rose and fell beneath the sea's gritty, evershifting surface. As the mother rolled, her segments ground against one another, whipping her oily coating into pellets that migrated outward along the edges of her scales.

"Oh, look, Stephin. Maybe we'll get some fresh milka."

As they watched, several of the pellets, each easily the size of Teila's entire body, worked their way free of the mother whale's skin. Denser than the sand, the milka pellets would remain on the surface of the sea even as the whales themselves, fully fed from the sunlight, disappeared below. With no whalers or milkasloops in sight, the pellets would likely drift for days or weeks until someone discovered them or they eventually were ground to dust by the constantly grinding sands.

Teila didn't have a milkasloop, only a small scudder, but she was well skilled in the use of it and had all the tools to gather milka—at least for their personal use. She didn't have the room to store more than one pellet at a time, nor the licensing to sell it. It was, in fact, illegal (if overlooked by most of the local authorities) for her to gather it herself instead of reporting it. But there was nothing better than fresh milka.

Leaving Stephin in the capable hands of his amira, Densi, Teila quickly shucked her robe, leaving her in a sleeveless undershirt and leggings, and wrapped her hair and face in a scarf. Grabbing the long milka hook and some rope, she went down the long spiral stairs into the base of the lighthouse, then to the boathouse and the dock beyond it. Tilting the solar panels, she urged the scudder away from the dock and toward the smallest pellet.

She'd marked the location of it from the lighthouse balcony, but of course the swelling waves had shifted it. The first pellet she came across was too big—twice the size of the scudder. Teila shifted the solars to urge the scudder a little farther from the lighthouse, skimming it along the undulating sands. The winds fluttered the edges of her scarf, and she wished she'd taken the time to slip on a pair of goggles.

The pellet she'd been aiming for came into view. It was still easily as big as her boat, but when she hooked it and tied it behind, there was no trouble pulling it. The pellet's smooth surface skidded without friction on top of the sands, tugging a little at the scudder's back end as she steered it toward the lighthouse.

She could've stayed out here forever, or at least much longer. As a girl she'd spent hours on the sea in this boat and an equal number on her father's much larger whalecraft. It had been years since she'd been brave enough to leap onto a breaching whale in order to scrape free the smallest and freshest pellets, the most coveted. But once she'd been one of the best milka harvesters.

Nobody bothered to do it that way anymore. Now the whalers came with their nets, capturing the whales and holding them above the surface while the mechanical harvesters crawled all over the creatures and scraped them raw. Then they left the poor things behind without so much as a lic of oil to coat their skins against the sea's rough caress. Many of them died.

By the time she got back to the shore, Billis and Vikus had come to greet her, their curved knives at the ready. They made short work of the pellet, slicing it into thick slabs for storage, then smaller pieces for immediate consumption.

"It's a good one," Vikus said, showing her the smooth white coating and the layers of red and orange inside. The center was soft and pink and sweet. "You could live the rest of your days on what you could earn from the sea."

"I'll live the rest of my days a free woman, thank you," Teila said. "I don't have the head to be a criminal."

Vikus grinned. "Me and Billis . . ."

"Shh, I don't want to know." Teila waved her hands. She'd known these men since they were boys, which seemed like only yesterday. It made her feel old when she realized both of them had been of legal age for as long as Stephin had been alive.

They'd been good boys, and they were good men. Life out here could be rough, and Teila had needed to rely on Billis and Vikus for a lot. She watched them take care of the pellet, snagging a bite for herself, relishing the sweetness as it melted on her tongue. She tipped her face to the suns' heat, savoring that as well in the last few hours before sunsdown and the world turned to ice.

With her eyes closed against the glare, Teila thought the steady *thump-thump* was the rising wind. But when the sound got louder, she looked to see a large cruiser lowering itself onto the patch of rocky earth behind the lighthouse. The bits of scrub grass there had been burnt so many times by landing cruisers that there was little left to ignite, but the rocks glowed red from the heat of the thrusters.

"I have no room," were the first words out of her mouth when the man in the familiar uniform came down the short ramp toward where she stood waiting. "You've given me too many as it is. This is still a lighthouse, not a convalescent home. Or an asylum."

"Those convalescents," the soldier said, "are what keep that roof over your head and food in your stomach. Nobody comes this far in this direction any more. What use is a lighthouse without those who'd need guiding?"

He was wrong about that, but there was no use arguing with him. "There is always need for a light in the dark," Teila said.

The man studied her. He wore a scar over his eye like a badge, and in a way she supposed that was exactly what it was. His dark gray hair had been cropped short to his head, not because of his rank or service in the Sheirran Defense Forces, but because, she suspected, he liked the way it made him look. The Rav Aluf was the highest-ranking commander in the SDF. He was also her father-in-law.

"Bring him," he said over his shoulder to the two soldiers manipulating the gurney on which a covered figure rested. "Take him inside. There's a room at the top, put him in there."

"I think I should decide where to put him," Teila said mildly. "Seeing as how he's going to be my charge."

The Rav Aluf raised a hand, effectively stopping the soldiers halfway down the ramp. He twitched back the magblanket covering the man beneath to show his ravaged face. Starburns feathered over his forehead and cheeks. His mouth and eyes were swollen and the blisters scabbed over.

Teila drew in a breath, though she'd seen soldiers in far worse condition come to her. She looked at the Rav Aluf. He jerked the blanket with its healing magnetic properties back over the man's face.

"Put him in the top room," Teila told the attendants. "Make him as comfortable as possible."

2

Darkness.

It was better than the light had been, the unending, burning glare he'd thought would be the last he'd ever see. There'd been a period of time when he'd wished for it, the end of everything. Now, with the pain in his face and limbs eased by time and whatever the medibots had done to him, he lay in the dark and wished for something to ease the monotony.

How long had he been here? Not a clue. He remembered the battle in which he'd fallen, his ship attacked by a swarm of the small, stinging ships they called hornets. The advanced fleet for the much larger ships of the Wirthera. Hornets normally would've been no match for a full-sized Sheirran battlecruiser, except for the damage they'd taken on in the solar storm just hours earlier. The ship's hull had been breached by the myriad of hornet lasers and their scuttling robotic destroyers that ripped and tore at metal like it was made of paper.

He remembered all of that. The smells of fire and screams of dying men. The whine of the ship's engines as they struggled to provide enough power to keep it running when the repair systems kicked in. He remembered the agony of the shields going down, letting in the flares of starfire that burned on contact. And he remembered the metal pincers and claws all over him, the slice of his skin, the burn of the injections. He remembered so much pain.

But he couldn't remember his name.

3

Teila had never trained as a medicus. She'd learned how to stitch wounds and mix herbs as remedies in the lighthouse because here in Apheera, the furthest outpost on the edge of the Sea of Sand, there was no city. Not even a town. The closest medica was a half-day's journey away across the sea on one of the islands, where they'd built waystations for the whalers and tradeships. She could soothe a fever and bandage a wound, but the greater injuries done to most of the men and women who'd found their way here to her care were not of the flesh but the mind, and for those, she was still learning.

The man in the top room, the one closest to the glass dome containing the solar-powered lamp, had been sleeping for days. That was from the drugs they'd pumped through his veins on the medicruiser, and also the nanobots still working to repair all the internal damage. When they'd finished their duties, they'd flush out from his system in his waste, but until then they'd work at keeping him mostly unconscious. She'd made sure the room was kept dark for him, the temperature comfortable, that his bandages were clean. Beyond that, all she could do was wait for him to wake up.

"You understand," the Rav Aluf had said, "how important it is that his mind be taken care of. The traumas he suffered, the damage done to those neural pathways that hold his memories, his personality, all of that was done by nanotriggers implanted in him by the Wirthera. You know what will happen to him if they're triggered."

All Sheirran schoolchildren had heard the horror stories. "He will become part of their hive."

"He will be lost to us." The Rav Aluf had shaken his head sharply before straightening his shoulders. "He will become the enemy. He will have to be put down, but before he can he might do a lot of damage."

As a top-ranking soldier in the SDF, the man in the top room had been fitted with internal and external enhancements that made him a better warrior. Injuries incurred during battle would've resulted in additional enhancements, not all of which she'd ever discover even with full access to his medical records—which she didn't have. If he went rogue, if he were triggered to join the Wirtheran hive, the enhancements that made him such a good soldier also meant that he could easily become a machine, destroying everything in its path in order to create the chaos the Wirthera promoted as part of their plan to take over Sheira and all the other worlds they'd yet to conquer.

"I understand," Tiela had said.

The Rav Aluf had leaned closer. "Do you? Do you understand how important it is that he return to himself without prompting?"

"Yes," she'd said, irritated by the man's condescension. It wasn't new, so she ought to be used to it. But it still stung.

"And that he may never?"

This had been harder to answer, but she'd managed. "Yes, Rav Aluf. I understand. You've brought me a man I'm supposed to heal but I'm not allowed to help."

A smile had twitched his lips, and she'd seen a shadow of the man he must've been when much, much younger. "You were ever so much smarter than I could give you credit for."

With that, he'd turned on the heel of his polished boots that had always thudded too loudly on her tiled floors. He'd left her there with this man who could be so dangerous if she wasn't careful. And why? Because, she thought as she moved around the darkened room, straightening and tidying, listening to the sound of his uneven breathing, the Rav Aluf trusted her.

His name was not Jodah, but that was what the Rav Aluf had told her to call him. It was the most common birthname on Sheira, though not many kept it beyond their adolescence when the adulthood rituals allowed children to choose what they wanted to be called for the rest of their lives. It suited him, she thought as she dipped a cloth in cool water and dabbed at the crust surrounding the edges of one of the bandages on his forehead.

When his hand came up and grabbed her wrist hard enough to grind the bones, Teila bit back the cry that would've had Vikus or Billis running to help her. They wouldn't take kindly to seeing her charge handling her so roughly—but Teila hadn't grown up surrounded by her father's less-than-savory friends for nothing.

Calmly, though his grasp hurt, she put her hand over his. "You're awake."

"Where am I?" He didn't let go. In fact, he yanked her closer, hard enough to make her stumble on the hem of her robe. He sat up, legs swinging over the edge of the bed, and caught her before she could fall.

Reflexes, not consideration. She reminded herself of that, even as the harsh grip on her wrist loosened and his other hand went automatically to her hip to steady her. It had been many circuits of the suns since a man had held her this close.

He smelled good. Yes, there was the odor of blood and stale sweat, scents she'd sadly grown accustomed to since the Rav Aluf had started bringing her patients. But below that was a spicy, rich scent. Not of dust and heat but of green and growing things. Of black earth, not scorched sand. Of . . . water. Oh, how he smelled of fresh, clean water, of the air after a rare storm.

"Where am I?" he demanded, his fingers gripping and bunching her robe. "Who are you?"

"I'm Teila. I'm a lighthouse keeper, though in recent years I've been put into practice as something a little more." She paused, considering how to answer him. "You're in the lighthouse at Apheera, on the edge of the Sea of Sand."

"Which one?"

She laughed, because although there were indeed a multitude of sand seas on Sheira, along with only two saltwater seas, both so small as to be barely significant, there was only one Sea of Sand. The others had different names and were broken by islands and inlets and peninsulas and civilization. The great body of evershifting sands outside her windows was vast and mostly uninterrupted, the only body of sand large enough to provide haven to the whales.

"The big one," she told him.

He peered at her through heavy lidded eyes. The starfire that had burned his skin and caused internal radiation damage hadn't ruined his eyes. She knew they were a pure and vivid gray—or would be so in the light and once the swelling and redness had gone down. Now she could only glimpse a hint of the color. She put a hand on his shoulder, her fingertips brushing the skin of his neck.

"Are you thirsty? Hungry? We have fresh milka. I could bring you some water or juice. It would be best if you didn't overindulge yourself too much at once."

The hand on her hip gripped yet harder, shifting her closer so that she stood between his legs. Seated, he had to look up at her, but not by much. Jodah was as tall as the Rav Aluf, if not a few inches taller. His mouth parted and his tongue swiped along his lips.

"Hungry," he said.

"I'll bring you something." Teila didn't move. This close to him she could see the pattern of crimson veins and arteries raised against the lighter brown flesh of his forehead. Starfire burned from the inside out. She traced the map of his injuries with a fingertip, not trying to cause him pain.

He winced anyway. She leaned a little closer, unable to stop herself from looking him over as best she could in the dim light. Her eyes had adjusted, but there were still details she couldn't make out.

She drew in a breath when he pulled her still closer, bending her at the waist to get his mouth and nose close to her neck, exposed by the way she'd arranged her hair. At the touch of his lips there, she shivered. At the brief tickle of his tongue against her skin, she shuddered. And when he breathed her in, giving a low moan of need, she let him pull her onto his lap.

The man called Jodah mouthed her throat while his other hand slipped under the hem of her robe, finding her bare skin above the thigh-high leggings. His fingertips traced her heat there. Then higher.

"Who are you?" he breathed, his fingers painting pleasure on her skin.

She whispered, "My name is Teila. I'm the lighthouse keeper. And I'm going to take care of you."

His hardness pressed against her. Everything about him was hard—legs, arms, the chest against which she was so firmly nestled. Teila was used to the bodies of soldiers, but Jodah was more than a mere soldier. He wore this skin like a shield, his bones beneath replaced or covered by metal. She could guess that his lungs and kidneys had been replaced by artificial components too.

"My heart," he muttered, pressing her hand to it. "It's beating so fast."

His heart was still real.

She couldn't keep herself from kissing him, then. She cupped his face and opened his mouth with hers. Their tongues met, stroking. It had been so long. So achingly long.

He growled when she moved against him, the sound low and chilling. His eyelids fluttered, and for a terrifying moment she thought she'd somehow set off the Wirtheran nanotriggers roaming the channels of his brain. But no, arousal moved him. Not pain.

He ground her rear onto his cock, his hips pushing upward while the hand between her legs found her clit as easily as if she'd directed his touch. She wore nothing under the robe but the thin slipcloth undergown and her leggings, and at the press of bare flesh on hers, Teila cried out. When he slid one thick finger into her, she had no voice and could only shake.

A life without pleasure is no life at all. That old Sheirran saying had been one of her father's favorites and one Teila had taken as her own. But her life had been without pleasure, at least of this sort, since before the birth of her son. Her own hands had never been an adequate substitute for a man's rough caress, and though she'd had many offers over the years, she'd declined them all.

Waiting.

"I want to taste you." He moved so fast, so smooth, and he'd pushed her onto the bed before she could blink. Then he was between her legs, pushing her robe up, his mouth following the path his fingers had made.

He kissed between her thighs gently, the heat of his breath like fire. His tongue found the tight knot of her clitoris and stroked along it, then lower to dip inside her labia. Teila's back arched when he moaned against her. At the press of his tongue inside her, she had to stifle her own cry by biting her fist.

It felt so good, so good, and her hips lifted, pressing herself to the delights of his lips and tongue. Bright threads of pleasure wove themselves into a tapestry of ecstasy as he licked and sucked at her clit. When he pinched it gently between two fingers, jerking it slowly while he flickered his tongue over it, Teila lost her mind. Her orgasm rose inside her like the surge of sand on the wind, rolling and shifting, and all she could do was ride it.

There was no biting back her cry this time, not shattering with climax as she was. The pleasure tore through her and left her spent and gasping, shuddering with the aftershocks as Jodah continued to lap at her clit and fuck deep inside her with his fingers. It was no substitute for his cock, but when he curled his fingers just so against the hidden spot inside her, Teila shuddered again with a second climax that came hard on the edge of the first.

"So sweet," Jodah said when she'd finally quieted. He pressed a gentle kiss to her cunt and withdrew just long enough to shuck out of his trousers. Again moving so fast and seamlessly she didn't have time to react, he moved forward and slid inside her, so deep that at first the press of him inside her passage, so long without such attentions, made her squirm.

But only for a moment, because when he began to move, her body surged along with his. She raked her fingernails down his bare back, not wanting to hurt him but helpless to keep herself from the reaction. Jodah muttered in wordless pleasure, fucking into her harder. He supported himself with one hand while the other moved beneath her knee to lift it, opening her to him further. Deeper. She moved with him, this dance a familiar one and never out of fashion, no matter how long it had been since she'd last made the steps.

He bit down on the softness between her neck and shoulder when he climaxed, and Teila relished that pain. When he collapsed on top of her, she ran her fingers over and over through his hair, down his back and finally cupped the back of his neck when he went still. She listened to the sound of his slow breathing, felt the weight of him grow heavier as his body went slack in sleep. Then, she carefully pushed him off her, and he rolled onto his side, curling against himself and going quiet.

She lay beside him only a moment longer after that. She had no time to spend in this bed, even if her legs felt boneless and she wasn't sure she'd be able to walk. She listened to the rattling in-out of his breathing, reassured that it was harsh but not labored. She touched his hair gently; he didn't stir.

In the hallway outside, she quickly arranged her robes and smoothed her hair. There was nothing to be done for the marks he'd left on her skin, but she answered to nobody even if any of them should ask. In the lamp room she made sure all the switches were on, the solar cells charged. The light was built to last a millennium without burning out and would come on automatically, but she still checked and would check again as the suns dipped below the horizon and darkness fell. She'd check in the middle of the night, too, because while only once had the light ever gone out, it had left behind the wreckage of three whalers. That had been the night her father died.

One of the mechbots whirred and chirped at her as Teila checked the switches once more, and she paused to touch it lightly on its "head." It let out a series of low hoots that made her smile. It was programmed to react to petting, though of course it had only the lowest level of intelligence and had no emotions whatsoever. Its reactions had been built to make people think of it as a pet, not a robot, and therefore be more likely to treat it nicely if and when it malfunctioned. Vikus kept all the 'bots in the lighthouse working, but it did require constant tinkering, especially now that the parts for repairs were so hard to come by. Someday and maybe soon, 'bots would be made illegal and she'd have to decide how on earth she'd manage the lighthouse without them. Though for now the subject was cause for debate and controversy each election, but it had not yet been changed.

Downstairs, she checked with the kitchen to be sure the meals had been prepared. The other residents, each with their own room in the lower parts of the lighthouse, would serve themselves as they were hungry, but Teila had implemented a communal dining time for the evening meal. It was good for the residents, many struggling with socialization or other mental issues related to their traumas, to have the company of others even if the rest of the time many of them preferred solitude. With that task taken care of, she climbed again to the top level and her own quarters, down the hall from the room the Rav Aluf had insisted on giving Jodah.

Stephin was still too young to stay awake for the night meal. He'd been given his dinner by his amira, who'd been Teila's amira and also her father's before that. Amira Densi would probably be the amira to Stephin's children, too. Curled in his small bed, one fist tucked beneath his cheek, her son slept without stirring even when she stroked his hair. But when she made to leave, his wide gray eyes opened.

"Mao?"

"Yes, love."

But he only smiled and sank back to sleep. She sat with him for a while, her hand on his back, testing the rise and fall of his breath. This boy was her life. He was all she'd had of his father since many months before his birth, and all she'd come to believe she would ever have again. Until now, she thought with a prayer of gratitude sent up to the triple Mothers who'd seen fit to return Teila's husband, though his own father, the Rav Aluf, had told her he'd been lost in battle.

Now, her husband had come home.

4

He could no longer tell the passing of time. Day or night, nothing mattered with the blurriness in his eyes. Looking too long
at anything made his head hurt so bad he swore it was going to
explode, and perhaps even wished for it to happen, if only to stop
the pain. The rest of his body was slowly healing, but there were
times he swore he could feel the skittering touch of insects scuttling
in his brain.

He still couldn't remember his name or how he'd come to this
place, but the taste of a woman was something he'd never forget.
Now it coated his tongue and lips, making his cock so hard it
ached. There was softness beneath him; a bed. He remembered the
touch of her hair against his face, the stroke of her fingers on him.
The smell of her.

He slept and did not dream.

He woke at the sound of her voice. She called him "Jodah,"
which didn't sound right. Didn't fit or feel right. Still, he rubbed

at his sticky eyes and tried to find her in the room's dim light. It
had a different feel to it, a paler gray. Rectangles of light marked
the windows he realized had been covered, probably to protect his
vision.

Her name was . . . Teila. He remembered that. She was taking
care of him. But was she the woman he'd spent himself inside?
Yesterday, the day before, a lifetime ago, Jodah couldn't remember
if it had been real or a dream. For that matter, was this happening
now or was it another of his brain's attempts at getting him to leave
behind the pain?

"You'll be well enough to join us for meals soon," she said. There
came the clatter of plates on a tray. The smell of something good.
She moved close to him, the bed dipping when she sat. "Here. Let
me help you."

The broth was thick and rich, but he could take only a little bit
before his stomach urged him to stop. The flavor of it was familiar
the way so much else seemed to be, but then it was overlaid by the
memory of thick ration paste, the nutritionally complete meals
that never tasted of what they were supposed to. And another
memory flooded him with bitter and sour, making him wince.

". . . They made me grateful for ration paste," he said aloud.
The sound of his own voice was as unfamiliar as a stranger's.

Teila said nothing at first. Then her gentle hands took away the
tray and wiped at a spill on the front of him. "Who did?"

But that was as lost to him as everything else. She moved closer
to him to press a damp cloth to his forehead. He was sweating and
hadn't known.

Need rose in him again, and he pulled her close. She was
beneath him in a heartbeat. Her body, open and slick and willing,
drew him in. It felt so good he couldn't speak, could only move.
Thrust and grind and fuck.

She tightened on his cock, and he slowed, remembering what it was like to draw out the pleasure. To make a woman scream with it. Not to simply pound away and find his own climax, though it was close and he had to fight it. He forced himself to steady his pace. To slide in and out, adding a grind of his hips to press himself against her clitoris when he was fully inside her.

He kissed her.

Her mouth was a sweet heaven. He plundered her mouth with his tongue, stroking in and out in time with the thrust of his hips. He lost himself in her mouth, her cunt. Her arms around him, her legs around his waist. She urged him to move faster but he kept the pace slow and steady until she writhed beneath him and her body clutched and fluttered around his cock. Only then did he move faster again, deep and deeper inside her until ecstasy overtook him and made him blinder than any injury.

Then there was dark again, the soft sound of her singing and the press of another cool cloth on his face. Some time after that, the whirr of metal on metal. The stink of blood. The sounds of screaming, and he was screaming and running . . . running . . . and they'd pinned him down while the bonesaws buzzed and the sting of needles pressed him all over. Then all he had was pain.

5

Vikus looked up at the sound of far-off screams. "Should he be here? This isn't a medica."

"The Rav Aluf thought this place would be best. And it is," Teila told him as they walked along the edge of the sea. Dust powdered the edge of her robe. A few steps in one direction would take her onto rocky, barren soil. A few in the other would have her up to her neck in the slickly sliding sand. She kept herself carefully on the edge.

"He's worse than any of the others ever were. He screams every night. During the day, too. He's mad."

She gave him a sharp look. "Wouldn't you be? And you act as if he's the only one who ever came here with bad dreams."

Vikus had the grace to look ashamed, but he shielded his eyes to look up at the windows at the top of the lighthouse. "You know he could become one of them at any time."

"Not if we're careful. Not if we keep him safe. Anyway, all of them could." Stubbornly, Teila refused to look where he was looking. She forced herself to think of her husband as Jodah, not Kason, because she didn't dare slip up and call him by his real name. It could be the worst sort of trigger, worse than her own name, which she'd given him despite the risks. "He needs to come back to himself, Vikus. Slowly. That's all. On his own."

"What if he never does?"

Her heart leapt into her throat at the thought of that, and she glared at him. "Bite your Mothers-forsaken tongue. He's strong. He's a soldier, for the love of the Mothers!"

"And been one for a long time." Vikus' expression went dark. "And he's not . . . the same, Teila. I loved Kason—"

"Jodah," she corrected sharply. "You must call him that."

Vikus began to speak, but Teila cut him off by grabbing the front of his robe. "You must promise me, Vikus. If he's mad, it was done to him in service to this world. For me, and for you too. My husband would've given his life to protect us from being enslaved by the Wirthera."

"And if he turns, we will likely give ours." Vikus had never looked so serious in all his life. But then he took Teila in his arms and hugged her tight. "I would fight him, if it came to that. To protect you and Stephin. And the others. Even Billis."

"It won't come to that."

But, no matter how much she loved him, Teila knew it was entirely possible that her husband, if he turned, could very well slaughter them all in the name of the Wirthera. Without a second thought. Without remorse.

As she'd told Vikus, all of them could. The difference was simple, she realized as she watched Vikus head back toward the lighthouse to finish his chores. None of the others who'd ever come here would've had any reason to be triggered by something in the lighthouse. For Jodah, on the other hand, everything could be.

Inside, she took her handheld into her bedroom and closed the door firmly. She tapped in the Rav Aluf's access code, expecting to leave only an angry message and surprised when the man's status showed him as online. She didn't bother to choose visual access as she had no desire to look at him.

"Why did you bring him here?" she said without preamble, her words automatically converting to text and being delivered to him. "Of all the places for him to recover, you chose the one most likely to trigger him! Is it your intent to lose him?"

His answer didn't come right away, but when it did, it was entirely unsatisfactory. "No."

"He would get better care in a medica."

"Nobody could care for him better than you," came the reply.

"He is insane," Teila said after a moment, hating herself for it. "Worse than most of the others you've sent me. And there's too much here we have to avoid. Anything could tip him over. Anything could set him off. You need to come and take him away."

The instant the words left her lips, she wanted to reclaim them. But it was too late since they'd been translated and transmitted. The small blinking indicator on the handheld screen told her the Rav Aluf had received the message and was replying, and Teila didn't quite have the courage to disconnect before she heard his answer. She wasn't in the military, and she was his daughter-in-law, but he was still one of the most powerful men in the world. Some said the Rav Aluf had more power than the Melek himself, and Teila understood how that could be true. The Melek of Sheirra might rule the world, but the Rav Aluf was in charge of keeping it safe.

"Once you told me I had no right to take him from you. Do you remember that?"

Of course she did. It hadn't mattered then. "Yes. But that was different."

"Was it?"

There was no way to hear tone from reading words on the screen, but she could well imagine the sound of her father-in-law's voice. His son had mastered the same supercilious lift at the end of a sentence, though Kason had only ever done it to mock his father, never her. She took her time in voicing her reply, careful to be sure not to give him any reason to call her hysterical or irrational, or even rude.

"Of course it was. Then you were taking away my husband from me, when we both knew he didn't want to go. This time . . ."

"You think he'd want to go away from you again? If he knew?"

"But he doesn't!" she cried, then lowered her voice. The hand-held wouldn't interpret her tone any more than it had his, but she didn't want to give him the satisfaction of even guessing at her distress.

"He might, someday. And when he comes back to himself, do you want him to remember that you sent him away?"

"He would understand," Teila said slowly.

No answer came for some time, while she waited impatiently. Finally, the indicator light blinked to show his message was being translated. It was not the reply she was expecting.

"Please," said the Rav Aluf. "You are the only one I trust with my son's life."

6

Days passed, as they do, and if the man in the top room seemed to grow no better, at least he grew no worse. His daily nightmares had become so commonplace they no longer woke anyone but Teila, who often stopped to check on him when she was doing her nightly check of the lamp. She told herself it was what she'd have done for any of the wounded who'd been sent for her care, but she knew the truth. She went to him at night because that was when he took her.

Kason had always been a tender lover, over careful of bruising her. Even before he'd gone into the SDF he'd been a big and strong man. His hands had once been able to span her waist. But that was no longer, she thought ruefully as she bathed herself in the quiet of her chambers. Childbirth and age had made that impossible.

Kason had kissed her gently, held her with soft hands. He'd made love to her for hours, sometimes until both of them passed out from exhaustion, only to wake her with his face savoring between her legs. Then he'd make love to her again. He'd studied and learned her body so thoroughly she'd never thought of taking a lover, not even after the Rav Aluf had come to her with the news Kason had been captured and would never be likely to come home. No man could ever know her the way her husband had.

Jodah, however . . . Jodah was a different man. Bigger in some ways than Kason had been, his shoulders marginally broader. Thighs thicker. The differences might've been minor to someone else who hadn't studied his body as well as he'd known hers, but to Teila it was as though she traced the lines and curves of someone else who wore her husband's face. His cock was the same, long and thick and delicious. It filled her the same, brought her the same pleasure, but he didn't use it the same way. Kason had made love to her. Jodah fucked her. Rough and raw and hard, full of need and greed. And Teila loved it.

The first time it happened, she'd acted on instinct, reacting to his touch. But since then she'd grown to expect and crave the way he reached for her. Now as she used scented oils to clean herself and dressed in soft robes that would open without struggle, Teila's nipples peaked. Her cunt slicked. She was ready for him before she even went inside the room.

He was sleeping fitfully when she opened the door. At the thin crack of light from the hall, some of it spilling over from the lamp, he stirred. She'd taken care to block out his windows from the sunslight to protect his damaged eyes, but soon they'd heal well enough for him to start to be exposed to the brightness. He threw up a hand, wincing at even this faint spill of gold across the floor.

"I heard you cry out." She crossed to him, not waiting for him to reach for her but settling herself next to him on the bed. The heat radiating from him was immense. Not a fever, but a by-product of the enhancements in his system. He'd run hot for the rest of his life. "You were dreaming."

"I'm always dreaming." Jodah, for he was Jodah now, not Kason, rubbed at his face. His broad shoulders flexed, along with his back muscles.

She kept herself from touching him, but only barely. Everything about his body cried out for her caress. She said nothing.

Jodah leaned toward her. "I'm dreaming now, aren't I?"

"Do you want this to be a dream?"

He seemed to study her, though she knew she had to still be nothing more than a blur. He could smell her though, and he did just that, nuzzling at her neck. Teila's eyelids fluttered from the pleasure of that simple touch.

"They give us this to keep us hoping," Jodah muttered against her skin.

Teila froze, every muscle stiff and tight.

"Keep us hoping," Jodah said again in a low, sing-songy voice. Gruff. A broken voice. "They give us this to keep us believing we might someday get out, get home. Isn't that right?"

She turned to him, but before she could speak, he'd captured her mouth. He rolled her, one of his big hands pinning both her wrists over her head. With one knee, he shoved her legs apart and pressed his erection against her. His other hand went between them to tug up her robe so he could get at her bare skin.

He paused, fingers tracing light patterns on her inner thighs, and pushed himself off her. He'd been fully naked with her, but so far she'd always been almost completely clothed—his eagerness to get inside her had never allowed for the time to take off her robes. Tonight, though, Jodah toyed with the laces at her throat. He tugged them free, loop by loop, until her breasts lay exposed.

Again, Teila froze at this change. She lay still beneath him, but only until he bent to tug at her nipples with his mouth. One, then the other. He sucked at the tender peaks until she gasped, writhing, her back arching. The pleasure was so intense on her super-sensitive flesh that it edged on pain.

Pressing her breasts together with his hands, Jodah nuzzled and licked at her until she couldn't stand it anymore. With a low, sobbing cry, Teila shattered. When the pleasure eased, she found him staring at her.

"I want to see all of you," Jodah said. "I want to see all of this dream."

She wanted nothing more than to be bare with him, but she hesitated. There were no guidelines. No standard practices, other than his mind would either break or heal on its own. He believed this was a dream, that she was a projection provided to him by his enemies as a way of controlling his mind.

What would happen when he saw tangible proof that she was his wife?

The tattoos covering her ribs, hips, and lower back had all been expertly marked with her family crest as well as Kason's. Later, Teila had added markings for the birth of her son. If her husband came back to her mentally as he'd done physically, there would be celebratory markings for that event, too. Her marks were unique and distinctive to her alone—but more than that, they told a story. If he could read it, would he remember her?

And if he did, would that set off the nanotriggers that had taken up residence in his brain?

Jodah eased her robes further off her shoulders and undid the laces all the way to the hem, then opened her clothing as carefully as a gift. On his knees on the bed in front of her he hissed an appreciative breath, though there was no way he could see more than the shape of her. His hands moved over her next, fingers spread. His palms skidded over her skin. Rough.

His mouth moved on her throat, teeth nipping. Then down the slopes of her breasts, her nipples still tight and tender from his earlier attentions. Over her ribs, tickling, though she was too breathless to laugh. The slope of her belly was no longer unmarked or as flat as it had been when he last knew her, but his lips lingered on the silvered scars almost reverently. Then lower, lower, until at last, oh, by the Mothers, his tongue slipped delicately against her clitoris with light, feathering strokes that had her vibrating with tension in the span of a few heartbeats.

"You're a blur." He kissed the inside of her thigh, adding the slick, wet press of his tongue.

"It's your eyes," she managed to say. "They've been injured. You have to give it time."

"Such a pretty trick." Surprising her, he chuckled, low.

Tears burned the back of her eyes at the sound. She'd heard it echoed in their son, but so many nights she'd lain awake in her lonely bed, wishing more than anything to hear the sound of her husband's laughter. She put a hand on his head, then dug into his hair to pull him again to her mouth.

"I can taste you." He sounded wary. His tongue stroked hers. His hands slid up her thighs, one finger, then two pressing inside her. "I can feel you. I can hear you. I can smell you. As though you're real."

Arching under the pleasure he was bringing her, Teila found it difficult to think of anything but how good he felt against her. Her words were not as cautious as they should've been when she gasped, "It's because I am real!"

Kason pushed himself up on one hand to look down at her. Jodah, she reminded herself. Jodah, or else he might be forever lost to her. His fingers moved inside her, slowly but without hesitation. He was bringing her to climax again, and she was helpless against it.

Her pleasure rose in tightly spiraling coils. Her muscles tensed. She held her breath, aching for release, every nerve straining toward that pinnacle to which Jodah was so expertly bringing her. Just before she reached it, he eased the pressure inside her and slowed the pace, holding her off.

Teila lost track of how many times he edged her. She was vaguely aware of begging him, pleading against his mouth for him to make her come. Imploring him to fill her with his cock until finally he moved over her and did as she'd asked. Her orgasm began as he entered her, and she cried out from its strength.

When her body clenched around him, Jodah fucked deeper inside her, his thrusts ragged. He found her neck, nipping and sucking as she bucked beneath him. They finished together, and he collapsed on top of her.

Teila relished the crush of him. When he moved off her to curl on his side, facing away, the loss was worse than it had been the other times, because it was the closest he'd seemed to be to the man she'd married. She wanted more than anything to align herself with him, to press her face into the space between his shoulder blades. To sleep with him that way until morning.

Instead, Teila eased herself from the bed and dressed quietly so as not to wake him. She stopped herself from kissing him before she left, though the desire for it was as fierce as any she'd ever had. His voice, though, stopped her at the door.

"None of the others," he said, "were ever like you."

They are stronger than you are.
    They are faster than you are.
They are more relentless than you will ever be.
They will never stop.

It had been drilled into every recruit since childhood. The Wirthera were the enemy that could not be defeated, only held back. No soldier joined the Sheirran Defense Force believing he or she could be part of destroying the Wirthera, only that they would most likely give their lives in service to keep them from consuming Sheira the way they'd already devoured and ruined so many other worlds.

He was nameless, but not completely without memory. He knew the Wirthera could not be defeated. That had never stopped him from believing he should try. Three cycles, that's what he remembered. Three cycles he'd spent leading his troops in the fringes of his own galaxy, far from home. Far from the life he'd had before his father had shamed him into no longer ignoring the family legacy of service. But what life had that been? All he could recall were the three cycles of cold and lonely space, fighting an unseen enemy, defending the people and world he loved against the attacks not of the Wirthera themselves, but of their advance scouts. Keeping his world a secret to keep it safe.

Fire. Smoke. The clang of metal on metal. Screams. The brightness of starfire, so beautiful and deadly.

Pain, always pain.

He could not be sure what had gone wrong, only that the hornets they'd blown up had not all been destroyed. One must've gotten away, back through the fields of starfire that helped to protect this galaxy from detection. Found its way home. Returned with its bigger brother, an advance Wirtheran fleet.

There'd always been rumors, of course, that the Wirthera were sneaky, distrustful even of their own technology, that sometimes they send their own troops to explore rather than relying on the fleets of hornets. That was how his ancestors' world had been conquered, by suspicious Wirtheran ships scouting on the tail of a horde of hornets. His family had been one of the few that managed to escape, fleeing ahead of the giant cruisers that had surrounded the small planet and systematically began consuming every resource and obliterating all traces of life.

Those ancestors had found a second home far away, not like their home planet of lush green jungles and vast seas, but instead of deserts and sand. They'd mingled and joined with the native population and homesteaders from other nearby worlds to make a new life, and generations later, their people were still hiding and fighting against the insidious, never-ending Wirtheran forces.

Stronger. Faster. More relentless. His captors had proven themselves to be that and so much more. The Wirthera had an inhuman capacity for cruelty and an insatiable curiosity.

They made . . . experiments.

He had listened to the sounds of his shipmates' screams for days. Locked in a featureless cell, no visible door or window, just smooth, polished metal that vibrated without cease and made his entire body ache. Naked, with nothing soft to lay on. Nothing to eat or drink.

Periods of blackout, when they took him. When he woke, only the pain was left to show something had been done to him. It had been better than when they stopped making him unconscious, when they left him awake to watch the slit opening in his cell in place of the nonexistent door.

Metal arms had cuffed him, dragged him free. The Wirtheran 'bots were different than the ones he was used to—perhaps constructed with the faces of their makers, they were alien, insectile things with multiple limbs and jointed bodies. They made no noises, no cooing chirps or whirrs or buzzes. Their silence was terrifying.

In a different room, full of tools and instruments, they strapped him onto a gurney. They'd probably done it dozens of times before, but this time he was awake, fighting the bonds. It didn't matter that he knew he couldn't get free; the instinct to fight and survive overwhelmed all reason.

And then . . . they came. The Wirthera, covered in their plated armor. He choked and gagged on the stink of them. He screamed at them to show their faces, but they made no answer. Always silent. Never ceasing.

After a while, he begged for them to make him unconscious again. Not long after that, he begged for them to let him die. That was when the dreams began.

Then it no longer mattered what they did to his body, because he had the dreams. In some small part of his mind, he knew the sexual pleasures offered to him were all part of the experiment, though what purpose they served he couldn't begin to guess. He knew the flavors of the food he ate at the banquets they laid out for him were as false as the caresses of the women, that all the other joys he experienced were also not real. And yet the dreams were so much better than the pain or even the monotony of being in the cell that there came a day when he begged for them to take him, to do whatever they wanted, if only he could be in the dreamworld again.

That was when the real pain had begun.

8

How is he?" The screen flickered, first stretching, then shrinking the Rav Aluf's face.

"He's . . . improving."

Teila didn't bother fiddling with the controls. The sound was fine, and she didn't need to see her father-in-law's expression to know he looked disapproving. She continued slicing the pellet of milka as she talked. She knew it would annoy him to see her doing what he'd call menial labor, but he seemed to forget that even with the money the SDF paid her for the care and keeping of its cast-offs, it wasn't like she could afford a retinue of servants. Besides, she liked working in the kitchen.

"What does that mean?"

She gave the screen a sideways glance. It would also irritate him that she wasn't giving him her full and direct attention. "It means that he's improving. As they all do. Slowly. It takes time."

"His memory?"

"He remembers plenty," Teila said. "But only the bad things. Much of the time, he thinks he's dreaming this place. Me. That he's still being held by the Wirthera."

The Rav Aluf muttered angrily. "I thought being here would be best! That he'd return to his own mind sooner, but now I see I was wrong. I should've taken him home."

"This is his home!" Teila put down the carved blade and turned to the screen with her hands on her hips. "This was his home for years before you played upon his guilt and made him a soldier!"

"He was my son and an excellent soldier!"

"Yes," Teila said. "And he was also an excellent husband. My husband. And he'd have been an excellent father, had he been given the chance."

The Rav Aluf looked suddenly so much older. Defeated. He rubbed a hand across his eyes. "Would that he be given the chance now, daughter. For that, we can both ask the Mothers."

"My hands are tied," she said after a minute. "I can't tell him his real name or who I am to him. All I can do is be a wife to him as best I can, even though he doesn't know me. I told you to take him. You didn't want to."

"Do you still want me to?"

She hesitated, then shook her head. As his nightmares had eased, she'd seen more and more glimpses of the man she'd married. In fact, Teila was ashamed to have even suggested his father remove him—though she'd never have admitted it to him.

"Do your best." His tone made it clear he didn't think it would be good enough.

It was futile to retort. He would never soften toward her. Still, her anger manifested itself in words she had no time to say before he'd ended the call, and Teila had to satisfy herself with working out her anger on the milka pellet. It was in shards by the time she was finished. Ruined for anything but pudding.

Stephin was the only one who liked milka pudding—everyone else took theirs solid or not at all. So after the treat had set and was ready to be eaten, Teila climbed the stairs to look for him. At this time of the day he was supposed to be taking lessons from his teachbot under the watchful tutelage of his amira, who was skeptical about the benefits of trying to educate a child so young. She often tried to sneak him out of the lessons, claiming there was plenty of time in adulthood for him to learn different languages or career skill sets, so it was no surprise to Teila when she found her son missing from the study room, though the 'bot was operational and droning the first one hundred useful words in Fendalese.

It was a little more disconcerting when she couldn't find him in his bedroom, or the living space they shared. Nor could she see him from any of the room's three glass walls, overlooking most of the lighthouse property. Amira Densi was supposed to know better than to allow the boy to play along the sea unattended. Fenda children were born knowing how to swim, but Stephin was not Fenda. He could so easily step out to a depth over his head and be swept away.

"Stephin?" Teila moved through their shared quarters, but her boy was nowhere to be found.

Amira Densi she found dozing in a patch of sun at the end of the corridor. For an instant, Teila was furious, but when the amira let out a small snore that vibrated her whiskers, she reminded herself that Densi was an old, old Fenda. The Sheir natives lived so many more cycles than the homesteaders who'd come to populate the world. A nap in the sun was probably unavoidable for her.

That understanding did nothing to stave off Teila's growing unease. But before she could shake Amira Densi awake, she heard her boy's familiar lilting laughter from down the hall. From Jodah's room.

Teila set off at a run—Stephin didn't sound like he was in distress, but she wasn't going to take a chance. Slipping through the doorway, she stopped short at the sight of Jodah sitting upright, Stephin on his lap. Both heads of identically curly dark hair bent over the tablet in Stephin's hands. The boy was showing Jodah some of his favorite animations.

Teila had watched them all a dozen or more times, could've recited them word for word, and her son had watched them far more often than that. He pointed excitedly at the screen, bouncing on Jodah's lap. Jodah looked puzzled, but he was looking at the screen from a normal distance. Almost as though he could see it.

"I don't understand," he said. "Why do they have to catch the colored balls with those straws?"

"Because it's an excuse for them to dance around singing silly songs," Teila said.

Jodah looked up. He definitely saw her. His eyes widened and his lips parted, just a little. He looked . . . ashamed.

"Your eyes?"

"I can see," he told her. "Everything was blurry when I woke up. But then this little one came in with this tablet, and at first everything was still unclear. But then as I watched, I noticed I could see the figures on the screen, not just fuzzy blobs."

"That means you're healing."

He looked at her, his pale gray eyes narrowed. Despite the scabs and bruising still so prominent, it was a look she'd seen many times. Calculating. Working through the pieces of a puzzle. "Where am I?"

"Adarat vi Apheera. The lighthouse."

His lips curved and his head tilted. "A lighthouse. I'm in a lighthouse."

"Yes. On the edge of the Sea of Sand." She'd told him this before, but kept her voice carefully light, her expression neutral, trying to see if there was any sign of recognition. This had been his home for ten years. The place where he'd met and married her. It was the place his father had chosen to bring him so he could find his way back to himself.

Jodah's gaze grew shuttered. He shifted Stephin off his lap. "I'm tired now."

"Stephin, come." Teila held out her hand for the boy, who reluctantly did as he'd been bid. "We'll let you rest. I'll be back with something for you to eat—"

"I'm not hungry."

"You should eat," she said gently. "I'll bring a tray."

"I said I'm not hungry!"

His shout startled the boy, who began to cry. Teila gathered him close, but Jodah was already on his feet, advancing on them both. She hadn't forgotten how tall he was, or how broad. But she'd never seen him this way. Menacing and dangerous. She'd never seen him as a soldier.

Instinctively, she pushed her son behind her and held up a hand. "You're scaring the boy! Stop it!"

Jodah moved fast and was on her in two long strides. One arm reached for her and he closed on her throat. Not squeezing or hurting, not yet, but the promise of it was there.

Teila kept her voice steady. "Stephin. Go find Amira Densi. Now."

Her boy was so good, so obedient. He went at once, yelling for the amira. Teila met Jodah's gaze without flinching or showing the fear rising in her.

"Who are you?"

"My name is Teila. I'm the—" His fingers squeezed a little, still not hurting, but the pressure gave her pause. "Lighthouse keeper."

"Why am I here?"

"To rest and recover."

"Why a lighthouse?" Jodah's pale eyes went dark from the wideness of his pupils. "Why not a medica?"

She had no easy answer for that question. Why were any of them sent here to recover instead of a medica, other than they all had injuries that mere medicines and surgery couldn't cure? That there were too many soldiers who came back and not enough places for them to recover? Before she could answer, Jodah moved closer, his hand still at her throat, the other moving to fist in her hair and tip her head back a little. His breath gusted over her face as he muttered into her ear.

"You aren't real."

Teila closed her eyes. He could kill her in a heartbeat. Snap her neck. Throttle her. If she gave him the wrong reply, the nanotriggers could be engaged. He could turn. The problem was, she didn't know what she was supposed to say.

"I'm real," she breathed.

He let her go so suddenly she sagged forward and had to grab the doorframe to keep herself from falling. Jodah backed away from her, disgust splashed across his face. She couldn't tell if it was for her, or for himself. He turned his back, shoulders hunched.

"That's what they want me to think," Jodah said. "So they can break me."

9

She'd told him his name was Jodah, but that felt like a lie, and if the name she'd given him wasn't true, how could any of the rest of it be?

He worked his fingers, one by one. His wrists, elbows, shoulders. Feeling every ache along every nerve, in every bone. He'd been broken, he remembered enough to know that. Put back together, but like a shattered vase, incapable of holding water.

He studied his reflection. The eyes blinked when he wanted them to. The mouth opened and closed. This was his face in the mirror, but he didn't recognize it.

The ever-present agony was becoming memory, but that too could be a trick. They took the suffering away, only to return it a deca-fold. When he shattered the mirror with his fist it made a new, fresh pain, the shards of glass slicing at his skin. Making him bleed. Dispassionately, he watched the bright drops splash from his wounds onto the white tile floor. Then he wrapped his hand in a towel until the bleeding stopped.

The woman had brought him a tray as she'd promised. The food on it was real—not broth or pudding or ration paste, but thick slices of bread and milka, a portion of grains and greens. He hadn't touched any of it, wary of what it might contain, still half-believing that it was figment and would leave his body hungry no matter how much of it he ate. He'd had no real appetite for so long that the ache in his stomach had first seemed like just another torment, but now he fell upon the food ravenously and devoured every bite to the point of sickness.

When his vision had cleared, so had a brightness in the edges of it. A long stream of numbers, images, and words, constantly scrolling so fast that none of them were clear. When he blinked or closed his eyes, the brightness was still there. If he concentrated on it hard enough, he might be able to bring it into focus, but doing so flared agony inside his skull sharp enough to keep him from trying it more than a few times.

That was not part of the dream; he knew that much. But the rest of it . . . He paced the length and width of this space, measuring and mapping it with every stride. If this was a dream, the room could change at any time. If this was real . . . if all of this was real . . .

Something inside him wouldn't allow himself to believe that. Hope could kill him faster than his captors. So he paced the room and stored the calculations, and he fed his body with what he was convinced was nothing but imagination.

Yet when he woke in the morning, the tray was still there, littered with crumbs. And his hand still stung, the blood crusted in the myriad of cuts. Glass scattered the tiles, along with the spatters of blood. The room had not changed size or shape.

And there was the woman again. Teila. She looked at the mess on the floor, the breakage and the blood, and when she spoke to him her voice was cold and stern.

"If you're strong enough to break that mirror, you're well enough to clean it up," she said. "I'll bring you a mop and broom."

She did, too, and left him to the task. She brought him fresh clothes when she came back. A bar of soap, another towel.

"Clean yourself up too," she told him. "You stink."

Some dream, Jodah thought as he went into the bathroom and ran the water as hot as he could stand it. The world swam as he stood beneath the spray, head bent to let it pound over him. The wounds in his hand stung afresh when the water hit them, washing away the dried blood. He put them both against the shower's stone walls.

When they came for him, it was always without warning. How many times had he woken in a place he didn't know? At first believing he'd been rescued or had escaped, later knowing none of it was real—later still, knowing and pretending he didn't so that he could cling to whatever relief the dreams brought.

What was this, now?

She said she was real, but they always did. And though his hand burned and ached from the cuts, he believed they would make anything happen in the dreams to convince him it was truly happening and not just in his head. Even giving him pain.

Shaking, he clutched at the shower, trying to find the part of his brain that stored the memories he'd marked as real. He couldn't find it. He could access faded recollection, bits and pieces of events—a birthday as a child. The sound of a song playing while he danced with a woman in his arms, though she had no face. The smell of baking bread. The sound of laughter.

"Jodah?"

Turning, he found her looking at him with concern. He could see all of her now. What had been a blur of curves and shadows had become her face. Dark eyes beneath arched, dark brows. A lush mouth, red as . . . red as a whale's backbone, he thought. Remembering.

He reached for her, pulling her beneath the water. Her startled laugh cut off beneath his kiss. She gasped when he tugged at the laces of her sodden robe, and when she was naked in his arms, pinned against the wall, she said his name. Once, softly, then again, louder.

"That's not my name," he told her.

Naked, he pushed against her. His cock rose against her slick flesh. She smelled so good. She tasted good too, her mouth like sweet berries. Her lips soft and warm. When he put a hand between her legs, the heat there sent a shudder of pleasure through him.

He went to his knees in front of her, water sluicing over them both as he feasted on her. He lapped at her clit until she moaned and thrust herself against him. Then he slid a finger inside her, stroking at the spot just behind her pubic bone. Her fingers tightened in his hair, pulling him hard against her. He licked and fucked inside her until she cried out, the walls of her cunt clenching tight on his finger. Her clit leaped under his tongue, and he drank her sweetness until she went still.

He looked up at her, the water spattering on his face, blurring and blinding his vision. Yet her face was still clear. She cupped his cheek softly.

"What *is* your name?" she asked him.

Pain like a knife in his skull split his head, doubling him onto his hands and knees. It pried at his brains. He shook with it.

She knelt beside him, her hand stroking down his back. Over and over. She said nothing, just offered comfort, until he could stand no more. Pushing her back onto the hard tiles, he fitted himself inside her. He hated himself for it, this hunger that drove away all rational thought. This need, this greed. But the pleasure forced the pain away, and when he thrust harder, she cried out and wrapped her arms and legs around him to draw him deeper into her.

Desire crested. It took away everything else, and he got lost in it. In her. And when at last shuddering, he spent himself, she murmured soft words in his ear and cupped the back of his neck until he pushed himself off her.

His knees and elbows felt bruised, and he didn't miss the way she winced when he helped her to her feet. Dreams didn't feel pain. No matter what had ever happened in them, what force he'd ever used—and sometimes there'd been a great deal—none of the dream women had ever shown so much as a glimmer of discomfort.

The shower water had tangled her hair over her shoulders, and she raked through it with her fingers before wrapping it in a towel. She was free and easy in her nakedness in a way that suddenly shamed him. How many times had he taken her like this? No words of love or even kindness, just simple, hardened lust. Selfish.

"Here." She handed him a towel and turned off the water. "Come on, you should get back into bed. I've put fresh sheets on it for you."

She startled when he grabbed her wrist, and he eased his grip, mindful for the first time of how much bigger he was. How easy it was to hurt her. When he let her go, she stepped back with a small but wary smile.

"Thank you," he said. "For . . . everything."

For a moment, she said nothing, but her eyes glimmered. She cleared her throat, her voice rough when she answered, "I'm paid very well to keep you here."

No dream would ever have said such a thing. Those women cooed and fluttered. They seduced.

"I'm sorry," he told her, "that I'm such a terrible patient."

"You always—" Her teeth clamped down on the words. She backed away from him. "You should get some more rest. You're not well."

He couldn't argue with that. He didn't feel well. He felt uneasy, unsettled. On edge. And that, too, told him this was no dream. So, if he was not in his cell at the mercy of the Wirthera, and he was not on board the ship he could just barely remember, doing what he could only vaguely recall, and he wasn't in one of the hallucination dreams . . .

That meant all of this *was* real.

10

"Venga. You shouldn't be wearing that. You're going to broil."
Teila tutted at the older man, clothed head-to-toe in the garments of his youth as a whaler. The full-length heavy robes, including the face covering. She couldn't begin to think where he'd found them, but since he was here in the lighthouse sitting room and not on the sea, battling the heavy winds, he was going to pass out from the heat.

"I like it." His voice was a little muffled through the veil. "They can't find me in here."

She didn't have to ask who. It didn't matter because the answer changed from day to day. "At least have something cold to drink."

Venga shook his head. "I'm fine."

Teila sighed and patted his shoulder through the bulky robes. "If you want anything, let me know."

She made her rounds of the others, making sure everyone was accounted for and not in need of anything. All of the residents had been here long enough that they didn't really need much from her any longer, but it was still her responsibility to check on them, just as it was her job to make sure the lamp was working. Rehker, as usual, was reading in the parlor with his feet on the stool. He charmed her with a smile when she came in, tried to flirt with her. She was used to that. Pera, on the other hand, was busy working on some sort of long document in the other corner. A viddy script, she said sometimes. Other times, a memoir. At any rate, she ignored Teila completely, which was fine with her because Pera could be uncomfortably intense.

In the dining room, Teila found Adarey and Stimlin. No surprise that the women were together, as it was rare for either to be apart from the other. They'd been strangers when they came here, both suffering the after-effects of their time in battle and both having lost their partners, they'd quickly become a couple.

Adarey looked up when Teila came in. "The delivery ship came. Vikus said he'd sign for the shipment, but he's not around."

Stimlin said nothing, but then she never did. She ate a bite from the plate between them, then passed the fork to Adarey. The kitchen had plenty of tableware, but Teila had stopped trying to convince the pair they didn't need to share.

In the kitchen she found the delivery 'bot waiting patiently in standby mode. This far out there'd be no other deliveries it had to make, and it had probably been programmed to hold as long as necessary for the appropriate authorization. When she passed her hand over the 'bot's control panel, its faceplate lit up. The 'bot whirred and clicked. Rust had bruised it all over.

"Stay tuned," the 'bot said in its grinding metallic voice. "Stay tuned."

Whatever that meant, Teila had no idea. This 'bot was so old it probably hadn't had its dialogue functions upgraded in a long, long time. It didn't seem to matter when she didn't answer, because as soon as she'd finished punching in her acceptance codes, the 'bot went to the back door where the delivery ship's transport scooter waited. The ramp extended and the carrier 'bots began transporting the boxes and bags of supplies into the kitchen. Teila knew better than to simply trust that they'd get everything off the scooter—there'd been too many times when it had pulled away without fully emptying its cargo and she'd had to wait another full cycle before it came back. But when she checked the flatbed, the scooter was empty. She watched it trundle back to the edge of the sea, where it was hooked by the delivery ship's wires and pulled aboard. Habit made her wave at the ship, though she could see no signs of crew.

It wasn't true, what the Rav Aluf had told her when he returned her husband. Yes, the days of the sea being black with whalers had ended, but there were still plenty of pleasurecraft and tradecraft that passed by. They stayed far out to sea, very few of them ever coming close enough to even risk running aground. She sometimes watched the enormous luxury party boats from the lamp room. When the wind was just right she heard the sounds of their music, though she had to rely on her imagination for visions of the food and drink and dancing the passengers enjoyed.

Her father had told her stories of the tables set with gold-rimmed plates, utensils forged from platanium. The finest wines and best cuts of flesh, not farm-simulated but genuine. He and her mother had taken such a voyage for their wedding journey, and he'd promised Teila that one day he'd take her, as well. That had been in the days when whalers made their cycle's fortunes with a single haul, before the government had stepped in to regulate the milka trade. Before the war had escalated, before the rationing and new laws. Now only the wealthiest could afford to take pleasure cruises, and though she had her father's estate to keep her from poverty, Teila was far from wealthy.

She didn't regret it. Life on a whaler was hard. Life in the lighthouse at least was steady, if not occasionally dull. It wasn't the life her father had chosen for her, but what she'd chosen for herself. She might dream of luxury, but she'd seen what too much money and power did to people. She'd never be poor, and she'd never be rich, but she could at least be content with where and who she was.

At least she *knew* who she was.

She found a surprise waiting for her in the kitchen. Jodah stood in front of one of the mechbots, both hands up defensively, while the 'bot itself clicked and whirred brokenly. Jodah turned when she came through the door, his stance aggressive enough for her to pause before he relaxed. Just a little.

"It came at me," he said.

Teila's brows rose. "It's a mechbot. It can't hurt you."

"I know that. Now," he added angrily. "But it took me by surprise."

Somehow, she thought, that had been the problem, and not anything the poor old 'bot had actually done. That it had managed to take Jodah by surprise. She put a hand over her mouth to hold back a giggle, but a little bit slipped out.

"Let me see if I can fix it." She pushed past Jodah, who stepped back. Fortunately, the 'bot had only been dented a little. Vikus could probably fix it, and the irony of that—needing him to fix a 'bot whose sole function was to repair things around the property, was not lost on her. "I'm not sure I should bother. It's so old, and there are no more replacement parts since the SDF commandeered them all."

She paused, wondering if her mention of the SDF would cause

him to react, but Jodah said nothing. She opened the poor 'bot's control panel and punched in the keycode that would send it back to its charging station. Its gears ground, and for a moment she was certain that was it, it was irreparable. But then it moved, clanking and wheezing, down the hall. She'd found them in odd places before, their batteries run down before they could make it back to their docking stations. She'd check later. For now, she turned to Jodah, who still looked ashamed.

"Are you hungry?"

"No."

"Then . . . why are you in the kitchen?" She gestured at the boxes of supplies just as Vikus and Billis came in from the dining room. "Boys, we need to get this put away. Jodah can help."

"Not my name," he said through gritted teeth.

She paused, but kept her voice calm though her heart had begun to beat faster at his tone and the way he'd clenched his fists. "We can call you whatever you'd like."

"What's he doing down here?" Vikus asked brusquely.

Jodah was on him before the young man could take a second breath. His forearm went under Vikus' chin, pushing him against the wall while Vikus flailed. "You should be more respectful."

Silence, not a word from any of them. Billis, to no surprise, had retreated across the room at the first sight of violence. Vikus stopped struggling. Teila, remembering the squeeze of her husband's fingers on her throat, wasn't about to agitate him, even though she knew in her heart he wasn't going to hurt Vikus. Once he'd loved the younger man like the brother he didn't have.

"What would you like us to call you?" Teila asked quietly. "And please let Vikus go."

Her husband did and stepped back with a wary glare that faded into a grimace of embarrassment. He nodded stiffly. "Your pardon."

Vikus shook his robes to straighten them and gave Teila a narrow-eyed look, but he nodded back. "Granted."

"If I could call myself anything I wanted," Billis spoke up suddenly, "I'd pick something really silky."

"Silky?" One of her husband's brows lifted. "You think I should pick a silky name. Like what?"

Billis moved forward eagerly. "Like . . . Dentrel. Or Vesperil."

"Viddy performers." Teila laughed. "Billis, I don't think he wants to name himself after viddy performers."

"Anyway, he doesn't want to pick his own name. He wants to use his real name. Even if it's gritty and not silky, right?" Vikus put in a little snidely.

Teila frowned at him, but her husband didn't seem to care this time about respect. He nodded and ran a hand over his face. He looked at her.

"I must've come with records."

"Yes," she said hesitantly. "But they told me that your name was Jodah."

"Everyone's name is Jodah when they can't remember their own." This came from Billis in the corner, who gave Teila a shamefaced shrug when she whirled to glare at him.

She looked back to her husband, who'd never been Jodah even before he picked his adult name. It would be so easy right now to suggest he call himself Kason, but she couldn't do it. "Jodah is a fine name, but if it doesn't suit you, or if it makes you angry—"

"It's not right. I know that." He punched a fist into his palm. "It doesn't feel right."

Teila looked at the time meter hung on the wall. "It's almost time for the midday meal. Why not join us, and . . . maybe we can help you figure it out. Or at least figure out what you'd like to be called."

He nodded slowly. Carefully. "Yes. All right."

Teila snapped at Vikus and Billis. "Right, then. You two. Let's get these boxes unpacked."

She caught him looking at her, dark brows drawn, pale eyes fierce. The first time she'd seen him look at her that way, she'd fallen in love with him. Now it took everything she had not to throw herself into his arms and kiss him into remembering who he was.

11

He was not yet used to being up and about, amongst others. He ought to have been. They were soldiers too, if not exactly like him then at least similar. It wasn't that he felt like they were judging him. He was just one among many, he was sure, who'd come and gone from the lighthouse over the years. His problems were better than some and no worse than others had suffered. And yet, he still felt out of place and uncertain when he made his way downstairs after the monotony of being alone in his room became too stifling.

The day before he'd spent the midday meal at the table with the others, half-expecting them to clamor for information from him, but nobody had paid more than a moment's attention to him. It had been a comfort to sit and eat in silence while conversations went on around him. Not excluding, but not prying, either.

Teila had not brought up the subject of what to call him at the table. He'd asked her afterward to show him his records, and seeing it there on the viddy screen hadn't convinced him it was true. He knew in his gut he was someone else. He hadn't been able to think of something better for her to call him though, and he hated it.

That small interaction with the others had made it impossible for him to remain sequestered, however. His room had no viddy monitor and he'd have tired of it quickly even if it had. He needed to be active. He needed to move. He'd spent too long inside. He sensed a lot of weaknesses in himself. He wanted to work his body and make it stronger.

He wasn't hungry, though he looked in the kitchen and knew he could help himself to whatever he wanted. He didn't want to sit in the parlor, either—Venga had turned the viddy monitor to some program blaring discordant music and flashing so many pics it would surely give Jodah a headache. The old man sat too close to the monitor anyway, blocking the view. In the study, Jodah looked at the catalog of reading material on the communal handheld, searching for something he hadn't read.

As if he'd remember if he had.

"That's only for in here, you know." Pera had been sitting in the shadowy corner, unnoticed.

Jodah looked up at the sound of her voice. "What?"

"The handheld," she said. "That's for in here. For anyone to use who wants it. You can't take it upstairs or anything, because that wouldn't be fair to the rest of us."

"I won't." He held it up, weighing it. "How old is this thing?"

She had a gritty laugh, dusty as the sands outside. "Really old. Rehker told me Venga brought it with him when he came, and that was a long, long time ago."

"So it's Venga's handheld," Jodah said. "Not just for anyone who wants it?"

"No. He doesn't use it anymore. It's for the whole house." She got up and came closer, standing shoulder to shoulder with him. She wore her hair short all over but for the front, where the white strands fell forward over her eyes. "But if you want to order anything, you put it on the house account and Teila deducts it from your personal account."

This gave him pause. "What if I simply want to use my own handheld?"

"Do you have one?" Pera looked at him through the fringes of her hair.

"I could buy one, couldn't I?"

"I don't know," she said with a small smile that revealed tiny, perfect teeth. "Depends on how much money you have, heywhat?"

Along with the medical records, Teila had shown him the ones for his personal accounts. He had enough money for anything he could ever ask for or need. Certainly for a handheld newer than this one. He hefted it in his palm again, then put it down. The data stream brightened for a moment, and he winced.

Pera moved closer. "You're enhanced. In the brain."

Jodah nodded, fingers pressed to his temples. He blinked, hoping to force the constant stream of light to fade enough for him to be able to ignore it. "Yes."

"I was stationed with some enhanced officers. If you ask me, it causes more trouble than it's worth. Filling people up with metal and wire. It makes you faster," she said, stroking an unexpected finger down the front of his robes. "And stronger. Sure. But it also takes something away, doesn't it? Something important."

"I can't remember," Jodah said hoarsely. "What it was like before I was this way."

"You can't remember anything, can you?" Her expression was cooing, but her tone cold. A little mocking. Her fingers curled into the front of his robes.

She was on her tiptoes before he knew it, her lips brushing his before he could think to move away. The kiss, so brief it was barely anything, somehow stung. Jodah shook his head as Pera pulled away, and she gave him another of those small grins. The pink tip of her tongue crept out to press the center of her upper lip.

"It's okay," she told him. "It's the way we all are around here. Crazy as drywhales."

Drywhales, those that had been stripped of all their oils and left behind to suffer the grind of sand in their sensitive joints. If it didn't kill them, the agony sent them into a frenzy powerful enough to sink any size ship. It made the normally mild-tempered creatures fierce and violent and furious . . . and vindictive.

"I'm no drywhale," he said.

Pera smirked, tilting her head so the brush of her hair drifted across her eyes. They gleamed through the white strands. "Of course you're not."

When she leaned to kiss him again, Jodah turned his head so that it would land on his cheek rather than his mouth. Pera had a soldier's reflexes. She stopped the kiss before it got that far.

"No?"

"No," Jodah said. "I'm sorry."

Pera gave him a long look through the filter of her hair. "You're not sorry. But that's all right."

A discreet cough from behind them made Jodah turn, while Pera didn't move at all. It was Rehker, smiling that odd, wide grin of his that didn't reach his eyes. When he crossed the room to take a seat on the lounge, he passed Pera close enough to brush her sleeve with his fingertips. She closed her eyes at his touch.

Jodah didn't miss that.

Nor the way her breath heaved, or how her nipples tightened, poking the thin material of her robes. Or how she stood so still when Rehker passed, as though she were trying her best not to leap after him. Jodah sensed the tremor of her muscles.

"Don't let me interrupt," Rehker said smoothly.

"There's nothing to interrupt," Pera answered in a low voice.

"Then come sit by me. I'm sure Jodah won't mind." Rehker patted the spot on the lounger next to him, and when Pera took it, he leaned forward, hands on his knees. Not looking at her. Not touching her. His attention was focused on Jodah, yet the tension between Rehker and Pera was palpable.

Rehker clutched his hands together and gave Jodah a sincere look. "We haven't really had a chance to get to know each other. You and me. You've been here long enough, surely we should've had some time to spend with you by now. You kept yourself upstairs for so long, I thought you'd never come down."

"I've been unwell."

"So have we all, brother, so have we all." Rehker rocked a little on the lounger, his fingers linked tight. Pera couldn't take her eyes off him but he didn't even glance at her. "But you're no brother of mine, are you? I presume too much. You're enhanced. You were an officer, huh?"

"I . . . yes." Jodah set the ancient handheld on the table.

"But you don't remember what rank." Rehker laughed, not waiting for an answer. "It's okay. Hardly any one of us does. We come here broken. Teila puts us back together, doesn't she, Pera?"

"Sometimes," Pera said with a little startle when he spoke to her.

Rehker looked at Jodah. "Sometimes. But you . . ."

The other man got up and strode toward him to stand just a little too close. Jodah had known men who favored the company of men before. Not that he remembered, exactly, just that he knew without overthinking it that he could tell the difference between Rehker's interest in him and Pera's. Both felt predatory and both lacked any sense of sexuality.

"You," Rehker said when Jodah didn't give him any ground, "are very high ranking. Aren't you?"

It felt right to answer yes, but Jodah didn't. "How could you know that? Did you know me?"

Rehker tilted his head. "No. We didn't serve together. I think they're very careful not to place any of us together, in case of problems. But I can tell by looking at you."

Jodah gave the man a hard, unyielding glare. "Tell me, Rehker. What do you see?"

"Enhanced, definitely. You've lost weight, a lot of it, and your face is haggard, but you haven't lost muscle. You're still strong . . . even when you feel weak. Yes?"

"Yes." Jodah crossed his arms over his chest. "Anything else?"

"Your eyes. The pupil of the left is a little larger than the other. It opens wider. Closes smaller. It's recording everything you see, isn't it?"

Jodah hadn't thought about it, but now that Rehker had pointed it out, all he could notice was how much clearer the world seemed looking through his left eye. When he looked at the other man, the data stream brightened, white and glaring, but Jodah could do little more than blink at it as the string of words and images flashed past him.

"And you've got a lot going on in that brain, I bet. Oh, you can calculate the trajectory of a hornet as quick as that, can't you?" Rehker snapped his fingers. "You wouldn't even have to think about it. All the work would be done for you. They give the officers the best advantages, don't they? Of course they do. Not for the rest of us, of course, not the under soldiers. The SDF couldn't possibly do that."

Jodah had a memory of pain, vivid and yet welcome. He wanted to hold on to it, but it slipped away before he could. Even so, the flavor of it remained. The smell of something burning. An ache deep in his bones. An extra weight inside him as he got used to his new skeleton.

"Nothing comes without cost, Rehker. The SDF gave me what I needed in order to lead."

"And in the end, Jodah-kah, you ended up the same as all the rest of us. Didn't you?"

Kah. The honorific was an old one, appended to the end of his name in the Fenda style. The use of it had fallen out of favor years ago, then resurged in popularity in the viddies as a slang term, usually faintly insulting. Rehker had said it without a flinch, a simper, or a snide look, but somehow Jodah knew the man hadn't intended it as respect.

"Yes. I ended up just the like the rest of you. So there's no need to call me kah." Jodah looked at Pera, who hadn't moved from her spot on the lounger. Her eyes wide, her grin wider, she couldn't keep her adoring gaze from Rehker, who at last turned to face her.

"Sweet Pera. The past is a shadow to you, isn't it?"

"Mostly," she said.

"And you're glad of it?"

"Mostly," she said, this time with a pause before replying.

Rehker frowned. "We don't remember who we were or what happened to us, but we can look at each other and see the truth. I look at you, Jodah-kah, and I see a man who must've done great things. I'd have been proud to serve under you, I'm sure."

"Thank you," Jodah said, not sure he could believe Rehker, no matter how sincere he sounded. There was something off-putting about the other man. Something sly. Or maybe it was simply the way he allowed Pera to dote on him, keeping her close to him and feeding her just enough attention to fan the flames of her desires, yet never, so far as Jodah could see, giving her what she wanted.

"You're welcome, Jodah-kah."

Irritated, Jodah frowned. "You don't have to call me that."

"But it fits you so well," Rehker replied with another of his wide grins that didn't reach his eyes. "It suits him, doesn't it, Pera?"

"Oh, it does. Absolutely."

Jodah looked from one to the other, knowing the pair of them were somehow mocking but unable to figure out a way to say so without sounding too sensitive. He put a hand on his belly and gave each of them a formal half bow. "Thank you, Rehker-kah. Pera-kah. I'll say the same for you."

This brought a sour giggle from Pera, but Rehker only looked at him with that same flat gaze. Jodah stared at the other man until he looked away. What they were up to, he couldn't be sure and didn't really care. Both of them were not well in their minds, which he could forgive. But disrespectful, that he had no time for.

"Another time. I look forward to getting to know you better, Jodah-kah." Rehker returned the formal gesture, though as with the use of "kah" it had a flavor of mockery. He turned to Pera. "Pera, a game of golightly?"

Rehker's dismissal of Jodah was so clear it almost made him laugh, but he took the chance for escape, instead.

12

The simple food had been expertly prepared. Several courses of grains and greens with sliced milka and milka pudding for afters. He dove into it like a starving man, savoring every flavor as though he'd never tasted it before. And maybe, he thought, watching the others at the table, he hadn't. Or at least had not in so long that they might as well have been brand-new.

The table conversation was lively and disjointed, but as with the other meals he'd shared at the table, nobody seemed to care if he joined in. Instead, he sat back and watched the others. Gathering information. Observing. Details formed patterns in his brain, making shining strands of color that became rapidly scrolling lines of analysis he could barely decipher.

Venga, the old man. Not dressed appropriately, moving slowly, but faking much of his decrepitude. He also hoarded food beneath the heavy robes, a sure sign he'd been held for a long time in near starvation.

Adarey and Stimlin, the women. Partners. Adarey spoke for Stimlin, but it was clear if you watched them how she relayed her needs and thoughts through subtle hand signals. Where would she have learned them? Data he hadn't been aware he had filtered into the stream of details and patched them together, but he still didn't know.

The chatty and vibrant Rehker, who kept up a never-ending stream of jokes to hide the constant tremor in his voice that didn't come from fear. The sullen Pera, who looked with hidden longing at Rehker, but only when she thought he couldn't see. Pera was the only one with visible scars, burns across her face and on her arms, exposed by the sleeves of her robes when she reached to serve herself.

They were all military except for Vikus, Billis and . . . Teila. The woman. And of course her son and the ancient Fendalese female who served as the boy's amira. All were soldiers, none of them as high ranking as he, though there was no way for him to know that for sure. It was just a feeling.

He'd started having a lot more feelings.

None of them treated him like an outsider. If he stood off from them, they didn't seem to notice, or at least not enough to care. Nor did any of them try to pull him into the discussion, for which he was grateful. His head had begun to ache from the noise of conversation. Too much stimulation. He couldn't stop collecting and compiling details into his mental data stream, even though none of the information made sense or triggered any responses.

"Enhanced," he said aloud, suddenly, startling himself and causing everyone else at the table to fall silent and stare at him. "I'm enhanced."

"In my day, we called it built up," Venga said after a moment. "Got a chip in my brain, supposed to help me take pictures with my eyes like a camera. Never worked right."

Rehker laughed and struck an exaggerated pose. "Take a picture of this."

Venga snorted. "Like I'd want that stuck in my brain, no thank ya."

Jodah pushed away from the table, his head spinning and his meal unfinished. The chair clattered to the floor behind him hard enough to break. Rehker's laughter stopped.

"It was an old chair," Teila said. "Don't worry about it."

"I think I should go upstairs," he said.

"Everyone cleans their own plate from the table," Vikus said.

Teila gave him a stern look. "Vikus."

"Well," the younger man said, "we do."

This time, Pera spoke up, the first time she'd said a word the entire meal. "A Rav Gadol wouldn't clear his own plate from the table."

Rav Gadol. The term lit up something in the part of his brain that was constantly calculating. A sudden flare of agony caused him to press his fingertips to his temples. A chittering sound blocked out everything else for a moment, but then passed along with most of the pain. He straightened and looked at all of them.

"I was the Rav Gadol. But now . . . I'm just a man." With that, and a significant look at the now-sulking Vikus, he picked up his plate and took it into the kitchen, where he put it in the sanitizer.

When he turned, Teila was behind him, smiling. "Vikus doesn't mean to be disrespectful."

"Yes, he does. It's fine." He tested the title again. Rav Gadol. It tasted right, felt right. It fit. But it wasn't his name any more than Jodah was. "How did she know?"

"Pera?" Teila moved past him with her own plate. "She knows a lot of things. You'd have to ask her."

"She's right. I was a Rav Gadol. I can feel it."

"Do you remember anything . . . else?" Teila put her plate in the sanitizer and turned to him. She tilted her head, looking curious.

With only an arm's length between them, it would've been so easy to reach for her. Grab. Pull her closer. Slant his mouth over hers and . . .

No.

He backed away. If this was not a dream, she was a real woman and not here to slake his desires. He'd done her a great disservice by forcing his attentions on her. If it had not been rape, it had certainly been something close to coercion, and his stomach felt sick at the memories of her beneath him.

"About your name? What we should call you?" She moved a step closer.

He moved a step away.

A flash of what seemed like disappointment shone in her face. "We could call you Rav, if you'd like. I said I'd be happy to call you whatever you like. Nobody else here likes to use their military titles."

"I don't mean for them to treat me like their Rav," he said stiffly. "It's just a name. And no, I don't want to be called that."

She nodded after a second's hesitation. "All right, then. If that's what you'd like. So . . . shall we keep calling you Jodah? Until you remember your own?"

"What if I never do?"

She studied him for a moment, her wide, dark eyes kinder than he deserved. When she reached to put her hand on his shoulder, he suffered her touch though it sent flames rippling through every nerve and left him raw. She squeezed him gently and when he didn't respond, at least not in a way she could've seen, she let him go.

"You will," she said. "I know you will."

13

n the bright light of morning, two of the three suns risen and the smallest one, Elaris, peeking over the horizon, it was time to put out the lamp. It was one of Teila's favorite parts of the day, when everyone else was still sleeping but she could look out across the Sea of Sand and see the whales at play.

As a girl, her father had often brought her up here when he wasn't at sea, to point out to her the different whales and their young. He'd learned them so well he could tell exactly when they'd breach and for how long, though he never gave them names.

"They're not pets, Tee," he'd always told her solemnly. "And we can't ever own them. Never forget that. They give us something precious, but they don't belong to us."

Her father had lost his life to one of those whales. A cow, threatened by the whaler's proximity to her baby, had unexpectedly turned on him. Not even the whaler's metal hull could stand against an angry whale. None of the bodies of the whalers had been recovered.

Teila had already taken over the lamp by then. She'd spent her days looking out across the sea to see if her father's ship was coming home. Instead, the Sheirran Battle Fleet had sent her a viddy message telling her the wreckage had been discovered and that the ship's final moments were recorded by its security systems. It had been foolish of her to expect a message from her father, and yet she'd wept when the footage showed only the whale rising out of the sand to slam its body onto the ship's deck, over and over again.

Two cycles later, she'd been out on the sea in her scudder, netting a milka pellet, when a pleasure cruiser had appeared on the horizon. They weren't as uncommon back then, before such ships became luxuries only the wealthiest could afford and this edge of the Sea of Sand too far and difficult to reach. So much had changed even in these past few years, she thought, shielding her eyes to look out across the sea.

No whales this morning. No pleasure cruisers like the one that had brought Kason to her. No whalers. Just the seemingly unending expanse of rolling, golden sand and the hint of a storm coming closer.

There'd been a storm that day, too. Rare clouds had made the sky dark, and the winds had tossed the sands high into the air. Without the sun, the solar panels on her small craft hadn't been able to provide her with enough power, and she'd needed to use her sail. The pleasure cruiser, which was much larger, had been in a similar situation except that it had no sails. Boats like that required so much power they were more often equipped with solar cells. She'd find out later that he'd drained them without making sure they were full again before the storm hit, and that was why the cruiser had gone dark. But at the time, all she could do was fight the wind to get herself to shore.

By the time she'd made it there, the sea had been whipped into writhing, boiling hills and valleys, and a fine choking dust had clouded the air. Teila had watched for a minute or so before realizing with sick horror that that the lamp had not been lit. She'd run, taking the stairs two at a time, reaching the top in a thick sweat and ready to faint from the effort. By the time she got everything working, the visibility outside had become nil. With no sight of the pleasure cruiser, all she could do was make sure the lamp was working and entertain Vikus and Billis, mere toddlers belonging to the women who'd kept house for her father—and who'd obviously shared his bed more than once or twice.

She hadn't been able to get the thought of the cruiser out of her mind. It had been far enough away when she first spotted it that it might not even be close to shore or the jagged rocks hidden under the deceptive layers of golden sand. It might've gone in another direction or found a place to anchor on one of the few islands out of her sight. But, pacing, trying to see through the storm, Teila had known that the cruiser was edging closer and closer to shore. She could only hope the light warned it.

The lighthouse, as it turned out, was the only reason the pleasure cruiser had not ended up completely destroyed. The craft's captain and only passenger had seen the light and been savvy enough to head for it, but the stormy sea had been too violent. Unable to fight the twisting sands, he'd aimed the craft for shore and initiated the escape sequence. However, without enough power, which ran out just before he crashed, he was unable to eject the metal pod that would've protected him from the sand and rocks and whales and anything else.

Through the glass at the top of the lighthouse, Teila had watched the pleasure cruiser getting closer and closer, just a great dark shape in the shadows of swirling sand. She'd watched the interior lights gutter and go out. She'd held her breath, wondering if the passengers had managed to get out, or if they were going to be on board when it inevitably hit the reefs a few hundred septs from shore.

The crack of the cruiser against the rocks now exposed by the shifting sands had been loud enough to vibrate the glass in the tower room. Though she had strained to see, all Teila had been able to make out was the dark shape a short distance off shore. When a swirling gust of wind parted the dust cloud long enough for her to catch a glimpse of the cruiser, broken and being sucked into the depths of the sea, she hadn't thought twice.

She'd run.

At the base of the lighthouse, bored into the solid stone foundation, were two enormous platanium rings with several coiled lengths of rope made from the same metal hung between them. They each had hooks on the ends and were too heavy for her to lift. Luckily she didn't have to. The rescue ropes were designed to be shot with an air gun toward a stranded ship and hooked onto it or whatever escape craft it had, then reeled in to pull the craft to shore. She'd never had to use the system, though when her father was home he had been fond of running practice rescue missions.

The first shot had gone wild, taken by the wind. Heart in her throat, sand gritting her eyes to slits, Teila had set the trajectory for the second rope and hook. With a silent prayer to the Three Mothers, she'd let it fly. The hook hit. The rope had gone taut. She'd pushed the button that would reel it in.

Halfway to shore, the rope had gone slack. There was no way to shoot it again without reeling it all the way in, a complicated process that required more attention than she could've spared in the middle of this storm. Already her throat and mouth had gone dry, caked with thick dust. She'd barely been able to see.

The lamp, on its round-about flash, had illuminated something in the sea. Teila had forced her way through the wind and dust to the edge of the rocky grass to where the sea began. Something had floundered there, grabbing onto the rope but going under. Coming up and going under again.

She hadn't been able to toss out the hook, but she could hold on to the rope and wade out into the roiling, rolling sands. It had gone over her head in a minute, soft and loose and getting into every part of her. She'd pulled the hood of her robe over her face and could only feel along the metal rope, kicking her feet steadily and climbing the hillocks of fine sand that shifted endlessly all around her. Some planets had seas of water under which a person couldn't breathe, but even covered with sand she could manage to sip a few breaths here and there. The hood's filter had helped a bit with the dust, but not enough to keep her from getting dizzy.

She'd been unable to yell out. All she'd been able to do was reach blindly into the clouds of dust, groping for what she'd seen clinging to the end of the rope. And then, just before she could go no further, a hand had gripped hers.

And that had been Kason, the man she married.

She turned at the sound behind her, knowing already it would be him. It was in the way the air moved around her when he was close. She said nothing, just watched as he entered the lamp room. He didn't see her at first, and something broke a little inside her that he wasn't as attuned to her. Once it had been the same for him.

"It's a storm," she spoke up when he noticed her. "Out there. Far off, but it will be here by the afternoon, I think."

"Do we need to do anything to prepare for it?"

It was an interesting question. She studied him as she answered, wondering if any of this would trigger more memories. "No. Just be prepared for the solar panels to go dark, make sure all the backup cells are full so the lamp doesn't lose power. That's the most important thing."

He looked out the glass again. "Why do you do this, Teila?"

She broke again a little at the way he said her name. "The lighthouse?"

"No. The rest of it." He kept his gaze focused outside, not on her.

The truth was, his father had been the one to coerce her into opening the lighthouse to fallen soldiers who needed a place to recover and, in some cases, live out the rest of their lives. He'd convinced her the money she'd get from the SDF would be worth it, but what she'd discovered was that the satisfaction of giving people a safe haven had become more important than the financial security. But again, she was hampered by what she thought she might be able to reveal without forcing something into his mind. Not for the first time, she cursed the Rav Aluf. He'd returned her husband to her in a way that made it nearly impossible for her to ever get him back.

"There are so many soldiers who come home from battle needing a place to rest, and not enough facilities to house them. I had this entire huge place just for myself and Stephin. Even with Densi and the boys, we didn't need this much space. It seemed natural for me to offer it to those who needed it, when I was asked."

He looked at her then. "I think I've been gone a long time."

"Yes," she said before she could stop herself. "I mean . . . yes, I think you're probably right."

He pressed his fingertips to his temples. "There's this constant stream of data. It's in my mind, but I can see it." He gestured just beyond his eyes. "I can't describe it. Strings of information, pictures, and colors, but they make patterns. Like fitting together a puzzle, only too many of the pieces are missing. This must've been useful at some point, but now it only hurts. It's distracting. I can't seem to shut it off."

They'd both known he would be enhanced when he went into

service. They'd talked about it every night in those last few hours before he'd gone into training, in between their sometimes frantic, sometimes leisurely lovemaking. There was no way to know in advance what would be done to him, but because of his father's rank, they'd assumed he'd get the highest grade of enhancements.

"It hurts?"

He nodded with a grimace. "Like lights flashing in the corners of my vision, until I focus on it. Then I can see the data stream. If I ignore it too long, the pain starts up. Here." He tapped his temples. The center of his forehead. Each inner eye socket.

"I can give you pain relief—"

"No," he said sharply, then softer, "I'm tired of being unfocused."

"Then . . . I can still help you. Come." She gestured, pulling out a chair from the small desk in front of the lamp control panels. Sometimes she'd penned letters to him there, the old-fashioned sort with quill and paper, because electronic communications could be intercepted. She'd never had an answer. Never knew if her letters had reached him.

He hesitated, but came with dragging feet. He sat when she indicated the chair again. When she put her hands on his shoulders, he went instantly stiff.

"This," she told him gently, kneading at the tight muscles, "is probably a big part of the problem."

He'd always carried a lot of tension in his shoulders and neck, and she knew where to find the trigger spots. One on the left side from an old injury incurred before they'd met. There had to be others now. Many others. She worked at the muscles. Slowly, slowly he relaxed under her touch.

She moved around to the front of him and, without thinking, straddled his lap. She took his face in her hands, meaning to use her thumbs to work at his temples, but both his hands came up to grab her wrists. Her heart leapt at the heat that rose between them. Her lips parted at once, ready for his kiss.

It didn't come.

Instead, he put her from his lap firmly and without hesitation. He stood, moving the chair so he could get away from her. He wouldn't meet her eyes.

"If you need help getting ready for the storm, let me know," he said.

Stunned and embarrassed, Teila nodded. "Yes. Um, thank you. I think we'll be fine. But I'll let you know. Yes."

"I'll be in my room. If you need help."

She nodded, turning her attention to the dials and switches of the control panel. Nothing there needed her to fiddle with it, but she did in order to keep herself focused on that and not on him. Only when he'd gone did she let herself sag a little, a hand over her mouth to hold back the sobs threatening to slip out.

It had been better, she thought before she could stop herself, when he'd been convinced she was a dream.

14

The storm had teased the horizon for the full of the day, striking hard only as night fell. The others had gathered in the sitting room to watch a viddy program, but shortly into it the picture flickered and sputtered, turning to black as the rising dust outside blocked the signal. No amount of fussing with the tuner would bring in the picture, much to the grumbling Venga's disdain.

Thinking of himself as the Rav still felt more right than as Jodah, but it wasn't quite natural. It was a name others were meant to call him. Not how he should think of himself. When someone said it though, it turned his head.

"Rav," Pera repeated. "Do you play cards? How about a game of golightly?"

All soldiers did, of course. It was sometimes the only way to pass long hours in transit, when electronic entertainment units were forbidden because the transmissions they used could be picked up by enemy scanners. He'd perfected his shuffle, his deal, even

the art of a few cheats that everyone knew and used so they couldn't
really be considered dishonest.

He took the pack of cards from her, demonstrating until she
grinned. "Don't call me that. What are we playing for?"

He supposed she could've asked him to play for money. Instead,
she pulled a bin of colored marbles from a closet and put it on the
table, separating them into colors and choosing one set for herself.
The other to him. It made the game a challenge, but not a real risk.
She won the first. He won the second.

Outside, the winds began to howl. The lights flickered but came
back on. Eventually Stephin came into the sitting room along with
his amira, a bowl of milka pudding in her hands.

Jodah's stomach rumbled as the child settled in the chair next
to him. "What do you have there?"

Stephin showed him. "It's good."

"I know it is."

Pera shuddered. "Disgusting. It's the only way I won't eat milka.
How can you stand it that way?"

He and the boy shared a smile. "If you let me eat some of your
pudding, I'll show you how to shuffle these cards."

The boy grinned, but gave his amira a look. The ancient Fenda
waved a languid hand and ambled toward the long, low couch in
the corner, where she promptly settled herself and fell asleep. Jodah
took a bite of pudding and then handed Stephin the pack of cards.

"Here. Like this."

They passed the time that way for a little longer as the storm
began to lash the lighthouse. Pera, abandoning the game now that
the boy was involved, got up to look out the windows. Venga
grumbled some more about the viddy program he wasn't able to
watch. Adarey and Stimlin, who'd both been reading, went to bed
without saying a word.

Though he'd waited for her all evening, Teila hadn't come into the sitting room. Now Densi woke and took the protesting Stephin by the hand to get ready for bed. The boy hung back.

"Will you take me?" Stephin asked.

"Don't you bother him now," said the amira with a shake of her head, though she gave Jodah a curious look. "He don't need to be messing with the likes of you."

"I'm going upstairs anyway," Jodah said. "I'm tired, too. C'mon then. Let's see if you can count how many stairs there are."

"Oh, I know how many," the boy said importantly. "I've learned them!"

In the boy's room, Jodah tucked him into bed after making sure he brushed his teeth and changed into sleeping robes. Stephin's eyes closed, his breathing soft almost as soon as his head hit the pillow.

"You have a way with him," Teila said quietly from the hallway when Jodah ducked out of the boy's room and toward his own. "Thank you. Amira Densi is old and sometimes impatient with him at bedtime. And I needed to check the lamp."

Jodah had never considered before why he'd been put into the room in the quarters belonging to Teila and her son, but he was glad for it now. This high, with the lamp sweeping its circle of light out across the sea, he had the best view of the storm. Uneasily, he paced in front of the windows. The pain in his head that had subsided so nicely under Teila's ministrations had crept back slowly over the course of the night. Playing cards had distracted him from the data stream, but now here in the dark, he was finding it hard to put it aside again.

And then . . . there was the storm.

The spatter of grit against the windows set him back a step, though there seemed little chance of anything breaking the glass.

In the sweep of light, he looked out to the sea, catching sight of what he thought might be a pair of whales cavorting in the whirling sands. If not whales, perhaps two ships being tossed on the roiling sands.

A ship in a storm.

15

"You're a fool and what's more, an idiot."

The words are no surprise, coming from his father, though the tone is harsher than he feels is necessary. In front of him, shining in the bright sunslight, is the cruiser. He restored it himself, spent hours rebuilding and repairing. It was worth twiceten the amount he'd spent to pull it from the junkyard, even if you included what he'd paid to have it hauled to the docks and the rent to keep it there. He'd done all of this on his own, too. That's probably what made the old man so mad.

"She's a beauty, Pao. Even you have to admit that." He ran his hand along the hull. "And I can sell it for more than I spent on it, if that's what you're worried about."

His father glared. "What I'm worried about is the time you wasted on this project. Time you could've spent in training. And now what are you going to do with it? Because for all your bragging about how much you could sell it for, I can see you've no plans to do so."

"Not right away. I'm going to enjoy her first." Grinning, he hopped over the railing to stand on the deck. Looking up at the suns, he calculated how long he had until nightfall. Plenty of time to get out onto the open sea.

And from there . . . freedom.

"You don't even know anything about the sea!"

Those were the last words his father had said to him, and they'd been the truth. Now he was in the middle of the Sea of Sand, the largest sea on all of Sheira. But what was there to know? The cruiser had been built with an autopilot and needed no more than occasional intervention. He had enough supplies to last him for a year if he ate amply and for much longer than that if he were meager in his consumption. And as for company, well . . . the world was a big place. He was sure there'd be plenty of people to meet.

Then came the storms, a series of small ones. The cloud coverage was just enough to require a few hours of supplemental power from the storage cells every day. Nothing that should've mattered much, if he'd known there was a break in the circuitry that was draining the supplementals all the time. To save some power while he worked on the repairs, he let the ship go wherever the sea took it. Far off the course he'd set, the tides and winds took him. And there, the biggest storm hit.

His cruiser was lost, but he was found.

16

Teila found Jodah crouched on the floor below his window, the heels of his hands pressed to his temples. When she knelt in front of him, he startled, pushing her away. She grabbed a handful of his robe to keep herself from falling and didn't let it go, even when he grabbed her arm hard enough to bruise.

He stared at her with wild eyes. "Where am I?"

Her heart sunk, but she kept her voice steady despite its desire to shake. "You're in the lighthouse at Apheera, on the edge of the Sea of Sand."

"Have I been here before?" His grip relaxed, and blinking, he let himself slide down the wall to sit against it.

Her mouth opened and closed on the reply. She cursed the Rav Aluf. How could she answer that question without risking Jodah's mind?

Outside, the wind howled. The lights dimmed and went out. Teila looked automatically toward the window to watch for the lamp's sweeping circle of light—it was still on. In a minute or so, if Vikus or Billis didn't get there first, she'd go downstairs and switch the rest of the lighthouse's power over to the supplementals. Without the sunslight, the cold would quickly permeate even the lighthouse's thick stone walls. They needed working heat.

He stared at her steadily now. "Teila. Keeper of the light."

"Yes," she said. "Jodah."

"That's not my name either, and you know it. Don't you?"

She drew in a slow breath. "It's not anyone's real name forever."

With a grunt, he doubled over in pain, hands pressed to his head. She put her arm around him, feeling the heat coming off him like he was his own sun. He didn't fight her off, though at her touch he definitely straightened his spine.

"Let me help you into bed."

"I don't need you."

That stung, though she tried not to let it. "I know you don't want to. Let me help you anyway."

"I don't need to go to bed!" His cry echoed.

She got to her feet. "Fine. I'll leave."

He snagged her by the elbow and forced her to kneel again in front of him. "Have I been here before?"

"Do you feel like you've been here before?"

"That's not an answer. Would I be asking if I didn't feel it?"

The lamp's sweep lit his face through the windows. Shadow. Light. Shadow. Light. She wanted to cradle his face in her hands and kiss away the anger and fear in his eyes, lit so briefly. Then darkness. It might've been easier in darkness.

Instead, she didn't touch him. They knelt in front of each other, only the heat and brush of breath connecting them. If she listened hard enough, could she hear his heartbeat?

"Where was I before I came here?"

"In a military medica." That, she could tell him. Only the parts of his life that had happened before the SDF rescued him from the Wirtheran war ship could set off the nanotriggers.

"I don't remember that."

"You were sedated," she said.

Another sweep of light. His gaze met hers without flinching. She found it harder to do the same.

"Before that . . . I was somewhere else. Captured. The Wirthera."

She refused to allow herself hope. "Yes. That's what they told me."

"How long?"

"I don't know," she answered honestly. "Long enough, I should guess."

Silence, then, but for the sound of his breathing. In the next sweep of light she could see him pressing the heels of his hands to his eyes. She ached for him.

"Before that, I was on a ship. I was the Rav Gadol. I remember that much, at least I think I do. Was it true?"

"Yes." Teila inched closer, still not touching but well within his grasp if he wanted to reach for her.

"What did they do to me?"

"I don't know, sweetheart." The endearment slipped out, bittersweet.

She felt him shudder and reached for him, unable to stop herself. He let her pull him closer until his head rested on her breasts. She ran her fingers through his hair, over and over. They sat that way for a long time in silence marked by the constant sweep of the lamp.

Slowly she became aware of the delicate caress of his fingertips on the inside of her knee. Then a little higher. The muscles of her thigh leaped under his touch when he made small circles there on the tender skin.

She gasped at his mouth on hers, then moaned at the slide of his tongue inside. Her hands threaded through his hair, pulling him closer. He covered her with his body, the heat rising even higher as he unlaced the front of her robe.

His mouth found her breasts and then her nipples, sucking gently. Teila arched under his touch. When his lips moved lower, his hands pushed her legs apart so he could get to her clit.

When he touched her, it was like fire. It had always been that way, from the first time he'd kissed her. And this . . . this was more like it used to be between them. Tender, sweet, almost too gentle. Teasing.

It took a long time for her to get to the edge, but any time she tried to move or shift to get at him, those big hands held her in place, until at last she simply gave in and let him have his way. She drifted on the pleasure until she couldn't stand it anymore.

His name, his real name, rose to her lips before she could help it. It was swallowed in her cries of pleasure and became no more than a moan, but even in her ecstasy how close she'd come to slipping frightened her. Shaking, she settled into the afterglow, her heartbeat slowing.

She waited for him to enter her, but he didn't. He kissed her thighs softly, then her belly. Her hipbones. Over her ribs, her breasts, and at last again to her mouth where he brushed the taste of her over her own lips. They lay together in the dark and quiet through three passes of the lamplight before he spoke.

"You're real."

"Yes," she told him.

He cleared his throat roughly. "I . . . took you. Before."

A small smile tugged at her lips, but she did her best to keep it from her voice. "Yes. You did."

"I'm sorry," he told her in a stiff, formal voice. "I shouldn't have."

She gathered her robes in front of her, holding them closed as she rolled to face him. "You think I couldn't have stopped you, if I wanted?"

"You couldn't have." In the next pass of light, she saw that he was staring at the ceiling, one arm behind his head.

"No. You're right. But you didn't force me, if that's what you were thinking."

He was silent for a moment. "Still. I shouldn't have . . ."

"Did you do what you just did as an apology?" Teila pushed herself up on one elbow, wishing she could see his face. The sound of the wind had gone quieter, though the occasional spatter of sand against the window told her the storm hadn't yet died.

He said nothing.

Stunned, moved, touched, her heart full, she leaned to kiss him. "You didn't make me do anything I didn't want to do."

The lights came back on. At the look on his face, awkward and clearly uncomfortable, Teila sat up and moved away. Giving him space.

Kason—because that was how she thought of him now—sat up too. "I'm a stranger to you."

It was her turn to stay quiet.

Frowning, he gave her a long, steady look. "You fuck a lot of strangers, Teila?"

Her chin went up, though his tone wasn't accusatory as much as merely curious. "No."

"It's not your habit, then?"

"No," she repeated and got to her feet. Her fingers fumbled with her laces as she closed her robes.

She felt it when he got up behind her. Waited for him to turn her. He didn't touch her, at least not with his hands. He didn't have to. She felt him all over her anyway.

"Teila."

She wouldn't look at him. Couldn't. She half-turned to give him the illusion of it, but cut her gaze from his.

"Have I been here before?"

Teila kept her words careful. "Do you think you have been?"

"Curse it! Answer me!"

She braced herself for his grip. His fists clenched, but he didn't touch her. Her throat dried even as her eyes burned; she closed them against the tears and his look.

"Am I a stranger to you?"

Her breath hitched inward, choking. She backed up a few steps, her head spinning, the Rav Aluf's warnings echoing in her head. *Don't tell him anything. Don't lead him. Above everything else, do not trigger him.*

"You've been here long enough," she said, thinking desperately of how to tell him something, anything, that would open the locked door between the present and the past. "No. You're not a stranger."

"But when I came here? Was I a stranger then?"

"Did you . . ." She had to swallow hard. "Did you feel like a stranger?"

Kason's back straightened. His eyes narrowed. "Yes. I did. All of this felt new to me. But now . . ."

"Yes?" Teila couldn't stop herself from hoping.

"Now, I doubt."

Everything inside her began to shake—joy or terror, she couldn't be sure. "It will take time for you—"

"Did you know me?" His tone brooked no more confabulation.

Without waiting for her to answer, he did it for her. "You did. I can see it in your eyes. You knew me, Teila. Before I came here this way, you knew me."

So close, so close, but she couldn't risk it. Not for any reason. "Do you remember me?"

"No." He shook his head, fingertips working at his temples again. "I don't, and I don't remember knowing you. But I did."

She couldn't say yes. But she could not say no. She let her silence answer, and that wasn't good enough for him.

Kason let out a low, angry growl. That was the only way to describe it. It was a sound of animal fury, culminating in a roar that had her cowering. With one swift motion, he swept the nearby table clean of the glass vase and tray. Both shattered on the floor. The table was next, toppled and broken.

Was this it, Teila wondered, terrified. Had he been triggered? Was he gone over?

When he turned on her, she stood her ground. Not from any bravery, but because she had no time to move before he had her in his arms. She'd been in just this place so many times before, sometimes with love or lust and a few times, lately, in anger. All she could do was look up at him and beg the Three Mothers to let him see her for who she was.

His fury drained as she watched. His grip loosened, though he didn't let her go. He leaned in, and she thought he might kiss her. Instead, he closed his eyes and took a long, slow breath. His nose traced a line up her throat to her jaw, the heat of his breath not quite a caress.

When he looked at her again, his gaze was flat. "You knew me. But you won't tell me how. Or who I am."

I can't. But even that was too much to say. All she could do was stare.

Kason put her from him so firmly it was as painful as a slap. He gave her his back. "Get out."

"Everything takes time—"

"Get out," he repeated. Softer this time, but far more dangerous.

The man she'd married would never have turned his back on her that way, no matter how angry. Perhaps it was time to admit it, Teila thought as she left the room. He was no longer the man she'd married.

17

This was a dream, but a real one. Knowing it gave him no more control over it than he'd had during any of the hallucinations, but that was all right. This dream wasn't full of sex or gluttony.

It was filled with flowers.

A field of them, red and blue and yellow, on a carpet of lush green. That's what had tipped him off to knowing this wasn't really happening. Sheira was a planet of dust and sand, its foliage gray and brown and dry. The only time he'd ever seen plants like this had been in his mother's greenhouse, grown at great effort and expense, or on the Sheirran sister planet of Asdara. That world had all the green Sheira lacked. He'd only been there for a short time during his training.

Training.

For the Sheirran Defense Force.

He remembered that.

His time as a soldier had been so much a part of him he'd never lost it, no matter what the Wirthera had ever done to him. Just as he'd never lost the Wirthera themselves. He could've gone without remembering them forever.

He wasn't training, now. He was in uniform, his hair shorn, his feet weighted with the heavy boots he remembered that had been so hard to get used to after wearing sandals for his entire life. He was alone, though, not paired with his training partner who'd never leave his side until one of them got promoted or died.

He'd been promoted, he remembered that. But only after his partner, Leora, had been killed during one of their initial missions. A Wirtheran hornet had launched a laser missile, catching a stupidly vulnerable section of the scouting craft they'd been in.

Leora. She was not a dream, even if this was, and he'd forgotten her until just now. He looked around, expecting to see her—after all, the dead did come back in dreams, didn't they? But there was still nobody. Just him and the field of green and red and blue and yellow. And the blue sky. Brown earth. But she had been real. He knew it and clung to that memory even though it tried to slip away and become fantasy.

Here, at least, he didn't suffer the constant stream of scrolling data in the corners of his vision or the pain that went along with trying to constantly suppress it. The relief of it set him to laughing. Then running. Leaping. Turning handsprings, backflips, athletic feats he'd have been hard-pressed to manage in the waking world even with all his enhancements.

If he tried hard enough, he thought, maybe he could even fly.

A soft breeze tossed the flowers. He drew in their scent, heady and rich and unlike anything he'd ever known. He wanted to throw himself down into them and roll around, and with that thought he was in the thick of them, the sweet stink all over him. Then, as is the way of dreams, he heard his name being called.

Rather, he heard a voice calling and he knew it was calling for him, but the name was muffled as though whomever it belonged to had covered her mouth with a scarf or filled it with stones. He strained to listen for it.

Far in the distance was a woman. Her long hair blew in the breeze and covered her face. He couldn't see the color of it, or of her dress. Not a dress. Robes, long robes. She didn't move toward him, and he couldn't move toward her, but she kept getting closer. She stopped an arm's length away. He should've been able to see the curve of her features but all he could make out was the faint shadow of eyes and mouth. Her murmuring rose above the wind, but the words remained unclear.

"Who are you?"

She didn't answer.

Everything began to turn dark. The sky. The ground. The soft breeze grew no fiercer, but the sound of it became something else— the chittering, terrifying sound of the Wirthera.

He ran, but there was no escaping it. The sound was everywhere. The air grew thick as syrup, and he fought against it though his fists punched nothing but empty space. He went to his knees, crouching, his hands over his ears. Still the furious chattering stabbed at his ears. He couldn't see them, but that didn't mean they weren't there.

He fell to the ground in the softness of the flowers, though now instead of bright colors they'd all gone black and gray. Their tendrils bound him, holding him tighter the harder he struggled. The woman came closer. Her soft murmuring, still incomprehensible, nevertheless blocked out the relentless, grating sound of Wirtheran voices.

Calming, he looked up at her. "Do you know me?" The gripping vines released him so that he could get up, but no matter how many steps he took toward her, he could get no closer. "Do you know who I am? What is my name? What's my name?"

He woke with the question shouting from his mouth, so loud he thought at first someone else had asked it. Breathing hard, he collapsed back onto the bed, the delicious scent of the flowers fading fast. But something had remained, captured from the dream and imported into that cursed fucking scrolling data stream.

The woman.

18

t's ridiculous." Teila gripped her handheld communicator hard enough to turn her knuckles white before forcing herself to relax. "We can't keep this up. It's not right!"

"Would it be better to tell him and risk triggering him into going over? Do you want to be responsible for that, when he goes mad and slaughters all of you?" The Rav Aluf was far less intimidating in the small screen than the large.

Teila shook her head. "He won't. I know he won't."

"Let me tell you a story, Teila—"

"About Lorset Deen? I've heard it," she interrupted coldly. "Every schoolchild has. He was the soldier who came home from the war, suffering what seemed to be the mildest of injuries, after being rescued from one of the Wirtheran prison ships. How he returned to what seemed a normal life, only to go suddenly crazy and kill everyone in his housing complex before infiltrating capital headquarters. He was caught trying to access high security information before being shot down by the SDF. I've heard it."

"That story was propaganda. It wasn't true. Lorset Deen was never held by the Wirthera. He suffered from a non-related mental break due to his addiction to opiates. He never made it past the capital's front steps, and he didn't kill anyone."

Teila's jaw dropped. "What?"

The Rav Aluf didn't crack a grin. "His family was paid very nicely for the scandal. None of them have suffered any hardship."

"Except that their son, husband, brother and father is known throughout history as the first soldier to go over for the Wirthera!" She grimaced, sour bile rising in her throat at the thought of Kason upstairs, fighting demons only he could see.

"Deen's story wasn't true, but that doesn't mean it doesn't happen. It does. The ones who come back are . . . damaged. Several cycles ago we had an internal attack at the capital much like the one in that story. The soldier, a former Rav Gadol, managed to get close enough to the Melek to get her hands around his throat. She could've killed him. Sent the entire government into confusion."

Teila didn't believe the government could be so fragile. "But she was stopped."

"Of course she was. You think we'd let anyone kill our world leader?" The Rav Aluf snorted.

"You let her get close enough to throttle him," she pointed out.

"He was fucking her," the Rav Aluf said flatly. "He has a thing for the ones who come back."

Teila's lip curled. "As if it's not bad enough for them to be captured and held in prison ships, they have to put up with that sort of harassment after being rescued?"

"We don't get our men and women back from the prison ships."

The Rav Aluf rubbed at his temples in an eerie echo of his son's habit.

Teila propped the handheld on her desk so she could sit to talk to him. "I don't understand."

"As far as we know, there are no Wirtheran prison ships. The only crafts we ever see from them are the hornets, their scouting crafts. Anyone who's ever seen a true Wirtheran warcruiser—if they even exist, we have no idea—has never been able to talk about it. And the only soldiers who ever come back to us are never rescued. They're returned."

Sickness twisted her guts. "What are you saying? The SDF doesn't save our soldiers?"

She thought he might be angry at her tone, but the Rav Aluf only looked grim. "Do you think we wouldn't, if we could?"

"Why can't you?"

"We fight a battle against an enemy we never see until they're defeating us. The Wirthera remain hidden, always, except for their hornets. The best our troops can do is destroy the hornets before they can relay any information and alert the Wirthera about our presence." The Rav Aluf sipped quietly from a mug of something steaming. He wasn't in uniform, Teila realized uneasily. It was the first she'd ever seen him in civilian clothes.

"But . . . if they capture our ships and troops, how is it that nobody's seen them? Nobody escapes? Not ever?"

"Never."

This stunned her into silence for a moment. "But . . . the viddy reports. The lists of our wounded and rescued, the stats about the numbers of Wirtheran warcruisers destroyed, the battles won . . ."

"Fabricated. We win nothing except the defense of our borders from their hornets. They take our ships and our troops, and the only ones we get back are the ones they give us. My son was found in an escape pod, naked and completely shaved, evidence of their experiments all over him. He was alone. The rest of his crew, his ship, disappeared. No trace. They sent him back."

"But . . . why? Why don't you go after them? Why don't you look for any of them?" She could tell his answer before he gave it, but it sat no better with her than if she'd been unable to guess.

"We suffer the loss of a few," he said, "for the good of the many."

"You're lying to all of us," she whispered. "Having us believe the Wirthera are our enemies!"

"They are the enemy."

"How do you know that?" Teila cried. "When you've never even seen them? All you hear are stories of other places they've conquered and destroyed—"

"From within. The way they try to do with us, by sending our people back to us, ready to break. They seek to destroy us from the inside out!" The Rav Aluf's shout sent a squeal of static and feedback through her handheld's tiny speaker. "That's how they do it, Teila! Believe me when I tell you, they've done it in other places. Entire planets wiped out in battle amongst themselves, their people triggered into homicide and rage! Even in Sheira's history, we had in-fighting among our own people. But united against an enemy, we stand together."

"Everything you've ever told us has been a lie," she said. "And you sent your own son into that knowing it."

"We've been keeping Sheira safe for the past decacycle, girl. Don't you tell me we haven't kept the Wirthera from breaking our borders."

She put her finger on the button to disconnect the call. "It sounds to me like they just haven't decided they want us bad enough yet. And what will happen when they do?"

She didn't wait for his answer. The screen of her handheld went blank. A moment later it vibrated angrily, but she ignored the call from her father-in-law and went instead to gather her son in her arms and cradle him close.

Stephin suffered the embrace for just a little while before struggling to get down. He was more interested in playing with his toy boats and whales than letting his mother cuddle him. She watched him play for a while, wondering what she would do if she ever had to watch him become a soldier the way his father had.

Leaving him under his amira's sleepy care, Teila checked the lamp room for the coming night. Downstairs, she made sure everyone had what they needed. Adarey and Stimlin were, as always, self-sufficient. Pera and Rehker were mysteriously absent, though when Teila passed Pera's room she thought she heard the faint sound of murmuring voices from within. She didn't knock.

"Venga," she said, surprised when she found him in the parlor. He usually preferred to sate himself on viddy programming, not read. "Are you all right?"

He wasn't overdressed today, and his gaze was clearer than she could remember seeing it in all the cycles he'd been here. "I had a wife, once. And a daughter. A son. Did you know?"

"No." Teila took a seat across from him. "But I'm glad you do."

"I have grandchildren."

She smiled. "How lovely for you, Venga. Would you like to contact them?"

He shook his head. In front of him was his ancient handheld, a unit so old she was surprised it still connected to the transmissionate. "I looked them up. My children. I saw pictures. That might have to be enough."

"It doesn't have to be. You know you're not tied here." Teila moved a little closer to him to cover his hand with hers. "If you like, I can help you get in touch with them . . ."

"No. I'm a stranger to them. I'm a stranger to myself." His expression was bleak, but in that moment she saw what a handsome man he'd once been.

She squeezed his fingers. "You are not a stranger to me."

"You remind me of my daughter. She had hair like yours. Long and dark. And she laughed a lot, like you do." Venga's smile was tentative. "You've been kind to me, Teila. Thank you."

His gratitude moved her and made her uncomfortable, too. She hadn't opened her home to these people out of the kindness of her heart. She was paid to take care of them.

"I know it's your job," he said before she could answer. "But you don't have to do it with as much concern and caring. I'll guess there are many who, in your place, would be less than kind."

"Is there something I can get for you, Venga? Do you need anything?"

He shook his head again. "I think I might lie down in my room for a bit. All of these memories . . . they were gone for a long time, weren't they?"

"Yes," she told him gently. "A long time."

"Some I wish I still forgot."

She didn't ask him which they were; she could guess there were many painful reminders. She gave his hand one more squeeze and got up from the table, but caught a glance of what he'd been looking at on his handheld. It was a government news page. Many of the interactive features wouldn't work with Venga's old unit, but Teila had seen the page before.

"Venga . . ." She had to ask him. Had to know. In all the time he'd been here, he'd never shown any interest in the gov pages, only viddy entertainments. "Why were you looking at this? Is it what helped you remember, or did you look at it after you started?"

"The handheld was on my bedside table when I woke up today. Set to that page. Looking at it, I started to remember."

"But why did you look at it today?"

He shrugged. "I don't know, Teila. Maybe it was just . . . time."

She nodded, still curious but willing to let it go. He said something else as she was leaving that stopped her. "What?"

"I said," Venga told her, "that I do know one thing that isn't a memory. Not something I remember, just something I know now."

"What's that?" She thought he would tell her about his grandchildren again, or perhaps more about his daughter.

But Venga gave her a narrow-eyed look cold enough to send a frisson down her spine. "They've been lying to us for a long, long time."

Chilled, Teila didn't know what to say. Outside, she found Vikus and Billis to help her with the cleanup outside. The storm had done some minor damage to the lighthouse outbuildings, but it had almost ruined the boathouse and left behind a lot of debris on the shore.

"There might be something we can use," she told the grumbling Vikus. "Remember the time we found all that scrap metal and sold it? That bought you a trip to Salvea, Vikus. I don't remember you complaining about that."

"Only when he came home," Billis told her.

Vikus frowned. "I should've stayed in Salvea. More people there."

"We'd miss you here," Teila said mildly. "But you know if you want to go, Vikus . . ."

Billis grinned and punched his brother on the shoulder. "I'll go with you. We can get jobs in the viddy shows, Vikus. You can dance and I'll sing."

Considering neither of them had any talent in either area, Teila laughed behind her hand. "Remember me when you're rich."

At this, Vikus put an arm around her shoulders. Seriously, he said, "We could never leave you here alone, Teila. You and Stephin need a man here."

Her brows rose at this—both at the idea that she couldn't manage on her own without a cock and balls, but also at how sweetly serious he was. Vikus and Billis had known her all their lives, though the fact they were likely her brothers had never been discussed even when both their mothers passed on.

"Why would you say that?" There hadn't been a man in charge of the lighthouse for years before Kason's cruiser wrecked, and there hadn't been one in charge since he'd gone, either.

Billis looked embarrassed. "Vikus is right. We can't go away from here."

"You certainly can," Teila told them both sternly. "I've always told you that you could make your own way in the world, if that's what you wanted. Go to school, get training. Go off to Salvea or anywhere else. I never meant for either of you to be stuck here forever, like . . . well, like me."

"I thought you loved the lighthouse!" Vikus looked shocked.

His brother, too. "So did I!"

Teila tipped her head back to look up at the stone lighthouse, rising so high against the backdrop of the pale sky and three bright suns. She did love the lighthouse. She'd lived in it for her entire life. That had never meant that she didn't wonder what it might've been like to live in a city. To pursue an education beyond what she could learn herself through correspondence courses. When she was younger, it had meant imagining finding love . . . but the light-house had brought her that.

"Of course I do. But that doesn't mean you both have to. The lighthouse won't be the same without you. But it doesn't mean you shouldn't go, if you want." She knuckled Vikus' head, though he'd grown so much taller than her it was difficult to reach.

He slowly pulled away from her. Billis had walked ahead just enough to reach the bleached bones of a whale jutting from the ground. They'd been there for several cycles, home to the nests of seabirds. Just beyond it the shore took a meandering curve farther out. Much of the debris tended to collect there after the storms.

"You go on," Teila told him. "See what you find. I'm going to start making a list of repairs we'll need to handle."

Walking in the opposite direction, she put her face into the wind and let it whip her hair around her face. It felt good. Cooling under the suns' relentless glare. In a few hours at sunsdown the wind would bite, but now it caressed her. So intent on looking over the damaged buildings, Teila didn't pay attention to anything else until she rounded the base of the lighthouse and found Kason.

Wearing only a pair of loose trousers low on his hips, he stood at the edge of the sea, facing out. He worked through a familiar set of motions, sweeping gestures with his arms and legs. How many times had she seen him do this, usually in the early morn-ings before the heat of the day? Every day that she'd known him.

He was bigger than he'd been before, but too thin. The knobs of his spine jutted like the whale bones out of the ground. His hipbones looked sharp enough to cut. She watched the play of his muscles beneath his tawny skin and thought about what his father had said.

Not rescued. Returned. The Wirthera gave up the ones who

came back, but riddled them with nanotriggers before they did. It didn't seem like the most effective method of infiltration to her, but what did she know? She wasn't military.

If he knew she watched him, he didn't acknowledge her. She tapped notes into her handheld, taking stock of the worn paint and splintered bits of wood in places the wind had gouged on the lighthouse. The stone base would weather storms far worse than any she'd ever seen, but she checked them too for cracks or missing mortar. When she'd finished, she looked up to see him standing with his feet together, palms pressed against each other at chest level.

This was the man she'd loved. Borne a child with, who he'd never had the fortune to know. She'd have done anything for him before and would do anything for him now to keep him safe. Sane.

She thought of Venga, a man she'd have sworn would never return to his right mind, yet this morning he'd been clear as glass. And from what? An unexpected prompt. Had he opened the page on his handheld and forgotten it, only to see it in the morning and set his own recovery in motion?

Or had someone left it there for him?

The idea disturbed and intrigued her. Who would've done that, and had it been on purpose?

The Rav Aluf and the SDF and the Melek himself had lied to them all for years. What if they were wrong about the soldiers who'd been returned and the nanotriggers they all carried inside them? What if they didn't need to remember all on their own, without any help?

What if she could prompt Kason to come back to her?

19

"You must be feeling better," Teila said to him.

"I couldn't stay inside any more. The others just sit around doing nothing."

She laughed ruefully. "They do, indeed. I guess they feel entitled to a little rest."

He didn't feel entitled. He felt restless and bored. He felt weak. The exercises he'd been doing had come from the data stream, the first good use of it he'd been able to make. He hadn't had any more luck in muting it or controlling the flow, but he'd been able to pull something out of it that made sense, and that was quite an accomplishment.

"They'd probably feel better if they worked on something other than their bad moods. You should make them help you out here." He eyed her handheld upon which she'd been typing. "I'm sure you have a list of chores that need taken care of. Even old Venga could help around here."

She shrugged and tucked the handheld into the pocket of her robe. "It's not Venga's job, or any of theirs, to help here. They're here to rest and recover however they choose."

He squinted to try and read her expression. Her tone held no hint of condescension or contempt. "Has there been a lot of damage from the storm?"

"No. The lighthouse was built to withstand even the worst storms. The boathouse will need a new set of doors and nearly all of the windows will have to be replaced. The rest can be repaired, but I can't fix or replace the scudder."

"What happened to it?" Without thinking about it, he'd started following her around the curve of the lighthouse and along the shore toward the boathouse.

Teila tugged at the double doors, both of which had splintered and sagged. When she couldn't get one open enough to get inside, he reached around her to grab it. He might feel weak and out of shape, but he still had the strength to pull the entire door off its broken hinges. In fact, he pulled it so hard with so little resistance that the door flew backwards and broke into several pieces on the hard earth behind them.

Teila stared at him, mouth parted, brows raised.

"Sorry," he said gruffly. "It wasn't as stuck as I'd expected."

Inside the shadows of the boathouse, away from the glare of the suns, it was so much cooler that he drew in a grateful breath. Teila showed him the small scudder, victim to a fallen roof beam. The whole boathouse, as a matter of fact, looked ramshackle and ready to fall over at any minute.

He ran a hand over the punctured hull. "This wouldn't take much to fix, not with the right tools and materials."

At first she didn't answer, but when she did, she put herself directly in front of him. "You could fix this boat."

He knew he could, but the fact that she seemed to know he could caught his attention. He'd been angry with her before. Furious to the point of violence. But something about the dream he'd had had calmed him. He tilted his head, studying her now.

"I think I could."

She smiled slightly. "You could. There are tools in the shed. We could order the other supplies for delivery on the next boat. If you want to make yourself useful . . . keep yourself occupied . . ."

"It would be better than sitting around playing cards," he told her.

"Come on then," she said. "I'll show you where they are."

20

The shed had survived the storm a little better than the boat-house with only minor cosmetic damage. Some of the tools had fallen from their pegs from the wind that had broken one of the windows, and a fine layer of seadust had settled over everything, but that was the worst of it. Teila turned to look at Kason, who'd followed her inside. This had been his place. His tools. Would he remember?

"Nice setup," was all he said. "This should have everything I need. I can get you a list of materials for the boat repairs once I've checked it out." He turned and caught her staring. "I'll pay for them, of course. I'm sure my pension will cover it. At least . . . I think it will."

"You have plenty of money," she assured him. "But you don't have to pay for the boat. It's mine. I'll order the supplies. I'll pay you for your labor, too."

"You won't."

She tucked the inside of her cheek against her teeth to keep herself from smiling. "Of course I will. I'd have to pay someone else, and there'd be no guarantee the work would be any good. Plus, I'd have to wait forever for anyone to get here, and I'm sure they'd expect room and board while they stayed. I could buy a new scudder for a fraction of the cost of repairing it, if I had to bring someone in. You're already here. And I know you can do the work to my standards."

He eyed her. "Do you?"

"Yes," Teila told him, her gaze locked on him. "I do."

Tension spun between them, thin as a glass filament and as fragile. She waited for his anger and wouldn't have blamed him for it. His eyes narrowed for a moment, but the corner of his mouth twitched upward.

"You know more than I do, then. I'm not sure I know what half of these do." He gestured at the tools.

She looked them over, remembering the times she'd come in search of him for the evening meal and found him in this very place, using those same tools. He'd made her many lovely things, though he'd never worked on another pleasure cruiser.

"You'll figure it out," she told him. "I have faith."

He caught her sleeve when she turned to go. "I had a dream last night."

She waited for him to go on, and when he didn't right away, she said, "I'm sure you had more than one."

"It seemed like more than a dream."

"Ah." She moved a little closer, though not so close as to make this awkward even though she couldn't stop herself from remembering what it was like for him to pull her into his arms.

"Not like the other sort," he said in a low voice. "The ones from the Wirthera. It wasn't like those, either."

"I'm glad."

Kason looked at her. "I think you were in it."

This surprised and pleased her so much she couldn't hide it in her expression. "What was I doing?"

"I think you were trying to help me."

"I would like to help you," she said, swallowing around the lump of emotion she didn't dare let overtake her.

He studied her. "You help everyone here, Teila. Don't you?"

She thought of Venga, who'd been in her care for so long but had never improved from anything she'd ever done. "I try."

Kason went to the bench and lifted several of the tools, blowing off the dust. He turned in a slow circle to look all around the shed before focusing on her again. "Is there a reason why you can't tell me what you know about me?"

"Yes," she said hesitantly.

He nodded. "It's because of the Wirthera? Something they did to me?"

Rules. Guidelines. The training she'd undergone before they would allow her to take on even one soldier. All of it shuttered her mouth. It was hard to throw it all away, even knowing about the lies. Even believing there was a way to help him.

She took a deep breath. "Yes."

He looked thoughtful. "You think it would be dangerous to tell me."

"Yes," Teila said.

"But you did it."

She nodded. "Yes. I did."

"Because you want to help me."

She smiled. "Yes. Because I want to help you."

"Why do you want to help me, Teila?"

That question was far more dangerous to answer, but as he stared into her eyes, she thought that maybe he'd begun to know.

21

It was disheartening to realize he still had physical limitations. He'd spent much of the day cleaning the shed, wiping each tool and inspecting it for damage and also to familiarize himself with them. They felt right in his hands, more right than anything else he could remember.

He discovered something else as he returned each tool to its place and tested a few on some pieces of scrap wood from the pile in the corner. When he focused on the tools and their functions, the data stream faded. It didn't disappear. He thought it probably never would. But when he worked with the tools, he found he could ignore it, at least for a little while.

He found Billis in the yard with Vikus nearby. "Hey. I need your help with the scudder."

Billis nodded, but Vikus gave him a narrow-eyed look. "What are you going to do with it?"

"It got damaged in the storm. I told Teila I'd try to fix it."

"That makes sense—" Billis began, but Vikus elbowed him hard enough to make him double over.

"Shut up," Vikus told him. To Jodah, he said, "You better make sure it's safe for her."

Jodah frowned. "Of course I would. Why would you think I'd do anything else?"

Billis looked shame-faced. Vikus didn't. Squaring his shoulders, he moved closer to Jodah. "She goes out it in alone, you know. So you'd better make sure it's fixed right, that's all."

"I will." The younger man's belligerence might've made him angry, except that he so clearly acted out of concern for Teila. Jodah clapped him on the shoulder. "Trust me."

"I don't." Vikus shook his head and backed away. "But she does."

The three of them were easily able to pull the damaged scudder from the boathouse and carry it to the shed, where they put it up on the wooden frame Jodah had built. The younger men left him there to pursue their own tasks, and Jodah got to work.

When he began, he wasn't sure if he remembered what to do from previous experiences or if somehow the progression of tasks just seemed natural. He decided that it didn't matter. As he moved from step to step in the project, all his tensions began to fade. He worked as the suns moved across the sky, so absorbed in his work he didn't even stop to eat.

"That's Mao's boat." The small voice piped up from just outside the doorway.

Jodah looked up to see Teila's son peeking in at him. He paused to make sure the whirring saw he'd been using to trim away the damaged wood was well out of the way. "Yes. I'm fixing it for her. Want to come in and help me?"

The boy looked solemn. "Amira Densi says I'm not to bother you."

"It's no bother. My father never let me—" Jodah stopped, flickers of memory rising to his mind's surface like the shadow of a reflection in a mug of caffah. "He never let me help him with anything. He always said I'd get in the way."

The boy sidled his way into the shed, but didn't come any closer. Jodah didn't try to make him, either, but he did keep an eye on him as he finished removing the damaged wood and tossed it into the pile of scraps. This left a fist-sized hole in the bottom of the scudder. Carefully, Jodah put the saw away and gestured to the boy.

"Come here, Stephin. Look at this."

Reluctantly, the boy came closer, though he looked ready to run at any minute. Jodah held out his hand, fingers curling. Stephin didn't take it, but he did move within grabbing distance. It was a start.

"You see the hole here?"

The boy nodded. "It will make the boat sink if the sand gets in."

"Yes. So we have to fix it. See how I cut away all the ragged pieces?" Step by step, Jodah walked Stephin through the repair. Smoothing the edges of the hole, cutting a new piece of wood big enough to repair it, affixing the patch.

They hadn't gotten further than picking out a piece of scrap wood big enough to make the patch when the shed door opened and Teila came in. "Stephin! By the Three, you scared the life out of us! Amira Densi has been looking everywhere for you. You know better than to just go away without telling anyone."

"She was sleeping," the boy said. "I couldn't wake her up."

Teila shook him a little by the shoulder. Not hard or rough, but firm. Then she gathered him into her arms for a hug, which he protested, as she looked over his shoulder at Jodah.

"I'm sorry if he was bothering you."

"He was no bother. Really. He was a great help. He can come help me anytime."

The way to a man's heart was well known to be between his legs, but the way to a woman's could very well be through her child, he thought. At this thought, that he wanted a way to her heart, the data stream became clear and blinding again. Wincing, Jodah put his hand to his temples to press away the pain.

"Stephin, go inside and find Amira Densi and tell her you're sorry for scaring her." When the boy made a small protest, Teila gave him a serious look. "Go. Now."

When he'd gone, she turned to Jodah. "It's not good for him to go off without telling anyone."

"The boy's old enough to be allowed some freedom."

It was the wrong thing to say, he saw that at once. Her eyes narrowed and her mouth went grim. He might not remember much about his life, but he instinctively knew when he'd pissed off a woman.

"You think so? You think he should be allowed to wander around by himself? He's four years old. You think he should be allowed to go where he pleases? Maybe you think he ought to make himself at home in the sea, ride the back of a whale? That would be a fitting occupation for a four-year-old, would it?"

"If you never give him any freedom, how can you ever expect him to learn any caution?" Jodah set the tools to the side of the workbench and dusted his hands on the seat of his robes.

"I realize," she said in a voice as chilly as the sunless night, "that you think you're being helpful, but you're not."

He didn't need another hint. Jodah held up his hands, conciliatory. "You're right. I'm sorry. He's not my son, I shouldn't interfere."

Teila made a startled sound as he turned to face her. "It's just that he hasn't had . . . there hasn't been . . . anyone. To be a father to him."

The pride in her expression moved him. They stared at each other across the small space, a heat that had little to do with the suns overhead rising between them. He understood a lot about her now, or at least he thought he did.

"Nobody for you, either."

Her eyelids fluttered a few times before she ducked her head. Then she covered her eyes with her hand. Her shoulders heaved.

He'd made her cry.

The fucking they'd done hadn't been about seduction. He'd taken her—though not by force, at least there was that. He wouldn't have been able to live with himself if he knew he'd done that. But it had been under false pretenses on his part. He'd wondered at her motivation for allowing him the use of her body. Now he understood.

"Come here," he told her.

Teila looked up at him with wet eyes and parted lips. At first she didn't move, but then slowly, one foot in front of the other, she went to him. He pushed the weight of her hair off her shoulders so it fell down her back. Then, unable to help himself, he gathered it in his hands and pulled her close to him.

She smelled so good. He breathed her in again and again. Again. He pressed his face to the fall of her hair, his hands roaming over her back. She was so small, yet not delicate.

"You're strong," he whispered into her ear. "Do you know how strong you are?"

Her arms went around him. "I don't feel strong."

"You are." He rubbed her back in slow circles, feeling the knobs of her bones through her robes. Lower, over her hips and then to her rear, which he cupped to pull her against him.

It should've made sense. He'd been without real human contact for a long time. Without a real woman's touch. It should've been nothing but natural for him to want her . . . except that it was just her and only her who affected him this way. Pera's overtures had left him cold.

He needed her mouth. Her tongue. He needed to taste and feel her, to be inside her. When his fingers threaded through her hair, she moaned and pressed against him. Her breasts, so full, beckoned for his kisses, and he pulled open the laces of her robes to get at them.

The skin there was paler, more golden than the rest of her skin. Her nipples, the color of sweet wine and as delicious. He suckled them, groaning as her sweetness exploded on his tongue.

His cock was aching, rock hard. He lifted her so she could wrap her legs around his waist, her robes falling open so he could still get at the sensitive flesh beneath. She shook her head, murmuring what sounded like a protest but became a plea when he rubbed his erection between her legs.

He walked her to the workbench and settled her ass on it. Kissing her mouth, he worked a hand between her thighs to find her clit. She was wet already, her cunt slick and hot. He slipped his fingers inside, relishing the way she shuddered as he curled them upward. His thumb pressed her clit. His other hand captured the back of her neck, holding her to his mouth even as she squirmed.

He wanted her to beg him to take her.

He first spread her legs, then her labia, and found the pearl of her clit with his tongue. The workbench creaked as Teila arched under his mouth. Her fingers dug into his hair, pulling hard enough to sting. His hands lifted her ass, holding her still as he worked between her legs.

She cried out when she came, bucking against his lips. Her taste flooded him, sending shocks of pleasure straight to his cock. He looked up and found her glassy-eyed, mouth moist from the swipe of her tongue over her lips. Her hair had tumbled over her shoulders and forehead.

She drew in a breath and made as though to speak, but he didn't give her the chance. His mouth was on hers, silencing everything but her moan. He shifted her to the edge of the workbench. His cock nudged her entrance, but he didn't push inside. He pressed his thumb to her clit, moving it in infinitesimal circles, feeling the pulse of her orgasm still beating there.

His eyes met hers. She licked her mouth again, and though he desperately wanted to kiss her, he held off. His thumb moved, slow. Slow. His cockhead pressed her.

The suns had set. The automatic solar lights in the shed had come on, bathing her in golden light. The heater hadn't come on, however. Teila shivered. When he put his fingers to his mouth to taste her, never letting his gaze leave hers, she gave a low cry, her body jerking.

Jodah kept the circling pressure steady on her clit. It swelled under his attentions, her flesh slippery and swollen. He eased the head of his cock the tiniest bit inside her, the feeling of her wetness on him making it nearly impossible for him not to slam inside her—but he managed. The cold air had begun making him shiver too, though the heat between them rose so fiercely he barely noticed the chill.

"I want to know you want me," he told her.

"I want you," she said at once, her longing clear in her voice. "So much."

He shook his head. Slow, slow circles. A little deeper inside her. "I want to make sure it's me you want."

Teila blinked and wet her mouth again. She linked her hands

behind his neck and put her forehead to his. Her voice was hoarse. Raw. "I want you . . . Jodah. You."

With a low groan, he seated himself all the way inside her. She gasped, her fingernails digging into his shoulders. Her teeth sank into his neck. Her cunt clenched around him.

He pumped into her slowly, then faster as the pleasure built. Kissing her, he breathed in. She breathed out. Everything about her felt so good, better than any dream ever had. Better than anything he could remember.

Jodah spent himself inside her, her name on his mouth when he came. Blinking, he focused on her face. She smiled at him.

And all at once, he was overtaken by darkness.

22

The random string of words made no sense, but Kason spoke them as though they did. His gaze had gone shuttered, blank, his hands still on her. He was still inside her.

"Jodah?"

He withdrew so fast Teila almost fell off the workbench. He backed up, shoulders rigid. Face without expression. He muttered rapidly.

Not another language, she thought, pulling her robes closed and getting off the workbench to go to him. She said his name again quietly. Then louder. When he didn't respond, she stood on her toes to cup his face in her hands.

So fast she didn't even have time to blink, he'd grabbed her wrists and twisted her away from him. It hurt, but mostly she was surprised. She didn't struggle, even when his grip ground the bones of her wrists together.

"Jodah, it's me. Teila. You're in the lighthouse," she told him as calmly as she could. "You're safe here. You're fine."

He was breathing hard, his skin clammy. The heaters in the shed that would keep it at a comfortable temperature had not come on, and now the chill had become suddenly noticeable. Her teeth chattering, Teila let herself go still in his arms.

"Are you remembering something?" she asked him and sent a silent plea to the Three Mothers that he'd answer her.

He did, to her relief, though his reply wasn't comforting. "Data stream. It won't stop. More and more and more and more . . ."

His voice trailed off, but then he shook himself. He let her go. His gaze focused on her. He grimaced when he saw her rubbing at her wrists.

"Teila. I'm so sorry. Did I hurt you?"

"No. I'm fine." He had, a little, but there was no point in telling him so.

He'd put distance between them, and she wasn't sure if she should close it. She concentrated on lacing up her robes and smoothing her hair, making herself presentable as though nothing strange had happened. She watched him from the corner of her eye as he got dressed.

"You're doing a wonderful job on the scudder," she said. "Thank you."

His expression cleared, and he went to the scudder, touching it with almost reverent hands. He looked at her. "I'm not sure exactly how I know what to do with it. It just seems right, though."

He took her by surprise when he pulled her close again. Tentatively, as though she might pull away. He cleared his throat, his voice low. Such a change from the man who'd owned her body so thoroughly such a short time ago.

"This feels right too," he told her. "Maybe it shouldn't, but it does."

She couldn't stop herself from stretching onto her toes to kiss him then. "Take each day as it comes, Jodah."

His arms tightened around her. "You know when you say it, the name almost feels like it's mine."

Teila wasn't sure what to say to that—it wasn't his name and if he got comfortable with it, would that prevent him from remembering his real name? It was all so complicated. She frowned.

"I'm sorry," he said. "I shouldn't."

Teila shook her head, forcing a smile past her frustration. "No. You can. I'm glad I can help you."

His gaze grew serious. "You are helping me, Teila. So much."

23

My father told me I was a fool," Kason had told her. "He was right."

Both of them had stared out at the sea, calm after the storm. There were no signs of the pleasure cruiser, not even any bits or pieces of it tossed up onto the shore. The sand had swallowed it whole and might spit it out tomorrow or in a full cycle from now, or a hundred cycles from now. Or it might keep all of it forever.

She hadn't known what comfort to offer him, not then. He'd seemed a mighty fool to her indeed, to have gone out onto the sea alone without making sure every part of his craft was in top working order. It would be the only time she'd agree with his father, but she didn't know that then. All she'd known was that the storm had wrecked his cruiser and that she'd had to rescue him, and that he'd eaten all of the milka pudding for breakfast, leaving none behind.

"I'm sorry about your ship," she'd said.

That's when he'd given her the widest, most shining grin she'd ever seen. "It's okay. There will always be another ship, but how often do I get to enjoy the company of the most beautiful woman under the three suns?"

Another woman might've melted at that, especially one who'd been so little courted. But though Teila had never been in love, she *had* grown up around her father's crew, all of them to a one masters of flirtation. She'd raised a brow at him.

"Does that line usually work for you?"

He'd had the grace to look a little ashamed. "Yes. Usually."

Teila had laughed at his honesty. He had a good face. Strong body. He came from money. If the pleasure cruiser hadn't proved that, she'd have been able to tell that right away from his clothes, as filthy and wretched as they'd been after the sea had had its way with him.

"Are you hurt at all?" The night before she'd shown him to one of the small rooms on a lower floor, far away from her quarters. In the bright sunlight, she could see scrapes and bruises all over him, but that was to be expected.

"Mostly my pride."

"Better that than your bones," she'd told him.

That was when he'd given her his hand. "I'm Kason."

"Teila." Their fingers had touched, then linked briefly before she'd pulled away. "Do you want to contact your family? Let them know you're all right?"

Kason had tipped his face to the suns, squinting, before looking back at her. Another grin, this time one that warmed her so thoroughly it might as well have been made of flames. "Nope."

"They'll wonder where you are."

"Yes," he'd said. "But then they'll want me to come home."

She hadn't meant to smile at that—he was clearly working hard on being charming. "And you don't want to go home?"

"Nope," Kason had said. "Not yet."

24

The nights were hard. He could turn on the lights, and the lighthouse was never cold, but the night was never the same as the daytime. During the night it was impossible not to dream.

Part of him welcomed the dreams, since they seemed to lead him closer and closer to his memories. He was more and more convinced the female figure who led him toward his recollections and kept him safe from the grasping claws of the Wirthera was meant to be Teila, even if he'd never seen his guardian's face.

She'd become so much to him. Her smile. Her laugh. The way she made sure everyone here was taken care of, even when he could see sometimes that the burden weighed on her.

She was a true woman of valor and he . . . he paced, pushing the thoughts away.

Sheira had three suns but no moons. At night the stars pierced the black sky but cast very little light to the ground. He could look out his windows to the Sea of Sand, but it had become shadows.

The dark and cold beckoned to him, but not like a lover. Like an addiction. He wanted to lose himself out there beyond the safety of the lighthouse, to run and jump and fight and destroy. The worst part of that was that he had no idea if that was how he'd always been—a man of violence—or if something the Wirthera had done to him had infected him with the need to feel fury.

Teila would soothe him, but she'd be sleeping now. He couldn't wake her. She'd get up to check the lamp the way she always did, and maybe he could see her then. But if he saw her, he'd want to touch her, and if he touched her he'd want to kiss her. If he kissed her, he'd want to make love to her. He wanted to lose himself in her body, and that need was almost as strong as his desire to attack the night.

When it got too strong, when his fists began their ceaseless opening and closing and his breath went tight in his throat around the urge to scream, Jodah gave in to the urge to flee the comforts of the lighthouse. Pulling on a thick overrobe with a hood, he ducked out of his room and into the hall beyond. A shadow moved in the lamp room. His heart thudded.

"Teila—" But it wasn't her.

Rehker turned when Jodah came into the lamp room. He had nothing in his hands, yet his expression was of a child caught with his fingers in the milka pudding. The man's grin was wide and bright and without guile . . . and utterly suspicious.

"Jodah-kah. What a pleasant surprise."

"You don't have to call me that. I told you that before." Jodah frowned. "What are you doing in here?"

Rehker gestured at the vast expanse of glass. "I like to come up here at night. It's very peaceful. And the view is marvelous. Not all of us are privileged enough to have a great view from our bedrooms."

Ignoring the subtle dig, if that's what it was, Jodah eyed him.

The view from the lamp room would be magnificent during the day, but at night the constant spinning of the light would make it impossible to look for more than a few minutes at a time. "You shouldn't be in here."

"Are you going to throw me out?" Rehker held up his hands, brows lifted. "I didn't realize you'd become the guardian of the lamp as well as the lampkeeper herself."

Jodah drew himself up, wary. "What's that supposed to mean?"

"Nothing." Rehker smirked and tried to sidle past him.

Jodah put out a hand to stop him. The other man tried to keep going, but Jodah was bigger. Stronger.

Rehker winced and backed off, rubbing his breastbone. "By the Three, Jodah-kah, watch yourself. We all know you're the biggest and the strongest. No need to brag on it."

"I'm not . . ." Jodah's fists clenched as he looked at the other man. The bright light swept over them both and left darkness behind. He looked with longing to the night outside.

"You want to go outside." Rehker's gaze followed his, and his smirk grew. "What do you want to do out there? Catch a whale? Grab it by the tail? Ride it to the suns and all around the world?"

Jodah knew at once it was a children's nursery song. The data stream brightened, pulling words from who knew where. Filling in the rest of the rhyme. "Ride along the sea, free as anything could ever be, just make sure to come back to me."

"You got it," Rehker said. "Think on that, Jodah-kah. Think on lots of things."

Jodah shook his head, but the data stream persisted, bright and glowing in the edges of his vision. Forever scrolling. He pressed his temples against the pain he knew was coming.

"I'm going now. I wouldn't want your *beshera* to lose her temper about me being in here. I guess only you get the special privileges."

Beshera . . . beloved. This, along with the second insinuation that somehow Teila gave Jodah special treatment, while true or not, set his jaw. "Do you have an issue with something, Rehker-kah? If you do, you should tell me right out. I've never been one for dancing."

At the honorific, Rehker's smirk twisted into a sneer, but only for a moment before it was replaced by a bland smile. He backed out of the doorway into the hall, and Jodah went after him. He snagged the other man by the back of the shirt as he made to get away.

Rehker turned, hands up again, his face full of guile disguised as innocence. "Back off."

Jodah didn't, but he did let him go. "If you're not going to hold your tongue, then you'd best explain yourself."

"Everyone knows you're fucking Teila and that you have been since you got here."

Jodah's eyes narrowed. "And what business is it of anyone's? Adarey and Stimlin are lovers, and I don't see anyone minding about that. And you and Pera—"

"Pera," Rehker said coldly, "is not the lampkeeper."

"What difference does that make? Do you really think she gives me any better treatment than any of you? And what difference would it make," Jodah said, "if she did? This isn't a prison, or a hotel. So far as I can see, Teila makes sure all of you have what you need and how you need it. Why should it matter to you?"

"Oh, it won't matter to me. But it might make a difference to her husband."

Jodah's mouth opened. Then closed. "Her husband?"

"Yes. The father of her son? Surely you know *him*," Rehker said. "The boy's all over the place. Did you think he was born out of a pile of sand?"

"No. Of course not."

Rehker shook his head. "Far be it from me to judge who she

takes into her bed, but I think you'd at least have the consideration not to make a fool of another man."

"Her husband is . . . gone."

"Gone? Is he dead?" Rehker asked, brows raised.

"I don't know."

"Of course you don't. Because she hasn't told you, has she? There are no pictures of the man about, are there? She must keep some, don't you think? Wouldn't a widow have at least a few holos of her *beshera* to remember him by?"

"Maybe they sundered."

"Or maybe," Rehker said slyly, "he's off fighting against the enemy while his lovely bride stays home and fucks whoever tickles her—"

In a flash, Jodah had his fists in the front of Rehker's robes. He shook the smaller man until his teeth rattled. "You shut your fucking mouth before I shut it for you."

"Isn't that delightful, the wounded warrior going all feral over his lady love—"

Jodah punched him in the mouth. Blood ran from Rehker's split lip and Jodah's knuckles. The pain in his hand was instant and exquisite, and the urge to keep pounding, pounding, punching and hitting and kicking rose inside him like a separate entity. He barely kept himself from hitting the other man again, and only by sheer willpower.

Rehker grinned, blood lining his teeth. He licked his mouth, blood staining his tongue. "Like I said. I don't really care, as far as I'm concerned. I just thought you had more honor, that's all. As one soldier to another, how would you feel if you came home from the war to discover your wife had been spreading herself for someone else?"

Jodah hit him again. This time, Rehker dropped to his knees, both hands over his spurting nose. Blood spattered the soft golden tiles, and even in the hall's dim lighting, it was the crimson of a whale's back. Incredibly, the man laughed.

"What's going on?"

Jodah had been getting ready to kick Rehker, but at the sound of Teila's voice, he stopped. Rehker got to his feet, one hand pinching his nose to stanch the flow. His laughter faded, and he gave Jodah a sly look before turning toward her.

"We were in disagreement over the results of a game of golightly," he said smoothly. "That's all. I came to get my winnings, and Jodah-kah insisted I allow him to pay me the full amount he lost to me, though I didn't want to break him. It was for fun, after all."

Teila didn't look convinced. She crossed her arms over the front of her almost-sheer sleeping robe. Her hair had been pulled to the nape of her neck with a ribbon, but tendrils of it escaped and hung all over her face. She pushed them out of the way in irritation.

"You're being very loud," she said. "And I don't allow fighting in here. If you must beat each other, you'll have to do it outside."

"Do you have a problem with many of your charges beating each other?" Rehker said from around his hand. He gave Jodah another snide look. "I don't seem to remember any of us ever raising a fist to someone else before."

It was meant to shame him, and her look did. His reaction was not to hang his head, but to lift it. He met her gaze squarely.

"Rehker was just leaving."

The other man nodded, all wide-eyed innocence. "Oh, yes. I was."

With that, he pushed past Teila and went to the stairwell. Jodah listened to the sound of his boots on the metal stairs growing fainter before he turned to her. She was still frowning.

"What's going on?" she asked. "Why were you fighting?"

"He was in the lamp room."

Her mouth pursed. "Hmm. Why?"

"I don't know. But he shouldn't be."

"No, he shouldn't." Teila moved past him and into the lamp room, checking the light as it swept in its unending circle. She gave cursory attention to the panel of instruments before turning to him. "Did he say what he was doing here?"

Jodah shrugged. "He had an excuse. Have you had trouble with him before?"

"No." She paused. "We didn't ever have trouble . . . before."

They stared at each other. Without a word, Jodah left the lamp room and headed for the stairs. Behind him, he heard Teila's shout, but he ignored it. He took the spiral stairs two at a time, heading for the bottom floor. She came after him, calling his name.

He was still ignoring her when he burst out of the door downstairs and onto the rocky grass, so cold it stung his bare feet. Shivering at the instant chill, Jodah headed in the direction of the sea. He could hear the constant *shush-shushing* of the moving sands, though he could see nothing in the blackness until the lighthouse swept it with bright white light.

He remembered stepping into the sea. Not this one, maybe. Something smaller. He remembered easing his feet from rocky ground into the soft, shifting sands, shallow at first, then deeper. To his knees. His calves. He remembered wearing a formfitting sandsuit coated in whale oil to keep the sands from abrading him. He did not remember what he'd been doing.

Jodah closed his eyes, breathing in the night air, cold enough to freeze the delicate hairs of his nostrils. He spread his arms and tipped his face to the sky, waiting for memories to rush over him, but nothing else came. Behind him came the soft step of feet on the rocks. He didn't have to turn to know who it was. He could smell her.

"You're going to freeze," Teila said.

"I'm fine. I can't freeze." He had no idea if that were true, but it felt like it must be. He could feel the cold, but after those first few minutes of shivering, his body's internal enhancements had raised his temperature to normal.

"Well, I can," she snapped. Backlit by the light from the lighthouse windows, she looked taller than normal. Her robes fluttered. "Come back inside."

"You go. I need to be out here." Already he was thinking of running along the edge of this sea, which did not lap with shallow edges at the ground beyond, but instead fell off, sharp and deep. He needed to run, to work himself into exhaustion.

"I can't leave you out here alone."

He turned to her. His eyes had adjusted, his pupils ratcheting wider to capture any stray light. He had the advantage over her, for she'd still be blinded by the night.

"I don't need you to hover over me," Jodah told her. "I'm not your responsibility!"

She came after him when he started heading away from the lighthouse. Jodah stopped, though the urge to run was now strong enough to make cold sweat trickle down his spine. He heard the rattling of her teeth and cursed under his breath.

"You're not even wearing the right clothes!" he cried. "You're the one who's going to freeze!"

"Then come back inside with me."

He could've just told her about the need burning inside him, but it felt too similar to the fury that had made him take her so fiercely in those beginning days when he still confused dreams with reality. He knew better now—lots better, more than he wished he knew. Rehker's words about her husband echoed in Jodah's head.

"I can't leave you alone out here," she said again, each word cut into pieces by the chattering of her teeth. "It's dangerous!"

He moved closer to her. "You think I can't take care of myself? Really, Teila? I'm a Mothers-forsaken Rav Gadol in the Sheirran Defense Force. There's more technology in me than flesh. I've been torn apart and rebuilt. Torn apart again. There's nothing out here, not beast or sea, that I can't withstand."

"Please," she murmured. She found his hand with hers in the dark. She tugged him closer. "I'll worry too much about you out here. Come inside."

The words came out of him before he could stop them. "Is that what you used to say to your husband?"

In the silence that came after he spoke, the wind rushed across the sea, stirring the sands. To him they sounded like the whispers of the flowers in his dreams, the real dreams that he'd been having since he came here, and not the ones the Wirthera had given him. He waited, listening.

"Yes," Teila said. "I did."

He wanted her so much it was a little like dying.

"The sea brought him to me," she said. "And I lost him after that."

"To the sea?"

She moved closer to him again, this time so close the heat and scent of her washed over him, making him shiver worse than the night air had. "No. Not to the sea."

"What did you lose him to?"

She was silent. There was something there, something he was missing, if only he could put the key into the lock. It eluded him. Angry, Jodah sighed.

"You're not a widow."

"I've never claimed to be a widow," Teila said. "If you thought I am, that's your assumption. Not my truth."

When she kissed him, he let himself get lost in the taste of her. He let her part his lips with hers, stroke her tongue inside. He let her press herself against him. But when she murmured something that sounded like the name he couldn't claim, he pushed her from him.

"What would your husband think?"

"He doesn't think anything of it," she told him. "He doesn't know."

Jodah persisted, holding her at arm's length while the night wind whipped up around them. Her hair tickled his cheek. In the corners of his vision, the data stream brightened, ticking downward with a list of internal computations as his body adjusted to the temperature. She had to be cold, though he wasn't.

"What I did in the beginning, I take responsibility for that. It was wrong. I used you—"

"I told you before," she put in sharply, "that you didn't force me. Stop blaming yourself for what happened when you were not aware of where you were. If anything, I should be blamed for it, since I fully knew what was going on. If one of us took advantage of the other, it was me."

He would not bend to that, no matter how many times she said so. It would always be his fault. He was bigger. Stronger. "You couldn't have stopped me."

"I didn't want to!" she shouted. Softer, she added, "If you'd forced me, Jodah, if I had any resentment toward you for it, would I be here now? Would I have made love to you again?"

The memory of her slick heat stirred him, but he pushed the thoughts away. "What happened in the beginning was wrong for one reason. What happened after is wrong for another."

She drew in a breath. "You think it's wrong for us to be together."

"Yes," Jodah said. "It's wrong for me to be with another man's wife."

"I am a woman! Not just a wife," she cried. "I was myself long before I ever knew him, and I am myself now."

"You think it's all right to be with me when you're still married to him?"

"My husband was a soldier," she said slowly. "He chose to leave me behind, knowing he might never see me again. He chose that path for the greater good, for what he believed would be his efforts toward protecting not simply Sheira, but me specifically. He chose to leave me because he loved me. He told me more than once . . ." She broke, then, and it broke him to hear it. "He told me he would do anything to make sure I could be happy. So you ask me what my husband would think, if he knew, and I will tell you that he would want me to be happy."

He kissed her until she gasped and writhed in his grip to be set free. He knew his fingers would leave marks, but he couldn't make himself soften. "This," he said, shaking her a little, "this makes you happy?"

When he kissed her this time, she bit his lip. The pain, sharp and instant, was accompanied by the bitter tang of blood. He let her go. Stepped back. Already the blood had stopped. Soon the wound would mend.

"Do I make you happy, Teila?"

She said nothing. The wind whispered and sang as the sea shifted behind them. She was still so close he could grab her again, if he wanted to, but he kept his fists at his sides.

"Sometimes," she said finally. "And sometimes, Jodah, you only make me very, very sad."

25

She'd fallen in love with him that first day. Teila could admit that now, though at the time she'd done her best to deny what she felt for her handsome gift from the sea was anything but lust and possibly affection. But not love, definitely not that. It had taken almost losing him to realize that she couldn't live without him.

They'd become lovers without effort. He'd been bold. She'd been willing—surprising him, she thought, when she took him up without hesitation on his charming offer to take her to bed. And after, surprised him again when she waved away his attempts to cuddle her.

"I've work to do," she'd explained. "I have to check the lamp, for one thing. For another, I don't want to spend the night in this narrow bed when I have my own much nicer one."

Naked, she'd laughed at his snort of affront and left him there. The next day he'd cornered her in the kitchen while she sliced up a milka pellet. She'd allowed him to seduce her, but later had laughed again when he suggested he join her in her "much nicer bed."

"You have your own," she said. "The bed for guests."

"But surely," he'd said, trying again to charm her, "I'm not a guest any more."

She'd put him in his place quickly enough with a raised brow and shake of the head. "Why would you presume that?"

He'd had no answer for that other than his furrowed brow. It had almost made her change her mind, that stubborn look. She'd always had a weakness for arrogant men.

"Make yourself useful," she'd told him after that. "If you're not a guest, then you should work."

And he had. Kason had taken over much of the maintenance work that Vikus and Billis had been struggling with, not because they weren't eager to pull their weight but because as boys they were simply incapable of some of it. Kason, despite his wealthy upbringing, had proven himself more than handy. It had surprised him as much as her resistance to his affections had, she thought, and was glad for his sake that he'd discovered himself to be more than a wealthy man's son.

She hadn't known then, of course, that it was more than that. Kason's father was the Rav Aluf, the man in charge of the entire Sheirran Defense Force, which made him more than simply rich. It meant he was powerful, too.

They'd become a team as effortlessly as they'd become lovers. For nearly a full cycle, Kason had infiltrated her life, learning the ways of the lighthouse and also of her. She'd learned him too. How he liked his caffah, how he looked when he was sleeping, the sound of his laughter. The smell of him. The flavor. And yet still, though she might visit him in his narrow guest bed and they'd done their share of lovemaking in almost every part of the lighthouse that offered space for it, he did not share her bed. They didn't speak of love.

Not until the day his father found him.

Teila had been outside, bringing in her scudder with a good-sized milka pellet dragging behind, when the cruiser appeared in the sky. It had been a long time since she'd seen one, and the noise of it startled her into nearly running the scudder ashore. At first, she'd thought it was the authorities coming to arrest her for illegal milka harvesting—the rules had become so much stricter over the past few cycles, she wouldn't have been surprised to learn she'd inadvertently been breaking a handful of them. It wasn't until she went around the back of the lighthouse and found Kason there with a man who looked so much like him it could only be his father that she noticed the crest on the side of the cruiser.

The Rav Aluf had sneered at the first sight of her. She'd never forget that he'd given her no chance to prove herself to him, that he'd immediately presumed she'd set out to seduce his son. She'd never forgiven him for that, and probably never would.

"Come home, Kason," his father had said. "It's time. You've spent long enough shirking your duties."

Kason hadn't seen her come around the base of the lighthouse, so his answer hadn't been for her benefit. "I'm not coming home. I don't want to join the SDF. I've found something here that I want to keep."

"What's that? A warm bed? Please," his father had said. "You can find a hundred women more suited to you than her."

"You don't even know her."

Another sneer. "I don't have to know her."

"I'm not coming home."

"If you don't come home," his father had said with a long, hard look at Teila, "you will forfeit everything. Do you understand?"

Kason had turned then to look at her. "Yes. I do."

"Will you stay?" she'd asked as though she'd just come around the base of the lighthouse and hadn't heard anything else they'd said. "I'll make something to eat."

"I'll stay only long enough to convince my son to leave with me," the Rav Aluf had told her.

He'd been true to his word, and a terrible houseguest, too. Teila had bitten back every retort that rose to her tongue, determined not to give him the satisfaction of being right about her, but it had been a bitterly won battle. Kason hadn't seemed as bothered by his father's constant sniping. If anything, he'd seemed to enjoy baiting him.

"You let him speak to you like you're a child," Teila had said one night when Kason had tried to make love to her and she'd turned her back on him, too aware of the Rav Aluf's presence.

"It doesn't bother me."

"It bothers me," she'd said. "And you allow him to speak to me like . . . like I'm worthless."

That had made him sit up. "No."

"Yes," Teila had said. "And you say nothing."

"It's just talk. He'll leave soon, when he sees that I'm not going with him."

She'd turned on him fiercely. "And why aren't you? Why would you stay here, so far from anything, working so hard, when you could go home and live a life of luxury?"

His hand on her wrist had kept her from going far. Little by little, he'd pulled her closer, then onto his lap. He'd brushed her hair from her face. "Why do you think, Teila? Tell me why you think I'd rather stay here."

She couldn't bring herself to say it, in case she'd overassumed. The thought of looking like a fool in his eyes was too much to bear, so she shook her head and stayed silent. Kason had kissed her, soft at first. Then harder. His hands roamed, making her sigh. Making her squirm.

"Don't you want me to stay?" he asked her after, when both of them, spent and naked, lounged in his bed. "Teila?"

Pride and fear had bound her tongue. His hand on her bare back had gone still. He sat up to look at her.

"Answer me."

"I need to check the lamp and get some sleep."

He caught her wrist again, this time harder than before. "Check the lamp, but come back to me. I want you to sleep here."

"No. Your father—"

"It's not his business." Kason's voice had gone hard as lightning-seared sand and just as brittle. "Say you'll come back here."

She hadn't been able to make herself form the words. Silence had filled the darkness between them, colder than the air outside. When she left him, he didn't try to stop her.

The next morning, the roar of the cruiser's thrusters had woken her from restless dreams. She'd leaped from her lonely and too-empty bed before her eyes were even open to run to her window. He was leaving her; she knew it without even seeing him board.

Teila had never taken the stairs so fast in her life. She'd tripped at the bottom and broken her ankle; the pain had been distant and faint until much later, overshadowed at first by her desperation to reach him before he went away forever. Limping, she hurtled herself through the back door and toward the cruiser, which was just closing its doors. Vikus and Billis had been pressing their goggle-eyed faces to the glass.

She'd said nothing, made no cry. It was too late. He was going to leave her because she'd been stupid.

And then, the door had opened. Kason came down the ramp.

She'd run on her broken ankle and launched herself into his arms. She'd covered his face with kisses and vowed to never let him go. And, until his father had returned a few cycles later and convinced Kason that his duty to protect her meant serving in the SDF, she hadn't.

26

He smoothed a hand over the curved wood, testing it for splinters or imperfections. The pads of his fingertips caught briefly on a tiny rough spot, so he went over it with the smoothing paper again and again until the wood was as slick as glass. Only when the entire hull had been smoothed to his satisfaction did he get out the jar of whale oil.

He held it to the light, swirling the golden contents. This oil was what lubricated the whale's jointed segments; over time and with the right amount of grinding, it would become milka. It was far more precious and expensive in this state, because it was so much harder to gather. It was also poison if you tried to eat it, unlike its nutritious and delicious other state.

He knew these things the way he knew the color of his hair and eyes, that he liked milka pudding, that his favorite color was blue. None of that came from the data stream, which, though still prominent, had begun to bother him less. He knew about whale oil and boats, he thought, because he'd known about them *before*. And Teila had known he would know.

Carefully, he poured some of the oil on the wood and began rubbing it in. He used his fingers because it was easier that way to make sure he got the oil into every crevice and pore. Something happened while he worked.

He relaxed.

The aches and pains he'd come to count as commonplace began to ease, despite the way he'd been stretching and using his muscles while working on the boat. The tension in his neck disappeared, which in turn erased the throbbing pain in his skull he'd thought would never go away. This was what he was meant to do, he thought as he got lost in the rhythmic motions of his hands working the oil into the wood. Fix. Not break. He was a builder, not a soldier . . .

"Hey! You!"

Startled, he turned and nearly knocked the jar of oil off the counter. Pera stood in the shed doorway, her eyes wide and her white hair mussed. She looked shiftily around the shed before settling her gaze on him.

"You need to go inside," she said. "Something's happened."

He didn't move, not right away, though he did reach for a rag to begin cleaning his hands. "Something like what?"

"Something with the Fenda."

He carefully wiped each finger, making sure to get his skin clean. "What about her?"

Pera danced, impatient, clearly having expecting him to have run out the door the moment she arrived. "She's probably dead!"

"She was old," he said. "It's not unexpected."

The woman in front of him looked blank for a moment. Then something else filtered into her eyes, an expression he couldn't quite read, though it wasn't sorrow or fear. "Teila's really upset. She's crying, hysterical. Says she needs you."

"Why would she need me?" His words had nothing to do with how he felt, but there was no way he was going to give away anything emotional to Pera.

"I don't know, she just does. You should come."

He gave a last glance at the boat, which ideally needed another few coats of oil, but it wouldn't hurt it to be left for a while. Again making sure his hands were completely free of any traces of the poisonous oil, he tossed the rag onto the workbench. "Fine. Let's go."

Upstairs in the lighthouse, the boy wailed in his bed while his mother, Vikus, and Billis had gathered around the slumped figure of the ancient Fenda in her rocking chair on the other side of the room. Teila looked up when he came in the room, and though tears streaked her cheeks she didn't look hysterical. She did look surprised to see him.

"Pera came for me."

Teila nodded, stepping away from the Fenda's chair and giving a quick glance over her shoulder at her weeping son. "She's gone. Stephin found her."

At the sound of his name, the boy wailed louder. Crossing to the bed, Jodah sat next to him. "Shh. It's all right."

Stephin buried his face against Jodah's chest. "I thought she was sleeping!"

Jodah passed a hand over the boy's thick, dark hair. He pulled a milka bud from his pocket. "Here."

The boy took it, sitting up to look at him. "Mao says not before dinner."

"It's fine," Teila told him before Jodah could answer. Pera had arrived a few minutes behind Jodah, and Teila gestured at her.

"Stephin, go to the kitchen with Pera. She'll get your dinner for you. I'm going to take care of Amira Densi, all right?"

Stephin nodded, giving another tearful look toward the Fenda. "Can I say goodbye to her?"

"Of course you can." Teila took him by the hand and led him to the chair.

Pera watched the boy tentatively put his arms around his amira, then hug her completely as he sobbed out a goodbye. "Disgusting."

Teila hadn't heard her, but the men had. Jodah shook his head at her, only to earn a wide-eyed look of innocence and a shrug. Vikus glared, while Billis looked uncomfortable.

"Go with Pera," Teila told the boy. "Pera, can you please make sure Stephin gets his dinner?"

Pera's smile stretched her mouth and showed her teeth, but looked more like a grimace. "Of course. Come on."

When they'd gone, Teila turned to him. "We'll need help wrapping her and carrying her outside. She'll return to sand soon. I'd like to say some words over her before she does. I think Stephin would like to be there too."

"Are you all right?" The question slipped out of him before he could stop it.

Tears still glittered in her eyes. "Yes. Densi was very old, and she'd been telling me for a while that it would soon be her time. I didn't want to believe it or think about it, of course, because . . . well. Because I love her."

Billis burst into muffled, snorting sobs. Vikus clapped him on the back, but the younger man couldn't be soothed, even when Teila put her arms around him. Over his shoulder, she said to Vikus, "Take your brother to the kitchen and get him a drink. A strong one. Hush, shhh, Billis. It was her time."

Even with her own pain at the forefront, she was so good at taking care of people, Jodah thought as he watched her comfort the younger man and send them both off. She turned to him, her features strained, weariness evident in every movement. She opened her mouth to speak, but all that came out was a long, slow sigh. Then her shoulders slumped and she put her hands over her face.

He didn't think about anything else, not his anger or her lies. He gathered her against him and held her close. She gave a low cry but then melted against him. They stayed that way in silence while he measured the beating of his heart.

"Thank you," she said finally, pulling away from him. Her eyes were dry, her smile sweet but a little wary.

Suddenly, he hated that he'd made her feel that way about him. Distrustful. He wanted to pull her close again, breathe the heady scent of her hair, but that would be selfish. Instead, he let her go.

"You're welcome," he said gruffly. "Let me help you."

She hesitated, then nodded. "Yes. I'd like that."

27

All Fenda returned to sand when they died and, despite the sorrow of it, watching Densi's disintegration was beautiful. They'd carried her wrapped in a canvas sheet, then laid her on the rocky earth by the edge of the sea. Teila had removed the old Fenda's robes, laying them respectfully aside. Then they'd each spoken of some good memories they'd had of her. Vikus, Billis, and Stephin, too. Venga had even spoken, for though she'd never been his amira, he'd known her for a long time.

Her skin had begun to flake just as Venga finished. Moments after that, her body crumbled and became fine golden sand. The wind picked it up and blew it toward the sea. It comforted Teila do know the old Fenda had become part of the sea again, but she stood for a long time watching even after the others had gone inside. As the suns began to go down and the world became dark and chilly, she rubbed at her arms and murmured a private goodbye.

When she died, Teila thought, she would not become sand or

one with the sea. Her body would be burned according to the Sheirran custom brought from her ancestor's world. Her loved ones would commemorate her by etching her name on a rock at the lighthouse base, perhaps next to her father's and mother's. She'd always known that—death was a part of living, after all. She'd done it for her father as he'd done it for her mother when she was too small to remember. She'd somehow always imagined her husband's name would go beside hers there on the rocks, but now . . . would that ever happen?

Upstairs she sat with Stephin until he went to sleep. Her boy, her sweet boy. For so long he'd been all she had, and now he was still all she had, really. She stroked the hair back from his forehead, feeling the dampness of his skin, flushed from all the crying. She pressed a kiss there too, grateful for the chance. All too soon he'd be grown up and not interested in letting his mother love him, at least not this way.

In her own room she stripped out of her robes and ran the shower as hot as it would go. When steam wreathed the room she stepped into the spray, tipping her face to it and letting her mouth open to wash away the taste of her grief. It didn't help.

It was more than the loss of Densi, who'd been part of Teila's life since birth, and it wasn't just the problems with the lighthouse or the strangeness with Venga. It wasn't even just the cold silences with Kason, the man she'd once loved so much it was like being on fire.

Suddenly, everything was too much, and sobbing, she sank to the floor and let herself go.

He'd been kind to her earlier tonight, and she hated herself for being grateful for what ought to have been simple compassion. The man she'd married could be arrogant and boastful, but he'd always been kind. The man who'd returned to her had shown glimmers

of kindness, though his anger and mistrust had more often covered
it up. She couldn't blame him for it, but it hadn't made any of this
easier for her. Would any of it ever be easier?

She sobbed into the shield of her hands, wishing the world away,
if only for a little while. The coolness of air moving over her lifted
her head. She expected to see her son, seeking her comfort, but
Kason stood outside the shower looking down at her.

She'd been naked in front of him so many times there should
be no shame, and yet she curled into herself to cover herself from
his gaze. When he bent to lift her, she fought him. Her skin, slick
with water, slid under his grasp so that he had to grab her harder.
Bruising. Her protests were futile because he pulled her out of the
shower no matter how she kicked and hit at him.

He wrapped her in a thick towel and carried her into the bedroom, where he lay her on the bed and pulled the blankets up over
them both. Cocooned in the towel and the sheets, Teila struggled
as soon as he let her go, but she hadn't managed to get free before
he'd curled himself along her back. His strong arms pinned her
until she stopped struggling.

He was naked, she realized as he entwined his legs with hers.
His breath caressed the back of her neck as he held her still. Slowly,
slowly she relaxed. She was exhausted, but she she couldn't sleep.

The towel unwrapped a little when he slid a hand inside. Heat
on her belly. Heat lower, between her legs, when his fingers brushed
her there. She closed her eyes, feeling the sting of tears again. Her
lips parted, but all she could manage was a sigh.

He did not touch her for a long time, but when he did, the
stroke of him on her flesh was so tentative, so gentle, she thought
she'd imagined it. His lips pressed the back of her neck. She felt
the press of his cock against her bare ass just below the towel. She
wanted to move, to get away from him, but couldn't make herself,

and not simply because she knew that it would be no use—if he wanted her where she was, he would keep her there.

There'd been a time when she hadn't given up to him so easily, back in the earliest days when he'd believed nothing more than his charm could win her. She gave up to him now, helpless against the pull of her heart no matter how her mind protested. He was a stranger; he was her husband.

She loved him and would always love him.

With a subtle shift of their bodies, he eased inside her. His fingers circled on her clit as he filled her, and she couldn't hold back her moan. She rocked her hips, urging him deeper. They moved together, no hesitation or fumbling.

She lost herself in the pleasure. Too late for her to hold it back or worry that it might've triggered him, she cried his name when it overtook her. Shuddering, she turned her face to give him her mouth. His tongue stroked hers, his fingers never ceasing their magic. His teeth snagged her lower lip as he came, and the taste of blood flooded her mouth as another rush of climax washed over her.

Relaxing against him, still connected, Teila wanted to let herself take the comfort of his bare skin on hers and couldn't. Without moving, she whispered, "What changed?"

He didn't reply at first, and she wasn't surprised. She wasn't sure she really wanted to know. What answer could he give that would satisfy her?

When he drew in a breath, she tensed, waiting for him break her heart anew. Before he could say a word, the door flew open. Pera shouted from the doorway, "Come quick! Stephin's sick! He's really sick!" And after that, all that mattered to Teila was getting to her son.

28

I t should've been easier than this. They ought to have been able to put out a call for the closest medicus, but a fresh storm outside had cut off external communications again. They'd sent Vikus and Billis in the landcruiser to the next town, but it would be hours before they returned with any help. They needed to help the boy now.

"Input symptoms," intoned the voice from the monitor. The medprogram was old, probably out of date, but this far out it was the only option they had.

"Vomiting. Lethargy. Thready pulse. Pallor." Jodah looked at the boy who lay in Teila's arms without moving. He'd been that way for the past hour.

The medprogram's face was so neutral in its features it was impossible to tell if it were supposed to be male or female. It wasn't three-dimensional, either. It clicked as it took in the information Jodah fed it, its face expressionless. It would've been better, he thought, if it had no face at all.

"Diagnosing," it said, then fell silent.

"Mothers-forsaken thing," Teila said. She dipped a cloth in water and tenderly wiped it over Stephin's brow. The boy moaned a little but didn't move. "He's never been this sick before."

Jodah rapped the side of the monitor, hoping to jolt the program into action, but all that happened was that the screen flickered and went black. He muttered a curse and hit the power switch again, but when the blank face swam into view, not even the monotonous voice came out of it. The lips moved in silence.

"It's useless anyway. We need a medicus," Teila said.

In her arms, Stephin lay limp. Jodah touched the boy's forehead. He was glassy-eyed, cheeks flushed, but no fever. When Jodah pushed open his mouth to examine inside, a cluster of white blisters caught his attention. They meant something, though he couldn't remember what.

He cursed again. "I'm missing something."

Teila bathed her son's face again. "Vikus will be back soon, won't he? Oh, Mothers. Please let him get back soon."

"I can help him. I know it." Jodah reached for him, intending to put the boy on the bed, but Teila covered him protectively with her body.

"What are you doing?"

"Put him on the bed," Jodah said gently. "I want to look him over. I feel like I can figure this out. I know I can."

"You're not a medicus." Teila shook her head sharply.

The distrust on her face, so different from the way she usually looked at him, twisted Jodah's guts but also thinned his mouth. He didn't have the right to be angry with her, yet fury rose inside him at being balked. He fought it by backing up and turning his back on her. His fists clenched. He breathed in. Breathed out. The data stream scrolled and scrolled, spitting useless trivia at him

instead of making the connections he knew were in there and
would help him figure out how to help the boy.

Blisters. Pallor. Lethargy. Vomiting.

"Whale oil. Oh, Mothers," he said. "Teila, the boy ingested
whale oil."

"What? How?"

"He must've gotten into it in the shed . . . I thought I put it
away, but—"

"Get out!"

"I can help him," he said in a low voice.

Teila's hoarse shout turned him. "No, you can't! So why don't
you just get out! Get out of here! I can't deal with you right now!
You poisoned my child!"

He opened his mouth to protest, but even an enhanced soldier,
a Rav Gadol of the Sheirran Defense Force, was no match for a
mother driven by terror for her child. Jodah nodded and backed
away, closing the door behind him. Downstairs, he went to the
kitchen, thinking to try the monitor as though the system might
work better there. It didn't, of course, since all the monitors were
serviced by the same network.

Which he could probably fix.

It meant trying to access the data stream again. Pain throbbed
in his skull and the base of his neck. It wasn't a matter of simply
focusing on the unending scroll, any more than he had to tell his
legs "walk" before they'd move. Pulling what he needed from the
constant analysis of his surroundings and putting it together into
what he needed required concentration, yet couldn't be accom-
plished with something as simple as a command.

Thoughts rarely come in words. They're images, memories,
sounds. He needed to think his way to the solution. Stop trying

to force it. He needed to embrace the data stream as part of him, not some alien thing.

Standing in the kitchen, Jodah opened himself. His muscles went loose, fists uncurling, head drooping. He remembered the smell of the flowers in his dreams, the tickle of flowing hair on his face . . . His mind reached, reached for the memory of how to fix a viddy network . . .

So entrenched in what he was doing, Jodah at first didn't move when the back door flung open and Billis staggered in with a bleeding Vikus in his arms. Vikus was screaming. Billis too, but Jodah couldn't understand a word either of them were saying. Their screams brought Venga running, but the old man skidded to a stop at the sight of all the blood.

"No," he said. "It wasn't supposed to—"

"Get out of the way, old man." Rehker came from behind him, pushing him aside. "By the Three, Billis. Stop hollering and put him on the table."

As Billis struggled to get his brother on the flat surface, all hope of accessing the data stream for any useful purpose vanished. Jodah went with Rehker to the table, both of them reaching for Vikus, who spat and struggled despite the many gashes all over his face and arms.

"Wrecked," he cried. "Someone cut the landing wires, we only got a few cliks before we flipped into a ditch!"

Billis, pale and shaking, clutched Vikus hand. "We rolled into a ditch. We were going really fast."

"Someone," Vikus panted as his eyes rolled up in his head, "did it on purpose."

Then he passed out.

"Move away." Rehker unlaced the front of Vikus' robes. "We need to stop the bleeding."

Pera had appeared as well, dark circles shadowing her eyes. She hovered to one side, a hand over her mouth as she watched Rehker press a cloth to one of the worst wounds. Jodah thought she was holding back a sob but, to his disgust, the bitch was laughing.

"You're making it worse!" Billis tried to shove Rehker away, but was no match for the soldier.

Rehker shoved back twice as hard, sending Billis to the floor. Apparently it wasn't enough for him to toss Billis to the ground, because he then kicked him in the ribs. When the younger man howled and writhed, Rehker slammed his foot onto Billis' chest, pinning him. "Stand down! Stand the fuck down!"

Pera laughed from the corner, both hands now covering her mouth. She sounded both desperate and pained, like every guffaw ripped something inside her. Jodah didn't have time for her. Grabbing the back of Rehker's robes, he tore him away from Billis, who'd gone as silent as his wounded brother.

Rehker came up swinging, one fist connecting with Jodah's jaw hard enough to send them both sprawling apart. Pain bloomed, but Jodah shook it off. Truthfully, the pain only fueled him. Triggered him into action.

He grabbed Rehker again, holding him close enough to punch his face several times in succession. Blood spattered. Jodah's knuckles split over the same wounds from the last time he'd hit the man. More pain. Baring his teeth, he snapped them at Rehker, who jerked out of the way at the last moment.

Behind them on the table, Vikus stirred. Pera was on him in a flash, her hands on the front of his robes. Busy with Rehker, Jodah couldn't do more than glance their way, but Venga had come forward. He and Pera struggled. Venga was bigger, but Pera younger and stronger. She pushed the old man down and bent over him. A blade flashed in her hand.

"No!" Jodah cried as she stabbed the old man in the chest. Blood gouted in a thick, pumping stream.

In that moment of distraction, Rehker grabbed a cooking pot from its place on the counter and slammed it against the side of Jodah's head. The world tipped and spun. Then went black.

29

Sunrise was Teila's favorite time of day. It hadn't always been so—as a child her amira had always had to pull her from the covers, and as a young woman she'd taken on the habit of staying up late and waking late, too. Becoming a mother had changed those habits out of necessity, not desire, but her reluctant embrace of the early morning had become genuine appreciation after too many interminably long nights sitting up with Stephin, who'd suffered from night terrors for one full cycle. Only daybreak soothed him, and Teila had come to cherish the first rising glimmers of pink and gold in the black night sky. She could only pray now that sunrise would see her child recovering.

He'd never been so sick. This was more than random childhood illness. There'd been a few times in Stephin's brief life when Teila had feared losing him—once when he'd been missing for half a day after hiding in an empty cupboard and being trapped there.

Once when he almost fell from an upper balcony as she watched, screaming, until Vikus managed to pull him back inside. And now, when no matter what she tried, he got sicker and sicker.

More blisters had broken out all over his mouth, spreading across his pale, plump cheeks. He no longer even moaned when she shifted him. His skin had been cool and clammy before, but now heat had risen all over his body. He lolled in her arms.

"C'mon, baby," she whispered. "Please, come back to Mao."

Carefully, she put him on the bed so she could go to the monitor again and see if the medprogram had come back online. The screen crackled with noise when she tried to tap in a few commands, but nothing happened. Acid burned her throat when she looked at her son, lying so still. She needed to know what to do to treat him. They needed a medicus or the medprogram and now, or her boy might be lost to her before sunsrise.

She went to the door, hating to leave him for even a moment but needing do find out if Vikus had come back or if Jodah had been able to get the network running. The moment she set foot in the hallway, the lights flickered and went out. Teila froze, waiting for her eyes to adjust to the dark.

And it *was* dark, she realized. Completely. No light sweeping back and forth from the lamp room. She hadn't checked it at nightfall, her attentions focused on Stephin, but it still should've turned on automatically.

Outside, lightning flashed as another storm came in close on the heels of the last one. It might've explained the lights going out in the hallway, but not the lamp. If the main solar cells were somehow disrupted, the lighthouse went on auxiliary power from the backup cells. The only way the lamp wouldn't go on was if something had happened to it.

Fresh worry warred with her, not coming close to displacing her growing terror about her son but adding to it. Teila put a hand out, seeking the wall. She found something else instead.

A solid body. Warmth. Before she could recoil, a hand grabbed her wrist. Held her tight. Another hand covered her mouth before she could scream. She was backed up against the wall hard enough to slam her head. An arm came up beneath her chin, pressing her throat.

"What do you think you're up to?" breathed a low and trembling male voice directly into her ear. Rehker. Teila shuddered, but couldn't answer. He didn't seem to expect one. A knee nudged between her legs, a fierce pressure devoid of any sensuality. "How's your boy?"

She made no attempt at even a muffled retort; she bit, instead. She choked on the foul taste of his blood, but didn't let go even when he began shaking her. He dug his fingers into her hair and slammed her head against the wall. Again. Once more, until she fell from him, slack and faint. She went to her knees, ears ringing, stars bursting behind her eyelids.

"Oh, look," the man said from above her as another flash of lightning illuminated the hall. "It's a whaler. A big one, a crew of sixty or more I'd say. I surely hope they know enough to stay far away. Not run aground."

"The lamp," Teila managed to say.

"The lamp is out." More lightning and at last she could see his face. Rehker sneered and nudged her with his toe. "The lamp will stay out."

"Why would you . . . ?"

"Let's just say I needed that equipment for other things." In another flash from outside, his grin was wide and terrible. He bent in front of her face, the heat of him so close she knew if she snapped her teeth it would catch his flesh. "Other, other things."

From outside, far away, she thought she heard the slap of a ship against the sands. It had to be her imagination, just like the sounds of men screaming had to come from memory, not whatever was happening out there now. When Rehker moved away from her, Teila struggled to her feet.

"You have to turn on the lamp."

"No. I don't. I told you," he said in a low voice that was not very much like the one she was used to but still eerily familiar, "I need the equipment in the lamp room for other things."

"What could you need it for?" With the wall at her back, Teila was able to orient herself. Her bedroom door was across from her and to her right. The lamp room, all the way to her left at the end of the hall and up another short flight of stairs.

"They will all die. All of them die. All of you die, too. That boy of yours, Teila. He's going to die. Did you know that? You can fix the lamp or you can fix your boy, Teila. Which do you choose?"

"You shut your mouth," she said fiercely. "Vikus is bringing—"

Rehker laughed. "Vikus? That useless pup. He isn't bringing anyone. If he's not dead yet himself, the dear Pera will have taken care of him. Much the way she took care of your boy, though much more swiftly, I'd think."

Teila staggered toward the sound of his voice as another flash of light lit them both. "What do you mean? What have you done?"

"Chaos," whispered Rehker in a voice that sounded like love. "Anarchy. Disbandment. Downfall. You want to know why?"

She didn't have to ask him why. She already knew. She'd known the moment the first flash of lightning had lit his face.

Rehker had gone over.

30

Jodah wasn't out for long. His enhancements kicked in, sending blood flowing to the places that needed it, expanding his lungs to bring in fresh oxygen. He was on his feet before he actually became aware of what he was doing.

He didn't remember grabbing her, but he had Pera by the back of her neck. She flailed, but unlike Venga, Jodah wasn't old or infirm. The fragile stem of her throat threatened to snap when he shook her.

"What are you doing?" Jodah demanded.

The lights went out. It didn't matter to him—he could see as well in the dark as in the light. But Pera fought him harder, kicking and biting at him like a wild animal. She began to scream in breathless, panting gasps. He didn't have time for a temper tantrum. He shook her again until her teeth rattled.

"Don't worry about me!" she screamed through horrifying

laughter. "You should be paying attention to something else, something other than that bitch's spawn! You can't help him anyway, there's no cure!"

Jodah went still. Pera still dangled in his grip. Vikus groaned from the table as unsteady Billis leaned over him. Venga didn't move and made no sound.

Jodah brought her very close to his face and bit out each word. "What did you do?"

"Whale oil. I gave him whale oil!"

"Why?" Oh, by the Three, Jodah's stomach twisted as he remembered now, Pera in the shed while he put away the whale oil. He stopped himself from breaking her neck right then, but only barely. "Why, Pera?"

Her eyes fluttered. She couldn't see him as anything more than shadows, but every line of her face, every pull of her expression were clear as glass to him. Her features shifted rapidly through every emotion. Hilarity, fear, desire, surprise, all in rapid succession and not as though she had any control over it. A low, grinding noise came from deep in her throat, and froth appeared in the corners of her mouth.

"I remember," she said, jerking in his grip.

Her eyes opened wider, staring into his though he knew all she could see was darkness. All of her muscles twitched and spasmed, making her kick and squirm. Then, she calmed.

"Oh, Mothers. I remember everything now."

She'd dropped the blade she'd used on Venga, but all good soldiers carried more than one weapon, and no matter what she'd become, Pera must've been a very good soldier. The knife came up and across before Jodah could step back, so the blade caught the edge of his arm. But her slice wasn't meant for him. She'd aimed for her own throat, gouging deep and without mercy. No chance of saving her. The suicide act was a maneuver they'd all been trained in.

If only, Jodah thought as the heat of her dying covered him, she'd done it before being captured by the Wirthera.

He dragged her corpse to the corner and let her fall. He knelt next to Venga, certain the old man was dead, but he found a faint throb of a pulse. The blood flowing from his wound had slowed, but only because his heart was going to stop soon.

Jodah hadn't been medically trained. He knew that much without having to force a memory. But as a Rav Gadol he'd been given the information necessary to provide care in the field. Programmed into his auxiliary data sources, accessible via the data stream, if only he could finally figure out how to access it. He was so close and still too far.

Pressing his hand to Venga's, Jodah murmured a prayer to the Mothers to take the old man under their fiery skirts, should he not survive. Venga didn't move. Vikus did though, when Jodah checked over his wounds.

"Billis. Are you hurt?"

"Not too bad. No."

"Is there a handlight or something down here?"

Billis gestured wildly. "Yes. There's a box of them in one of the cabinets. For emergencies. We've never had to use them, the backup power always comes on."

Jodah went to the cabinet and found the handlights, cracking the inner tube to get the light glowing. He gave a few to Billis and tucked a couple into his sleeve pocket. Also from the cabinet, he pulled a medkit of sutures, surgical glue, and bandages. The seal on it had never been opened, and the box hissed when he cracked it.

"Take this," he told Billis. All of this came from common sense, not from the data stream, which still danced elusively out of his grasp. He rifled through the contents, searching for poison antidotes, but there were none. "Pressure on the wounds. Use the glue to seal them. That bottle is anti-infection meds, make sure he takes some."

"Where are you going?" Billis cried.

"I need to get the power back on. And help Stephin and Teila." Without waiting for an answer, Jodah left through the back door.

Lightning bathed the sky when he ran out. In the flash, he saw the dark shape of a whaler, dangerously close to shore. Without the light, it would surely crash.

The crack of thunder, flash of lightning, the crackle and sting of smoke. Rope skidding on his palms, burning them. The rough kiss of sand against him, over his head as he held his breath and tried not to drown.

Jodah shook his head free of the images assailing him. Breathing hard, he spat the taste of sand that had become so thick on his tongue he passed a hand over his face to convince himself he was on land and not suffocating beneath the sea. In the next crack of lightning, the ship had come closer. He needed to get the power on.

The mechanical equipment was all housed in a small shed connected to the lighthouse. Jodah had never had reason to be inside, yet when the door opened with a tug instead of being locked, he froze in surprise. Bathed in the amber glow from the handlight, the interior of the shed gleamed with machinery and solar cells.

He had been in here before.

A vision overlaid itself on top of the one he was actually seeing. Most of it was the same, except for the stream of golden sunlight through the windows and a few pieces of equipment that were shifted. He blinked and blinked again, but the vision didn't fade. From behind him, he heard a woman's voice and turned even though he knew she wasn't there for real. Only in his mind.

In his memory.

In moments it was gone, nothing but darkness behind him. Focus, he told himself grimly. Get the power on. Find Rehker. Get help for the boy.

The problem with the solar cells was clear at once—a tangle of wires that had been torn apart. There'd be no fixing it. Whoever had done this, whether it was Rehker or Pera or even Venga, they'd known what they were doing . . . and Jodah did not. Helplessly, he shone his light over the shredded wires, components hanging from the ends. The solar cells had been smashed, all but one, and that one was still connected to the main power grid. One small green light glowed on the circuit board, showing it was live.

One live connection, but where did it go? He scanned the board but couldn't tell where any of the wires went. Jodah held the light closer, but none of the ports had been labeled. The data stream brightened as he looked, and for one miraculous moment he thought he was going to be able to access it, figure out the schematics, find a solution. But it was only so much distracting gibberish. Useless and annoying. He blinked it away as best he could.

From far away, he thought he heard the sound of screams. Teila's voice, so familiar to him now, brought to his ears only because of his enhancements. He still couldn't make out her words, but the fact she'd raised her voice enough to carry to him with this much distance between them told him more than he needed to know. She was upstairs with her son, and he needed to get to her.

31

You don't need to do this, Rehker." Teila, her head spinning and woozy with pain, did her best to stand upright.

Rehker had dragged her by the hair all the way down the hall and up the stairs to the lamp room, where he'd tossed her against the low wall below the windows. He barely gave her a glance when she managed to get to her knees, but when she put a hand on the windowsill to pull herself higher, he hit her hand with the long metal pipe she used for hooking the storm shutters.

"Shut your mouth," he said mildly. "Or I will beat it so swollen you can't speak."

She shut her mouth, but not out of fear. If he beat her any harder, she'd be unable to stop him from whatever he was doing in the lamp room. She'd be incapable of helping her son.

"Let me go back to Stephin. He needs me."

The pipe slammed onto the wall so close to her head she felt the breeze of its passing. Rehker bent over her, the stink of his breath sour enough to choke her. His hand cupped her chin, forcing her to look at him though the lamp room was so dark she could see nothing but the faint glint of his eyes.

"The lamp or your son, Teila. Which would you choose?"

She thought of the ship on the storm-tossed sea, but there was no question. No doubt. "My son. Always my son."

"Sentimental bitch." He didn't sound angry, only thoughtful. "Do you know when they took me, I was one day away from being sent home. To my family. I'd been injured in a hornet attack. My face. I was meant to be blind. They hadn't done anything to my eyes, they said when I got home I could apply for surgery and might be eligible. The money's there for the Rav elite, to be sure, but for us plain soldiers, we have to limp along with what scraps we can glean. When the Wirthera took me, I didn't even care. What life could I have led back here, supporting a family without my sight? Before I joined the SDF I was a sculptor. I made beautiful things, Teila. How could I do that without being able to see?"

She thought better of speaking, and Rehker clearly didn't care to have an answer because he kept on.

"The Wirthera took me and the rest of the crew on the mediship headed for home. One minute we were cruising along. The next, I was naked in a metal cell with no windows or doors, no sound. Just like that. They don't tell anyone back here that truth, do they? That the Wirthera don't need to cross our borders to get to us. We never see their ships because they don't need to leave them. Maybe," Rehker said, "they don't even have them. Maybe they've never left their homeworld at all. However they take us, it has nothing to do with a ship. They take us and keep us while they study us . . . and then—"

"Then they send you back," Teila said quietly. She wanted

desperately to turn her face away from his to keep the stink of his breath from making her want to gag, but she didn't dare. "I know."

"They gave me back my eyes."

Teila closed hers. She cringed at the brush of his mouth against her cheek, then to her neck. He sniffed her, and she shuddered.

"They are the enemy and yet they gave me what my own government would not. Better than the ones even that the Mothers themselves gave me. What do you think of that, pretty Teila?"

"I don't think it gives you the right to kill anyone," she said.

His teeth tore at her flesh, bringing blood before she shot up a knee to catch him between the legs. With a roar, Rehker fell back enough to allow her to roll away from him. Teila didn't need light to find her way around the lamp room. She crawled with one shoulder along the curved wall, heading for the door.

Rehker caught her by the ankle at the last moment, dragging her back. "No. Get back here. You need to help me with this. It doesn't work."

She kicked at him, but he dug his fingers into the soft meat of her leg below the muscles. The pain was instant. She kept herself from screaming only by biting her tongue. He grabbed her by the hair with his other hand, yanking her to her feet. The leg he'd grabbed buckled, but Rehker kept her upright.

"You need to make it work," he said into her ear as he marched her toward the control panel.

"The power's out—"

"I know that, you stupid kilta. I cut the wires to the solar cells for everything, including the lamp. All except the one to the control panel. I need access to it."

Teila tried to focus, but all she could think about was getting back to her son. "I don't understand."

"Of course you don't. Nobody could. They put it all into my brain, my brain. Of course your lover, the Rav Gadol, he thinks he might understand, he thinks he could figure it out, him and his Mothers-forsaken data stream. Oh, by the Three did I get sick from listening to him whinge about it. He. Knows. Nothing."

He shook her. "Make this work!"

"I can't see it!" she cried, furious and terrified. "My eyes don't work in the dark like yours do."

He stilled. "Of course. Of course. Here."

Without letting go of her, he shuffled with his robes. She heard the distinctive crack of a handlight and then the glow. It was so bright after being so dark that she threw up a hand in front of her eyes. In that flash, she caught sight of his face.

It had changed. Rehker had always been a handsome man. Charming with it, knowing he had a face that could get him whatever he wanted. Out here in the lighthouse his appearance hadn't been as beneficial to him as it might've been in other places—Teila had turned down his advances, one after the other, since his arrival, but since she'd never treated any of her clients any differently no matter her level of fondness for them, the only suffering he'd felt had been in his imagination. He'd stopped trying to seduce her after one late dinner when the others had all gone to bed and she'd allowed herself the luxury of one too many glasses of beer. She'd been silly. He'd been insistent. He'd tried to kiss her and she turned her head at the last moment, her hand on his chest to keep him from coming closer.

It had been enough at the time. He'd never bothered her again, at least not beyond the flirtation that had been his interaction with any female in the lighthouse. He'd taken up briefly with a woman who'd stayed for only a cycle before she'd deteriorated so badly she'd had to be moved to a full-service facility.

His handsome mouth had pulled down on one side in a grimace that didn't seem intentional. His lips didn't move right when he spoke, giving him a slur. The eye on that side of his face drooped as well. He didn't seem to notice, but the shock of it made Teila gasp.

"What?" Rehker asked. "What's the matter with you?"

"Your face."

He touched it, fingers exploring the sagging skin. The unaffected side of his face hardened. The lighter in his other hand flickered and went out, and Teila realized he'd let her go. He realized it too, and grabbed at her again before she could get away. His grip seemed looser with this hand, the one on the same side as the other changes.

"They did something to you," she told him. "Something in your brain. You need medical attention, Rehker. And soon."

He managed a sneer. "From who? The medprogram's down and even if it were up, all it could do is diagnose me and tell you I need to be seen by a medicus. You think the government would help me? No. They will help me. They'll fix me. Once they come for me."

"Who?" she cried.

"The Wirthera." The lighter flicked on again, highlighting his even further ravaged face. Now a silver string of drool leaked from the corner of his mouth. The hand gripping her loosened. "I'm calling them."

32

Up the stairs, two at a time, Jodah pushed himself to the limits of his speed. On the top floor he went first to Teila's room, where he found the boy lying in sweat-damp sheets, limbs sprawled. His breathing was shallow his pulse thready.

"Mothers," Jodah breathed, cradling Stephin to him. "Please, let me figure out how to help him."

But no matter how he tried, the data stream remained inaccessible, just out of reach. He laid the boy gently down and searched the room for Teila, but she wasn't there. He listened for her, though she was no longer screaming.

The lamp room. He heard both her and Rehker, their voices low and indistinct but definitely theirs. Jodah gave the boy one last checking over, then ran for the stairs.

He burst into the lamp room to find Rehker bent over Teila, her hands moving rapidly along the buttons and switches of the control panel as Rehker held up a burning lighter. At the glare of

Jodah's handlight, Teila turned with a cry of relief, but Rehker shoved the light into her face.

"Work!" he screamed almost unintelligibly. Saliva spattered. He glared at Jodah from one rolling eye, the other narrowed. His mouth had twisted into a curved sneer.

Jodah didn't think. He moved. He tore Rehker away from Teila and threw the other man to the floor hard enough to make the metal floorboards ring. Then he fell upon him with his fists and feet. From behind him, Teila let out a shout as the control panel whirred to life.

Rehker fought like a wild thing, writhing and biting. One hand caught the edge of Jodah's jaw, sending him back enough for Rehker to get a foot up, kicking Jodah in the chest. The other hand swung ineffectually, the fingers limp. Jodah caught it and crushed it in his own while Rehker howled.

"It doesn't matter, anyway. That kilta got it working. They're coming for me. I called them and they're coming!" Rehker collapsed in Jodah's hands, no longer fighting.

Jodah looked at Teila, who stood frozen next to the control panel. "What's he talking about?"

"The Wirthera. He says he rigged some sort of signal to alert them to where he was, so they can take him back." Her fingers moved over the controls swiftly, flipping switches and toggles.

"Don't! You can't let them!" Jodah shouted.

She didn't even glance back at him, her attention on the panel in front of her. "The lamp. We need the lamp, there's a ship out there!"

Rehker writhed free of Jodah's grip, falling to his knees with a howl. Both hands gripped his head as he shook it. His scream became a piercing shriek that went up and up until he choked on it. He went to the floor, his body arching so impossibly far it seemed he'd break his own back. His feet thudded on the metal floor.

"What's happening?" Teila cried.

The lamp glowed dimly, barely lit, before going dark again. From the base came a low vibration that faded immediately. Teila cursed and bent back to the controls while Rehker convulsed. Jodah knelt next to him, putting his hands on the other man's shoulders to still him. It didn't work. If anything, Jodah's touch exacerbated Rehker's writhing. He'd begun muttering a string of senseless words over and over, getting louder and more vehement.

Not senseless words. Jodah knew the sound of them, and they made him cold. Rehker was speaking Wirtheran. Jodah didn't know what he was saying, but it didn't matter. He backed away like the man had burst into flames.

"What did he do to that control panel, Teila?"

With a hitch in her voice she answered, "I don't know. He kept the power connected to it but somehow not the lamp, which I'd have said was impossible. He arranged some sort of signal with the outgoing network, and it's hooked into the lamp controls. But I can't figure it out, and Stephin needs me . . ."

"You go," he told her. "I'll get the lamp running. I'll be there as soon as I can. I'll take care of Rehker."

She didn't hesitate, just took the handlight and ran from the room. Leaving Rehker on the floor, Jodah went to the control panel. It looked simple enough, aside from the tangle of wires spilling everywhere. Teila had done something to it, but not enough. Thinking quickly, not sure where the knowledge was coming from, he untangled them. Two wires spit sparks at him as he did, and he twisted them together as the shock tore through him. His nerves sizzled, colors bloomed in his vision, and the stink of electricity bloomed in his nose along with the coarser stench of burning hair.

The lamp came on.

"Noooooo!" Rehker shrieked. "You've ruined it!"

Jodah turned with both bleeding and burned palms held in front of him as Rehker launched himself toward him. He caught the other man by the front of his robes, the pain in his hands somehow distant. As Rehker snapped his teeth in Jodah's face, the lamp's bright white light spun past them. It blinded Jodah in those few moments, long enough for Rehker to dive at his throat and gouge out a mouthful of flesh.

That was the end. Jodah did not go blank—everything became as sharp and clear and white as the now-turning lamp. His fists came up.

Rehker went down.

In moments he was still, and Jodah gave him no more attention. He ran down the stairs toward Teila's room and burst inside. Lit by the amber glow from the handlight, her face was streaked with tears and blood. She looked up at him as he came in, the boy in her arms.

"Kason," she said in a moan that raised the hair on the back of his neck. "Oh, Kason. Our son is gone."

All at once, everything came back to him.

33

She'd lost him. Teila held her son in her arms, willing him to breathe and unable to make him. The man in front of her staggered forward, going to his knees in front of her with a low, moaning sob.

"No," he said. "No. He's not gone."

Her own sobs came then, stealing her voice. She reached for him. He pulled her close, one of his hands on Stephin's chest. He looked into her eyes.

"Teila, I can save him. But you have to trust me." He kissed her swiftly, saying against her mouth, "I remember."

She gasped and choked, her grief too vast for any amount of joy to find its way in. When he tried to take the boy from her arms, she couldn't even find the strength to fight him. He lifted Stephin gently and moved toward the door.

"Come on," he told her. "You can make it, Teila. You're strong enough. Come on."

The lights came on as she reached the hallway. The brightness hurt her eyes, but even squinting against it she kept moving after him. Down the stairs, along the corridor, to the kitchen where Kason laid Stephin on the bloodstained kitchen table.

Billis burst through the back door. "I fixed the—Is he dead?"

"Salt," Kason barked, arranging Stephin's limbs into straight lines. "As much as you can find. A barrel of it, if you have one."

They did, of course, for storing the milka in. Several barrels, as a matter of fact, in the store room. Billis ran at once to bring one while Teila moved to the table. Every part of her ached and stung and the world threatened to spin out from beneath her feet. She clung to the table edge, head down, unable to do more than that.

"Water," Kason said. "Make a paste. Cover him with it. It will draw out the poison."

Billis moved to help him while all Teila could do was take up her son's limp and lifeless hand. "It's too late, Kason."

"No. The data stream," he said. "I know how to do this."

With the water and the salt, Kason made a thick paste and covered as much of Stephin's skin as possible, even tucking some onto the boy's tongue. Then he tipped the boy's head back and positioned his mouth over Stephin's and blew hard enough to raise the boy's chest. Then again. Again. Teila could only watch, horrified and overrun with grief.

Kason worked for a long time, many heartbeats, too many to count. Until at last, defeated, he sagged into a chair with his head in his hands. His shoulders shook.

"I'm sorry," he said. "I failed."

Teila couldn't speak. She took her son's hand with both of hers and brought it to her lips. Her tears wet the gritty paste covering his skin. She tasted salt and the sting of whale oil beneath that.

Let me die from it, she thought, numb. *Let it kill me, too.*

From the corner, Billis began to cry. At her side, her husband buried his face against her. Teila wept without sound.

In front of her, Stephin opened his mouth and let out a long, choking cough.

34

Her husband touched her with slow but certain hands. Smoothing fingers up the backs of her calves, the insides of her thighs. He teased her soft flesh, stroking along her seam and parting it to slip inside. His thumb pressed her clit as the heat of his breath caressed her. Teasing.

"Kason." Pleasure pushed his name to her lips, intensified by the simple ability to use it without fear. She breathed it out with every sigh. "Kason, Kason, Kason . . ."

His murmured laughter sent shivers of desire pulsing through her as his lips found her clit. Then, his tongue. He worked her body with his mouth and fingers until she arched and shuddered under him. But he didn't let her go over. No, he knew her better than that.

Easing off, he kept her on the edge until everything else faded away but his touch. Teila lost herself in it, greedy and not ashamed to urge him with the lift of her hips, her gasps, the tug of her fingers in his hair. She gave herself up to him even as she demanded more from him. And he gave it to her. He gave her everything.

Her orgasm rippled through her, tickling and then coming in a rush. She bucked helplessly against the waves of pleasure devouring her. It consumed her. She went up in flames and became her own fiery sun.

"I know why the poets call climax 'joining the sun'," she said lazily when she'd found her voice again. Her fingers threaded through his hair.

Kason had rested his head on her belly, his hand still cupping between her legs. He looked up at her with mischievous eyes, his mouth still wet from her arousal. "Oh?"

"Yes. Yes, yes, yes," she said. "Yes."

She pulled him to her mouth, open for his kiss, and sucked his tongue. She licked him with feathery strokes and nibbled his chin, his jaw. She pressed her mouth to the beat of pulse in his throat. She dug her nails into the muscles of his ass and urged him to press his cock against her.

"Yes?" Kason asked. "This?"

He rubbed his cock back and forth over her clit, sliding with ease from her slickness. It seemed impossible that she could rise to pleasure again, but he took his time until both of them were shuddering and she ached with an emptiness she desperately needed him to fill. Yet still he teased her, though the muscles on his arms corded with effort and a thin sheen of sweat coated him.

Teila opened herself to him as he moved, and though Kason might've intended to keep on stroking his cock over her, she'd tilted her body at just the right angle to urge him inside with nothing more than a well-placed wriggle. He laughed and groaned at her trick, but seated himself balls deep. He kissed her, long and wet, not moving anything but his mouth. The beat of his heart thumped against her, and she clung to him, tight.

"I love you," she said. "I love you, love you, love you."

"And I love you, wife," he murmured between kisses.

With him filling her, all she had to do was tighten her internal muscles to bring them both another wave of pleasure. She laughed at his groan and sighed at his shudder. Hooking her heels behind his calves, Teila ran her nails lightly down his back, urging him to fuck into her. He didn't at first, resisting, but with another shift, another squeeze, he gave in at last.

He moved. She sighed, her hips rocking. They made love for a long time, slow and steady, until once more she could no longer hold back the fire inside her. No explosion this time, more a steady growing flame that eventually consumed her. Consumed them both.

Shaking, Kason kissed her as he spent himself. He crushed her with his full weight for a moment or so, but then slid to the side to cradle her against him. He nuzzled into the hollow of her shoulder.

"I could stay here forever. Never get up," he said.

She stroked his hair. "I would let you, sweetheart. But the lamp . . ."

He sighed, put-upon, but she knew he didn't mean it. He looked up at her with a faint grin. "I'll still be here when you get back."

"Oh, you." She knuckled his side, which turned into him pinning her arms above her head . . . which became him kissing her breathless.

With his hand flat on her belly, Kason propped himself on one elbow. "You stay in bed. I'll check the lamp. You need your rest."

She gave him a lifted brow. "I appreciate the sentiment, husband, but somehow the time we've just spent doesn't reflect that attitude very well. In fact, it sounds like more of an excuse simply to keep me abed for your own pleasure."

"Guilty," he told her, then slid down her body to kiss her stomach and the slightest of bulges there. "But there's this, as well. Tell me, Teila. You feel all right?"

She didn't laugh at his concern. "Yes, sweetheart. I feel totally fine. I'm all right."

He moved to kiss her mouth again. "Because we could have a medicus come—"

"I've seen one." They'd all seen one after the horror with Rehker and Pera and poor Venga. Vikus would need months of care but was well on his way to recovery, and Stephin's blisters had left scars that were slow to heal.

She'd known before the exam, of course, that she carried Kason's child. But it had relieved her fears to know that the medicus had found nothing wrong with her or the child swimming inside her. Rehker's abuse hadn't harmed either of them, but against her and Kason's wishes, the Rav Aluf and the SDF had used his story as a further example about the horrors of the Wirthera. They were out there, she believed that. But she'd become unconvinced that sacrificing Sheirran citizens in the constant fight was effective, or would ever be.

But that was a problem bigger than any of them in the lighthouse for now, something to work toward solving over time. For now, she settled against her husband, whose eyes had closed, his breathing steady and regular. In a few moments she'd get up and check the lamp to keep the sea safe for the ships that traveled on it.

For now, it was enough to be safe in her bed with the man she loved beside her.